FEATHERED SERPENT 2012

JUNIUS PODRUG

TOR®

A TOM DOHERTY ASSOCIATES BOOK
New York

This is a work of fiction. All of the characters, organizations, and events portrayed in this novel are either products of the author's imagination or are used fictitiously.

FEATHERED SERPENT 2012

Copyright © 2010 by Junius Podrug

All rights reserved.

Pioneer F Plaque image on p. 88 courtesy of NASA

A Tor Book
Published by Tom Doherty Associates, LLC
175 Fifth Avenue
New York, NY 10010

www.tor-forge.com

Tor® is a registered trademark of Tom Doherty Associates, LLC

ISBN 978-0-7653-4735-0

First Edition: March 2010
First Mass Market Edition: December 2010

Printed in the United States of America

0 9 8 7 6 5 4 3 2 1

For Hildegard Krische, who not only climbed out the window to be with me, but whose love and courage are my salvation, and whose grace and beauty are my delight.

For Carol McCleary, whose beautiful smile is a bright light, whose heart is big and generous, and whose friendship is a guarantee that your back will always be covered.

For Bob Gleason, a friend to ride the river with, a phrase cowboys of the Old West used for friends whom they could always rely upon.

And for Captain Crunch (1917–2009), a mother to us all, and whose spirit of working hard and thinking positive will always stay with me.

ACKNOWLEDGMENTS

I want to thank editors Eric Raab and Ashley Cardiff, copyeditor Steven Boldt, Jane Liddle, and the many unsung heroes at a publishing company whose hard work and talent go into turning a rough manuscript into a polished book. I am also grateful to Steven Jones, Michael Youngs, John Bevard, Jr., and Ginger Bevard for their help and encouragement.

THE RETURN OF THE DARK-PLUMED
FEATHERED SERPENT

Quetzalcoatl was gone; but *he would return*.

He was not dead. He had indeed built mansions underground . . . the abode of the dead, a place of darkness . . .

The opinion was widely accepted that the present is the fifth age or period of world history; that it has already undergone four destructions . . . and that the present period is also to terminate in another such catastrophe. The agents of such universal ruin have been a great flood, a worldwide conflagration, frightful tornadoes and famine, earthquakes and wild beasts, and hence the ages were respectively called . . . Water, Fire, Air, and Earth. As we do not know the destiny of the fifth, the present one, it has as yet no name. . . .

A change is to come, the present order of things will be swept away, perhaps by Quetzalcoatl, perhaps by hideous things with faces of serpents.

**—Written by archaeologist Daniel Garrison Brinton
in 1882 . . . *over 125 years ago***

BOOK I

THE CITY OF THE GODS

1

"We'll drive you from our land, we'll drink your blood."

Caden Montez watched men performing as werejaguars, legendary man-beasts of ancient Mexico, strike at one another with wooden swords, drawing blood to satisfy the covenant with the gods—blood for rain. With snarling jaguar headpieces, claws on their hands and feet, bare chests, and legs covered with gray ash and black spots, they were in the chilling guise of the infamous night creatures of the jungle. *But the blood is real,* she thought.

Watching the performance from the steps of the ruins of the Temple of Quetzalcoatl, the Feathered Serpent, Caden found the brutality ugly. And the taunts bothered her. The show was for tourists at the ancient ruins of Teotihuacán, Mexico's largest tourist attraction, and the crowd that had gathered to watch the performance had no idea that the words sung in the old Nahuatl tongue, the language of the Aztecs, were threats.

An expert in both astrobiology, the scientific search for extraterrestrial life, and archaeology, the study of antiquity, her specialty was ancient Mexico. She spoke Nahuatl, and she didn't find it amusing that the men were using the ancient tongue to shout murder threats at unsuspecting tourists.

The shouted threats had increased the sense of unease she'd felt all morning after a strange phone call from her assistant, Julio. Wrapped up in research for her into a dark legend of the ancient city, he appeared to have enmeshed himself in the project in unhealthy ways. That the research had been related to the ancient tales of Nawals, the blood-drinking werejaguars the dancers were mimicking, intensified her concern for Julio.

"We'll drink your blood," they sang to a *norteamericano* with a camcorder who stepped in for a close-up.

"What exactly do the performers represent?" Laura Gillock asked.

Gillock had come to the site to do a *National Geographic* piece on Caden's work at Teotihuacán. This was Caden's first meeting with the magazine writer, and she wanted to make a good impression.

"They're performing a blood covenant dance. The small cuts are sacrifices of blood so the gods give rain for the maize crop. The men snapping whips make sounds that mimic the thunder god."

"Why do the gods want blood?"

"The gods of ancient Mexico were nourished with human blood. It gave the sun god the strength to rise each day, the rain god the strength to water the earth, the war god the strength to win battles. So the gods made a covenant with mankind: Feed us blood and we will give you rain and sunshine for a good harvest, and strength and courage for victory in war."

"Those black spots and ash make the players look like leopards."

"Jaguars, they're dressed as werejaguars."

"*Werejaguars?* You mean like *werewolves*?"

"Exactly, with vampires thrown in because werejaguars also drank their victims' blood. Legends of shape-changing beasts exist all over the world—European werewolves, African leopard-men, tiger-men in India. Here, it's jaguars because the beasts have a special place in the lore of Latin America. They're the only great roaring cats in the Americas, creatures of dangerous grace and savage power, but at three or four hundred pounds, not something you'd want to pet. The indigenous people have always feared and revered them. The word *jaguar* comes from their word *yaguar*—he who kills with one leap."

"Wasn't there a murder cult like the Thuggee of India here in Mexico?"

"Cult of the Jaguar, a secret society that arose to drive out the invaders after the Spanish conquest. Members dressed as jaguars prowled the night, stalking and murdering Spaniards. A legend arose that they were shape-changers who could transform into were-jaguars, hideous creatures called Nawals. The king's men finally put an end to the cult with the hangman's noose, but the legend of Nawals didn't die in the jungles of Mexico where modern culture is still barely felt even today."

Caden knew millions of people still lived in jungle areas and had never assimilated into the general population, even though it had been nearly five centuries since the conquest. Periodically, these people whose culture lagged behind modern Mexico were in open warfare with the government. She hoped that shouting threats to tourists was just a private joke among them.

At the time of Christ, Teotihuacán was the largest city in the western hemisphere, the center of a powerful empire and a metropolis that rivaled ancient Rome in size. Now it was Mexico's biggest tourist attraction. Thirty miles northeast of Mexico City, the ruins of the ancient city had two magnificent pyramids: Pyramid of the Sun and Pyramid of the Moon. The pyramid dedicated to the sun god was only a hair smaller than the Great Pyramid of Giza in Egypt.

"How do you pronounce the name of the city?" Gillock asked.

"*Tay-oh-tee-wah-kahn.* Most people just call it *Tay-o* or *Tee-o. Teotihuacán* meant 'city of the gods' in the Aztec language. No one knows the real name of the city or the culture that built it. Or even why the largest city ever built on the American continent before Columbus was abandoned.

"All of the civilizations that rose afterward in Mesoamerica—the Aztecs, Mayans, Toltecs, and others—mimicked the structures they found here in building their own temples and pyramids, but never created ones this large. And none of them tried to populate the deserted city."

"Why?"

"They were afraid. Even the Aztecs, the storm troopers of ancient Mexico, feared the ghost city. They sensed dark magic at the huge pyramids and temples along the broad boulevard called the Avenue of the Dead. I suppose they sensed something we moderns can't relate to. All the cultures that came afterward adopted the infamous blood covenant and sacrificed humans to the gods. And Teo was where the covenant began. The main god and legendary builder of the city was said to be particularly bloodthirsty."

"Sounds creepy. But great stuff for my article. Is the dark mystery of the city part of your research project?"

Caden knew there was a possible connection, but the theory that the magazine writer had come to interview her about was controversial enough without adding an ancient-murder-cult angle. Besides, it wasn't a pleasant subject with her. Research into the dark legend was the assignment she'd given to Julio.

"Not directly, though I'm back in Teo because of the legendary figure that began the blood covenant. Are you familiar with the field of astrobiology?"

"I looked it up before I came. Search for life on

other planets. NASA has you astrobiologists looking for life on Mars. SETI people with those enormous satellite dishes are waiting for ET to call. Jodie Foster had that job in the movie *Contact*, didn't she?"

Caden laughed. "Well, I suppose that's the public's conception. Astrobiology is usually thought of as the search for life outside of Earth, but it's really the study of life in the universe, Earth included. We begin by studying life on Earth and extend the investigation into the far reaches of space."

"I read that you search for water on other planets."

"That's one focus. Water is the universal elixir, the magic potion that is necessary for life as we know it. Science believes life began in the ocean. When our primeval ancestors crawled onto land, they carried water with them inside their skin. I'm sure you know, humans are about two-thirds water, which is about the same percentage of water on the surface of the planet.

"So if we're going to look for life as we know it in other parts of the cosmos, we look for water. So far, the prime candidates for having water are comets, a couple moons of Saturn, and maybe beneath the surface of Mars."

"Water's the blood of Mother Earth." Gillock grinned. "Something I read when I was doing a piece on a Gaia group, people who view the planet as a living organism. Speaking of water, have you heard about the incident in the Gulf of Mexico?"

"The dead fish? I know a few weeks ago dead fish

suddenly started surfacing, but I've been so wrapped up here, I haven't followed the story."

"It's getting worse. My editor wants me to check it out on the way home. The government says there's a leak of methane. I understand that's essentially natural gas, the stuff we use in our stoves. Apparently the bottom of the Gulf is full of it."

"There are enormous methane deposits in many places under the seas. Some scientists believe that methane eruptions on the ocean floor are what's behind the mysterious disappearances of ships in the Bermuda Triangle. Methane is also called swamp gas because it kills life in water, creating dead ponds."

"So if it's a search for water, why Teo? Not much around here."

"My search is for life *on* Earth that originated *elsewhere*. It's a theory scientists call panspermia. The concept is that the seeds of life are scattered and carried throughout the universe, with planets like Earth having a friendly environment for life to evolve into higher states."

"How would life get here . . . from there?"

"A comet carrying microbes is the best candidate. There's even evidence that an impact with a big comet billions of years ago left the water that got our oceans started. That water could have contained organisms in microform. For sure, over eons, we've been hit with ice from space millions of times. And any piece of it could have carried microlife."

"Comets are big chunks of ice, aren't they? They call them dirty snowballs?"

"Halley's comet is a potato-shaped chunk of ice about five miles wide and ten miles long. Many other comets are also enormous. Earth is also constantly being bombarded by much smaller pieces of space ice that usually vaporize in our atmosphere."

"How could microbes survive in space?"

"On Earth microbes survive in volcanoes, under miles of ice pack, and under the floors of oceans. A ride on a comet wouldn't be that big a leap."

"So why are you at Teo if you're looking for comets?"

This was the tough part of the interview. Gillock was playing dumb, but Caden knew why she had asked for the interview. The controversy Caden had generated with a scientific paper had prompted the interview—along with unwanted attention from the media circus that thrived on stories about farm girls giving birth to two-headed babies after being raped by aliens.

She took a deep breath and plunged in. "Most scientists pursuing panspermia theories are looking for microbes that hitched a ride on a comet or a meteor. I'm sure you've heard, I have a different approach. My research focuses on the search for evidence of larger life-forms—"

"Aliens."

"I prefer to think of them as visitors. The word *alien* has a sensationalism derived from movies and tabloid stories." Caden stopped and faced the magazine writer. "Laura, I know how weird some of my theories sound, but I'm not a nutcase or someone deliberately provoking controversy. My paper on visitors was published in a scientific journal that only astrobiologists read. Now I'm getting the sort of ridicule that was thrown by the scientific community at the *Chariots of the Gods* type of books back in the 1970s."

"I recall most of those books claimed that evidence of ancient astronauts visiting us is found in the pictures drawn by the ancients on walls and vases."

Caden nodded. "And landforms that resemble giant airfields, the amazing movement of enormously heavy objects long distances, all kinds of things that seemed impossible for ancient cultures. Right off, the scientific community howled with laughter and derision— which is why I should have proceeded with more caution."

"What's your premise?"

"That because ridicule was heaped on the theories, scientists avoided serious study of many phenomena for fear they would be laughed at. Just because most of the theories lacked credibility doesn't mean we shouldn't investigate whether there's evidence of extraterrestrial visits in ancient times. But it isn't surprising that scientists don't line up to commit career hara-kiri."

"But you're into career suicide?"

Caden thought about the question. "I'm into finding the truth. I don't want to damage my career, but

I also don't want to hide my head in the sand out of fear that I'll take an unpopular stance. Science is not as open-minded or as friendly to new ideas as one might think. The numbers of scientists hounded for advocating theories that were later proved correct are legion."

"Isn't there a famous misconception about anatomy?"

"Right. For fifteen hundred years, medical students were taught human anatomy based upon a Roman study that used the anatomy of dissected monkeys, pigs, and dogs rather than the human body. Scientists who questioned the accuracy of the data were persecuted—one was burned at the stake. Which is about what I'm facing when I advocate that scientists do an in-depth analysis of whether ancient astronauts visited Earth rather than simply dismissing the idea out of hand.

"Scientists who have no problem theorizing that life could have arrived on a dirty snowball from trillions of miles away, or spend their lives listening to static from the cosmos in the hopes it's a message from ET, tremble at the notion of meeting head-on issues of whether we've already had visitors."

"Would you call it thinking out of the box?"

"I'd call it keeping an open mind and having the courage to question anything. The most important thing I've learned as a scientist is that science doesn't have all the answers. You can't find God in a test tube."

Laura raised her eyebrows. "Maybe God was an ancient astronaut?"

"Of course He was an ancient astronaut."

"Come again?"

"He wasn't of this world, was he? He created it. He lives in the celestial heavens, which are somewhere in the cosmos. How could God be anything other than a visitor from the far beyond?"

Laura laughed and shook her head. "Good Lord, I'll put my editor in an early grave if I turn in a story that God was an alien. Is that your theory?"

"Not at all, I was just playing devil's advocate—excuse the pun. The hypothesis I'm investigating is that the great civilization that suddenly rose at Teo—and disappeared as suddenly and mysteriously—was created by a being of superior intelligence. And that being most likely was a visitor from the beyond."

"Why someone of superior intelligence? What makes Teo so unique?"

"Its high state of civilization suddenly appeared in a region of the world isolated from the march of progress." Caden gestured at the enormous pyramids and ruins of temples. "This was a great city. In thousands of years, nothing to compare came about on the entire continent. It ruled an enormous empire and built world-class edifices."

"Egypt has pyramids and temples, the Greeks had—"

"Exactly. The great civilizations of the ancient world

all had incredible monuments. But the Greeks, Egyptians, Romans, Babylonians, Chinese, Hindu, were all physically close enough to have borrowed and learned from each other. Each succeeding civilization learned from the prior ones and improved upon it.

"What occurred here at Teo was a sudden explosion of progress and the rise of an empire with a territory larger than Western Europe. Even more astonishing is that the region basically relied upon a single crop—corn—and had no beasts of burden."

"No horses or mules?"

"And no donkeys, oxen, cattle. If you think about it, the horse was probably the greatest technological invention in history. Without it, Alexander wouldn't have conquered everything from Greece to the Himalayas, the Romans wouldn't have ruled the Mediterranean world, Genghis Khan's Mongols would never have conquered half the known world. But horses and other beasts of burden didn't come to the New World until the Spanish brought them.

"Look at the Pyramid of the Sun. As high as a twenty-story building, and if it were hollow, the Houston Astrodome could fit into it. It's bigger than two of Egypt's three biggest pyramids. And the city around it went for miles in every direction and ruled an empire that extended two thousand miles. Ancient Mexicans and ancient Egyptians who lived halfway around the world from each other and never could have interacted had amazing similarities—both worshipped feathered-serpent deities, built the largest pyramids on Earth, used hieroglyphics as their writing system, invented paper, developed sophisticated mathematics and astronomy, and had a 365-day calendar.

"How did this stunning relationship occur? We don't know. While ancient Egypt has been studied extensively for centuries, the wonders of ancient Mexico have been barely scratched. And for a scientist to even suggest the incredible similarities were anything but a pure coincidence would subject the scientist to ridicule."

Gillock nodded. "The cards were stacked against Teo, but a mighty civilization suddenly arose here. No one knows what happened to it. What's your opinion on why the city was abandoned and the civilization just sort of disappeared?"

"A significant event occurred in the first century around the time of Christ, shortly before Teo rose to become the greatest city of the Americas. A fiery object was seen flying across the sky from east to west. Astronomers in China, India, and Rome recorded the event as a comet but noted that it was much brighter and appeared closer to Earth than any comet seen before. Even more perplexing was a claim that the object changed course. It didn't take much for ancient people to decide that this was a god racing around the world in a fiery chariot.

"The observations recorded in Europe and Asia coincide with the report of a fiery god in the sky here in ancient Mexico. What really piqued my interest in terms of investigating the notion of an ancient astronaut was that the legend which arose about the god is connected to someone we know existed."

"Who?"

"Him." Caden pointed at monstrous stone heads poking out of a wall. "Quetzalcoatl, the Feathered Serpent."

The creature was grotesque, with the head of a giant snake, the jaws of a shark, and the plumes of a tropical bird.

"What we call an archaeobeast," Caden said, "an ancient supernatural spirit or preternatural beast, usually associated with an archaeological site. Cultures all over the world have them. Quetzalcoatl is just more ferocious-looking than most others."

"You're telling me this thing from a bad trip on Mexican mushrooms was real?"

"I don't know what he actually looked like. Hopefully he was prettier than the stonework, but Teo was ruled by a god-king named Quetzalcoatl. We're standing in front of the Temple of Quetzalcoatl. We don't know whether there was a single king with that name or a series of them using the name. The legend was that he was a frightful creature, a feathered serpent that flew in."

"What about the fiery chariot?"

"No chariots because there weren't horses to draw them. Instead, the ancient Mexicans identified Quetzalcoatl with the evening star, a flaming object in the sky. Like the biblical Genesis, the legend of him is a creation story in which he creates humans: Descending from the sky, he found a deserted world in which everyone had died. He gathered the bones of the dead and anointed them with his own blood so that they rose back to life. He, by the way, is the bloodthirsty gentleman who instituted the blood covenant."

"Sounds like *Night of the Living Dead.* What's your interpretation of the legend?"

"There's usually an element of truth in the myths of ancient peoples. Teo arose after another city not far from here, Cuicuilco, was destroyed by fire and brimstone. Could have been destroyed by a volcano . . ."

"Or the arrival of your visitor with a bang."

"Exactly. Many people were killed, we know that, and the city was abandoned. The survivors built a new city, Teo."

Gillock shook her head. "Bottom line, a guy comes down in a spaceship and makes people build a new city after destroying theirs?"

"I don't think that the story of a visitor from space building a city is any harder to believe than the biblical tale of a supernatural being creating the world in six days or a Darwinian theory that this incredible miracle we call life started with an accidental mixing of chemicals in a primeval sea."

"I didn't mean to get you mad."

"I'm not angry, I'm frustrated. I haven't accepted everything I just told you as gospel. I'm simply saying that legends supported by physical evidence ought to be enough to warrant a scientific investigation instead of everyone running and sticking their heads in the sand out of fear of being ridiculed. Here's how I break it down: Something happened about two thousand years ago. An object was observed racing across the sky, making a maneuver no comet can make. It was observed by astronomers around the world. Around that same time, a city is seeded that grows at an incredible rate to dominate all of Mesoamerica. The city is dominated by a god said to have descended from the heavens.

"Someone—or something—brought the knowledge to build immense pyramids, among the largest in the world, to a culture that had not built anything higher than the roofs of their mud huts. And I'm not willing to simply abandon a search to find out who or what it was because some people will poke fun at the notion that we've been visited before."

"What about the Mayan 2012 theory? Does your flaming-star god fit into that?"

Caden smothered a groan. She had enough problems with the scientific community already and didn't need any more controversy. But she couldn't risk antagonizing the writer by sloughing her off.

"The ancient peoples of Mesoamerica, the Mayans, Aztecs, and all the others, shared gods and legends, including Quetzalcoatl. The Mayans called him Kukulkán. It's said he invented the calendar, the one that ends on winter solstice, December 21, 2012. To those ancient people, the world was not just a threatening place, but was one that changed and shifted."

"How did it change and shift?"

"We believe that the world we were born into is the only world that has ever existed. That's not true at all. Repeatedly over the eons, world-shattering calamities have wiped out the major life-forms on Earth. Not just the dinosaurs, but other mass extinctions. The ancient Mayans and Aztecs had a more realistic view of history. They realized that the world around them was just the latest in a series of worlds that had previously existed. Each of the previous worlds fell to shattering, cataclysmic events."

"What kinds of events?"

"What we would call hits from planet-killing asteroids, earthquakes, ice ages, fire, and flood, but what they thought of as the violent whims of the gods. They believed civilizations lost their way and were wiped out by angry gods."

"Civilization losing its way? Doesn't that describe the world around us? Crazies going berserk with killing sprees at universities and malls, religious fanatics around the world trying to kill off everyone else, humans killing the planet with their excretions from cars and factories, a total lack of leadership by the people who are supposed to be protecting us. You know what this world needs?"

"A flood," Caden said.

Gillock screeched. "God, wouldn't that clean up the mess in this world!"

Caden smiled and shook her head. "I have to confess that despite all the excesses of mankind, I still have hope for the future. I don't disbelieve that we will see changes in the near future. But there's a good reason why ancient prophecies like the apocalyptic 2012 one are so thought-provoking—they came down to us over the ages because they have an element of truth. Earth has suffered repeated cataclysms. But I hope and pray that the changes coming will be positive ones, and will make the world safer and healthier for all of us—including the poor polar bears, who seem to be a gauge of the terrible things we've done to the environment."

"We will drive you from our land, we will drink your blood."

The werejaguar performers had caught up with them.

"We are of the jaguars," they sang, *"Nawals, lords of the night, servants of the Feathered Serpent."*

Thunder pounded from dark clouds pushing over distant mountains.

"The gods must be lapping up that blood," Gillock said.

A performer moved in close to Caden, and she made eye contact with a pair of bloodshot eyes glowing with hate.

2

As they walked toward the Pyramid of the Sun, Gillock noticed Caden glance up and down the street.

"Looking for someone?"

"My assistant, Julio, an archaeology student. He was supposed to meet me and come along with us. He knows a lot about Teotihuacán, sometimes I think too much."

"What'd you mean?"

Caden shook her head. "I don't know. I—" She hesitated.

"You seem worried. If you want to share it, I promise you won't read about it later on."

"Thanks. I really like Julio and I'm worried about him. There are all kinds of unusual customs associated with the Mesoamerican cultures that we'd find weird today."

"Such as?"

"A list that would fill a book or even a set of them. In Julio's case, he's taken a keen interest in one of the provocative, uh, I guess I'd call it a potion."

"The kind of mind-altering concoction you'd get from brewing peyote mushrooms?"

"Something like that, but more complicated. Julio isn't into drugs per se, it's more of a historical research thing. The pre-Columbian cultures were quite sophisticated when it came to medical pharmaceuticals, most of which came from plants. An early study categorized a thousand plants the Aztecs used in medicine. They had medical schools, with training in specialties like surgery and pharmacology. And, like all cultures, they had their uppers and hallucinatory drugs, like peyote. There was also a legendary concoction called *teopatli*. It wasn't very appetizing, a concoction of scorpions, spiders, poisonous snakes, and a hallucinatory morning-glory seed called *ololiuqui*. It was said to have magic powers, could turn a person invisible, permit them to shape-change."

"Shape-change?"

"Turn into animals, like those performers back there changing into Nawals, werejaguars."

"You're not going to tell me that Julio is trying to mix up a batch of this black-magic potion to turn himself into a Mexican Dr. Jekyll and Mr. Hyde?"

"*God, I hope not.* But when I asked him what he thought he'd achieve, he said the drug can be used to call back the dead and shape-change."

"That's a charming thought. Sounds like Julio's

been eating too many of those Mexican 'shrooms that make you see things that aren't there."

"You're probably right." Caden didn't add that Julio had been saying other strange things. During her last conversation with him, on the telephone the previous day, he had been almost incoherent as he babbled, saying things she didn't even want to think about. She regretted now asking him to meet them.

She changed the subject. "The temples built atop the pyramids were where they held sacrificial ceremonies. The victims were led up the stairs to the top, where priests performed their own version of heart surgery."

"Ripping out hearts?"

"Yes, the victim was bent backwards over an arched stone mound so their head and feet would be down and their chest pushed up. A priest ripped open the chest with a razor-sharp, obsidian knife and reached in and pulled out the heart while it was still beating."

"A charming custom. No wonder the indigenous people of Mexico have such a violent history."

"It wasn't any more barbaric than the Romans putting thousands of men, women, and children to death in the arena, often letting them be ripped to pieces by wild animals as crowds cheered, the Inquisition burning people at the stake, the French executioners holding up the 'talking heads' of people guillotined, the murder of six million Jews during—"

Gillock threw her hands in the air. "You win—I surrender. The history of humanity is a chronicle of inhumanity."

"In the pre-Columbian world, it was thought of as a matter of survival. The people believed that there were constant power struggles in the form of war and chaos among the gods. They believed that it was up to humanity to maintain order in the cosmos, and that order could only be maintained by pacifying the gods with blood sacrifices."

"Sounds like the same theory wild-animal trainers use to keep from being eaten by lions and tigers—they keep them well fed. Is that your friend Julio?"

A man gave them his back and walked away as Caden turned to look.

"No, that's not him."

Caden had noticed the man before. He had Japanese features, but his clothes, sandals, and straw hat were those of local men. Japanese tour groups weren't unusual at Teo, and some Mexicans were of Japanese descent, but she had heard him buying a Coke from a vendor, and his Japanese accent wasn't consistent with his being a native Mexican. She had caught him watching her out of the corner of his eye. Now he was back at Teo for the third day in a row.

"Someone you know?" Gillock asked.

"No, just curious about him. The way he's dressed and has his hat pulled down, at first glance I thought he was Mexican, but then I realized he's Japanese." Caden looked around. "I noticed that there are more soldiers and police here, too."

"Probably a terrorist threat."

"Isn't that the truth." Caden took Gillock's arm. "Let's continue toward the Pyramid of the Sun. Julio will be coming from that direction. His mother lives in a village not far from the site."

Caden was more worried about Julio than she had let on, and not just because of his sudden interest in ancient drugs. But it wasn't something she wanted to share with the magazine writer: She had him researching the resurgence of the Jaguar Cult. A week ago he claimed he had "infiltrated them," as if he were on a spy mission. After that, he had clammed up about his meetings with the group.

No, not clammed up, she thought. *Secretive* and *evasive* were more accurate. He said he'd met a girl in the cult that turned him on. Caden realized now that after he mentioned meeting the girl, he started being vague and evasive about what he'd seen at the cult meetings.

"You're worried about your friend," Gillock said. "It shows."

"Yes, I'm worried about him. I'm drawn between minding my own business and helping a friend who doesn't really want the help. Julio's been assisting me as part of his master's thesis. Over time, I've seen him get deeper and deeper into the occult lore of Teotihuacán. It really is addictive, the mystery of the place. But there's also a dark magic, a feeling I've never experienced anywhere else in Mexico, as if the city is still haunted by those bloodthirsty ancient gods. Like the Delphic mysteries of ancient Greece, there's a host of esoteric rituals and alchemy from Teotihuacán that influenced the entire Mesoamerican world, most of it revolving around the Feathered Serpent."

"I understand that you've learned more about the Feathered Serpent because of an earthquake," Gillock said.

"Yes, the quake shook things up. Researchers previously found tunnels under the site, but there's never been the money to do the excavation necessary to study them. It's always been suspected that they run all the way to the mountain. Tales of the Feathered Serpent often referred to an underground palace or tomb in the mountains, but without clues as to where it was located. Back in the 1500s a scientist sent by Philip the Second of Spain to research Teo reported a story of a tunnel that ran to an underground palace in the mountains north of the city."

"You think the tunnel runs to something in the mountain?"

"I'd bet on it." Caden pointed at a mountain north of the city. "The Avenue of the Dead points directly at Cerro Gordo, a peak that's been sacred since ancient times. Unfortunately, there's little money in the country's budget for archaeological sites. It will be a long time before we'll know whether the tunnel reaches the mountain and what else is down there."

Laura Gillock stared around at the ancient ruins and enormous pyramids. "I'm like the Aztecs, this place spooks me. I get feelings about places, my sixth sense starts beeping when I'm somewhere weird. A ghost city, that's what it is. I know a little about your Spanish scientist, I read about him in my research for another article. He also reported having found the bones of people and beasts over fifteen feet tall in the Cuicuilco-Teotihuacán area. That report takes on a stranger hue when it's matched up with an Aztec legend that Teotihuacán was built by giants."

Caden laughed. "If we come across the bones of any fifteen-foot-tall people, you'll have an exclusive on the story."

"Don't laugh, places don't get weird reputations without some basis."

"Did you read about the alien sighting?"

"The ones over Mexico? I know they've had some amazing sightings in Mexico City and by the Mexican air force. Apparently the sightings have made air force pilots true believers in the UFO phenomena."

"I was actually referring to one here at Teo. Back in the 1920s an American archaeologist reported his team was visited by a UFO when they were examining the Teotihuacán ruins."

Gillock shook her finger at Caden. "When the stories start piling up about how weird a place is, you better start wondering why. And those Aztecs, they were said to be pretty tough hombres. Ever wonder what they knew about Teotihuacán that scared the hell out of them?"

"Something's going on." Caden nodded at the Pyramid of the Sun. A large crowd had gathered at the foot of the pyramid.

The monument to the sun god was over two hundred feet high and had a wide, almost vertical stairway up the front. A *step-pyramid*, it had five narrow platforms, called steps, cut into its side. The steps came about every forty or fifty feet up the sides and were wide enough to walk on.

As they approached the pyramid, they heard tourists talking about the "show" being presented. Two figures, an adult dressed as an Aztec priest and a younger person, a boy perhaps ten or eleven, were on the edge of a platform about a hundred feet up the twenty-story-high pyramid. The two struggled beside a convex-shaped stone slab used in ancient times to perform sacrifices on.

"Did I hear right?" Gillock asked. "Those are actors up there putting on a show?"

"My God."

"What's the matter?"

"That's Julio with the boy." Caden pushed forward through the crowd, straining to see. The struggle was going on near the edge, where the sacrifice slab had been placed as a tourist attraction.

Julio clubbed the boy with a stone, knocking him down.

"Wow, that looks real," an American tourist near Caden said.

It looked real to her, too.

Julio picked the dazed boy up in his arms and lay him on the arched sacrificial stone. Caden felt a growing sense of horror. Gillock grabbed her arm and said something. Caden didn't hear her. She jerked her arm away and pushed her way through the crowd. Something was terribly wrong.

Julio stood next to the sacrificial slab and reared back, raising a large blade above his head, holding it with both hands.

Obsidian blade, she thought, *an old ceremonial sacrifice dagger.*

A gasp escaped from her as he brought the blade down and plunged it into the boy's chest. The boy screamed, his body and legs convulsing as Julio wrenched the dagger back and forth, creating a bigger hole. His hand went into the hole and came out grasping a bloody mass.

Some people in the audience clapped. Others remained silent, mesmerized. Caden felt faint. She knew what it was in his hand—a beating heart.

Julio stepped to the edge of the pyramid. He looked down and she realized he had picked her out of the crowd. He called her name.

"Caden! Caden!" He held up the bloody trophy and shook it. *"You see! I told you, I told you he came back!"*

For a moment he teetered on the edge, shouting and swaying. Then he threw himself forward as if he could fly, the heart still clutched in his hand. He fell headfirst, fifty feet to the next level. She heard rather than saw the impact of his body. She didn't realize until later that the screaming in her ears came from her own mouth.

He came back!

The Feathered Serpent had come back.

That was what Julio had told her on the phone.

3

Julio's mother lived eight miles from the Teo archaeological site. Caden drove her VW Bug to the woman's house three days after she observed the distraught woman at Julio's funeral. Knowing from discussions with Julio that his mother had little money, Caden had arranged through Julio's academic adviser to pay for the funeral.

Poor Julio. Mentally deranged on psychedelic drugs, had been the official verdict. She felt some blame even though he had told her of his prior interest in the mind-bending pharmacopoeia of ancient Mexico. Still . . . if she hadn't asked him to check out the Jaguar Cult, he might still be alive.

She wondered if her own obsession with the ancient history where much of her cultural roots lay and which caused her to push the envelope with her career had now helped send a student over the edge.

Her interest in Mexico's history was natural—she was a first-generation *norteamericana* of Mexican ancestry. Prior to her birth, her parents entered Texas illegally, crossing the Río Bravo (the river called the Rio Grande on the U.S. side) at night. In their day, political correctness hadn't yet been born and people called them wetbacks. But it was also before illegal entry became epidemic and a national issue. Back then, sneaking across the border at night was seen as an act of courage by people desperate for a decent life for their future children. They did farm jobs no one else would do, making fruits and vegetables cheaper to harvest—and buy. No one got excited about the influx because America was a big country, and in those days the Southwest and West could hold a lot more people.

Her mother and father worked farms every waking moment at dirt wages to scrape together enough to survive on. When her mother was pregnant, she gave birth to Caden in a lettuce field.

Raised in a Texas town thirty miles from Austin, Caden was in the third grade when her parents bought a one-bedroom, flat-roofed, plywood-box house on the outskirts of town. Her father repaired cars in the backyard, and by the time Caden entered high school, he had his own two-bay car-repair shop in a business district.

Although her parents lacked formal education, they encouraged Caden to succeed, and she was valedictorian of her high school class. Her grades got her into the Austin campus on scholarship. Tragedy struck in her second year of college when her parents were killed in a head-on collision with a drunk driver.

During college, she developed an interest in both Mexican history and archaeology. She became fascinated with the great civilizations that existed on the American continent before the "New World" was discovered and the indigenous cultures were destroyed by Europeans in their lust for treasure. Not that the history of the Americas jumped out at her—education in America was slanted toward European history because that was the ethnic background of the vast majority of the population.

The education system rarely got across that before the arrival of Europeans, the American continent had flourished with civilizations that left behind a rich heritage in architecture, math, astronomy, medicine, and calendaring.

Caden's interest in the ancient Americans wasn't just a matter of her roots. She had a little detective in her, and ancient Mesoamerica, the "middle America" region that stretched from much of Mexico to Panama, offered a tantalizing mystery: Who were the people who built the largest and most wondrous city of pre-Columbian America . . . and what happened to them?

It wasn't an easy transition to get an interest in Teo and then pursue it as a scientist. Archaeology, an old and very established field of science, didn't have an open door for a young woman to advance as rapidly as she wanted. But her background in archaeology opened the door to astrobiology, also called exobiology and space biology. An exciting field, its doors were wide-open for anyone with ability who took up the challenge. The search for extraterrestrial life involved all the sciences, so her background in archaeology provided a way in, including a job at NASA.

Investigating Teo was a perfect fit for her career goals. She believed that Teo, harboring the answer to a great mystery of archaeology, also perhaps held the answer to the question of whether other life existed in the universe—and whether any of it had made its way to Earth.

Her hypothesis was daring . . . and now she needed to find the answer before she was burned at the stake for scientific heresy.

Driving down the street where she expected to find Julio's mother's house, she thought about the young man who had committed a terrible act. He'd pop into her head for hours at a time, disrupting her work or robbing her of sleep, then slip away for a while, giving her some peace. The police report said that he was high on hallucinatory drugs when he murdered the boy in front of a crowd of people and tried to fly off the pyramid. She didn't fault the report. But Julio's acts made her wonder about Laura Gillock's statement that she got "feelings" about places.

As a scientist, Caden had never given much thought to metaphysical aspects of the places she explored.

Archaeological sites were not good or evil—cold, lifeless stone didn't have a soul.

Her mother believed that places picked up an essence from the people who had occupied them, that a room in which a murder was committed is tainted by the emotions of the victim and the killer. That was superstition, not science. But over the past weeks in Teo, an unpleasant feeling about the city had been growing in her, even before Julio began acting strangely. Walking the Avenue of the Dead, past the ruins and temples and staring up at pyramids where thousands— perhaps hundreds of thousands—had had their hearts ripped out, she felt something about the city, an emotion that she had never felt before about a site: a growing trepidation she now recognized as fear.

Working the city a number of times over the years had not created any strong emotions in her except enthusiasm. In her mind the unease she felt began with the arrival of the police and military guards—some sort of terrorist threat, people said. The Japanese man who stared at her and followed her movements without ever smiling or speaking had added to the growing sense of foreboding she experienced.

The presence of armed soldiers and the threat of violence had changed the vibe of the ancient site, as if it had aroused an essence that had lain dormant for millennia. Like bacteria spores that sprout to life under the right conditions, she wondered if Teotihuacán's evil side had suddenly been awakened. And if Julio's mind was twisted from pervasive evil around him rather than from the drugs he experimented with.

Stop it! she told herself. She couldn't permit herself to think about evil. Her mind was ruled by science, not superstition.

Julio's mother's house was whitewashed mud-brick with window flower-boxes and a flat roof. The street was unpaved and lined with similar houses, a neighborhood of small, one-story houses and children, a great many of whom were on the street with bikes, skateboards, and hula hoops as she drove up.

She hadn't met Julio's mother, Ana Rodriguez, and had not approached her at the funeral. Julio had told Caden that his mother worked at a laundry and had only a grammar-school education. His father had gone north when Julio was five and started a new family in Los Angeles, but had sent money home regularly until Julio was out of high school.

The woman didn't have a telephone. Caden had sent a messenger to the house yesterday to see if Ana would speak with her. The response was to come today.

After answering Caden's knock, Julio's mother quietly greeted Caden and invited her in. As soon as Caden was seated, Mrs. Rodriguez set a bowl of fruit on the end table next to her. The older woman's eyes were red and puffy.

Caden started to explain her deep regrets about what had happened to Julio, and the woman interrupted her.

"It was them, they killed him."

"Who?"

"The evil ones called Nawals."

"Julio was researching a group that call themselves the Cult of the Jaguar. Are you saying some of them are pretending to be Nawals?"

She shook her head vehemently. "Not pretending. My Julio said they were real. He said they drank a potion that turned them into jaguar beasts."

Caden didn't know what to say. She didn't want to tell the woman that her son was deep into mind-expanding drugs that altered perception. God knew what ghoulish things Julio "saw" when he worked up his imagination about ancient creatures of the night, then inhaled a drug that sent his mind soaring. With her lack of education, his mother might be superstitious enough to believe the old tales about werejaguars.

"You don't believe me," Ana said, "but that is what Julio told me."

"Was he afraid of them?"

"He was until she fooled him."

"She?"

"The girl, Marica. She's one of them. Julio met her when he went to their meetings." Ana's eyes watered. "He told me he loved her, but she tricked him. She was the one who gave him the drugs."

"Julio always had an, uh, interest in drugs."

Ana wagged her finger at Caden. "He talked about the drugs because they were part of his study at the university, but he didn't take them. Not until he met that girl. She told him he would become famous when he told you about the old painting."

"What old painting?"

"The one they found after the earthquake. Like the ones they did on walls long ago."

"What did it portray?"

"The Feathered Serpent, Quetzalcoatl."

"I don't recall any recent—"

Ana shook her head. "No one knows about it, only them. They found it in the mountain." She pointed toward the north.

"Cerro Gordo?"

"Yes, in a cave."

"Are you telling me that this Marica claims to have found an ancient image of the Feathered Serpent?"

"Yes, they found it, the ones who worship the beast."

Mother of God. The finding of a pictograph of the Feathered Serpent would create a sensation in archaeological circles. Not only would it be a rare and important find, it might lead to the tomb of the god-king that legend had long placed in the mountain. Could a cult of weirdos worshipping the ancient god-king have really found something that sensational in the mountains?

"How do I find Marica?" Caden asked.

"The girl is evil. Stay away from her."

Caden knew there were good people and bad people in the world, though her science-trained mind still fought against accepting the presence of evil. Good

and bad were based upon objective criteria, not metaphysical ones. And her good sense told her to stay
away from the girl named Marica and her bizarre
friends who were reviving an ancient murder cult.

All her training and common sense blew away in
the face of a chance to make a stunning archaeological find. A find that would go a long ways toward re-
habilitating her career. And if she found the tomb of
the Feathered Serpent, who knew what antiquities and
knowledge about mysterious Teotihuacán might be
found inside?

Howard Carter found King Tut's tomb, enriched the
world with its magnificent artifacts, and made history.

Why not her?

Naturally, one strange aspect of Howard Carter's
breaking into the ancient tomb came to mind as she
left Mrs. Rodriguez with the phone number of Marica
in hand. Eleven people associated with the King Tut
dig died of "unnatural causes" over the next five years.
The mummy's curse became the stuff of legends and
Hollywood box-office success.

Thinking about the warning of "evil," she rolled
down the window of the VW Bug and told the wind,
"Evil is a metaphysical concept. I am afraid of bad
people. I fear no evil."

That will be my mantra.

OLD WORLD EVIL

A great . . . lesson is to be learned from Old Mexico, for our own world is demon-haunted, the powers and principalities of Black Magic beset it, as never before. . . .

Evil is tireless. All evil works through a magic of its own, a black magic which expresses itself in forms so numerous and so protean that it is frequently indistinguishable from goodness and beauty.

—**Lewis Spence,** *The Magic and Mysteries of Mexico* **(1930)**

4

Marica, a dark, skinny, somber girl with large eyes, didn't leave Caden with the impression that she had been affected by mind-altering substances, though she wasn't talkative when Caden asked her about Julio's experiences with drugs. But she loosened up when Caden told her she wanted information about the Feathered Serpent image—and offered the universal motivator: money. A thousand dollars if there really was an image of the god dating back to antiquity. *Mucho dinero*, but she wanted the girl's complete loyalty.

"I can show it to you if you come to our meeting, but you can't take it. They wouldn't let you."

"Who? Members of the Cult of the Jaguar?"

"Yes. The group was formed after a man found an opening created by the earthquake on the side of the mountain," Marica said. "Like Juan Diego."

Not quite, Caden thought. Juan Diego was an Indian convert to Christianity who said he observed apparitions of the Virgin Mary about ten years after the Spanish conquest of the Aztec empire. He told his priest that the Virgin had commanded that a church be built on the spot where he saw her. News that one of their own had seen a miraculous image of the Virgin swept like wildfire among the indigenous people, whose pagan gods had been defeated by the Christian one. The incident sped up the conversion of the conquered peoples.

Marica's reference to Juan Diego and the Virgin of Guadalupe story implied that the girl expected the Quetzalcoatl discovery to sweep the nation into worship of it.

Marica was vague about what the image looked like. "It's on a wall, inside the cave. It's dark and hard to see, but it shows the god above the mountains."

Caden wondered if the girl had actually seen anything or just repeated what others had told her. But a claim of a previously unknown image of the Feathered Serpent was too much for Caden to resist.

"He's come back to fulfill the prophecy," the girl said.

"What prophecy?"

The girl waved her arms in the air. "You know, the world's going to end and another will take its place."

Caden now understood what Marica meant. The Feathered Serpent, like the apocalyptic Four Horsemen, was one of four gods of the Mayans and Aztecs that were destroyers of worlds. The lore about him since ancient times was that he would someday return to destroy the world, just as he and the other gods had destroyed previous worlds.

"He came back when the earth shook."

Jesus. They believe that the earthquake had un-tombed the ancient god. And that it will fulfill the 2012 End Time prophecy. No wonder so much excitement had been created in people like Marica.

Marica stared at Caden. "You don't believe me. But you will see." She leaned forward and locked eyes with Caden. "You will see."

The cult meeting took place at night in front of the cave on the mountainside. Caden went on the back of the girl's motor scooter, dressed in black clothes with a heavy shawl pulled over her head. The only equipment she brought was a flashlight and a small camera that fit in her pocket.

They left the scooter where a recently made dirt trail petered out and went by foot another half mile up the side of the mountain. As they climbed, a gust of wind made an eerie sound as it swirled around them. *Weeping woman* was what the locals called the wind because it reminded them of the moans of an old woman.

A collector of legends, Caden knew the tale behind the weeping woman: Each year an ancient village sought to be free of its transgressions by designating an old woman to bear the guilt—then stoned her to death as punishment for "her" sins.

Caden realized the economic reason behind the

ugly tradition—old people could no longer contribute as much to the village as when they were young. In essence, they became a burden and strained the meager food resources.

Not a nice story, but history wasn't always kind.

She heard voices before they came around a ridge and into a clearing to find people milling around a bonfire. The area was sheltered on all sides by a rock formation, making it unlikely anyone in the valley below would see the fire.

As they came into the clearing, Marica slipped on a jaguar mask. Caden estimated forty or fifty people were mingling around, and everyone she saw had jaguar paraphernalia, ranging from rubber masks to the elaborate costumes that the blood-covenant entertainers wore in Teo.

Wonderful. She was the only one without jaguar trappings. She felt as inconspicuous as glowing in the dark.

She spotted the "cave," or at least a crack in the mountain that could lead to a cave, on the other side of the fire. A narrow crevice about five feet high, it appeared barely wide enough for a person to slip through sideways. A little rubble on the ground indicated it could have been opened by an earthquake.

She moved closer to get a better look. Two guards stood silently outside the opening. They wore elaborate uniforms, unlike the makeshift costumes of the blood-covenant entertainers. As she got closer, flickering light revealed features on the dark masks.

Caden got the same chill she felt when she'd looked into the crazed eyes of the performer pretending to be a werejaguar. For the first time since setting out on the journey to find an ancient tomb, she felt genuinely frightened.

Marica's mask and the others she saw were the stuff of Halloween, but these struck her as expertly crafted studies in *evil*. That word again came to mind, and this time she didn't try to blow it away with her scientific training.

Nawals are real, Julio had told his mother. *He came back,* Julio shouted to Caden over the phone and at the pyramid.

The masks portrayed a preternatural blend of human and bestial features. Who—or what—would have gone through such trouble to make them so real? And frightening.

Between the fire and the opening was a large block of stone. As Caden stared at it, she realized it was a sacrifice slab, like the one Julio had used when ripping out the heart of an innocent child.

The people in the clearing had stopped moving around and become quiet. She turned slowly. Fifty jaguar faces stared at her.

The girl was no longer by her side.

Something was terribly wrong.

What have I gotten myself into?

Caden bolted—running for the trail that led down the mountain. She got only a dozen feet before two men dressed as blood-covenant entertainers grabbed her arms.

She fought to break loose. "Let me go!"

Her arms were released, but more people surrounded her and blocked her from leaving. Their ranks parted and the two Nawal guards that had been standing by the opening stepped forward.

"No!"

A guard put what looked like a hollow reed to his lips and blew powder into her face. She involuntarily breathed in the charged air. She knew the history of ancient Mexico and realized that the substance they blew was a narcotic, something that would rob her of her senses and her will, a drug that ancient temple priests used to rob sacrifice victims of their resistance.

They took her by the arms and pulled her along. Their grips were powerful. She knew instinctively that she had to resist, that she was being led to an unimaginable horror, but they led her along without resistance. Her mind rebelled but her arms and legs were rubbery.

They led her past the sacrifice mound and turned her sideways to pull her into the opening. It was pitch-black beyond the opening, and she only knew she was in a cave because of a sudden cooling of the air and that she wasn't bumping into walls.

An illumination started as a spark that grew, not a light that glowed, but as if the darkness were being sucked away. Her mind left her body and wandered around the cave.

Out of body, she thought. *I'm having an out-of-body experience.*

The first thing that struck her after being pulled sideways through a small opening was the size of the space. The ceiling was many times her height, and the walls seemed far from her.

As her consciousness floated in the shadowy realm, she realized that the cavern had expanded . . . it was no longer a hollow cave but an illimitable realm. She felt as if she had left the known dimension of her world and stepped through an opening into the cosmos.

She wondered if this mind expansion was what Julio had experienced when he took a psychedelic drug. But what had he encountered in his trip that led him to commit a horror?

Her universe slowly became limited as the cavern took on a shape.

I'm in the tomb of the Feathered Serpent.

The tomb was almost egg-shaped inside, smooth and hollow. Rich colors appeared and sparkled as light grew.

Such dazzling colors. Like standing inside a Fabergé egg turned inside out.

Fine etchings, produced by incredible workmanship, of beasts and gods covered the walls. The detail was superior to what appeared on the temples and pyramids of Teotihuacán and the hundreds of other archaeological sites in the country.

The colors were stunning in their glory of reddish orange hues, shades of green and blue, with fine weaving of gold, silver, and turquoise. Although the modern tourist and the archaeologist only saw dull, colorless ruins, both the Egyptian and ancient Americas originally used brilliant colors in the artwork that covered the inside and outside of buildings. Sheltered by solid rock in what Caden suspected was almost literally a vacuum seal, the original colors were as vibrant as when they were applied an eon ago.

An etching on the ceiling showed a flaming entity soaring across the sky, a fiery ray hitting a mountain, and a deluge of rubble crushing a city. Another panel showed a city being raised.

She understood the message of the scenes. The arrival of an entity. The destruction of Cuicuilco. The birth of Teotihuacán.

The painting on the walls and ceiling came alive. No longer inanimate pictographs, the scenes played out as terrible wars with warriors hacking at each other with razor-sharp obsidian blades, long lines of sacrifice victims stretching endlessly back from the steps of the great Pyramid of the Sun, priests at a temple atop the pyramid cutting open chests and ripping out hearts, holding the still beating bloody masses up for the spectators to see.

The scenes faded and she sensed something else.

I'm not alone.

The awareness raised the short hairs on her soul. It wasn't the Nawal guards who had led her in. The presence was larger, a force field that engulfed the entire cavern, her entire universe.

She felt herself swimming in a liquid dust that grew thicker every second. For a fleeting moment, a shape in the dimness, neither human nor animal, appeared before her, something more fluid than the mist, a form she could neither comprehend nor even describe.

I'm awake, she thought, awake yet dreaming. Awake but in a twilight state. Her mind no longer free-floated; she was back in her body, back on her feet, her knees feeling mushy. She felt nothing underfoot and began to float again, her body rotating back so she was supine. She sensed another presence in the shadowy mist she floated in.

Horror and repulsion suddenly gripped her as she felt first her shoes and then her pants come off. Her blouse came off next, then her panties and bra. She floated naked, exposed and helpless.

Someone—something—touched her. She felt it on the bare skin of her face. An exploration of her face and hair.

Her breasts were touched.

Jesus Joseph Mary Mother of God.

Her legs spread apart.

She felt a movement between her legs.

She screamed. But no one was there to hear her.

5

Pulled back out of the narrow opening, Caden's feet moved and her mind worked to catch up. She understood only that she was no longer in the cave, that the strange creatures who had taken her in had now brought her out.

They led her to the sacrifice block. Julio plunging a knife into the chest of a young boy flashed in her mind. As a costumed figure stepped in front of her with a blowpipe again, she turned her face away and twisted out of the grip of the two men holding her. She broke free but was quickly grabbed by a Nawal. She screamed and fought back as clawed fingers dug into her arm.

Bright light and loud noise exploded in the clearing as a helicopter suddenly rose above them. A powerful spotlight from the chopper lit up the whole clearing.

"Federal police—don't move!" was broadcast in Spanish.

Everyone ran. Breaking loose from the Nawal holding her as people stampeded in panic, Caden was knocked down. She got back up and almost ran into the arms of a dark figure standing before her.

The person dressed as an Aztec priest had a foot-long obsidian dagger in hand.

Caden backed up as the dark figure came toward her.

"You are meant to die."

"Julio?"

Gunfire erupted from the chopper. The priest jerked and staggered back as bullets ripped into him. He fell to the ground and convulsed for a second before going still.

Uniformed police came down ropes from the chopper. Caden ran to them as the first one hit the ground.

"Thank God you're—"

He sprayed her in the face with an aerosol from a canister. She pitched forward and he caught her.

6

A hospital. That much she understood when she awoke. From the monogram on uniforms, Caden realized it was a small hospital not far from the Teo site, one she had driven by several times. Other than that she was alive, the only thing else she could gauge from the hospital bed was that she was strapped down and nobody bothered listening to her pleas.

After she regained consciousness, she had told the doctor and nurses checking her who she was and why she had been at the clearing. No response came from any of them. They weren't mute—they spoke to each other—but acted as if they didn't hear what she said.

She knew she wasn't hallucinating. They heard her. And ignored her.

Something else she noticed was that under their white smocks, all the staff wore military uniforms.

When her door was opened, she could see more uni-formed personnel in the hallway.

The military had taken over the hospital. That was a given. But why were they holding her? And refusing to communicate with her?

Another mystery was the man she heard in the hall-way speaking English with an American accent. A moment later a nurse entered the room and gave her a shot. She closed her eyes, but a window was still open in her mind, and she didn't go completely under. She heard voices by her bed and recognized the male American voice she'd heard earlier. He hovered over her as he conversed with a man who spoke English with a Mexican accent.

"She's been thoroughly examined since her experi-ence in the tomb," the Mexican said.

"Our people will want all the reports, blood tests, scans, everything."

"Of course."

"Too bad," the American said. "She's young. Sup-posed to be really big in her field."

"Your people are certain they want her zeroed out."

"It's necessary."

My God—were they talking about killing her? She wanted to scream at them, tell them to free her from the madness she'd descended into, but her lips wouldn't move.

She was still groggy but awake when a male nurse came in and placed an oxygen mask over her face. As he started to turn a lever, he was clubbed from behind and collapsed to the floor.

A man hovered over her. He stuck something under her nose and her brain exploded, jerking her awake.

He put his hand over her lips as she started to scream. "Shh. We'll get you out of here."

Staring into his face, she realized he was the middle-aged Japanese man she had seen at Teo.

He helped her out of the hospital bed and into a full-length raincoat.

"We're going out the window. It's a short drop. We're on ground level."

She hadn't realized it was pouring outside, a thunderstorm pounding down. A woman outside the window helped her to a waiting van. The Japanese man got aboard, and the van moved down the dark street.

Still a little zonked, she stared at the people in the van. Besides the man who helped her escape from the hospital and the woman waiting by the window, whom she identified as American from her accent, a man of Mexican descent was driving.

"Who are you people?" she asked the group.

No one answered.

"Please say something."

The woman said, "We're friends. They were going to kill you."

"Why—*why*?"

"You saw too much."

"It's the Feathered Serpent," the Japanese said. "The disaster in the Gulf of Mexico. It's started."

"What's started?"

The woman leaned toward her, her eyes unnaturally wide. She spoke in a whisper, "The End Time."

Caden's mind swirled. What was the woman talking about? The end of the world? Armageddon? Caden had used up all the adrenaline rush she could muster. Her eyes wanted to close and shut down her brain. "This is insane. Who are you?" she asked again.

"We're frogs." That from the Japanese man.

"What do you mean?"

"Like you, we've been dissected."

"I'm sorry you have to take this, but it's better if you sleep." The woman held out bottled water and a pill.

"I'm not going to—"

"Please. We can force you, but we don't want to."

"It's just a sedative," the Japanese man said.

She pushed aside the woman's hand and passed out from the drugs already in her system.

BOOK II

LIVING WATER

7

Sedona, Arizona

Caden stood at a window and sipped tea as she gazed at the dramatic rusty-blood crimson of Cathedral Rock set against a cornflower blue sky. In and out of sleep for two days, she finally was alert enough to get out of bed and take a shower. When she stepped back into the bedroom, fresh clothes, a pot of hot tea, and a simple breakfast of granola with a banana and yogurt had materialized.

She was somewhere in Sedona, Arizona's New Age capital, with its artists and red-rock vistas, that much she knew, having spent time in Sedona a dozen years before, a romantic hiking trip with a college lover. Later, she came back alone to experience the quiet and tranquillity while working on her doctoral dissertation.

The only window in the room looked out at the famed monolith-shaped red sandstone peak and its two sisters. She didn't know the names of the other two mounds, but had once pencil-sketched Cathedral Rock.

A tap sounded at her door. The door didn't appear to be locked, at least not from the inside, but she hadn't bothered to open it and peek out. She wasn't ready to face the world, but now the world had come to her. Without moving from the window, she said, "Come in."

The man who had rescued her from a strange hell in a Mexican hospital opened the door and paused politely in the doorway. He gave her a short bow, more of an accentuated nod. "Good morning. How are you feeling?"

"Better."

He nodded again. "Excellent. Many people, including myself, believe that Sedona lies in a vortex of spiritual energy that can revitalize one's self."

"Why did you bring me here?"

"I assume that is just one of many questions you have. You deserve answers and shall get them." He offered his hand. "My name is Koji Oda. I am Japanese, but have been living in your country for the last twenty years."

She recognized the name and slowly pronounced it aloud. "Ko-jee, Oh-da. Scientist . . . water studies . . . unorthodox views. I read one of your papers when I was in grad school. Translated from a University of Osaka journal, I recall. You became a NASA scientist. I thought you were dead."

He smiled and gave another little nodding bow. "I

am sure there are many who have wished that result."

"No—I mean, you disappeared, fell off the radar.
Lots of controversy, then nothing for years. I'm an
astrobiologist, as you are."

"Your comparison gives me too much credit. You
are a true scientist. I lack both advanced degrees and
the desire to characterize myself as a scientist. I prefer to think of myself as a dabbler."

She knew this "dabbler" had a reputation as a world-
class astrobiologist with an expertise in water.

"What happened to you? About the time I was entering grad school, twelve years ago, there was a lot of
buzz about you, your experiments with water for
NASA, your predictions the world will run out of water before it runs out of fossil fuels, and that future
wars will be fought over water. My God, you were
constantly in the news."

"So much time has passed, it will take time to tell
it all. Let's take a walk and I will show you my oasis."

Sedona was desert country. The "oasis" was a seven-
acre complex with foot-thick-dirt-walled buildings
and buildings that were half-buried. The reason for
using dirt was obvious—the earth provided as much
insulation as concrete, keeping buildings cooler in the
summer and warmer in the winter. Palm trees were
everywhere.

"We grow and sell desert palms and many rare and
beautiful plants. The greenhouses over there produce
exotic plants that we truck to Phoenix."

"Where do you get the water? Artesian wells?"

"We capture part of it and create the rest out of thin air. The main reason I chose the site is that it's over the tunnels of an old silver mine. To store water during desert storms, we divert water into the tunnels for storage, creating a system of cisterns, just as ancient peoples in the Middle East turned deserts into gardens by storing storm water in cisterns. We use that water to grow the plants we sell. We also use part of a tunnel for cold store, using ice we've produced with the sun's energy."

"I recall reading you were working on some other exotic water problems for NASA."

"I worked on the Mars water project at NASA. We were reasonably certain that there would be water under the surface, probably in the form of ice. I worked out a plan to use the sun's energy to heat the water into liquid form and cause it to rise to the surface." He smiled a little shyly. "We had several other problems under study when I left NASA. Conserving water on a space vehicle by converting an astronaut's own sweat, respiration, and urine into drinking water, making drinking water from a vehicle's exhaust."

"Water from auto exhaust." She thought for a moment. "Hydrogen plus oxygen equals water. There's hydrogen in the exhaust fumes coming out the tailpipe. Add oxygen . . . and a stimulant, carefully."

"Yes, a very sensitive concoction."

She knew that if you combine hydrogen and oxygen, you can make water by lighting the concoction with a match. The problem is you would probably also blow yourself up. That's basically what happened to the 1930s German airship the *Hindenburg*. The eight-hundred-foot dirigible was filled with hydrogen, which sprang a leak. The hydrogen mixed with oxygen in the air and a spark from an electrical storm set it off.

"How are you making water from dry desert air?" She knew there were many ways to make water from the atmosphere, but the methods were generally more expensive than getting it by conventional methods.

"As you know, there is more water in the form of vapors in our atmosphere than in our oceans. If we had a cheap power source to convert vapor to usable water, we could economically create water out of thin air. The amazing thing about the desert is that it has a plentiful supply of the most powerful energy source in the solar system."

"The sun. Solar panels."

"Of course, Old Sol. We have a device to produce water in large quantities by using highly efficient solar panels as the power source. Again, it's a hydrogen-oxygen scenario. We create and compress vapors. To increase the supply of water, we artificially increase the relative humidity of the air in our chambers."

Using solar energy to turn water vapors into drinking water wasn't a new technique. She realized that the secret to his success must be that he had developed a method of greatly increasing the amount of vapor without a correspondent increase in the energy it took.

Watching people working with the plants, she asked, "Is this a commune? A cooperative to produce your own food, make a living off selling plants?"

"In a sense, that's exactly what it is, though none of us had set out to live in a commune. But all of us have something in common."

She stopped and faced him. "You called yourself a frog, say you've been dissected. What kind of nonsense is that?" As she spoke, she realized it wasn't any stranger than what had happened to her in Teo.

He took her arm. "It's time you got answers. Along with lunch."

Five of them, not counting Caden, were gathered around the lunch table. Koji sat at the head of the table and put Caden at the other end. The others were a middle-aged man called Pavlov, a small-boned woman named Joan who had haggard features and reminded Caden of a frightened bird, and Barney Hill, an older man who said nothing, hardly looking up from the food in front of him, nodding but not even saying hello when Caden was introduced.

The fifth person was the youngest of the group, a man in his late twenties with red hair and red freckles. He reminded her of the rawboned Texas farm boys she grew up with, and she was only a little off in geography—he was from Arkansas. He sat next to her and said, "Welcome to Roswell Two."

Roswell, New Mexico, was famous for one thing: aliens.

Lunch was simple—soup with cabbage and wheat dumplings, and a hunk of crusty bread. Caden slowly ate her soup and listened to the table talk. She noticed that Koji didn't join in. He was one of them, but apart, more the mentor to occasionally answer a question about how things worked than participating in small talk. She was the unspoken focus of attention and found the surreptitious stares disconcerting, feeling like a freak on display.

They're some sort of cult, she thought. And wondered when the table talk would progress to answers.

"I was abducted," the Arkie farm boy said.

The statement came out of nowhere and Caden didn't react to it. She finished a sip of soup before she looked up to meet his eye.

He'd said earlier that his name was Neo. It didn't fit him. Nor did the man who had the same name as the Russian scientist famous for his behavioral experiments fit him. She wondered if all of them were using aliases.

"We encourage everyone to tell their experience," Joan, the frightened bird, said.

Group therapy?

Neo went on, "It was back when I was in the air force, 'bout five years ago. I was stationed at Sheppard Air Force Base outside Wichita Falls. Me and my wife was coming back from visiting her parents in Utah. It was late, 'bout three in the morning. I had the pedal to the metal coming down Route 262. Wasn't much of nothing on the road except us and a coyote or two. My wife was asleep when I first saw it, seven points of light in the distance. At first I thought it might be a squadron of planes or choppers out of an air base, but they didn't act right for aircraft, at least not the kind we make.

"As I watched, these suckers flew up and down and around like they were giant fireflies, reaching speeds and doing maneuvers no aircraft on Earth could have done, not even the secret stuff I've seen."

Caden glanced at Koji while Neo told his tale. Nothing on his stoic face revealed his thoughts.

"They came right at me, all seven of them, spread out above the road like an attack squadron. Suddenly six of them split off, three to each side, and one came right at me, dropping down almost to the pavement, coming at me in a head-on. I went off the road, hitting a ditch. The car flipped and rolled over."

Neo's hands shook as he talked. "I went out, I guess I must have hit my head. I was unconscious, and then the next thing I knew, they had me, four little guys, maybe three, four feet tall, with black, shiny skin and big heads, oversized heads and small arms and legs, like the heads grew because they used their brains and the arms and legs weren't much because they didn't do much physical stuff."

"What did their hands look like?" The question came from Barney Hill, the man who had hardly looked up from his food.

"Like a baseball mitt, fingers webbed together with a thumb separate."

The man nodded. "Yeah, yeah." He went back to staring holes in his soup bowl.

"They examined me," Neo said. "Didn't take off my clothes, just looked me over as I lay there on the ground. I kicked at them but one of them hit me with a light, a red beam, like a laser. It hit me in the face and my face felt like it was on fire. I couldn't move my arms and legs, just laid there paralyzed. Then they took me aboard a ship and did a real examination. They took me apart, piece by piece, and looked it over. I still remember one of them holding my liver in his hands. They put me back together and you couldn't tell I'd been dissected. Didn't feel anything, either. They just put me back together and laid me out on the road. That's how I was when the state troopers found me, my car rolled over and me just laying there on the ground, unable to move."

Neo stared at Caden, pain in his voice as he spoke. "Those dumb bastards, the cops, they said I fell asleep at the wheel and ran off the road. Peg was thrown from the car and it rolled over her. They said I was making up the story because Peg didn't make it. But that's a big pile of bullshit, you know, just bullshit."

"Show her your face," Pavlov said. "Let her touch it."

Neo grabbed Caden's hand and rubbed it against his cheek. "You feel that, you feel it?"

She jerked her hand away. "I don't feel anything."

Neo jumped up from his chair. "That's right, that's right, you don't feel anything because there's nothing to feel. Five years and there's nothing to feel."

"He hasn't shaved in five years." Koji rubbed his own face. "The alien beam killed his ability to grow facial hair."

Caden bent over her soup, not knowing what to say. Should she tell Neo it sounded as if he fell asleep at the wheel and imagined alien abduction to rid himself of the guilt of accidentally killing his wife? But how was the lack of hair growth explained?

She now had insight as to why they had aliases. The Frogs were people who claimed they'd experienced alien abduction. Paranoia about alien control of the government and fears of being ridiculed went with the territory.

"Yeah, I know what you're thinking," Neo said. "I imagined it." He nudged her with his elbow. "I guess maybe you imagined you got examined by an alien down in Mexico."

The woman across from her, the frightened bird, suddenly volunteered that she took her name from St. Joan. "After Joan of Arc, you know. I always admired her. It was so awful that she was burned at the stake for being courageous and winning battles." She had a slight southern accent.

"I think she was burned by the loser of the battles," Caden offered.

That got a laugh from Neo.

"I was a prisoner in Dulce," St. Joan said.

Caden had never heard of the place. She wondered if it was a mental institution.

"It's an underground military base run by aliens," Koji said. "In New Mexico. Very isolated location near the Colorado state line."

Koji's tone was neutral, as if he was a moderator rather than a colleague.

"It was fifteen years ago that they took me," St. Joan said. "I had been attending school in Denver. During summer vacation I decided to check out some of the Old West and Indian reservation towns in New Mexico. I took back roads to cut across the mountains and deserts. You know what it's like out there, just rocks and snakes and maybe some sagebrush. I was traveling at night to beat the heat. That's when they get you, isn't it? When there's no one else around."

Neo said, "They always do it at night, on back roads or anyplace where there isn't traffic or houses."

Joan nervously brushed her hair back. "Anyway, there I was, on this blacktop road late at night in the middle of nowhere. No other traffic, maybe a car every few minutes, but nothing to speak of. The town coming up was a little place called Cuba. Really, that's its name, Cuba, like in Havana."

Caden nodded. "New Mexico has some funny names for towns. Gallup, Truth or Consequences, that sort of thing." She made the inane comment so the woman wouldn't think she doubted her word about the town's name.

"I was coming down this road, heading for Cuba, when something hovered above me. I couldn't see what it was, it was dark and the thing was black. There were no lights at all. I know everyone always talks about lights, but this thing didn't have lights. It was like a black void in the night sky, blocking stars and the light of the moon. Later I came to think of it as a kind of black hole."

St. Joan's hand shook as she took a sip of water. "The car just stopped running. Just stopped like that. The motor froze, you know, not like it died, you know how that sounds, kind of sputtering when it's going to die. It just suddenly froze in place. No headlights, the dashboard went black, just in a flash. It was like that thing above me had froze the car's motor. Me, too. I was frozen, too. Not cold, not at all, but I couldn't move, couldn't talk, couldn't lift a finger. I just sat there, frozen in my seat like a statue.

"You know how it feels when your arm or leg goes to sleep? You get that tingling, needle-prick feeling. That's how my body felt, like a million needle pricks on it. Maybe there was some sort of electric current going through my body, or whatever they use for electricity. I couldn't move, but I stayed conscious, even when they took me out of the car. They transported me to this place underground. It's out there, too, in New Mexico. I later learned it was called Dulce. A lot of people were there. *They* were there, too."

Caden listened quietly but with a growing panic attack as the woman described an army of human slaves being managed by alien "humanoid" taskmasters. Some of the slaves were used as servants and laborers, others were guinea pigs for experiments that made the laboratory horrors in *The Island of Dr. Moreau* pale in comparison.

She tuned St. Joan out as her mind replayed the helplessness she'd felt in the Teo mountain cavern . . . the feelings of repulsion she felt when her naked body was violated . . .

"They needed women to satisfy the sexual desires of the male slaves," St. Joan said. "I was put in a brothel and forced to—"

Caden knocked over her chair as she jumped up and ran out of the room.

8

Caden went back to her room because she had no place else to go. Making her way into town didn't seem like a good option until she had answers about what had happened to her in the mountain . . . and why the Mexican government, and probably even her own, wanted to kill her. She dismissed the idea that Julio had returned to kill her because anyone could have been behind the mask, but she couldn't dismiss the other strange events on the mountain.

Antsy, she didn't want to stay in the room, but wanted to be alone. She paced in the room, then sat down at a computer in the corner. She turned it on, hoping it was connected to the Internet. The Internet was an answer machine, and she had many questions.

Web news was same-old, same-old for a world that eternally managed to go from one crisis to another: An Islamic fundamentalist elected president of a former Soviet republic says his country will become the next nuclear power to challenge America, the Great Satan. The director of the Environmental Protection Agency told a press conference that the agency was working with the Mexican government on the ecological disaster created by methane exposure in the Gulf of Mexico. The problem was spreading, but the agency was confident that it could be contained.

The third story was about floods in Bangladesh that killed five thousand people. Sad, but so many terrible disasters occurred in Bangladesh that five thousand deaths only rated a short article.

She typed in the words *frog . . . alien abduction* and got over one hundred thousand hits. She skimmed through two hundred of the hits and came up with some revelations:

The Frogs were folk heroes in the alien-abduction world, but many people claimed that the organization didn't exist, that it was an urban legend like alligators in New York's sewers.

Koji Oda's name didn't pop up anywhere—not even in the news and scientific-articles archive of the official NASA Web site. She found that puzzling. He was a world-class water expert, a former top NASA scientist. If he didn't do any work for fifty years, there should still be mention of him.

"Where are you, Koji?" she asked the computer monitor after giving up trying to find any mention of him at NASA. She couldn't even locate a reference to the Osaka University paper she'd read.

She kept trying for Koji, expanding her search to the others.

Nothing. "Not one thing," she said aloud. Nada. Zilch. No hits on Koji, the Sedona facility, or any of the people she'd met at lunch. Plenty of Neos popped up, including the main character in *The Matrix* movies, but nothing about Neo the Frog, St. Joan, or any of the others she'd met.

Though the Frogs were not mentioned by name, the stories they had told her about their experiences were so similar to abduction stories in general that they were literally generic brands.

Like everyone else on planet Earth, she had some familiarity with alien-abduction stories. Now she searched the Internet for stories similar to what she'd experienced, beginning over sixty years earlier when the alien-visitation tales started grabbing headlines.

In the spring of 1947 reports came from around the world about strange phenomena in the sky. She found both the sheer number and that many of the sources were trusted professionals—commercial and military pilots—interesting.

But the sighting that would ultimately take the most prominent place in the lexicon of alien visitations occurred near the small town of Roswell in southeast New Mexico, about 150 miles from Albuquerque. The seat of Chaves County, it lies along the Rio Hondo near the Pecos River.

The air force was originally called the Army Air

Force, so a base established in the area in 1941 was named Roswell Army Air Field.

Rich in scientific history, New Mexico has not only Los Alamos and the Birth of the Bomb, but also Robert Goddard, the Father of Modern Rocketry, who used the Roswell area for his high-altitude research until his death in the mid-1940s.

Roswell ushered in the age of UFOs and extraterrestrials when something fell from the sky onto a remote New Mexico ranch . . . and an air force base commander and intelligence officer announced it was a spaceship.

In July 1947, a couple of months into the worldwide UFO sightings frenzy, a New Mexico rancher named Brazel discovered the wreckage of a strange-looking contraption in a sheep pasture. He called the local sheriff, who notified the air force.

The base commander, Colonel Blanchard, sent out his chief intelligence officer, Major Marcel, and an officer named Cavitt, who was in charge of the base's Counter Intelligence Corps (CIC), to check the site. Items from the crash site were picked up and returned to the base, then were flown to other air force locations for inspection.

At that point, things got really weird.

During the afternoon of July 8, the base commander put out a press release that they had recovered materials from a "flying disk." Later that night, the air force put out a news release rebutting the base commander's statement. The wreckage was from a "weather balloon," the air force said.

The situation remained dormant for about three decades, with only occasional grumbling. Then books began appearing that challenged the air force's weather-balloon version. It apparently dawned on someone that air force officers at the base were not going to confuse a weather balloon with an alien spacecraft.

Ultimately, at the behest of a New Mexico congressman, in 1994, forty-seven years after the crash, the air force released further information about the incident. The explanation admitted that it was not a weather balloon, but a high-altitude balloon used to monitor Soviet atomic tests, and that the weather-balloon story was released because the project was top secret. And the air force threw in a caveat—records about the incident had been destroyed, including ones that the air force was required to keep.

The air force's admission that it had lied, destroyed vital records, and was providing the "truth" nearly half a century later under congressional pressure, threw rocket fuel on the controversy.

One bone of contention centered around whether the bodies of aliens had been pulled from the wreckage. The air force reply was that people had seen "dummies" dropped as part of a different high-altitude experiment and confused them for aliens.

Critics of the air force response pointed out that the dummies were dropped years *after* the 1947 sightings, while witnesses at Roswell claimed to have seen the bodies immediately following recovery of the debris from the ranch.

One of the strangest twists to the story came from a Roswell resident who was both an ambulance driver and funeral-home employee. He stated that he received an unusual call soon after wreckage was recovered from the crash site. An individual from the air force base mortuary office called and asked if "hermetically sealed baby caskets" about "three and a half or four feet long" were available. When told the funeral home had two child-size caskets in stock, the man said that two more would be needed and asked how a body could be stored without using embalming fluid.

Later that afternoon, the employee transported an injured airman in an ambulance to the base hospital. The airman's injury was unrelated to the "flying saucer" incident, but when the ambulance driver followed his usual routine of walking through the hospital to get a Coke at a lounge, he found the hospital bustling with activity and staff members tense. He encountered a nurse he knew wearing breathing protection. She told him, "Get the hell out of here."

He was taken out of the hospital by two MPs and escorted off the base.

The next day he spoke to the nurse. Upset and crying, she told him that "strange creatures" had been brought into the hospital.

The hospital incident took place on the same day and at the same air force base where the base commander had announced that a flying disk had been recovered.

There were a number of other twists, including one involving strange writing that resembled "Egyptian hieroglyphics." The ambulance driver reported seeing unusual wreckage in the back of two ambulances parked at the hospital, some of which had writing on it that resembled hieroglyphics. The air force intelligence officer who recovered materials from the crash site brought some of it home to show his family. His son, who was eleven years old at the time and grew up to be a medical doctor, stated that he observed strange writing that reminded him of Egyptian hieroglyphics on pieces laid out on the kitchen floor by his father. The intelligence officer and his wife also reported seeing the markings.

Roswell alien-visitation theories became a cottage industry that has for decades supported hundreds of books, TV shows, and movies.

When Caden finished reading about the incident, she didn't know what to think. In the past when she was told about governmental incidents that were alleged to be conspiratorial, her inclination was to attribute the cause to pure negligence and stupidity—and to tell the person he or she was just being paranoid.

After her recent experiences, she was starting to think of paranoia as nothing less than "heightened awareness."

She also found out why *Barney Hill* was chosen as an alias by a Frog: The Hills, Betty and Barney, were

A-list celebrities on the alien-abduction circuit. They claimed that they were abducted by aliens on a lonely road in New Hampshire in 1961. Betty said the aliens took a sample of Barney's sperm and that she recalled their sticking a long needle in her belly button.

After the Hills' revelations, similar stories of abduction, and often even rape, surfaced.

When Caden had her fill of stories about visitors from the beyond, she hesitated, then typed in her own name.

Nothing came up.

She froze and stared at the screen. "Not possible."

Not possible at all. She had thousands of hits alone about the article that had stirred so much controversy about Teo. But there was nothing. Her name didn't generate a single hit. Not even the link to her employment at NASA and affiliation with the University of Texas, Austin.

She frantically did keyword searches, but no mention of Julio's ripping out a child's heart before hundreds of tourists popped up. And not a single news story about the incident in Mexico in which dozens of cult members were captured, with some even being killed.

Her heart stampeded for a moment. She leaned back and closed her eyes, calming her nerves.

Someone had spit on the slate and wiped her off. She was a nonperson. Nothing sensational had happened in Teo.

Koji had been wiped off, too.

* * *

She sat next to the window and stared at the night long after the sun had fallen. For hours, she had reconstructed what had happened in the past few weeks, going over everything she could remember.

Her world had taken a strange twist. Violence and danger were things she read about or saw on TV that happened to other people, often far away, not to anybody she knew, certainly not to herself.

Suddenly she was enmeshed in murder, bizarre events, and dark conspiracies.

Her meeting with the Frogs and Internet surfing had created more questions than answers.

One question that buzzed around her head concerned Koji Oda.

"What's *your* abduction story?" she whispered to herself.

9

Caden jerked awake when she heard tapping on her door. She had dozed in the chair in front of the window. The old-fashioned windup clock with a green-illuminated dial said it was eight o'clock.

The knocking came again. Koji's gentle tap. Answer time again.

She met him at the door. "Can we take a walk?" she asked.

Night brought to the compound the bright shine of a full moon and the song of crickets.

She had too many big questions and worked her way toward them with small talk, asking him where he had been for the past decade.

He told her he had never been satisfied at NASA because of the restraints. "Everything is done by committee. That's no way for a scientist to work. Science needs to be constantly nourished by new ideas.

Committees smother creativity. I was never completely accepted by the NASA people, anyway. I didn't have the advanced degrees and years of teaching at university that they felt comfortable with. I've always been more an inventor of new methods than a scientific theorist."

He stooped and lifted out a palmful of water from a small fish pond. "Oceanographers and hydrologists know far more about the chemistry of water than I do. But I believe that water is more than a chemical compound made up of atoms of this and that. Water has magical powers that no scientist can explain. We all know that it's the elixir of life, that it's necessary for life to exist. But no one has ever given me a satisfactory explanation as to how it creates life."

He stood up. "To me, there is living water and dead water. And only living water has the miraculous ability to form life." He held up a finger to stop her from speaking. "I'm not talking about just providing a friendly environment for chemical substances to combine and create life. Science describes water as a substance that assists life. We all know that we can't exist without water. Most scientists believe that a chemical soup in some primeval sea was the incubator for the creation of life.

"My belief is different. I see water as a living entity, an entity that is coeternal with living organisms. Poetically it's said that we are composed of star dust, and that statement has a scientific basis because living organisms and the universe itself are almost entirely composed of the same six atoms. I believe that this thing we call life is part and parcel of a *living* universe, that water and organisms have always coexisted along with their parents, the stars."

Too many thoughts were colliding in her head for her to concentrate on his theory of water.

"What happened to you? I'm talking about how you came to be part of this abduction group."

He nodded at a door he had led her to. "My quarters. Please come in for a moment."

Unlike the simple ranch-style furnishings she'd seen so far in the complex, Koji's décor had an exotic ambience, a little Far East elegance, a little Palm Springs desert rattan.

She accepted a glass of lemonade and took a seat next to a flowing fountain. The fountain was in the center of the room under an opening in the ceiling that would not only bring in some light, but rain and even dust when the wind blew.

Like an atrium, she thought, the style of Roman homes in temperate climates. She had always liked the concept of having some of the outdoors inside.

He came back carrying a black velvet pouch. He sat down opposite her and pulled a thin, gold-coated aluminum plaque a little smaller than a license plate from the pouch. He turned it toward her so she could see the etchings on its face.

She examined the etchings and showed her surprise.

"I see you recognize it."

"I've seen it before. Pictured in a book and a mock-up of it at the Air and Space Museum in Washington."

"Then you know the story behind it."

"A little. It looks like the plaque NASA put in spaceships to tell ET how to find us."

"Exactly. Back in the early seventies, Carl Sagan and other scientists came up with the idea of sending a message to extraterrestrials. A thin, gold-plated plaque, about six by nine inches in size, was placed on board the Pioneer and Voyager spacecrafts to be carried to deep space after they completed their missions in the solar system.

"The face of each plaque has an engraving that's intended to tell an alien race about where we are in the galaxy, what we look like, even how we think. Because there's no wear and tear in space, the plaques are expected to last forever—or at least longer than Earth and the sun. It was really a marvelous idea by scientists who had both imagination and knowledge."

Koji stared gravely at Caden. "Not that any of the information on the plaques would come as a surprise to extraterrestrials with civilizations advanced enough to understand transmissions from Earth.

"We've had radio transmissions for more than a hundred years, television broadcasts for over seventy, and high-powered broadcasts for more than fifty, transmissions that have been racing through space at the speed of light. Alpha Centauri, the closest star-cluster to Earth, is only a little over four light-years away, so our television broadcasts have been reaching there for at least half a century.

"The notion that for decades our television shows and news broadcasts have been soaring through space and might be picked up by an alien civilization is a nightmarish idea."

His hands went into the air in exasperation. "Heaven only knows what 'civilized' extraterrestrials must think of the images of sex and violence, war and hate, and the rest of man's inhumanity to man that have been vomited into space from our airwaves."

He shook his index finger at her. "All the space agency's attempts to make contact, what NASA scientists themselves refer to as 'messages in a bottle,' assume that whoever—or *whatever*—on the receiving end will be friendly. But none of us know when we toss a bottle into the sea where it will wash up. Perhaps in the vast galactic sea, there are pirates."

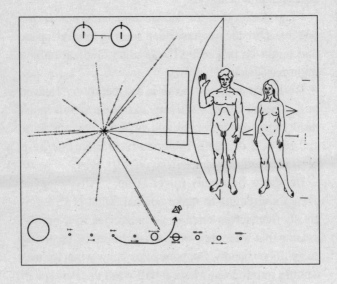

THE PIONEER PLAQUE

The plaque is intended to tell whoever finds it who we are and how to find us in the vast universe. It has a representation of the solar system; earth's position as the third planet from the sun; the position of the sun relative to the center of the Milky Way Galaxy; a man and a woman; and a hydrogen atom.

10

Caden had quietly listened because she felt he had things he needed to say, but now she posed the question that had been hanging in the air since he showed her the plaque.

"Are you going to tell me it's real?"

He sighed and put the plaque back in the velvet. "I don't know what's real anymore. Was Joan a prisoner in an alien brothel . . . or her own imagination? Is Neo's memory of abduction a security blanket against the terrible truth that he caused his wife's death? Did you experience an alien creature in Teotihuacán . . . or have a bad acid trip after an hallucinatory drug was blown into your face?"

"I didn't have an acid trip, thank you. How did you get the plaque?"

"A storm brought it to me. Like a gift from a Nordic god, perhaps Thor, the god of thunder. I was in a kayak in the ocean off Cape Canaveral back in the days when I was working on the Mars water project. I'd been at the Space Center attending a conference and stayed around afterward to take a vacation.

"I used a kayak for fishing because I didn't want to use a motor and found it easier to handle than a rowboat. This time I got caught in a squall that suddenly whipped up. I had drifted out farther from shore than I realized, and when I started in, wind and the tide pushed me back. The sky went black and exploded with lightning and thunder. My little kayak was tossed violently, whipped around like a toy, and I was certain that my end had come."

He paused and deliberately locked eyes with her.

"That's when I saw the light."

"The light at the end of the tunnel," she murmured.

He shrugged. "More like the light at the end of a maelstrom. It grew brighter and brighter until I was completely blinded by it. The storm around me faded away and I found myself in a room, more like a metal chamber, but metal that seemed fluid, unlike anything I'd ever seen. Dark shadows floated around as if they were weightless creatures. I sensed something attached to my head, and I found myself back in my mother's womb."

He paused and sipped lemonade.

"Your mother's womb. Were you a, uh, fully formed fetus?"

"I don't know. My mind flew, as the saying goes, a

million miles an hour. Every experience I ever had, my entire history from conception to being blown by the squall, things long forgotten or that I was never even conscious of, flowed from me in a steady stream as if it were sucked out by a conduit attached to my psyche."

He stared into the waters of the fountain for a long time. Not wanting to disturb him, Caden sat still and silent.

Finally he stirred and sighed. "The next moment I found myself lying on the beach, my kayak a few feet away. It was a beautiful day again, the sun was out, my clothes were dry. The only thing that was different was that the plaque was lying beside me."

She got up and walked around the room for a moment, gathering her thoughts. "What did people say when you told them about your experience?"

"I told no one. Can you imagine the ridicule I would have been subjected to had I told them? Yes, I suppose you could since you got a dose of it yourself when you proposed alien visitors."

"You had the plaque."

"They would have ridiculed that, too. How could it be compared to the originals? They were millions of miles away. And I feared something else. From the moment I woke up on the beach, I had a sense of fear and dread of the government. It was as if besides leaving me a gift to let me know how they had found us, they had left me a warning."

"What sort of warning?"

"I don't know. Perhaps that if they had found us . . . others might have come before them."

"And still be here running things? The standard alien-conspiracy theory. I'm surprised no one has claimed that it was an alien on the grassy knoll when JFK was shot."

"Oh, I assure you, many have. But before you make fun of the millions of people who subscribe to theories that the government is hiding the fact that aliens have visited us, let me cite you a very Anglo-American phrase: Where there's smoke, there's fire."

"I—I guess I shouldn't throw rocks at anyone's weird ideas. My theory was a glass house based upon ancient visitations. So that's why you dropped out of sight? The plaque thing?"

"I went back to my quarters, packed up, faxed a resignation to my superior, and started looking for a place where I could think. I chose Sedona because I had bought this piece of property years before." He smiled. "In my youth, I read Frank Herbert's *Dune* and became obsessed with the idea of someday bringing water to a parched desert."

"What about the others I met today? How did they get here?"

"Along with my water experiments, I began to research abduction stories. As time went on, I invited a few of the victims here, to help me with my experiments and my abduction research. It was Neo who first called us a bunch of Frogs. He said that after his abduction experience, he kept thinking about a frog he had dissected in high school."

Koji paused and raised his eyebrows. "By the way . . . none of them have heard my story."

"Why? They told you their stories."

"If they saw the plaque, I'm not sure they wouldn't tell the world . . . or even attempt to show it off to the world. I have spent a great deal of thinking and manipulation to keep this facility and the Frogs a secret from the government."

"The government must know about you." She told him about there being no reference to him, her, or the incidents in Teo.

He stroked his chin. "Interesting . . . not the fact that we have been spit upon and wiped off the slate, as you put it: I did that myself."

"Say again?"

"I employed a hacker to delete us off—you, me, the people in the compound."

"Why? How?"

"Elementary, my dear Watson." He giggled. "Actually, it was quite a challenge. In the old days when paper records were the norm, it would not have been possible to do. In the computer age, it's doable, especially if you're only involved in the mundane instead of military or spy secrets. A good hacker can eliminate vast amounts of material with just a stroke of the delete key. I first had myself eradicated, then the others as they came aboard, and you only in the last couple of days.

" 'Why?' you ask. For the same reason I've told no one about the plaque—anonymity. We live in an era of super-vast bureaucratic institutions that are so fat they can't see their own feet. If they focus on you, they can hang you with red tape. Or worse, if any of the conspiracy theories are true, they will do worse. You found that out in Mexico."

"You're hiding out here."

"In a sense. This is our base of operations, but now we have people in many places. Over the years, my own paranoia about government cover-ups has no doubt been aggravated by my associating myself with others of a like mind. The organization has grown far beyond what you see here in Sedona. We have members at all levels of government. One even in the White House. Many in the Department of Defense, NASA, even the intelligence services."

She felt warm, a bit faint. "I need some air."

They left his quarters and he slowly walked her back to her own room. She had absorbed an enormous amount of material. She felt brain-fried, but the most important questions of all to her were still hanging between them.

"Why did you bring me here? What's going on in Teo?"

"I was pointed toward Teo by an old friend from the University of Osaka. She's an oceanographer and became privy to secret information about a serious environmental problem in the Gulf of Mexico."

"The methane leak caused by oil drilling?"

"Methane, yes, but the stories being spread that it was caused by a natural disaster like an earthquake or a drill hitting a pocket of methane under the seafloor are lies. Even the extent of the disaster is much greater and much more out of control than what the government tells us. Methane is lethal not only to breathe, but kills water and all life in it. It's called marsh gas because it creates putrid swamps. As you know, it's the main ingredient in most natural gas piped to houses for heating and cooking. The Gulf of Mexico has an enormous amount of the stuff under its seafloor."

She recalled the magazine reporter's statement. "It started coming up, killing fish. And the government made up excuses for it."

Koji nodded. "Which begs the question—why did the government need to make excuses if it was just a natural disaster? Why keep it a secret? My friend learned that something very big and very secret was coming down, that the best oceanographers, hydrologists, meteorologists, and other water experts were being brought in from around the world."

"What does that have to do with Teo? It must be a hundred miles from the Gulf coast."

"She was asked to join a team investigating the Gulf problem. Some of the experts were sent to the Gulf . . . my friend and another group were sent to Teotihuacán."

Caden shook her head. "I don't understand. Why would she be sent to Teo? Wait . . . are you saying that the cause of it is in Teo? That thing that I—I ran into in the mountain?"

"Quetzalcoatl, the Feathered Serpent."

"It's doing this?"

"We don't know. My friend was sent to the antiquity site to take air, water, and dirt samples. There was special interest in getting samples from the mountain where the creature is said to have had its lair. When I learned that there was an undisclosed connection with Teotihuacán and the Gulf water disaster, I started researching it."

"And came across my activities at the site."

"Yes. I saw that like a detective, you had followed clues about mysterious visitors to antiquity sites. Your theories about an ancient astronaut presence in Teotihuacán, combined with my friend's information about a supersecret government cover-up at the site, were too tempting for a conspiracy-theory nut like me to pass up."

They walked in silence while Caden digested what Koji Oda had told her. An alien presence in Teo. A disaster in the Gulf.

"Assuming the thing I encountered in the cavern, the Feathered Serpent or whatever, is an alien . . . why a methane leak in the Gulf?"

"I don't know the how or why yet, but I'm sure the government does. I can think of only one reason to keep the information secret."

Caden knew the standard alien-conspiracy-theory mantra. "The government is conspiring with the alien or is controlled by it."

"From the fact they interceded to kill and capture

the alien's minions, I suspect it's more a power struggle. But one that the government wants to keep secret for fear of worldwide panic." Koji frowned. "Not just panic. The actual proof of an alien presence could cause a worldwide breakdown in civil order. Millions of people would fight to destroy it, millions would fight to join it, more millions would find their lives empty, as everything they've been taught about religion and an afterlife comes into question."

"Jesus. I just got a frightful insight as to why it might have chosen methane."

"Share it with me."

"During the Permian period about two hundred and fifty million years ago, about eighty percent of the life on earth became extinct. The mass extinction may have been caused by an extreme greenhouse effect, perhaps from massive volcanic eruptions. But recently it's been proposed that it could have resulted from excessive methane gas in the air. We can only breathe air with a small percentage of methane in it. If we get too much of the gas in the atmosphere, it's deadly. In fact, methane is one of those substances we know exist in other places in the solar system and we examine as part of our search for extraterrestrial life. This creature in Teo may know some way to release methane into the Gulf."

"What caused the methane imbalance during the Permian period?"

"No one's absolutely sure, but there are microbes that produce methane and ones that consume methane.

If something happens to the ones that eat the stuff, there'd be nothing to keep the production of methane in line." She grabbed Koji's arm. "Can this be true? Could an ancient astronaut have landed in Teo and built an empire? And now threatens the modern world?"

"You were comfortable with investigating the possibility of a visitor. You encountered it personally. To imagine that it now threatens the world is not a giant leap."

"I was searching for a god in a flaming chariot."

"Do you think he's a god?" Koji asked.

"More likely a demon who escaped from hell. Is this what the 2012 prophecy's all about? Some ancient creature coming back to destroy us? If it was somehow entombed nearly two thousand years ago . . . how could it have come back to life?"

Koji shrugged. "If it came from the stars, it may have taken an eon to get here. In science fiction books, space travelers go into deep hibernation. It might have that technology."

"There was an earthquake at Teo a few months ago," Caden said. "The Jaguar Cult arose soon afterwards." She faced Koji and slowly shook her head. "That quake ripped open Dracula's coffin."

BOOK III

ALLEN HOLT

11

Morgantown, West Virginia

Allen Holt was awake when the phone rang. He had drunk himself to sleep, awakening a few minutes before the phone rang at three in the morning. Waking up in the middle of the night had become routine to him—drinking himself into a deep sleep, then waking up a few hours later and staring up at the dark ceiling, no light in the room except the green glow of the clock radio on the end table.

Ten years had passed since he had lost his wife and daughter in an auto accident. He would live out his life remembering them every day, remembering their smiles and laughter, the scent of their hair. He had lost the two people who meant everything to him.

Still, he was grateful that they had not seen the world go to hell. A contagion in the Gulf of Mexico was destroying the ecology of the Gulf States, the Caribbean and Mexico. Doomsayers called it the beginning of the end, the greenhouse-gas tipping point that would turn the whole planet into a fiery hothouse like Venus. But he personally didn't care whether the world survived. He hadn't cared about the world since his own world crashed and burned.

He'd left the CIA, where he had been director for five years, a lifetime in the topsy-turvy Washington political climate. During his CIA tenure, he had successfully managed the most critical antiterrorist project in the history of the world. And he had voluntarily retired after the mission was over.

He had also moved, left no forwarding address, and put in a phone only so he could call for pizzas and beer so he wouldn't have to leave the house.

Only one person had his number, a longtime friend whom he owed too much to abandon the way he did the rest of the world.

It had to be her on the phone. From the White House. She was now president of the United States.

They hadn't talked for a while, but a call from her meant trouble. In the middle of the night, it spelled nothing less than the world on the brink.

And he was fresh out of motivation to save it.

"Yeah."

"What kind of way is that to answer a phone?"

"What kind of time is this to call a person?"

"I'm sorry. Next time an earth-shattering crisis arises, I'll be sure to time it so that it doesn't interfere with your sleep. How are you, Allen?"

"Excessive. I'm old and fat, I eat too much, drink

too much, think too much. And I feel too sorry for myself. Other than that, I'm fine. And how are you, Madame President?"

"Also excessive. I have one too many crises on my plate. The biggest one is something no other president has ever had to face."

"Kennedy brought us to the brink of thermonuclear war."

"The Soviets were rational."

He gave her the worst scenario he could imagine: "Let me guess. A terrorist cell got ahold of an atomic bomb. They've planted it on Wall Street or Pennsylvania Avenue."

She sighed. "Too mundane. This one has pushed the envelope on crises. It ranks with the biggest one."

She didn't have to tell him what the "biggest" crisis was. He had managed it.

He closed his eyes and thought about her. She'd be in bed now, sitting up, papers scattered all over. He'd never seen her in the White House bedroom, but he drew the image from years of dealing with her. As he had been when he was a crisis manager, she was a 24-7, hands-on, workaholic manager.

When they were Washington elites who communicated regularly, she as chairwoman of the Senate Select Committee on Intelligence and he as CIA director, a sexual attraction had arisen between them. He never closed the gap between attraction and pleasure because he'd never come to grips with the loss of his family.

"The world coming to an end," she said.

Jesus H. Christ. "An asteroid? Comet?"

"Worse. An *it*. We don't know if it's male or female, animal, vegetable or mineral."

"The Gulf crisis. Dead fish. Greenhouse gas. Global warming."

"All of the above and more. And it's nice to know you at least watch the news while you're wallowing in self-pity. Remember the Passage Project?"

That prompted a loud, unrestrained, coarse laugh. "Vaguely."

He was joking, of course. *Passage* was the name given to the intelligence operation that took on the "biggest" world crisis—the antiterrorist mission that had been his swan song.

The crisis began with a miraculous incident in which a scientific experiment accidentally broke a hole in time, opening a door that led two thousand years in the past to the time of Christ.*

"We're going to need you again—and time walkers. Along with the miracle machine."

She called the scientific facility a miracle. He thought of its use as making a deal with the devil—at some point there would be the devil to pay.

"I destroyed it. Remember? You were in on the decision to drop an A-bomb on it."

They both knew that the A-bomb had been exploded in the air so that it destroyed only the build-

---

*The incident was related in the novel *Dark Passage* by Junius Podrug.

ings aboveground. The "miracle" was produced in the vast underground tunnel system that was left intact.

"You've got the wrong guy. Call somebody who isn't burned-out."

"I called you because I know you can be the smartest and meanest bastard on the planet. I'm not asking you to volunteer. You're being drafted."

"I'm too old. Get someone that still has fire in their belly."

"The new people are all MBA types with a specialty in bean counting. What we're facing is an old-fashioned evil. That's your expertise. The bean counters wouldn't know how to handle it unless they were able to reduce its costs by taking away medical benefits."

"What is it?"

"Something that's been asleep for a long time has woken up. Like a bear that's been hibernating, it woke up hungry."

"For what?"

"For blood."

BOOK IV

THE BLOOD
COVENANT

12

Teotihuacán, Mexico

Blood. A river of blood. Iyo! The gods are thirsty and shall get their fill this day. I am Tah-Heen, the ball-player, and I stand in line with others waiting for the Knife of the Gods to cut out our hearts.

The line of those selected for sacrifice stretches from the great Pyramid of the Sun God—where I stand—down the Path of the Dead to the Pyramid of the Moon God. Along the way stand Jaguar Knights, with their double-edged obsidian swords and axes.

Atop the pyramid the Flay Lord, High Priest of the god Quetzalcoatl, the Feathered Serpent, performs the sacrifices that satisfy the blood covenant: a promise by the gods to bring rain and sun so the maize grows fat and tall in exchange for blood.

The Knife of the Gods used in sacrifices and flaying is made of obsidian obtained from the fire mountains that surround the valley Teotihuacán sits in.

Standing guard over the Flay Lord are Nawals, his protectors. No one has ever seen the features of a Nawal, but it is said that they hide frightening faces behind the man-jaguar masks they wear.

Iyo! To be chosen for sacrifice is a great honor . . . but the faces of those awaiting the plunge of the Knife of the Gods into their chest don't reflect joy. Their thoughts, like my own, focus on fear and hope for divine intervention. Escape is not an option because those caught trying will not die quickly, but will suffer the Slow Death: taken before the Flay Lord to be skinned alive, their skin slowly stripped off before they are sacrificed and their blood fed to the gods.

The Flay Lord skins people so exquisitely that they remain alive through most of it. He removes much of the skin in one piece so that he can slip it over his own body. When the skin has been removed, the Flay Lord pulls the hair and face down over his own head and parades around the top of the pyramid for the people below to see his work, the rest of the skin flapping behind him like a cape, the empty "hands" dangling from his own wrists.

The flaying ritual is a tribute to the gods, to encourage them to summon spring and spread maize and beans over One-World. The Flay Lord mimics spring by slipping into the "new skin."

All transgressions against the Feathered Serpent are punishable by flaying. It is said that the Flay Lord and his underlings discover many offenses against the great god. I have only seen stone carvings of Quetzalcoatl, but those representations of a beast with great fangs are more frightening than the masks of Nawals. Even the god's name speaks of exquisite terror: Quetzals are brilliantly colored birds—a coatl is a snake. Thus Quetzalcoatl is the Feathered Serpent.

For my own transgressions, I was placed near the head of the line by Jaguar Knights. They grabbed the man in front of me and dragged him to the foot of the steps, where the priest called Flower Weaver blew dream dust in his face. In seconds, the man was docile.

Extracted from the bark of a jungle tree, dream dust robs people of their senses and their fears of the obsidian knife.

Thousands of spectators gape up at the bloody work of priests on this festival day. The rich watch from the roofs of palaces and temples while the common people crowd shoulder to shoulder before the pyramid. The sacrificial block is at the edge of the first flat level of the pyramid, close to the stairway, so that all below can see blood flowing down the steps.

The now docile victim is led up the stairs by knights, who hand him over to the priests assisting the Flay Lord.

Taking the man by the arms and the legs, the priests place him on his back over the sacrifice block, a stone with a hump, bending him backward to thrust his chest up.

The Flay Lord drives his knife into the man's chest, widening the hole until he can stick his hand in and rip out the beating heart, thrusting it overhead to show the thrilled spectators.

A rivulet of blood flows down the steps, blood I will soon step in when it is my turn to mount the sacrifice block.

The Flay Lord and his priests eat some of the hearts raw, although they disperse most hearts among those who provided the sacrifice victim—usually a warrior had captured the victim in battle, or a great lord or wealthy merchant donated a slave. Often the meat is shared with guests at a feast following the ceremonies.

The victims in line today are men. Women are saved for the spring sacrifices when the fertility gods must be satisfied.

It's a bright, happy day for all except the Soon-to-Be-Dead. Festivities take place in the marketplace during the days leading up to the sacrifices—music, dancing, and games, along with the selling and trading of goods from throughout the empire and the One-World.

Why was I condemned to the sacrifice line? Was I a captive in war? A slave purchased as an offering by a wealthy lord? Guilty of sacrilege? Thief? Murderer? An adulterer? No! A Nawal spotted me and ordered my arrest. Some instinct told him that I had transgressed Quetzalcoatl himself, that I am to suffer the rite of Tlacaxipeuliztli: All my hair, except a long lock at the back of my head, will be shaved off. When I reach the top of the stairs, I will be dragged by the clump of hair to the stone of sacrifice. Along the way, Jaguar Knights will lash me with spike stems from the maguey plant. When my bruised, bloodied body arrives at the top, I will be spread-eagled over the stone of sacrifice. The Flay Lord will skin me like husked corn, a tribute to the maize god. Only after these indignities will the divine dagger cut out my heart.

Iyo! To be singled out by the Flay Lord is to be invited to a feast by the Lord of the Underworld in which you are a meal for worms and snakes.

Some of those in the Parade of the Soon-to-Be-Dead are prisoners of war, captured in battle. For them, the afterlife will be pleasant. They will ascend to the House of the Sun, one of the thirteen heavens, and traverse the sky with the Sun God from dawn to dusk as the fiery deity's honor guard. During the hours of darkness, they will wage mock battles. Afterward, there will be feasting, friendship, and female companionship.

Women who die in childbirth, people who drowned or were struck by lightning, and those who go willingly to the sacrifice slab also find a place in the thirteen heavens, though not as grand and privileged as that of the warriors.

After four years in the heavens, they metamorphose into birds. With rich plumage, they fly back to earth, flitting from flower to flower, imbibing of the nectars.

The heavens are only for those who die honorably. People who die of sickness—a straw death—will suffer my dark afterlife, a descent into Mictlan, a vast, bleak underworld divided into nine hells. The innermost hellworld is the abode of the skull-headed Lord of Hell, and his wife, the Lady of the Dead.

The daunting trials in Mictlan I must endure in the afterlife dominate my thoughts as I await my turn for the priest's blade. The first eight hells in the underworld are physical challenges—I must swim a raging river, crawl among deadly snakes and hungry crocodiles, survive between two mountains clashing together, climb a cliff with jagged edges sharp as obsidian blades, survive a freezing windstorm, battle raging beasts and eaters of hearts. After four years, if I reach the ninth hell, I prostrate myself before Mictlantecuhtli himself, the King of Terrors. If he finds me worthy, he will grant me the Peace of Nothingness by turning my soul to dust and scattering it on the parched sand that lies to the north of our lush valley.

Before I face the brutal challenges of the underworld, I must first mount the Great Pyramid of the Sun, where the Flay Lord and his priests will send me on my journey.

Behind me in the line is a frightened youth.

"You will go to a better place," I said gently.

"My master says I'll go to the nine hells."

"The nine are better than the tenth."

"What is the tenth hell?"

"You live in it."

He told me of the sin that brought him here. He had put his erected blade, the one men carry between their legs, into the daughter of his master, she who was already promised to one of her own station. For his transgression, his master donated him to the sacrificial mound.

Listening to the woes of the boy, I think of my own life. I am only a few years older than he, but have lived many different lives, moving from one wheel of time to another. Once a prince among men, I was a hero to women, a man other men feared and envied.

How I rose from the dirt to fall from great height is a tale worthy of the revered story of the flood that once engulfed the One-World—the waters drowning all but a man and a woman who clung to a huge tree.

The boy vomited his breakfast of maize soup.

"Do not fear death," I said. "You must not face the underworld with panic in your heart."

But even as I spoke, I knew the boy would not make it past the first hell, that he would fail. Unable to endure its brutal challenges, he will be eternally damned, his soul stuffed with snakes by the Lady of the Dead, Mictecacihuatl, and stitched shut with cactus needles.

Time is short and there is much to tell. Let me pinch your ear and bring you close so you may hear my words as if you were beside me when my life unfolded.

Though I am now called Tah-Heen, I have had many names. Know that Tah-Heen was not the name I received from my father at birth. My birth name was cast to the wind when I was still a babe in arms and given another. I was raised among the People of the Rubber in the wet-green tropical region near the Eastern Sea. In those days, I was young and innocent . . . perhaps not entirely innocent, but green as the frightened youth behind me.

I was forced to travel the One-World, sometimes eating dirt, other times festooned with honors and glory as I played olli, the ball game of life and death. I could have defeated the legendary Xolotl himself in a game played on the celestial field.

To understand my place in the One-World, you must know what passed in the eons before my birth.

It is written that mankind has been broken four times on the wheel of time. During each cataclysm, cities and civilizations were destroyed, and new ones rose in their stead. In the previous epoch dwelt a people created by Tezcatlipoca, the first sun. His time ended when the race of man was destroyed by giant jaguars in the era of Four Jaguar.

Quetzalcoatl, the Feathered Serpent, came to rule the heavens and the earth after the destruction and built the great city Teotihuacán so that he might be revered—and nourished—by many. This god had a great thirst for blood.

Come with me as I turn back the wheel of time, tell you how a fiery god came to the One-World and built an empire of blood, and how I fought for my birthright.

BOOK V

THE ARRIVAL

AD 42

13

Ancient Vietnam

Trung Trac, a young Vietnamese woman, stood on the wall of her fortress and watched the fire star blaze across the night sky. Her sister, Nhi, joined her. Dressed as warriors, they were ready for battle.

A wrinkled, old woman sitting nearby in the lotus position watched the fireball blaze across the sky as her fingers read a necklace of knucklebones. Phung Thi Chinh, the aunt of the young women, was too old to fight in the battle that would begin at dawn, but she was known and respected throughout the land as a sooth-sayer who could divine the future.

As she watched the ball of fire, she meditated about whether it was a good omen or a bad one. No one had seen anything like it before, although she had seen the "fuzzy stars" called comets and "falling stars," which left a brief streak of light as they fell to earth. This fire star was different. Many times brighter than any other star, it was larger than anything in the sky except for the sun and the moon. No actual flames were seen, but people called it a fire star because it appeared enveloped in a flaming red light.

A god in a fiery chariot racing across the sky was how the old woman thought of it. But what was its character? A god of light or of darkness? Good or evil?

A mile from the fortress a great Chinese army had gathered for the battle that would take place in the morning. Her niece Trac, the eldest of the two sisters, first conceived the idea of a revolt against the brutal Chinese rule over Vietnam—and was the first to pick up a sword. Now she led an army.

Vietnam had been suffering under the heel of the Han emperors of China for over a century. During that time, China had been busy battling tribes from the arid regions to the far north, beginning construction of a great wall that ran many li in an attempt to hold the invaders at bay. But conditions in Vietnam became insufferable when the Chinese governor, Su Ding, began the systematic destruction of the traditional Vietnamese culture and insisted that the people adopt Chinese ways. High-ranking Han officials—mandarins—seized land, displaced the hereditary overlords, and insisted that the Vietnamese people adopt Chinese dress, language, and customs.

Trac's husband, Thi Sach, had been lord of Chau Dien, a rich province in the north of the country. When he opposed Ding's efforts to destroy his people's values, Ding had him tortured and murdered and raped

Trac to send a message of terror to the Vietnamese people.

Su Ding made a mistake—he should have killed Trac. Unlike in China, where women were subservient to men and feared them, in Vietnam women played a prominent role in governing and in the army. Women held positions as administrators, judges, and soldiers.

Enraged by the injustices, Trac, aided by her sister, Nhi, led a rebellion, raising over eighty thousand troops, men and women, to fight the Chinese. Thirty-six of the generals were women. In the battles that followed, Trac became famous for her strategy and Nhi for her prowess in fighting.

During the first years of the rebellion, the Vietnamese defeated Chinese armies, driving the hated mandarins and their toadies from the country. Su Ding disguised himself as a female servant and fled with his countrymen.

Trac had been proclaimed queen of the land and restored traditional Vietnamese customs. But now the Chinese had come back, with a great army, one that threatened to overwhelm the much smaller Vietnamese forces.

On the heels of the army came the strange phenomenon—a ball of fire, moving slowly across the sky.

The gods controlled the heavens, and nothing that came from them was without significance. Seeing her commanders and troops frightened by it, Trac proclaimed that it was a sign of good fortune for them in the battle ahead. But her aunt wasn't convinced that Trac was right. The country had no tradition about a fire god appearing to help. People said that the old woman had the gift of prophecy and the eye that saw the future.

Staring up at the fire god, Chinh shuddered. She sensed a malevolence, a manifestation of evil unlike anything else she had experienced.

She thought about the impending battle against the Chinese as she quietly stared at the courageous sisters standing on the battlement, ready to draw their swords when the enemy advanced.

Taking off her necklace of human knucklebones, Chinh removed the bones from the string and gathered them in her hands. She shook them and tossed them onto the stone floor. The bones stopped in a shape that was vaguely familiar to Chinh, but one that her mind resisted acknowledging.

A grave.

She looked up at her two warrior nieces and had a vision: She saw thousands of Vietnamese soldiers falling in battle, the vastly superior Chinese forces overwhelming them, the fall of the kingdom that Trac had founded, and the return of Chinese domination.

And she saw water. Her nieces were in a river stained with the blood of their people. In the death-with-honor tradition of her people, the warrior-princesses drowned themselves rather than be humiliated by the enemy.

The old woman glared up at the fire god in the sky and silently shook her fist at the evil she sensed.

Leaving the battlement, Chinh retired to the bath adjoining her room. Laying aside her robe and sandals, she slipped into the warm water.

She thought about a time when she was a young woman, the same age as her two nieces. Life had not been as complicated then, though she had been betrothed once. She remembered the softness of her betrothed's lips, the firmness of his body, his man scent and the strength and security she felt when they walked side by side.

He passed beyond sorrow before the wedding from a fever. All the love she felt for a man followed him to the grave. After his death, she remained unmarried and devoted herself to her nieces.

Now she couldn't stand to see them suffer.

She slowly sank in the water, up to her neck, smiling at the memory of giggling with joy and anticipation when her betrothed arrived to be introduced to her.

Still smiling, she sank deeper, until the water was over her head.

14

Ancient India

As the fire god appeared in the sky over Pataliputra, the largest and grandest city in the land known as India, Dattaka, a noted scholar, worked on his magnum opus, the role of courtesans in the practice of the Kama Sutra, the rules of love.

Manuscripts describing the techniques of sexual intercourse were centuries old. His task was to add his own observations to the scholarly body of work. Over the objections of his wife, he had hired the services of the most exotic courtesans in the city to assist him in his study.

He had swept away his wife's objections with the wave of a hand. She was a mere woman in a land where a married woman could not own property—could not even claim ownership of her own body. A man and a woman were one—and *he* was the one.

He would not let her irrational jealousy spoil his research. His wife said it was not honorable that he was to engage in the acts with courtesans in their home, but he had corrected her, reminding her that it was his home, as were all the physical possessions of the family—including herself.

To teach her respect, he beat and humiliated her, making her walk through the marketplace with a dead hen hanging from around her neck.

The public embarrassment had just made his wife all the more combative. During the argument with his wife, she had made the outrageous statement that if he could lie with a courtesan, she would have the right to hire a man for sexual services to her.

The argument had solidified in his mind an aspect of marital relationships that he had given thought to but not acted upon either in his own home or in his scholarly work. The subject was the small button women had between their legs that give them pleasure when it was caressed.

After hearing his wife's statement—her threat of infidelity—Dattaka concluded that to ensure fidelity by wives in a marriage, women should have the object removed. After all, the only reason for a married woman to have sex was to produce children—no need existed for a married woman to experience pleasure in lovemaking.

Castration was used to create sexually impotent slaves that guarded the wives of kings and princes. But what of women? Excision of the female pleasure zone was not unheard of. It was practiced by some other cultures, including the Egyptians and Ethiopians— and varied from removing just the clitoris to also cutting off the lips at the opening of the vagina.

Over the objections of his wife, he had a doctor and a midwife come to the house. "Remove her pleasure button," he told them.

His wife did not willingly submit. They tied her down, gagged her, bent her backward, and spread her legs. The doctor performing the operation, a learned professional who prescribed rat dropping as a remedy for chest pain, took out a sharp blade he had earlier used to slice warts off a leper and showed it to her. Smiling, he clucked, "Do not worry, woman. Just a single slice and you will have peace. Those unhealthy urges will be gone."

A hot, wet night enveloped Dattaka as he awaited the arrival of a courtesan he had hired for his research. Passing the time, he worked in the cool of his garden with the light of a lamp as flying insects fluttered around. Occasionally he looked up to observe the fire star. The flaming star had been in the sky day and night for two days, causing consternation and panic. The king's astrologers said it was a comet, though no one had seen a comet as bright.

Dattaka was curious about the comet, but not distracted by it. He did not perceive it as a visitation from the stars or as an omen of good or bad fortune. An educated man, the most noted scholar in Pataliputra, he was not prone to superstition.

Pataliputra, like the rest of India, exchanged trade and knowledge with empires east and west. Located on the banks of the Ganges nearly three hundred miles from the Bay of Bengal, Pataliputra controlled river traffic, making the city not only rich but cosmopolitan from the goods and knowledge that flowed along the river.

Like a few other scholars in the city, Dattaka was familiar with the writings of Aristotle, the teacher of the boy-king Alexander, who had conquered much of India several centuries before.

Aristotle professed that the heavens were perfect and incorruptible. One had merely to look into the sky and see the permanency and orderliness. But comets were not orderly—they were erratic, appearing suddenly, traveling across the sky before disappearing. Because of their imperfect nature, Aristotle concluded that comets were not actually heavenly bodies but were exhalations of the earth itself.

Following this logic, Dattaka concluded that the comet over Pataliputra was in fact a ball of fire thrown into the air by one of the volcanic explosions that periodically occurred on islands in the Indian Ocean.

Dattaka ridiculed his wife when she said that the comet was an omen bringing her a message.

"Perhaps it will swoop down and carry you away!" he howled.

*　*　*

When the courtesan arrived, Dattaka examined her with his eyes, evaluating her by the criteria he had established in his book.

Not beautiful, but sensual and exotic, he thought.

She brought another woman with her, one whose face was hidden behind a veil.

"This woman is my best student," the courtesan told Dattaka. "She will assist in instructing you."

"Have her remove her veil."

The courtesan shook her head. "She will remove it when it is the right time in the lovemaking."

Dattaka and the two women retired to his room. He had earlier instructed his wife and servants to stay out of that part of the house to ensure he would have privacy.

"You are to show me the sexual movements that have proved most successful in your work," he told the courtesan.

"Then first you must watch rather than participate. Many times in your life you have had love made to your body, now you will have to learn how love can be made to your mind."

Dattaka watched as the courtesan knelt upon a soft mat. Slowly, with gentleness, the veiled woman removed the courtesan's clothes. As garments that were closest to the body went off, the veiled woman caressed the courtesan's naked flesh with her lips and fingers.

She's right, Dattaka thought, *I am as much aroused as if I were participating.*

The veiled woman guided the courtesan down on the mat and caressed her breasts with her tongue, teasing each nipple before she kissed the soft abdomen flesh, moving lower until the courtesan opened her legs.

"Stop!" Dattaka said. "Make love to me. Both of you."

"First we must shave you," the courtesan said.

"Why?"

"It will make your flesh pure and receptive to the touch. Hair blocks sensations to the flesh."

They removed his clothes slowly and had him lie on the bed. The courtesan disappeared, leaving him naked with her assistant bending over him with a straight razor.

The woman shaved him, using the blade, a bowl of perfumed water, and soap. As the razor-sharp blade worked around his penis, he first tensed, then relaxed as the touch of the blade began to thrill him. After he was shaved, the assistant rubbed scented cream around his penis and used her tongue to rub it in.

When he was fully aroused, he said, "Take off your mask. I want to see your face when I enter you."

The woman, sitting on the edge of the bed, slowly pulled off her mask.

He gawked at her. "You!"

His wife smiled at him. With bitterness. He started to get up and collapsed back down as he felt the bite of the razor against his scrotum.

"What are you doing? You're going to hurt me."

"Don't worry, Husband. You remember what the

doctor said. One slice and unhealthy urges will be at peace."

He started up again, and the sharp, cold blade against his tender, warm flesh caused him to fall back.

"You're crazy! *Put that blade down.* I'll punish you for this madness."

She slipped the flat of the blade up the underside of his sac, back and forth as if she were sharpening the blade. His legs trembled as shaking over took his nerves. "You will pay."

"No, my husband, you took away my womanhood. Now there is nothing more you can do to me." She pushed the blade against the soft sac. "Do you know what they call a man who's had his jewels cut off?"

He screamed as she cut off the soft sac.

15

Ancient Rome

Cornelius Sabinus, senator of Rome and scion of a great family of the empire, waited and watched as Emperor Gaius "Caligula" Caesar left the enormous Circus Maximus amphitheater at the end of the show.

Sabinus smiled and bowed as the emperor and his wife swept by, surrounded by Praetorian Guard. Nothing in Sabinus' body language revealed the hatred he felt toward the twenty-nine-year-old ruler.

At the games, Caligula announced that the comet they saw overhead was a golden chariot sent to take him on a ride into the heavens so he could consult with his fellow gods.

Knowing the emperor to be mad, the audience had not known whether to laugh or cheer. Fortunately for themselves, they had cheered.

The appearance of the comet that morning had aroused fears among the common people, but educated

Romans were taught the knowledge of the Greeks and believed that comets were not heavenly bodies, but debris coughed up from the earth.

Born Gaius Caesar Germanicus, the emperor was popularly called Caligula, "Little Boot," a nickname bestowed upon him by soldiers of his father's when he was sent to their camp as a child.

He had assumed the throne as emperor four years earlier at the age of twenty-five, upon the death of Tiberius. Since then, he had instituted a reign of mad terror, cruelty, and debauchery unlike anything the Roman world had before seen.

Caligula was maliciously drawn to any attractive woman he did not possess. He had the noblewomen of the city parade before him so he could select any that pleased him. He threw parties in which he had sex with the women in front of their friends before sending them back to their husbands and fathers. Afterward, he took pleasure in openly discussing the physical attributes of the women and what he had done to them.

Sabinus' wife was among his victims. So were Caligula's own three sisters, with whom he committed incest. He made love to one of his sisters, a virgin, before a small audience that included his wife. He married off one of his male lovers to his favorite sister and had sex with both of them. Attending a wedding, he desired the bride, so he stopped the wedding and married the woman himself, divorcing her a few days later.

His sexual transgressions were the least bloody of his excesses. He put to death whom he pleased, on whim, including the brother-in-law who had been his lover. When condemned criminals were finished off too soon by wild animals in the arena, Caligula had spectators dragged from their seats and thrown in the ring to face the beasts.

His madness was boundless. He rewarded his favorite horse, Incitatus, with jewels, a marble stall, a staff of servants, and threatened to make the horse a Roman senator.

Proclaiming himself a god, he had the Bay of Naples bridged with boats from Baiae to Puteoli. Wearing the breastplate of Alexander the Great, Caligula rode his horse across the "bridge," proclaiming that, like Neptune, he had "ridden the waves."

Despite Sabinus' knowledge that comets were physical objects and not omens, its appearance over Rome made him edgy. But he told himself that if it was an omen, it foretold the death of the emperor.

When Caligula's back was to Sabinus, Praetorian Guards around the emperor suddenly opened ranks, exposing the emperor. Sabinus, Cassius Chaerea, a tribune of the Guard, and others, threw themselves at the emperor, stabbing him with their knives. His fourth wife, Caesonia, was beside him. She screamed and fell under the knives. Her infant daughter was killed in the frenzy, the child's head bashed against a wall.

16

Ancient Mexico

Her name was Xilonen. Fourteen years old, she was gathering maize on a hillside above Cuicuilco when the fire star arrived.

Cuicuilco was a large town of nearly ten thousand in the Anáhuac Valley of the One-World. Part of a high, mostly flat plateau, Cuicuilco was ringed by mountains and active volcanoes. The town's influence was much greater than its size suggested because it had the highest pyramid in the world known to Xilonen's people. The pyramid was round and rose more than the height of a dozen grown men, with a base seven times its height. People from throughout the great valley came to it to worship and pay homage.

The residents of Cuicuilco were descendants of people who had built a number of revered sites near the great waters at the western end of the known world. These ancestors, called People of the Jaguar, had carved giant stone heads, some twice as tall as a grown man, and had built a tall mound on the coast of the known waters.

Xilonen didn't live in town. Her father had fields on the valley floor outside town and more upon the foothills of the mountains. Xilonen, her sisters, and four workers had been sent to these foothills, starting out when the sun first glowed behind the great eastern mountains. The mountains had snow on their summits, and two of them smoked and spit fire from the fiery furnaces within them. Occasionally, volcanic storms, with rivers of molten lava and clouds of deadly ash, burst from them, destroying whatever came into their path.

The girl and her group had reached the fields in the mountains when the fire star appeared. They heard it before it became visible, a piercing scream like that of a dying animal coming from the sky. They froze in fear at the strange, penetrating sound.

It came over the great eastern mountain as a ball of fire, as if a piece of the sun had broken off and fallen to Earth.

Xilonen only got a glimpse of the star as it streaked across the sky and struck near Cuicuilco. When it hit, a great explosion erupted, and the earth underfoot shook and heaved, knocking her off her feet. She fell, sliding into a ravine as a hurricane of dirty air struck. Lying on the ground in the ravine kept her from being shredded by the flying debris, but she was covered with dirt.

She had been in earthquakes before. The valley was as prone to the earth's shaking as it was to explosive volcanoes, but she had never experienced explosions and the earth rising under her feet. Day turned to night as dust and smoke from the blast filled the atmosphere.

Fighting the weight of the dirt, she rolled over and broke loose and got up, choking from the blackened air. The earth was still convulsing, explosions coming from the floor of the valley, the ground under her still trembling. She tried to call out to the others, but the sound came out of her dirt-clogged throat as a cough.

Her instincts were to climb, to get above the foul air, to get away from whatever catastrophe was gripping the valley. She climbed blindly, calling out when she could, but not hearing any reply from her sisters or the men who had come with them.

As she climbed, the air grew cleaner, but she still found it hard to breathe. When she looked back at the valley, she gaped in horror. A great hole had been torn into the earth, and lava poured from it, a wide river of molten fire racing down to the town. Dirty air and smoke made it too dark to see the town, but in her mind's eye she imagined thousands of people fleeing the fiery tidal wave.

Hundreds of feet above where she had been when the fire star hit the ground, she collapsed from a lack of oxygen and fatigue. She slowly got her breathing back and got dizzily to her feet, her back to the mountain. Her eyes stung and her sight was blurry, but the cataclysm gripping the valley below filled her whole world.

She heard the sound of rocks falling behind her. She turned, blurry-eyed. Someone was coming down the mountain. She almost cried out with joy. She rubbed her eyes, trying to get the person into focus.

She saw the feathers first.

And began to scream.

BOOK VI

LORD LIGHT

Sixty years later
AD 102

17

Teotihuacán

Yaotl, Lord Light, was napping in the bedroom of his hunting lodge near Teotihuacán when a disturbance in the courtyard awoke him. He had left the lodge before dawn that day to hunt deer in the forest and lay down after the midday meal. He was the richest and most powerful of the twelve High Lords of Teotihuacán, the mighty city-state whose empire composed most of the One-World. His own lands included over a hundred towns and villages. Only the High Priest, Xipe—Flay Lord and steward to Quetzalcoatl, the Supreme God of the One-World—held a more exalted rank than a High Lord.

He'd fallen sleep an hour earlier with the image of the deer hunt still in his thoughts. Peasants from the nearby village had come through the forest in a great half circle from the opposite direction, driving a herd of deer before them, as he waited in a clearing. As the frightened deer came into the clearing, he wounded a buck with his spear, catching it in the left haunch. The wound knocked the leg out from under the animal only for a moment. It shook off the spear and started to run, but Lord Light was on it, jumping on its back, bringing his obsidian knife across its throat, severing its jugular.

With the animal mortally wounded, he backed off to let his spear bearer finish the kill.

At thirty-four years old, Yaotl was the youngest of the High Lords. He'd inherited his title and lands from his father and increased his family's honors and wealth with his sword and shield, leading armies into the battles against territories that rebelled against the tributes levied by Teotihuacán. In war, he had not stood behind his warriors, but led them in battle, until he lost much of the use of his left arm to an enemy. Severely wounded, he killed the warrior whose blade had injured his arm and stayed on his feet until the battle was won.

He was a renowned warrior in a warrior empire. Teotihuacán was the largest city in the One-World even though it had been in existence for only sixty years. The city rose following the destruction of Cuicuilco. The Old Ones who are the Keepers of Memories say that Cuicuilco was destroyed when the Feathered Serpent, Quetzalcoatl, the fiery god of creation, fell upon the city from the eastern heavens. His impact melted mountains.

With two huge pyramids as anchors, one dedicated

to the Sun God and the other to the Moon God, and a great temple dedicated to him, the city the Feathered Serpent had built was unlike any other. And he made a covenant with the people—give blood to feed the gods and the gods will provide the heat of the sun and rain to ensure good crops of maize and beans.

The god enforced its rule with legions of Jaguar Knights, who acted as shock troops in the wars that conquered the One-World, a vast territory that took an army more than fifty days to march across it from north to south. The victories were not just due to the fierceness of Teotihuacán's troops, but to their special weapons that cut easier and deeper: swords and spears with obsidian cutting edges.

Obsidian was made by the gods that spewed molten lava from the guts of fire mountains. Of the two great deposits of volcanic glass that gave wood weapons razor-sharp cutting edges, one was located at Teotihuacán at the northern end of the One-World, and the other at the southern extreme. Quetzalcoatl's city soon controlled both.

Besides the Jaguar Knights, a special guard of the Flay Lord, Nawals, spread terror that paralyzed kings and commoners. Few in number, but large in the fear they created, Nawals were invincible warriors who didn't seem to need to rest or sleep and were rumored to also feed on sacrificial blood.

Not all people supported the covenant that sent thousands to the sacrifice mound.

Lord Light had growing doubts about the actions of

the Flay Lord and his minions. The Flay Lord had originally skinned alive only criminals for the most infamous crimes—treason or the murder of a nobleman. But his flaying knife had become increasingly bloody as he used it for lesser offenses, while his Nawals and Jaguar Knights kept the people in the city in constant terror and submission. The rumors about their atrocities were legion . . . as were the increasing demands for sacrificial blood that kept the sacrifice lines longer.

As a counter to the Flay Lord's legions, Lord Light had started another league of knights, one dedicated to the Eagle. Jaguar Knights fought under the banner of the great predator of the ground . . . Eagle Knights fought under the banner of the great predator of the sky.

The creation of a military force that rivaled the army of the Flay Lord was not welcomed news at the sacrificial mounds.

Lord Light had come back to his hunting lodge tired from the hunt. His crippled arm hurt, and he had taken an herbal drink given to him by Zolin, his steward, to relax and ease the pain. Instead of simply relaxing, he had fallen into a deep sleep almost as soon as he took the drink. Now, his sleep disturbed by noise, he awoke, his head still fuzzy from the sleeping potion.

When he heard the commotion, he first thought it was the sound made by the deer when he had landed on the animal's back to cut its throat. He lay for a moment confused, then realized the sound had been the scream of a woman. It came again, a scream of terror from the lodge courtyard. He got to his feet and threw open the shutters of the second-floor window that overlooked the courtyard.

The hunting lodge was laid out in a U-shape with a rectangular main building and two wings. Both wings were on fire and burned fast—unlike his palace in Teotihuacán, an imposing structure built from slabs of rock—the lodge was made of bamboo and hardwood.

The late-afternoon sun had fallen below the mountains, leaving the hunting lodge in shadows, but he could make out the courtyard below. His wife, two of his children, and servants were herded together.

Knights of the Jaguar, the special warriors that fought only under the authority of Lord Xipe, as the servant of the Master Lord, stood by with bloody swords. His wife, on her knees before a Jaguar Knight, looked up terrified as Lord Light stepped out onto the balcony.

He shouted in horror as the knight's obsidian ax came down, severing her head. The knights begin hacking his children and the servants as they screamed and cried out for mercy.

He grabbed his sword from where it hung on the wall and turned as Zolin, his steward, stepped into the room. Jaguar Knights came in behind him, four of them, wearing the headgear and uniforms of the feared order. Their swords were drawn.

"Zolin," Lord Light said. "You've betrayed me."

"You plot against the Feathered Serpent. You encourage the other High Lords to rise against him."

"He's evil and so is his demon Xipe. What did he pay you to betray me?"

Zolin smiled. "All that you have."

"Then take it to the Place of the Dead with you."

Lord Light charged, raising the sword.

Zolin faded back as the Jaguar Knights stepped in to meet the charge.

With two good arms, Lord Light would have been a match for even four of the knights. But the bad arm made his left side vulnerable. As he slashed out at the two knights to his right, a knight on his left hit him across the side of the head with his sword. He staggered backward as the blows kept coming.

Ome, the nurse to the youngest son of Lord Light, saw the smoke as she crested the hill. She stared in shock at the raging fire incinerating the hunting lodge. Men and women running in from the fields to fight the fire were intercepted by Jaguar Knights and cut down. Eagle Knights, the High Lord's house guards, lay dead on the ground near the front entrance.

As she watched the carnage, Zolin walked by the dead without looking down at them. Behind him, Jaguar Knights dragged Lord Light to a litter covered with black curtains and surrounded by Nawals.

Nawals, the personal guards of Flay Lord Xipe, stood in front of the litter.

Ome was not stupid. But like others of her social class, in many ways she was invisible to the upper classes. Lord Light, his wife, and his advisers spoke freely in front of her as if she didn't exist because she was a servant. From what she'd overheard her master say, she knew that he was angry at the Flay Lord for atrocities committed against conquered people and their own people. She had even heard him question whether the blood covenant with the Feathered Serpent should be honored.

She knew that if she took the baby down to the burning building, she would be killed. So would the baby.

Unable to have her own child, she'd transferred her love and maternal instinct to the infant child of Lord Light.

She fled, taking the baby, running through the forest to the river.

At the river she boarded a canoe used by the servants to catch fish for the hunting lodge. With no hesitation, she paddled into the current, knowing exactly where she was going.

A long journey lay ahead of her, by boat and foot, over mountains and through tropical forest. A journey to her own kind: the People of the Rubber.

18

"If you killed him, Lord Xipe will skin us alive," Zolin told the Jaguar Knights who had dragged the High Lord out of the burning compound.

Zolin knelt beside Lord Light and assured himself that the man was still breathing. "Take him before the Flay Lord. I will follow as soon as I'm certain all the family and servants are accounted for."

The orders from the Flay Lord were specific: All members of the family in the empire, to the degree of first cousin, and all servants and guards, were to be killed. The Eagle Knights were to be disbanded and all officers sacrificed. The estates and villages of the High Lord were to be forfeited to Zolin. The massacres would serve as a lesson and warning to those who plotted disobedience of the Feathered Serpent and those who served him.

Zolin was not bothered by his role as the betrayer

of his master and the murder of those he served as steward. He now served the mightiest god in the One-World and the nobleman who carried out his bidding.

He listened to a Jaguar Knight captain's tally of those who had been killed. "Fool! Two are missing. The High Lord's infant son and the servant girl who attends him."

"But you said that everyone in the household was within the compound."

Zolin stepped closer and shoved an obsidian dagger into the man's exposed gut. The officer gawked, jaw slack, eyes startled wide.

"And you must pay for the error." Zolin twisted the knife.

Zolin trembled as he obeyed the command to appear before the Flay Lord. A hunt for the missing nurse and child had failed. He had covered his own dirty tracks by killing the officer, "in self-defense," his messenger to the Flay Lord had reported while Zolin led the hunt, "after the blunder was discovered."

If it was suspected that the fault was actually his, he would get the ultimate punishment from his new master: his skin sliced off while he was alive, leaving the body raw and bloody with death coming only after hours of unimaginable pain and torment.

Worrying about his fate, he hurried to present himself before the Flay Lord. He had betrayed his master, Lord Light, for a reward. He now feared that reward would be the death of him.

When Zolin appeared before his new master to prostrate himself, the Flay Lord was out of the litter and seated on a throne shaded by palm leaves. Three Nawals flanked the chair on each side. A thousand Jaguar Knights were around the compound, but they created less electrified fear than the High Priest, who peeled people alive, and his nightmarish Lords of the Night, who were rumored to do things to people that not even the bravest whispered about.

Zolin's knees went weak at the sight of the Flay Lord and his jaguar-masked praetorian guards. He threw himself to the ground, facedown.

"Get up," Xipe said.

The Flay Lord was completely hairless. Those who saw him naked, slipping into the skin he had peeled off another person, knew that he had no hair anywhere on his body, not even his pubic area. His pale, unhealthy, milky flesh was drawn tightly across his bones, creating the impression of a skeleton. His eyes were pink, and it was known that he hated being in direct sunshine. In a land where people were almost as dark as a deer, he was pale as a fish's belly. Those who got close to him knew that he smelled like spoiled fish also.

A painted-on red streak ran from his right temple down to his neck, revealing the spot where flaying begins.

Zolin knew the Flay Lord wore the red line to remind others that he would start skinning them if they crossed him.

Said to be the only living person who ever saw the Feathered Serpent, he alone selected the victim whose blood was to be offered to the god. He also selected those to be skinned alive.

When Zolin got to his feet, he saw Lord Light off to the side on the ground, bound hand and foot, but still alive and conscious. Lord Light glared at him and said something, but his words were incomprehensible as blood foamed out of his mouth.

Zolin shrank back from the grotesque sight.

The tongue of his old master had been cut out.

"A child is missing," the Flay Lord said.

Zolin lowered his head and tried to speak without stammering. "A nurse took him away, but they will be found and killed. That fool captain permitted it. I—"

"This one did not get away." The Flay Lord gestured at Lord Light and rose to his feet. A priest sprang forward to hand him a knife.

Zolin knew what was going to happen. Lord Light would be skinned, with the only opening down his backside so the skin could be worn. He would die of shock and loss of blood. That would take a while. But Zolin had at least saved his own skin.

BOOK VII

PEOPLE OF
THE RUBBER

Twenty years later
AD 122

19

I am Tah-Heen, the ballplayer. My friends call me Tah. I was raised in the land of the People of the Rubber, which lies at the lush green foothills of the mountains that face the Great Eastern Sea.

The land of the Rubber People is nine days' journey from the most important city in the One-World, Teotihuacán, the City of the Feathered Serpent. That great city has more people than Mictlantecuhtli has souls in hell, while the tropical land of the Rubber People has more monkeys and parrots than people. In truth, more people live in a hundred paces of a Teotihuacán street than in the entire village where I was raised.

The jungle foothills of the great mountains and the coastal sands of the Rubber People are called the Hot Lands by those of the upper region because of the moist warmth that prevails year-round. Our land is not high up toward the celestial heavens, as is Teotihuacán

and the other large cities that lie in the great valley-
plateau on the other side of the snowy mountains.
Rather, the land of the Rubber People begins near the
bottom of the mountains and extends almost to the
Great Eastern Sea.

These Hot Lands are where Xolotl, the god of motion, put the trees called weeping women, which give
the milk that turns into rubber.

Because rubber is so desired by the rest of the One-
World, great wealth comes from the milk of the weeping women after it has been suckled and molded, but
the riches are for the Lord of the Rubber People, not
those who work the trees and mold the rubber. For
us, there are beans and peppers and maize for tortillas, with a little flesh—deer, rabbit, or dog—on feast
days.

The village in which I grew to young manhood is
in the northern area of the Hot Lands, in the foothills
of the snowy mountains, deep in the forest of weeping
women and vines. Beyond the rubber trees is jungle,
with foliage so dense and high that it blocks out the
light as the fiery Sun God travels across the sky. The
jungle is a place of rivers and swamps, of crocodiles,
monkeys, parrots, snakes, and great stalking jaguars,
of rain so thick you wonder if a celestial sea is falling,
and heat that is hot and wet and sticks to you like a
layer of damp, soiled clothes.

The people of my village are simple souls who work
hard, steal little, and help each other. I was raised by

my aunt Ome and her brother, Tagat. I call her my aunt because it is a position of honor, but she was not actually related to me by blood.

Ome married the servant of a trader and left the village to live in the Feathered Serpent's valley over the great mountains some twenty-five years ago. She was childless when her husband died five years later. She claimed that when she was returning to the village of her birth, she heard the cries of a baby and found me abandoned along the roadside after my parents, poor farmers, had fallen to a sickness.

Iyo . . . evil tongues in the village whispered that I was her own child, conceived without marriage after the death of her husband. But the wicked tongues didn't whisper where Ome or her unmarried brother, Tagat, could hear them. Both were exceptionally strong and would have repaid the insults with blows.

Tagat was a carrier of burdens, a member of the cadre of strong, swift-footed men who packed merchandise on their backs, carrying the products from town to town. He spent most of his life on the roads, traveling back and forth, a pack on his back rarely empty.

Our village had a hundred huts. Most were like the one I shared with Ome and Tagat, a dirt floor and three walls of mud-and-straw brick. The fourth wall was the one farthest from the afternoon sun and was made of palm thatch to let in an afternoon breeze. The roof was also palm thatch.

We slept in the common room and cooking was done outside, in front of the hut. Only the headman of the village had a walled courtyard with three rooms.

Everyone old enough to walk worked making the rubber that our people were famous for. The workday started before the Sun God began its escape from the dark cave where it was kept prisoner during the night. The men started the day by building cook fires while the women prepared a small meal, consisting usually of tortillas or corn mush.

In the twilight as dawn was breaking, each of us went off to our jobs, to produce the rubber that brought wealth to our noble lord, fame to our region, and maize and beans on our own tables.

Before we separated to begin each day's work, we gathered before the village headman, who selected the villagers who would perform the morning sacrifices to Xolotl. The households took turns making sacrifices, with two people each morning slicing a small cut on their body and dripping a little blood into a cup.

The headman spread the blood on trees that produced the milk of the rubber.

Before the midday meal, two others gave blood for the Moon God, who provided the "tears" that makes the rubber more pliable.

The trees that produced the milk of the rubber were slender, grayish brown, and grew higher than ten or twelve men standing atop each other. Dense green leaves started high up the trees.

When a tree was six years old, it was time to begin milking it, which would go on, with rest every few days for the tree, for about fifteen years. I have reached my twenty-first birthday, so most of the trees being milked today were not born when I was brought back to the village in my first year of life.

We started by wounding the tree. At a point on the tree about the height of a man, a slash was made about a thumb wide and almost halfway around the tree. A clay cup was hung under the wound. Soon the milk of the tree dripped into the cup, continuing for several hours.

We collected less each day from a single tree than would fill two hands cupped together, but there were thousands of weeping women, and the small cupfuls we gathered filled many clay jugs.

When our jugs were filled, we carried them back to the village, where the rubber was brewed and molded.

Fresh from the trees, the milk is white, thick, and gooey, but it starts to thicken as soon as it leaves its mother. The milk can be used almost immediately by draining off liquid and molding the thicker part before it stiffens.

Cloth sacks were coated with the liquid. After they dried, they were turned inside out to carry water.

Religious objects such as small clay images of gods and tiny rubber balls that are burned and resemble the teardrops of the gods when they drip were also prepared from fresh tree milk: We rubbed the still-gooey liquid on them.

Many other items were made from milk after it formed into rubber: soles of sandals that noble lords and rich merchants wore; mixed with copal for use as incense to burn; wood handles of pounding tools were dipped into it, as were drumsticks.

Even the priest-healers prized it, using it to cure sores and aches.

Olli was what my people called rubber; it was also what we called the ball game.

Iyo! To say "the ball game" is to say the purpose for life. Only war and death carried as much significance in our lives. Every town and village had a ball court.

Some courts were large, more than a hundred paces long and half that wide, with high walls and elaborate stone carvings of the gods. Others, as in my own village, were merely a long, flat, narrow area marked by stones.

Whether it was the grand arena of the great cities or the empty field found in a small village, the ball court was as important to the people as the temples dedicated to the gods.

Teams and individual players competing for the favor of the spectators and the gods battled the ball down the court; some to acclaim and victory—others to defeat and even death. That was why we called it the game of life and death.

A special type of rubber was used to make the balls.

Rough balls were made from the milk of the weeping-women trees by simply molding it as it hardened. Better balls were made from strips of the thickened milk. But to make balls with the best bounce, there had to be a mating between the milk of the weeping women and the tears of the Moon God.

While we gatherers collected the milk, other men cut and brought back vines of the moonflower, a vine that climbed trees and gave birth to a beautiful white flower the size of a man's hand.

My people believe that the Moon God and the Daughter of the Night fell in love. The Lord of the Night objected to the mating and turned his daughter into a vine when she refused to give up her love. But she never forgot her yearning for the Moon God. As her lover passed overhead each night, the Daughter of the Night showed her love for him by blossoming into a beautiful flower.

The tale must be true, because the flower blooms at night.

When the vine is cut down and flowers and leaves trimmed off, we beat it with stone hammers against rocks to soften it. After it is softened, we twist it, squeezing a liquid from it into clay pots.

The liquid is the tears of the Moon God, who cried each night when he saw the beautiful flower his lover had become.

When a concoction of one part moon tears to ten parts tree milk was boiled and molded, the balls made from the rubber had much better bounce than those made from tree milk alone.

The tree milk was likened by my people to semen,

a fluid that is indispensable for life. And so it was indispensable for the lives of the People of the Rubber.

Much of the rubber, mostly in the form of thousands of religious objects and balls used in games, was sent to Teotihuacán each year as part of the tribute the Feathered Serpent demands of the Rubber People. None would have dared deny the bloodthirsty Quetzalcoatl the tribute it demanded. To do so would bring a legion of Jaguar Knights and even the god's terrifying high priest, the Lord Flay Xipe.

Long before I was born, Quetzalcoatl, the Feathered Serpent, built Teotihuacán and came to dominate the One-World, with the Flay Lord doing its bidding.

It was not known if the Flay Lord was ageless, or if he died like other men and a new one took his place, but the Feathered Serpent was a god and remained supreme and eternal.

The god was worshipped not only in Teotihuacán, but the rest of the One-World, which acknowledged its mastery and sent tribute to honor it. In each large city, a lord who represented Quetzalcoatl collected sacrifice victims and other tribute and sent them to Teotihuacán to be judged and counted by Xipe and his minions.

As long as the demands for tribute were met, the other city-states of the One-World were permitted to govern themselves. When local leaders rebelled against the tribute demands, the response from Teotihuacán was severe: An army was sent, led by a legion of Jaguar Knights.

The slaughter that ensued would be horrific. The rebellious city was not merely brought to its knees, its nobility and warriors were sent to the sacrifice block and its people enslaved.

The city's king was always saved for last. After he was forced to watch the rape and enslavement of his family, he was brought by Nawals to the Flay Lord to be skinned alive.

Iyo! Not many cities failed to pay all the tribute demanded.

This then, was the land of the Rubber People, the place where I grew to young manhood. I would leave it with sorrow and heartbreak, with blood on the ground and demons snapping on my heels more terrible than those found in all the hells of Mictlan.

20

"Tah-Heen!" Ista, my friend, called as he ran to me.

I was outside the hut I shared with my aunt and uncle, with my uncle adjusting the pack I would carry. In my hurried excitement, I had made a mess of the straps that held it to my shoulders.

Early in the morning, the coming of the Sun God was barely visible as a faint light on the eastern horizon. Ista and I were excited—we were leaving the village for a trip to Kobak, a city three days' walk away. It was the first time we had ventured more than a day's walk from our homes, and the first time we would see a large city.

"A safe road," Ista said to my uncle. It was the standard farewell one made to a traveler, but not for one who also made the journey. He had forgotten that my aunt and uncle were also coming. But like me,

Ista was too happy and excited to remember his manners.

Ista was short and broad, while I was tall and slender, and my uncle called me the tree and Ista the stump. Ista was my age, but already he was second only to his father in being the strongest man in the village. Outside the hearing of others, he called me Tah, as did the other boys of the village.

"I have it," he whispered to me.

My uncle caught the whisper and frowned. "Make sure neither of you steal any of the Rubber Lord's goods—or you will find yourselves on the sacrifice block."

All rubber produced by the weeping women belonged to the Rubber Lord. He in turn was ruled by the king at Kobak. Rubber was everywhere about the village, but like those who mined the green jade far south of here, and those who made obsidian blades and mirrors at the Hill of Knives in the Fire Mountains to the west, all goods, and the villagers themselves, belonged to the lord who ruled the area.

Much rubber passed through our hands, my uncle was fond of saying, but none of it stuck there.

"We have stolen nothing," Ista said. "We have my father's permission to take the village ball with us."

Ista's father was the headman of the village. We villagers were permitted to have a rubber ball for playing the game, and we would carry that ball.

My uncle said, "I see, I see. You think that you will

find fools in Kobak to play the game and lose their sandals to you. Maybe you will find that the young men of the city can play better than you? What will you do if you lose the ball?"

"We can't lose. No one has ollin like Tah."

Ollin. Motion. Before the god Xolotl gave motion to the world, nothing moved, all things were set in place—water didn't flow, even the wind stood still. Xolotl waved his arms to create wind and took a great mouthful of water from the Eastern Sea and spat it onto the mountains, creating the rivers that flowed down from the heights. Xolotl was sent by the other gods to the underworld to find bones of different animals to create a being that would serve the gods. Bringing the pieces aboveground, he tossed them to the wind. They landed in two piles, creating man and woman.

Xolotl loved to play and used ollin to create the greatest motion game of all: olli, the ball game. Moving down the court, your body and the ball both in harmony, you scored points against the other team by getting the ball to the goal they protected. On some courts points were made by tossing the ball through a ring halfway down the court.

What Ista said was true: No one in the village had ollin like me. Even my uncle, who had carried rubber for sale and tribute to many great cities, said I moved like the professional players who traveled from city to city and played for honor and fortune.

"Be careful how you treat the boys of Kobak," my uncle said. "They're not like you. Some are the sons of nobles and will take offense if you beat them at olli. Others are thieves and would cut your throat for the ball."

"Do not fear, Uncle. If someone tries to steal the ball, I will run like the wind—and leave Ista behind to battle them."

In truth, we would fare better returning without our heads than without the ball.

We were joined by my aunt, and the four of us went to the east end of the village where ten others were waiting. As soon as we arrived, the headman selected Ista and me to make a sacrifice to ensure a safe journey. Everyone threw his or her staff onto a pile. Ista used his obsidian blade to nick the inside of his thigh and gave the blade to me. I did the same.

The headman collected the blood and sprinkled it onto the pile of walking sticks. The sacrifice was to Yacatecutli, the god of travelers.

Our packs were loaded with rubber—soles for sandals, rubber-coated clay figures of gods, balls of all sizes, the tiny ones to burn in honor of the gods and burials, larger ones for olli. Ome and two other women carried food for the journey.

We set off, my uncle Tagat in the lead, setting the pace with his staff, the rest of us following in a single line. Each man carried a staff with a piece of sharp obsidian embedded at the top. Traveling was safe on the roads of the One-World. The penalty to rob or harm anyone was to be bound hand and foot and carried to Teotihuacán, to be handed over to the priests of Flay

Lord Xipe. But some were always foolish enough—
or crazy enough—to risk being peeled alive.

We stopped to rest and drink water every two hours,
and for a long rest after the midday meal. An hour
before dusk, we stopped for the night at a clearing
next to a river where other travelers were camping.

Carriers who my uncle knew from his travels were
cutting up a crocodile they had killed. They gave us a
large piece to add to our meal.

The next day we left jungle behind and soon walked
along what appeared to me to be endless rows of corn-
stalks. For that day and until the evening of the next,
the corn, beans, and peppers that fed the people of the
One-World were never out of sight.

It was late afternoon of the third day before Kobak
became visible to us from a hillock. Most of the city
was awash in light earth colors, but I could make out
red and green and yellow also, colors my uncle said
were used for the palaces of the nobles and temples
and pyramids dedicated to the gods.

"Kobak is a large city," my uncle said. "People in
cities do not grow their own food. The food you have
seen growing as we walked is for the city."

"If they do not grow food, what do they do? Spend
their days playing the ball game?" Ista asked.

"They work as hard as we do. We make rubber, they
make other things. Many of the clay figures we cover
with rubber, the clay and wood bowls we eat out of,
are made in Kobak. They make blades, swords, and
mirrors from obsidian carried here from the Hill of

Knives. Bracelets, rings, necklaces, earrings, and nose plugs are made from shells brought from the Eastern Sea shore.

"There's trade in the cloth for clothes and blankets, needles from the maguey plant, the working of jade carried all the way from nearly the southern end of the One-World. Iyo! You will see, you will see. Our entire village is smaller than their marketplace. And ten of Kobak's marketplaces would fit into the great market at Teotihuacán."

"And the ball court?" I asked eagerly. "Is it a wonder to behold?"

"There are many ball courts, one for each section of the city, but professional games are played in the grandest one, the Royal Court. It's in the heart of the city, along with pyramids dedicated to the Feathered Serpent and local gods. It is not the finest court in the One-World, there are many larger, including the Great Court at Teotihuacán, but for people whose feet have never carried them from the village of their birth until now, the Royal Court of Kobak is wondrous. Professionals will play there for the king—"

"Will we see the game played?" I asked.

"No, it is for the nobles and rich merchants only, but there will be a parade before the game and you will see the players in their fancy uniforms with many bright feathers."

I knew from my uncle's stories that the uniforms that the players wore on the playing field were different from the ones they paraded in. Professional olli was a game of war—battles in which crippling injuries and even death were not uncommon.

"There is always a celebration when the professional players come to a city. The celebration will be even greater this time because the old king has died and his son is being enthroned."

Ista and I exchanged excited looks.

Professional olli players were the best in the One-World. They devoted themselves solely to the ball game, traveling from town to town, playing local teams or other traveling teams.

My uncle said the One-World had many professional teams, perhaps twenty-five or more. Some were well-known, with the most famous being the Jaguar of Teotihuacán. The team was legendary because its undefeated champion player was said to be the embodiment of Xolotl himself in movement.

The Jaguar only played once a year, a Skull Game against the team that had the best record in the One-World. The match was called a Skull Game because the ball used was a skull with thick rubber coating— the head of the captain of the team defeated the year before.

To play a Skull Game was the height of glory and honor for an olli player—even if it cost your life. We all knew that the game was more important than life itself.

For Ista and me, to see a ball game played by professional olli players was to watch the gods themselves play. Our earliest memories were stories brought home by my uncle and other carriers—tales of wins and losses, of players who had the ollin of gods and of those who ended up being sacrificed because they had lost during the Skull Games played before the Flay Lord himself.

There were wins and losses by the spectators, too, as they placed bets on their favorite teams. Uncle Tagat often told us of the conch merchant who gambled everything he owned on a single match. As he watched his team losing, he bled to death as he kept cutting himself to give sacrificial blood to Xolotl in the hopes the god would give his team the ollin necessary for a victory.

21

We camped that night outside the city and entered early the next day, getting to the marketplace as dawn was breaking. We unloaded our packs at the stalls of the rubber merchants. Our packs were soon filled with baked clay images of gods to take back with us, but we left them with the pottery merchants—we would not leave for home until the next morning and would pick up the packs that night before we headed for the encampment outside the city. That gave us an entire day to explore the city.

Before we parted from my aunt, she slipped several small balls of rubber into my hand. It was enough for us to buy food and treats in the marketplace. Little rubber balls, cocoa beans, pieces of obsidian, and bright feathers were used to buy other goods.

"Is it not amazing?" Ista asked as we walked through the marketplace.

So many people, so many things familiar and strange. Although traveling merchants occasionally came to our village, to sell the cloth used for clothes or trinkets worn at festival time, we had no idea that so many things were made for sale by others. Iyo! These city people must buy everything they need in the marketplace.

Most goods were made in the very shops that sold them. Shops of a like kind were located near each other—vendors of conch horns, animal-skinned drums with rubber-tipped sticks, whistles and flutes, were in the section devoted to merchants of musical instruments. Cloth merchants, who sold everything from the soft cloth from the vast fields of plants with white, fluffy heads that were picked and loomed into cloth, to purveyors of stiff cloth made from the maguey cactus and valuable animal skins, were in their own section.

We walked down the aisles, gawking at the goods: fruits and vegetables we had never seen, dried fish and the spines of stingrays from the Eastern Sea, obsidian blades and the shiny black mirrors that were said to reflect your enemy's secrets, green jade being worked by artisans into jewelry, gold and silver—a strange and exciting new world for two boys from a jungle village of the Rubber People.

Our wandering feet carried us out of the marketplace to get a look at the true heart of the city, the ritual center where the ball court and the temples were located. Before we got there, we saw three youths about our age playing the ball game. Like our own hoop at the village, theirs was makeshift, a slice of tree trunk with a hole in the middle.

"Fist ball," Ista said.

The three sizes of balls most often used in the game were the size of fists, coconuts, and heads. Actual heads covered with rubber were used only at the Skull Game in Teotihuacán.

The ball we brought with us was a coconut, but there would be little chance we would get the boys to play with it when they were used to a smaller ball. Besides, their hoop was only big enough to let a fist ball through.

We watched them for a moment. They were good players, better than the average person at our village, the huskiest of them as good as Ista. But none could move the ball as I could.

"What do you think?" Ista asked me.

"Back at the marketplace, my eyes saw beautiful feathers." I had seen bird feathers that would decorate the mantles of my aunt and uncle at festival time. But I had nothing to buy the feathers with. I could have stolen a piece of rubber for trade, but if I was caught, the sin would scandalize my family and the gods would feast on my blood.

"The ball they're playing with would buy many feathers and something for you to take home to your family," I said.

The boy who was the best player must have been of good family. His clothes were softer than those of the other youths, and he gave commands as if he was in charge. *It would be his ball,* I thought. Boys from lesser homes would not have owned a ball.

I took the coconut ball out of my pack and bounced it on the stone street. I bounced it to Ista and he bounced it back. It had the desired effect. The youth I took to be the ball owner stopped the game to watch us.

I backed up to put some space between us, and we hit the ball back and forth. The other youths came up to us.

"Where did you get a coconut ball?" one asked.

"They're Rubber People," the leader said. "You can see smears of rubber on their clothes and sandals."

He was right, of course. It was impossible to work the rubber without soiling clothes with it. My uncle had warned me that city people believed they were superior to villagers.

Ista bounced the ball to me. "Careful," he whispered, "he might be a nobleman's son."

The city boy's tone of voice and mannerisms had rankled me. At that moment I didn't care if he was the Flay Lord's son.

"May we join you in a game of olli?" I asked the leader, using the polite tone required when speaking to a superior.

He smirked and eyed me with scorn and arrogance. "We only play for prizes. What do people from a village have to bet? The dirt on your belly that you get crawling around like worms?"

Ista stiffened as the other boys laughed. "We should go, Tah, your uncle is waiting for us."

That was not true. I knew Ista wanted to avoid trouble. We both knew I could not reply back with an insult to the youth. If his father was a noble, he could have me beaten. If he was powerful enough, he could have me put to death.

I bounced our ball. "I have this."

Twice the size of their ball, it had a much better bounce. Their fist ball was almost solid rubber, but a coconut was made of strips of rubber wrapped around a core of palm fronds.

Ista groaned. He whispered, "The ball isn't ours, it belongs to the village."

"It's all right. When we're finished playing, the village will have two balls." I bowed to the arrogant youth. "Great Lord, would you honor us with a game and accept this coconut ball as a prize against your fist?"

"We will play. Three of us against you two—and we use my ball."

"That's not fair," Ista said.

"What do worms know about what is fair at olli?"

"We will play with your ball," I said, "and against the three of you."

Ista pulled me aside. "Are you insane?"

"I can beat all three by myself. We came here to play."

"Not against a nobleman's son. Humiliating him will cause problems. You know what your uncle said."

"Don't be an old woman." I grabbed Ista's arm and pulled him close. "You know we can beat them."

"I don't know—"

"Don't worry, I'll teach them a lesson that they will never forget."

Iyo! These pompous city boys would find out that the Rubber People have ollin in their joints and in the soles of their feet.

22

"How shall we play?" I asked the leader.

He indicated the areas at each end of the wall. "A point is made each time the ball stops in your end territory. Three points are made for putting the ball through the hoop."

"My friend and I need to handle your ball to see how it bounces."

As Ista and I tested the ball, three people—a middle-aged man, a young woman, and an old porter—stopped to watch. The spectators were city people, and it wasn't hard to see that Ista and I were country boys, especially after we put on our rude gear.

The game was played by hitting the ball with the wrists, hips, and knees as the players moved up and down the court. The only time the ball could be held in a player's hands was if a shot through the ring was attempted.

Ista and I both wore wood bracelets on our wrists, wood knee pads strapped to our knees, and a wide wood belt called a yoke around our waist. Rubber bounced, but it was hard enough to bruise skin. A fist ball, which was solid rubber, could knock a player unconscious or break bones if it hit hard enough.

The city boys had the same type of equipment we did, but much fancier. Their yokes even had the carved head of a jaguar on front, a tribute to the Jaguar players in the Feathered Serpent's city.

Their only advantage were helmets made of leather and wood. We were bareheaded and would have to keep our heads out of the way of the ball.

Play began when a city boy tossed the ball in the air. The ball was supposed to be thrown equally between the leader of the city players and me, but it was deliberately sent to the city boy. The youth kicked the ball to another player, who missed a shot through the ring. I went for the ball and was hit by a body block by another boy so their leader could grab the ball and take it down to the end zone.

"They cheated to score," Ista said.

"Of course." I had let them make a point to see how they played and make them think it would be easy. They didn't play nearly as well as I did, though the lead player was as good as Ista.

The people watching turned away, and I yelled to them, "Don't go yet. It's just begun."

From the end zone we guarded, Ista threw me the ball to get play started. I moved it down the court keeping it close to my feet, sometimes between my feet. The boy who gave me a body block before threw himself at me. I slid by him, turned, and pretended to kick at the ball. Instead of kicking the ball, I gave him a blow behind his knee that sent him crashing down.

Their leader kicked the ball to another player. I flew in between them and kicked the ball back at the leader, hitting him in the face. The ball bounced once before I was on it and had it downcourt and past their goal line.

I grinned at the people who had stopped to watch, then directed my attention back to the lead player. His nose bled and he gave me an ugly look.

They moved the ball back into play, and I quickly took the ball from them and danced it down to the ring and easily made a point.

Ista and I howled with laughter at the look on the faces of the city boys.

I beat my chest. "I have ollin! Xolotl gives it to me."

I never thought about how I would hit the ball. Movements were not planned, they just happened. But my body was not without direction—I gave my mind over to Xolotl, the god of motion, for him to direct. I went where his ollin took me.

When I touched the ball, it felt like a part of me, as if it were an extension of my body. I never felt fear that I would be beaten at the game. The score never affected my play. My mind and body acted together as one. Movement just happened.

I'd tried to explain to Ista and other boys in the village that they had to stop thinking about how to hit the ball and let Xolotl direct them, but none of them were able to connect with the god's motion as I did.

I easily scored a third point and bowed to the clapping of the onlookers. Ista was sweating and breathing hard, as were the three town boys, but I just felt a warm glow, as if a bright fire inside me was slowly burning down.

The middle-aged man who had been watching with the young woman and the old porter came up to me and asked, "What is your name?"

"Tah-Heen."

I wondered why he asked. He had the look of a wealthy merchant or even a minor nobleman.

He stared at me intently. "What's the name of your father?"

"My father is dead. I am of the People of the Rubber."

"What was his name?"

"I don't know. I was found after my parents died of a fever. Why do you ask me these questions?" I was bold to ask such a question to a man of authority.

"You remind me of someone."

His two companions came up and he pointed at me. "Mark this youth. His name is Tah-Heen and he is of the Rubber People. Remember the name. Someday you will hear it repeated throughout the One-World when people talk about the game."

The man gave me another intent look. "If it is the will of the gods, we will meet again, Tah-Heen."

I stood still, taken aback by his statements.

He gave me a little bow and turned away, walking briskly. As his companions followed him, the young woman paused for a moment and stared back at me. She was not just an attractive young woman; her muscle tone set her apart from other women. She walked with more confidence and authority than any other woman I had seen.

I gaped at her, an awed village boy, struck by her femininity and commanding presence, my body instantly reacting to her sexual appeal.

I watched them disappear into the crowds moving toward the festivities. I was suddenly breathless. My name proclaimed throughout the One-World as a ballplayer? Iyo! Who was this man who spoke this outrageous compliment?

The warm glow I felt when playing came back as I reveled in the praise I had been given. I heard running steps behind me. As I turned, I got the flash of something coming at my face. I started to duck, but was too late—the nobleman's son swung the wood yoke he wore around his waist at my head. He caught me with a glancing blow on the side of the head. I staggered sideways and fell, but recovered onto my feet. Ista was fighting off the other two. I ran to join the fray, and the two took off.

"They suddenly jumped me." Ista touched the back of his head.

I looked around in panic. "They have our ball."

Ista turned red. I was frozen with apprehension. The city boys were gone. With our ball and theirs.

"We've got to find them!" Ista almost spun in a circle. He didn't know which way to go. Neither did I. They were gone. The elation of victory and flattery instantly evaporated. We were doomed.

"What should we do?" Ista asked.

As always, he looked to me when a decision had to be made or a crisis surmounted. The sick feeling in my gut made me want to cry, but I pretended to be unfazed.

"They'll go to the festivities. We'll find them there."

Maybe we would. And when we attacked them, we would end up in the sacrifice line. What had I done? I felt like taking a club and beating myself. What had I got Ista and myself into?

We fell into the flowing crowd and let it carry us to the heart of the city where the tributes to the king would be made in the form of the two most popular sports in the One-World: watching the hearts being ripped out of those chosen for the sacrifice line and action in the ball court.

I was no longer excited by the prospect of seeing a ball game and the other wondrous festivities. Ista came behind me, not a word of blame for the mess I had got us into. Yes, I was right, I could beat city boys at olli. But I was naïve and stupid when it came to dealing with the machinations of city people.

Aunt Ome and Uncle Tagat were on a ledge across

from the main stand where the king and the high nobles were seated. I knew without asking that my aunt
would have been the one to shove and push her way to
the best place for common people to view the festivities. My uncle had a strong back, but was not as aggressive and assertive as his sister.

Ome took one look at our faces and knew something was drastically wrong. "What happened?"

I shook my head. "Our ball was stolen."

"Stolen? Or did you lose it playing?"

"We won the game, but the other boys ran off with
the ball."

Ome and Tagat exchanged looks.

"This is very serious," he said.

"We'll find them and get it back," Ista said.

Ome shook her head. "No, you won't, you'll just
make matters worse." She glared at Tagat as if he were
at fault. "When we get back to the village, you must
smooth this over. There are losses to thieves along the
road. This will be one of them."

Ista and I grinned at each other. Leave it to Ome to
find a solution. I squeezed her hand as Ista and I got
up next to them. They truly did have a grand view of
the festivities. Sounds of conch horns and drums came
from up the street. Excited murmuring in the crowd
reported that the two teams of ballplayers, the local
and visiting teams, were coming. My own excitement
shot up.

As I waited for the ballplayers to appear, I suddenly
realized that directly across from us was not only the

local king, but a much more impressive sight—Jaguar Knights. Ten of them in gold-and-black uniforms were lined up at the bottom of the stands. They looked much fiercer and threatening than the king's own guards, who shied back from the legendary fighting force.

The city was not part of Teotihuacán, but the great city dominated the One-World with fear. Pay tribute in goods and sacrifice victims, and enjoy the peace guaranteed by Teotihuacán. Fail to pay and a legion of Jaguar Knights march on the city. But these warriors of the great god Quetzalcoatl were not here to make war, but to escort a representative from the god to honor the local king.

The excitement of the crowd increased as the players came into view. Watching them marching toward us, I realized there were two visiting teams: male and female.

I had heard of professional women players, but had always thought they were a myth. And that was not the only thing that caused me to gawk—the stranger who'd complimented me about my play was at the head of the visiting team.

He was the manager, not a player. He and the players wore the uniform of the greatest bird of prey in the One-World: the eagle.

Each team in the One-World chose an animal—jaguar, rabbit, snake, coyote, monkey, or any of a dozen others.

Behind him came the female players, four of them. Then came the six male players.

"The Eagles are a second-rate team," Uncle Tagat said.

"Why do you say that?" I asked.

"I've heard of them. They don't play the big cities, not unless the local king wants them to make his own team look good. That's what they're best at—getting paid to lose."

I started to say something, but an expression on Ome's face caused me to stop. She was staring intently across the roadway. I followed her gaze. A man was standing perfectly still, staring in our direction. He was dressed as a great lord with many quetzal feathers adorning his helmet. A jaguar symbol on his helmet signified that he was a high official of Teotihuacán because only Jaguar Knights, the infamous Nawals, and nobles who served Quetzalcoatl were allowed to wear the jaguar symbol.

I'd heard talk on the streets that one of the Feathered Serpent's High Lords was attending the festivities.

As I observed the man, I suddenly realized that the lord was not staring at my aunt—*he was staring at me.*

"Zolin," Ome whispered.

I didn't know if she was speaking to me, Tagat . . . or herself. Her tone conveyed fear and repulsion. Before I could ask my aunt why she was upset, the man she called Zolin yelled something to the Jaguar Knights. While I didn't hear the words, his gestures were plain: The guards were being ordered to grab us.

"Run!" Ome shouted at me, but my feet were frozen. I was too confused to move. She shoved me. *"Run!"*

"Aunt—"

Chaos broke out around us as the Jaguar Knights charged and people stampeded to get out of their way. Shoved and knocked about by panicked people, I tried to push my way back to my family, but lost my footing and went down. I struggled back up and flowed back with the press of people. I got back on the ledge, and the man my aunt called Zolin spotted me. He pointed at me and again yelled to the knights, but his soldiers were battling the crowd just to keep their feet.

"Ome!" I spotted her in the crowd making her way toward Zolin. Smaller, faster and not burdened by a shield, sword, and elaborate uniform, she navigated the crowd much faster than the knights.

She raised the wood-handled obsidian dagger she carried. The Jaguar Knights spotted her also and turned to pursue her.

Zolin caught her dagger arm by the wrist. I started toward where they were struggling. Jaguar Knights were suddenly onto her, hacking at her with their swords.

Ista and my uncle were suddenly beside me.

"Ome!" I cried.

Tagat grabbed my arm. I pulled away and he jerked me back. "We'll die if we don't run!"

Panic over the bloodshed stampeded the crowd. I ran with it, stumbling beside Tagat with Ista as we worked our way through the chaos. Near the main marketplace we broke loose from the crowd.

Tagat led us down narrow alleys and byways until

we came out on a road leading south out of the city. It
was not the road to our village, which lay to the west.
There had been no time to ask questions until we
stopped to catch our breath.

I needed to know what had happened, why the man
Zolin had focused on me and why my aunt had tried
to kill him. For sure, I understood she had acted to
protect me.

Tagat shook his head at my pleas. "It is more dangerous for you if you know everything."

"I don't understand."

"Your ignorance will keep you alive, but you must
always be careful. From this day forth, tell no one you
are of the Rubber People. Forget your name and use
another. Forget your aunt and uncle and tell people
your family are all dead."

"But why? I must know—"

"Something happened a long time ago, in Teotihuacán. You were a baby when your father brought
down the wrath of Xipe, the Feathered Serpent's Flay
Lord, upon him and his family."

"My father? Ome said—"

"We didn't tell you the truth. Your whole life has
been a lie to protect you. Your father was a great lord,
but today to even speak his name would bring the
Flay Lord's Nawals at your throat. Ome had been your
nurse. When your family was murdered, she fled with
you, bringing you to be raised in our home.

"Zolin, the man who Ome tried to attack, must
have recognized you. Even I can see your father in

your face. And he would have recognized Ome, too. He was your father's steward."

My whole life had been a lie? What did that mean? Numb and confused, I just stared at my uncle.

Ista hadn't said a word. Rooted in place, he appeared as stunned as me.

"Keep on this road," Tagat said. "Go south as fast as you can. Fall in with other travelers."

"Without you?"

"I'm going to spread the alarm that you went in the opposite direction."

"But—"

"Go! As fast you can, don't look back."

Ista came alive. "Where am I to go?" he asked my uncle.

"Where do you want to go?"

"With Tah."

"Good. It would be worse if you returned to the village. The Flay Lord's men will go there looking for Tah, and people know you left with him. If you are there when they come . . ."

My uncle didn't have to finish. I understood. They would kill everyone in the village.

Tagat took off a pouch he had tied around his waist. "Rubber I was to buy supplies with. Use it when you need to, but don't let anyone see you have more than one piece."

The small, eye-size balls were commonly used to make purchases. One ball would buy enough food to last us days.

Tagat left us and hurried back to the city.

Ista and I set out down the road, walking fast. We were young and strong and could make time as good or better than a Jaguar Knight.

We walked in silence, in fear, my mind buzzing with questions I had no one to ask. I thought about Ome and began to cry. I tried to hide my tears from Ista, as he hid his from me.

23

We stayed on the road leading out of town. Unless one was wealthy and could afford a litter carried by slaves, the only method of traveling in the One-World was on foot. We kept our feet pounding, traveling on the main road only because we had no idea where other roads led.

"Small roads lead to small villages," I told Ista. "Not places we can disappear in."

Along the way we met travelers on the road, locals not far from their homes and porters carrying goods on their backs. I was tempted to have us fall in with a group of carriers for protection along the road and to appear less conspicuous, but with their burdens, they moved slower than we did.

We bought tortillas and fire stones at a village along the road. The two stones were struck together to create a spark for a fire. Even though our tortillas did not need to be cooked, a small fire would be a welcome companion tonight.

"We must sleep off the road," I told Ista. "They may have soldiers traveling at night searching for us."

As dark was falling, our fast pace was catching up with us. I could see that Ista was tiring. Spotting a hill a couple hundred yards off the road, I led Ista there because it would give us a view of anyone traveling below. Not even Jaguar Knights could see in the dark, so their torches would be easy to spot.

"We can't build a fire," I said, as soon as it occurred to me that our own fire would stand out more than a flaming torch below.

So we sat in the dark, fearful of the things we could hear and not see and things we could imagine.

"Perhaps they will send Nawals after us," Ista said.

A terrifying thought. "There are no Nawals in this area."

I didn't know that for a fact, but my uncle told me the dreaded man-beasts always stayed near the Flay Lord Xipe of Teotihuacán. Tagat also said the Feathered Serpent cast a dark shadow on the land with his high priest that skinned people alive.

"Xipe's spies are everywhere," Tagat had told me, more than once. And I knew his legions were ready to march against any king who failed to do his bidding. But nothing in the One-World was as terrifying as the stories of the Flay Lord and his creatures.

All I really knew was that the Flay Lord and Nawals were terrors that naughty children were threatened with by their parents if they misbehaved. I had never thought of them as real. Not until I found myself on the run from a blood feud with the Flay Lord.

Ista said, "My father told me that Jaguar Knights are the best warriors in the One-World. But that Nawals are not warriors. They are shape-changers who turn from man to beast."

"That's a story to frighten children."

"It frightens me, too. They say Nawals can track a man by his scent," Ista said.

"I don't know."

"They say that when they catch you, they rip out your heart and eat it, then drink your blood."

"Shut up."

An animal scream startled us—the sound of something killing or being killed.

"Nawals," Ista said.

"Shut up!"

We huddled next to each other on the hillock, wrapped in our cloaks, surrounded by silence and darkness. I tried once again to make some sense out of what Tagat had told me, but only one thing he said kept popping up in my mind: *Your whole life has been a lie.*

A lie created by Ome and Tagat to protect me.

I had often wondered about my parents. They were simple farmers, Ome told me. Now I knew I was the son of a great lord . . . but one who had fallen from grace with the Feathered Serpent and its denizens. A lord who had incurred the wrath of the mighty god enough that the sins of the father were carried to the son.

What had my father done to cause such rage that Nawals, the feared Lords of the Night, sought his son's blood—decades later?

Iyo!

Damp and cold, we rose before dawn after troubled sleep. Rain had fallen during the night, and we didn't dare light a fire to dry our clothes or warm our bones.

Ista was silent and grim. I felt more sorry for him than myself. He had been swept into the dark storm only because of me. I wished I could tell him to return home, but Tagat had traveled the One-World and was wise in the ways of all its peoples—and he had warned us against returning to the village. We would do ourselves no good and bring harm to our people.

As the sun broke, we started to make our way down from the hill, but had gone only a few paces when Ista grabbed my arm and pointed.

"Look!"

On the road below, soldiers at an encampment of porters had pulled aside two youths about our age.

We fled back up and over the hill, putting distance between us and the road. Ista led the way, crashing through the thick growth with strength born of panic. We had no idea how far ahead soldiers or news of us had traveled in the night.

We were both covered with sweat and welts from bushes and limbs by the time we reached a river.

"I can't go any farther," Ista gasped. He dropped to his knees and threw up.

My heart pounded. I caught my breath and shut my eyes, straining to listen. No sounds of pursuit came, but if we were spotted, the knights could be moving in a different direction to cut us off.

"We have to keep going," I told Ista.

We waded in and sloshed downstream, keeping our eyes open for crocodiles and snakes. We followed the bank until huts of a small village came into view. No more than ten huts, it was similar to a fishing village near our own homes that traded fish for rubber and used the rubber to buy other necessities.

Three canoes were beached on the bank.

Ista nudged me. "We need one of those."

I shook my head. "If we buy a canoe, the word will spread. It'll be worse if we steal one. The fishermen will catch up with us and use our livers for bait. Let's look for something we can float with."

Water transportation was tempting. We made our way in a wide circle around the village and back to the edge of the river. We walked and waded for another hour before we came across something that would help: a fallen tree trunk.

The branches had been cleaned off, probably by someone planning to make a canoe out of it. We pushed it into the water and sat on it, using long branches to fend off the bank and help the current carry us along. I feared getting a leg ripped off by a croc, but it was a superior way to travel.

We passed more villages and canoes, but there was little curiosity about us. People used canoes, rafts, and logs, anything that would float, to move along the small river. We blended in with the others.

We went downstream for two hours until we came into the outskirts of a small town. The river water turned salty and we began to move faster. I knew from my uncle that the Eastern and Western seas came higher on land and pushed up rivers each day for hours, then drew back a couple of times each day.

"We're being carried toward the Eastern Sea," I told Ista. "We'll have to get back onto land before we're carried out."

When an increasing number of houses and long fields of maize came into view, I decided it was time to get back onto land. "We're nearing a town and they may have been warned to look for us. We'd be easy to spot on the river."

We abandoned the log and got back afoot, circling the town. An hour's walk took us to the sands and waters of the Eastern Sea.

"It's incredible," Ista said, about the waters.

Not just incredible: the vast, dark waters were endless and ominous.

We People of the Rubber knew nothing about the seas except what Tagat and other carriers told us. And even carriers and people who lived on the coasts had no idea of the size and depth of the waters, though it was well-known that the waters and wind could sometimes fight and carry their ferocious battle onto land.

We also knew that the cave the Sun God came out of each morning was somewhere on the other side of the sea, but no one had canoed to it—at least, no one who came back to speak of the feat.

For three days, hungry and tired, we trudged along the coast. We knew fish, many bigger than us, were in the sea but didn't know how to catch them. Nor could we get a meal from the seabirds by chasing them and throwing rocks.

Finally, desperate from hunger, we made our way back to the road. Kobak was far behind us. We hoped our troubles were, too.

We were both miserable from fear and hunger when we came upon a roadside encampment. At the last moment, I grabbed Ista's arm.

"No. We can't take the risk."

"I'm hungry."

"We'll find something to steal. Let's get out of here."

I swung around and stared into a familiar face.

"What are you boys doing here?"

We froze in place, too shocked and terrified even to make a run for it. A throaty gurgle came from Ista as if a whimper had made its way up his throat and escaped out his mouth.

The team manager from Kobak who'd complimented me on my ball playing stood before us.

24

Others gathered around before we could run. I took them to be players on the team.

The young woman who'd seen me play, and who turned out to be a ballplayer, came up beside the man. From their features, I realized they were father and daughter.

The team manager suddenly grinned. "What a pleasant surprise. Isn't it, Daughter?"

His daughter didn't answer, but her features said that she wasn't at all pleased to see us.

He took Ista and me by the arm. "You boys look tired and hungry. We were just about to begin the mid-day meal. Come, join us."

As we sat in the shade of trees to eat, the manager asked, "What's your name?"

Ista gave his without thinking, and I gave the only one that instantly came to mind. "Tagat."

Only after I spoke did I realize the manager had been speaking to Ista only—I had told him in Kobak that my name was Tah-Heen. He said nothing about the contradiction.

While eating tortillas, I found out the team manager's name was Sitat and his daughter's was Ixchel.

"Where are you traveling to?" Sitat asked.

I cleared my throat to make way for a lie. "We're porters."

"Porters?" He raised his eyebrows. "Where are your loads?"

I couldn't say we had delivered them. No porter would drop a load at one location without picking up another.

"Robbed," I said. "They were stolen from us."

He nodded. Thievery on the roads was not unknown. "I imagine your master will not be happy when you return without his goods or payment."

Unhappy? Porters who lost their master's goods would likely quickly find their way to a sacrifice mound.

"I don't have a porter," Ixchel said. She gave me a look of contempt, as if I were not good enough to wash her feet. "He ran away."

Sitat laughed. "With welts on his back. My daughter has a short temper, little patience, and many demands. Right now we need a couple of porters. Our team travels the One-World, meeting other teams on the fields of olli. We have a dozen porters, but have a constant need for new ones because they return to their homes after journeying just so far. If you wish to join us, you may do so."

Ista and I looked at each other. It was not an offer, it was a miracle sent by the gods.

Half an hour later, Ista was turned over to the head porter, and Ixchel dropped a large, heavy bundle on the ground beside me.

"Get up and put this on your back. This is my uniform and equipment. I know everything in my pack. You lose anything and I will cut off your ears. You steal anything and I will cut off your head. You understand, boy?"

Boy? This young woman could not have been more than a couple years older than me. But I was smart enough to know that she was infinitely older in the ways of the world.

I slipped into the straps and mounted the bundle on my back. It was heavy. My glee at joining the company of ballplayers was tempered by a concern: Was she joking when she threatened to cut off my head and ears?

An hour down the road, we came upon a contingent of soldiers. Not Jaguar Knights, they were warriors belonging to the local king whose territory we were entering.

Sitat stopped and spoke to them and paid a fee before we passed.

I kept my head down, not knowing if there was still a search for me.

When Sitat was walking near me, a question popped into my head. "Does the team play at Teotihuacán?"

"We have never played there. Only the team that wins the championship for the entire One-World is invited there."

"The Skull Game?"

"Yes, the Skull Game. The best player that year in all the One-World plays the Feathered Serpent's champion. It is the greatest honor a player can achieve."

"No one ever beats the god's champion."

"The honor is not in winning, but in playing. There isn't a player in the One-World who would not willingly go to the sacrifice altar for the opportunity to play a Skull Game."

"Strange, isn't it? Teotihuacán has both the mightiest army and the champion ballplayer." I expressed a thought aloud that I should have kept to myself. Saying something that could be construed as a criticism of the Feathered Serpent was dangerous. "It's because he's the most powerful of all the gods," I added.

We walked along in silence for a moment.

Sitat said, "Do you know what the two most important things were that the great god at Teotihuacán used to bring the One-World to its knees?"

"Jaguar Knights?"

"No, not even Jaguar Knights can function without these two things. One is obsidian. The glass spewed from fire mountains gave his armies superior weapons. Put a sharp edge on a wooden sword and it can not only slice the enemy's sword in half, it can chop up the swordsman. The Feathered Serpent's forces quickly took control of the two main sources of obsidian and refused to sell the glass to other kings.

"And the other is tortillas."

"Tortillas?"

"Tortillas are prepared ahead of time, can be carried easily, and are filling. They permit an army to march greater distances in less time, while carrying fewer supplies, than foods that needed to be prepared. If soldiers had to carry raw foods like maize that required preparation, water for cooking it, a container to cook in, and wood for fires because they couldn't rely upon finding enough along the way, it would have taken much more time and energy to prepare meals. Three times a day. And an extra porter would be needed for every fighting man. Tortillas permitted the armies to make long marches, take on more supplies, and march again almost immediately."

We stopped and Sitat tapped my shirt with his forefinger. "Never forget this. Teotihuacán didn't come to dominate the One-World by brute force alone. Instead, it used intelligence to control the best weapons and extend the range of its army." He indicated the ballplayers passing us. "Olli is war, ball courts are battlefields. And wars are not won by brute strength alone. Players who try to muscle the ball won't win the war."

He left, leaving me wondering why I was supposed to remember the lesson about tortillas—and playing the ball game with intelligence. Was he hinting that I might someday be a ballplayer?

I had never seen professionals play. But looking over the players as they practiced en route and at rest stops, I decided I was as good as any of them. No—I was better. The best. On the field with a ball—

Something whacked me across the back of the head. I spun around. Ixchel raised her fist to hit me again and I stepped back.

She glared at me. "You're malingering."

"What do you mean? I'm carrying your things."

"You were daydreaming. You imagined yourself good enough to be a ballplayer, didn't you?"

I gawked at her. She was a witch.

"Well . . . so what if I was? I can—"

"You're here to carry my equipment. You're not a ballplayer. I watched you play, you're too weak."

"Weak? I'm as strong as any of your players."

"You have muscles in your arms and legs and none in your thinking." She sneered. "You're not tough enough inside to be a player." She pointed to her head. "You're weak here."

Ista came up beside me. "What's going on?"

"She treats me like I'm a slave and she's the wife of a king. Someday I'm going to teach her a lesson."

Ista stared at Ixchel strutting ahead of us and shook his head in wonderment. "I didn't know there were women like this in the One-World."

I didn't either. Ixchel was half-woman, half-wild-animal. All beautiful and graceful. And dangerous.

Ista saw something in my expression that gave him alarm.

"Tah—don't even think about it. The woman is too much. Bedding her would be like cuddling up to a jungle cat. After the act is done, she will cut out your heart and eat it."

"Listen, my friend, my only friend. Someday I will have the woman—and an invitation to the Skull Game. And I will master both."

For the first time in his life, Ista fled from me. He appeared genuinely frightened.

25

Three days later we came to a town about the size of Kobak where a game of olli was to be played against the local team.

Ista and I were once again excited about the ball game—we would finally see professionals play.

The day before the match, we watched our players practicing at our encampment.

"You're as good at handling the ball as they are," Ista said.

His encouragement emboldened me to boast to Sitat, "Let me play. I can handle the ball better than your players."

I could see from Sitat's face that I had not caught him in a good mood. He yelled to the chief porter, Vuk, an old man who supervised the carriers. He walked stiffly from age and had an arm that was twisted and of little use.

"Come over here, Vuk. This boy says he is a ball-player."

Sitat got a ball and bounced it to me. "Move the ball around him."

Play ball with an old cripple? My anger rose and I came close to giving the ball a good kick and walking away. But I was in no position to disobey a command of the team manager.

I bounced the ball, getting a feel of it. I didn't want to humiliate the old man, but it was necessary. I grimaced, but I had to do it.

Not being able to use hands or feet to hit the ball, I set up my move by bouncing the ball on my extended forearms and gave it a good hit, sending it bouncing, with me chasing it. The old man stepped to it, using his knee to stop the ball's momentum and keep it in front of him. I dashed around him to get at the ball, and he turned in a half circle. As I came around his side, crowding him, his elbow struck me in the middle of my chest. The blow caused me to stop and gasp. Stepping on my foot, the old man used his other knee to kick the ball up. It hit my nose and I stumbled on my heels and fell backward.

I sat up on the ground, holding my bleeding nose.

Sitat's feet crunched the ground beside me. "I told you, olli is a game of war. War is for men, not boys."

Vuk helped me up.

"You cheated," I said. "You hit me."

"Of course."

Vuk turned to leave and I said, "The way you handled the ball, it was incredible. Have you played the game?"

He smiled. And walked away.

As Ixchel watched me wash blood from my face, she shook her head. "You only know how to lead with your head, don't you?"

"He's just an old man."

"That old man was once one of the greatest players in the One-World."

"I never heard of him."

"What does a boy from a small village know? Vuk played at Cantona long before you were born. The winner was to go on to Teotihuacán and play the Flay Lord's champion."

I gaped at her. The winning teams from the entire One-World gathered at Cantona each year for play-offs for the prize as the best team of all. The city had twenty ball courts. The captain of the championship team went on to Teotihuacán to play a Skull Game.

"He lost at Cantona?"

"No, he won."

"He played the Skull Game?"

I instantly realized that wasn't possible. Vuk was still alive. Everyone who had played against the Teotihuacán champion had lost and was sacrificed.

"You saw Vuk's twisted arm? It was broken after the final game."

"What bad luck!"

"Not bad luck. The owner of the team had it broken because Vuk was supposed to let the other team win.

When he didn't, the owner had him punished. He was never able to achieve his destiny of playing at the Skull Game and being honorably sacrificed."

Iyo! That meant when Vuk died, instead of finding a place in the thirteen heavens, he would be doomed to the nine hells of Mictlan.

"I don't understand. Why would the team owner want to let the other team win?"

"Isn't it obvious? He was betting on the opposing team."

While on the road and preparing for the game, I learned a great deal about the team and the man who led it.

Sitat was a grizzled veteran, but not of the game. He could hit the ball as hard and fast as most players, but his scars came from his days as a warrior who had fought in many battles. But no one seemed to know exactly what wars he had fought.

Once I got to know more about the team, it soon became apparent that Sitat's vague background was the norm for the entire team.

"They're outlaws and outcasts," I told Ista, as we compared what we had learned about the team.

None of the players used their real name, not even me. From what I could judge, no one had a home or a family . . . at least none that they ever mentioned.

They traveled all year, every year. Like Sitat, they were tough, battle-hardened veterans, but of the ball court. Olli was their life, the team was their family.

Watching them practice, I was again struck by

Sitat's remarks that the game was not won by brute force. Yet the skill I saw them demonstrate was all muscle. Which made me wonder why the team manager was contemptuous of physical power on the ball court.

The game was tough and brutal. The ball was bigger and heavier than the one Ista and I were used to. Players got kicked, blocked, and had, as I learned, noses broken rather frequently. Sometimes players died or were crippled.

Not that there weren't benefits to being a player. They basked in the roar of the crowd, in recognition when they walked down a street. I learned early that my uncle had been right about this team's reputation for losing. Professional players, for sure, but not at the top of the profession. Rather, they were a team of minor players.

Unlike Vuk, none of the players would ever be invited to Teotihuacán to play in the Skull Game and experience the supreme death. They had never even made it to the finals at Cantona's twenty ball courts.

Each player had a porter assigned to help him dress for the game. In my case, the task was helping *her* dress.

The players had two sets of game clothes and equipment—a bright, colorful uniform for the festivities before and after the match, and the stripped-down, rugged uniform and equipment used on the playing field.

For their parade march, their helmets had the head

of an eagle mounted atop, with its white face and dark eyes. The rest of the helmet had black, white, and gray eagle feathers, and it covered almost the entire head, creating a mask over the player's face, leaving only the nose, mouth, and chin open. Below the headdress was a cloak of black feathers that covered the shoulders and fell to the back of the knees.

Worn around the waist was a thick yoke-belt made of black cloth with white feathers woven in and a large eagle's beak as its centerpiece. Pads for the shoulders, wrists, and knees were also woven and interweaved with feathers. Sandals had the tips of eagle-wing feathers swept back to give the impression that the feet could take flight.

The other team here was similarly dressed, only in the motif of a coyote.

As in Kobak, at the head of the parade were drummers and blowers of conch horns, followed by temple priests dressed as gods, and finally the ball teams. The managers, wearing the same uniforms as the players but of a higher-quality material, led their respective teams.

The procession paraded down the street and into the ball court where the city's notables had gathered. The local governor presented the game ball to the team captains. Each player in turn drew blood and smeared it on the ball.

After the festivities, the teams retired back to their encampments, where we helped them out of their parade clothes and into battle gear. The players stripped naked and we dressed them with thick leather and wood guards to repel the ball with. The only piece of clothing was a short deer-leather hip cloth that hung from their waist. Beneath the hip cloth was a buttocks strap that drew the fleshy cheeks together to make the rear a firmer place for hitting the ball.

Gone were the fancy feathered and woven materials. The equipment they wore in the game permitted them to move fast, hit the ball hard, and reduce injuries. Every player had scars. Stories of players crippled or killed during the games were legion.

Around their waists, tied on with leather straps, was the big yoke of heavy hardwood; each wrist, knee, and shoulder had a smaller yoke.

"The most powerful strikes of the ball come from the hips," Vuk told me. "That's why the yoke around the waist is so heavy."

Heavy gloves and sometimes hand-stones were used to strike small, hard balls, but the ball for today's game was the size of a skull.

I assisted Ixchel in dressing. Her uniform was almost the same as the men's. Her breasts were exposed, but her nipples were painted red. I also drew red stripes down the exposed parts of her face and down the sides of her legs.

The ball court was a typical professional one, Vuk told me as we stood together to watch the game and be ready to repair a player's equipment if it broke. The court was 120 feet long and 40 feet wide. The ground was worked smooth and hard. The court walls below where the notables sat had sloping sides. The players could send the ball along the wall, hoping to get to it as it rolled off.

A goal area was at each end of the court. Just as Ista and I had played at home, points were made by sending the ball into the opposing team's goal area.

The game could be played one-on-one, with two-man teams, and even with three or more on each side. Unless the players were famous, most games were not one-on-one, but played with two or three players to a side.

The action started in the center when the ball smeared with sacrificial blood was thrown by the highest-ranking nobleman. It was tossed so it hit the sloped side and bounced into the court where one man from each team was waiting. The second player on the team was positioned halfway to the goal area that was to be protected. When three players were on a side, the third player was positioned next to the goal area.

Just as in the game we amateurs played, the skull ball could not be touched by the hands or kicked with the foot. The ball weighed about nine pounds and was so heavy that feet and hands were not the best way to propel it, anyway. Rather, the shoulders, hips, knees, thighs, and buttocks were used.

Shoulder thrusts were powerful but not common because the ball was rarely bounced high enough to reach the shoulders—and hitting the ball with one's head was sure to cause injury. Knee shots were also dangerous because hitting the ball wrong could damage the kneecap despite the wood guard strapped on to protect the knee. Besides, a good knee shot could lift the ball high enough for the other player to shoulder it into your face, breaking your nose, knocking you unconscious, or even killing you.

Watching the game, I saw that Vuk was obviously right about which were the most powerful shots. The ball was too heavy to be launched well with a kick, so hip shots in which the player literally threw his body at the ball were the most powerful. The wood yoke around the waist protected the player from serious injury.

A good hip shot sent the ball bouncing down the court at high speed. Iyo! Nine pounds coming fast at a player. Hit it wrong and that was the end of your career.

The game was played with dazzling speed and brutal body blocks. Players were not permitted to kick or punch, but they threw body blocks against the opposing players to get control of the ball.

When a player went down, an "accidental" kick in the head often ended his career and sometimes his life.

I now completely understood why they called it the game of life and death. "Truly a game of war," I whispered to Vuk.

The female players went out onto the field first. Watching them play, I was amazed at their skill. "They handle the ball better than men."

Vuk chuckled. "Yes, they are faster with the ball. Because they are shorter, they are more often able to get under the ball with their hips to give it a more solid hit than a man."

"They can beat the men?"

"No, men are bigger and stronger. The women are more skillful, but if they played against men, they would be trampled."

Two players were on the field at the same time, with two players held in reserve. Of the players on our women's team, Ixchel was the best. She was better than any woman the coyote team could field, too.

Vuk said, "The women's games are just to warm up the audience for the men. The spectators want to see blood, not skill. But if we had a team of male players with Ixchel's skill, we would be invited to the Skull Game every year."

Our eagles were badly beaten by the coyotes.

As we walked back to where we would help our defeated warriors change, Vuk said, "Brute strength, that's all we have. None of our players know what to do with a ball except hit it hard—and that they do perfectly. They hit it to the other team, hit it out of bounds, hit it toward the wrong goal, they hit it everywhere but where it is supposed to go."

"Why doesn't Sitat train them to hit it correctly?"

Vuk shook his head. "He can't, they lack ollin. Perhaps some of them had it once, that gift of the gods that makes a ballplayer a winner, but our players are all too old and have been battered too many times. They can no longer soar like eagles, instead they crawl like snails. Did you see what they put in their mouths before the game?"

"Each chewed a piece of a green plant."

"The gods put something in the plant that makes a man stronger and faster after he chews it."

"Isn't that better for the players?"

"No. They need more and more of the plant as time goes on, and it has less effect on them. In my day, the great champions didn't use magic plants to increase their abilities. They looked within themselves for the extra strength. Today, most players use it."

"Can't Sitat get new players?"

"New players are expensive and the owner of the team won't spend the money."

"Who owns the team?"

I knew that olli was not just for commoners and professionals, but was played by noblemen. The great men of the realm played against each other as if they were captains on a battlefield, sometimes making large wagers on the outcome.

I wondered if the team owner was also a player.

Vuk told me he was not: "A wealthy Hill of Knives merchant whose slaves make mirrors from obsidian. He refuses to buy good players. When one of our players is no longer able to play, he replaces them with another player who is in the autumn of his career."

The players didn't look like old men to me. Most seemed just a few years older than me.

"Players age fast. And die young. It is better to die young. Then they do not have to dress others."

When we had finished assisting the players, Vuk kicked a ball to me and we moved it between us. This time I was careful not to use my nose to push it.

Vuk pointed at birds flying overhead. "Xolotl gave them ollin so they could be one with the sky. He made the fish one with the rivers and sea. That is why our players lose . . . they are not one with the ball. They move separately from it."

"I always thought I was one with the ball," I said. "I didn't plan my movements, they just happened. I gave my body over to Xolotl, and my mind and body and the ball became one."

He hit the ball to me so I had to extend myself to get it back to him.

"You were a boy when you played at your village. Now you must be a man."

He hit the ball and I scrambled to return it. Iyo! How did this old man have so much ollin?

"You are right," he said. "When you played against other boys, you used the ollin of your body. Great players use not only their own ollin, but that of the ball."

"I don't understand. The object is to hit the ball in the right direction."

"That is the tactic of mediocre players. They hit the ball this way and that way, sometimes it helps make a score, other times it doesn't. A great player must connect not only with his own motion, but with the ollin of the ball. Xolotl doesn't hit the ball when he plays on the celestial ball court, he flows with it, his energy connecting with the ollin of the ball."

We stopped and Vuk locked eyes with me. "Do you understand what it is to be a champion?"

"Champions win."

"It means much more. Great players get big rewards. They can afford not just a wife, but concubines. They live in a palace and eat the finest foods. They are praised by the public and favored by the gods. Not even war heroes get as much acclaim as olli champions. The heroes of songs are not the heroes of wars, but those of the ball court. And it is a profession fraught with the same dangers as war. Just as death reigns on the battlefield, the Lord of the Dead visits the playing field."

Vuk hit the ball to me, maneuvering it so I had to return it sometimes using my left side, other times on the right. I didn't realize for a moment that Sitat was watching. He came closer and Vuk said, "Did you see?"

Sitat nodded.

"See what?" I asked.

Vuk grinned. "I told him the gods had given you equal ability for both sides of your body. You just proved it. Most of us are better using either right or left."

I shrugged. "Is that important?"

"If a player can hit the ball well using either side, it gives him an advantage."

"I'm not a player."

"And you never will be," Sitat said, "if you don't learn to listen and do exactly what you are told."

"Are you saying—"

"Vuk will try to train you. If he can do it, you will be permitted to try out for the team. If he fails . . . I'll give you to the temple priests the next time we must provide a sacrifice."

26

When Vuk told me I had to be up every morning before the Sun God rose, I thought he wanted me to practice hitting the ball.

"If you hit the ball in the dark, how would you find it?" he asked, correcting my misconception. Instead I was to sit and feel the ball. "Like all young olli players, your relationship with the ball has always been to strike it."

"What good does it do to feel it? Wouldn't I learn more by hitting the ball?"

"Before you hit the ball, you must come to understand it." He ran his hands around the ball. "You must think about all the different ways that the ball can be hit when you transfer your ollin into it. Hit the ball in your mind. Only after you have imagined every way that a ball moves, will you be ready to hit the ball with your body."

I did what the old man told me even though I didn't completely understand. What he wanted me to learn didn't seem practical.

"You must learn all the ways ollin affects you and the ball because when you enter the ball court, you must never think about hitting the ball."

"I don't think about it, I—"

"You decide where to hit it—you just don't realize you are doing it. Oh, I know, I've seen you play with your friend. He is much slower and misses more than you because he thinks more about where to hit the ball. But you also think about it more than a great player would. The game is faster than your thoughts.

"We are not going to train your mind—you already know what you need to do. Your objective is to move the ball down the court and into your opponent's goal area. Your mind needs nothing more. It is your body that must be trained. Once the ball game starts, if you think, you will lose. Your body must react as one with the ball."

The old man pounded his heart. "Your heart must hit the ball, not your mind. It works much faster than your head. When the ball is hit by the other player, you have to know where to position yourself to meet the ball *before* it hits the wall. You have to be there before the ball."

Vuk showed me a stiff walking stick. The stick moved so fast it was a blur until it hit me across the thigh.

"Akkk!" I rubbed the side of my leg. "Why did you do that?"

"Pain is good."

"Good?"

"You must accept pain, embrace pain. Otherwise it joins your opponent's team."

Vuk hit me. Every morning. Every night. Hit me until I didn't yelp. Until I didn't flinch. Until I embraced the pain as part of my existence.

Vuk also changed the food I ate. "Rats and snakes are powerful for their size. You must eat them."

Worse than eating rats and snakes, Vuk made me play blind—completely in the dark. He took me into a field and tied a cloth over my eyes so I couldn't see.

As I stood there unable to see, a ball hit me in the face. I cursed, ready to kick to death anyone in range.

Vuk's voice came to me in the darkness. "You must not rely upon your eyes."

The ball hit me in the gut. Angry, I yelled, "May Xolotl turn your arms and legs into worms. How do I see without my eyes?"

"You'll see with the eyes that can look behind your head—*your ears*. You must learn to see with them because you will never have time to look behind and then get into position. The eyes in the back of your head must tell you what move you must make before the eyes in the front of your head see the ball."

You will live for the moment, Vuk told me, in a game where everything goes right, when the ball goes exactly where you want it every time. "You will have an invisible hand directing the ball for you. It will be Xolotl. He will have entered the game on your side. When Xolotl is your teammate, everything you do will be a success."

After three weeks of working with Vuk, I was finally given the chance of playing with the team. It was not a regular game, but a practice. I had watched the players carefully and was certain that I could handle the ball better than any of them.

"We will start with a one-on-one," Vuk said.

The player chosen as my opponent was the one who protected the goal. I considered him a lesser player, with the best player being the one who worked the ball to the opposing team's goal.

Vuk had the professional player and me stand ten feet apart. He bounced the ball between us. I shot at it. The other player bent down and head-butted me as I went for the ball. Blood squirted from my nose as my face exploded with pain.

Later, discouraged and humiliated, my nose swollen, Ixchel's pack on my back, I walked beside Vuk. He called the head-butt being "speared."

"It is a game of war. You went for the ball, your opponent went for you."

"He cheated."

Vuk shrugged. "He accidentally hit you while chasing the ball."

"It was no accident."

"I told you, it is war. Each member of the team has

been a soldier. Sitat is a captain of soldiers who has a blood instinct, an instinct to kill. There are two great predators in the One-World: the jaguar and the eagle. The jaguar rules the land, the eagle the sky. Sitat named the team after the eagle because he dreamed someday that his eagles would challenge the jaguar in a Skull Game.

"The team members do not dress as the eagle to impress spectators, but because they assume the character of an eagle. Like it, they become predators. Eagles have ollin, they move with all the grace and skill that Xolotl gave the wind. But they are also merciless killers. They attack without warning and rip their prey with their powerful beaks."

The grizzled veteran gave me a predator's grin. "To be a great player, you must have the blood instinct. In a battle, whether it's a fight between two men or two nations, the aggressor is almost always the winner. You must always attack. Never think about killing. You simply do it."

Vuk taught me many more things about handling the ball and myself on the court—hitting the ball when it came at me from different angles, getting into position to receive the ball from a teammate, faking the direction I plan on hitting the ball, and even reading another player's body language to see if he was positioning himself to injure me . . . so I could injure him first.

The most important thing he taught me was to be in continuous motion and let my body react without thinking. To achieve the state where my mind no longer controlled my actions, I had to let Xolotl take control.

Ixchel saw to it that my training with Vuk never interfered with my duties toward her. Iyo! The woman had neither mercy nor a gentle hand. The more I did for her, the more she demanded. But she fed me well and refused to let others use me for their chores.

I was attracted to Ixchel, admiring her both as a woman and an olli player. My blood grew hot when I was close to her or had to touch her body when I was dressing her. I wanted to experience her body as a man and a woman experience each other, but I knew that to lie with the manager's daughter, a woman who was above me socially, would get me a trip to the sacrificial block.

My mind knew it, but just as Vuk wanted my body to think for itself when I was playing olli, my body reacted with lust whenever I was near her.

Early one evening just before night was falling, I went looking for Ixchel because Sitat asked for her. I met her teammates coming back from bathing in a pond, and they told me she was still there.

Rather than disturb her . . . and warn her of my coming . . . I crept up to the pond and watched her through the reeds. She swam around on her back, exposing her breasts and the mound between her legs as I watched. She stood up in the water and rinsed her hair before stepping onto the embankment in front of me.

Instead of putting on her clothes, she stood naked on the embankment and bent over, her buttocks pointed toward me, as she reached to the ground in a stretching exercise. As I watched her doing the exercise, her rump facing me, my blood boiled.

Finally, unable to hold back my passion any longer, I burst out of the reeds and grabbed her waist to mount her from the rear.

She slipped sideways, twisting and grabbing the back of my shirt, sending me headlong into the pond.

When I came out, she was still naked, her hands on her hips, the nipples of her breasts stiff and pointed.

"I'm not a dog for a man to mount at his pleasure. I decide when I will lie with a man."

I was angry and had been humiliated enough by the woman. I came up to her until I stood only inches from her nakedness. "You better decide quickly . . . my body is not obeying my mind."

We went down together, my erupting stalk entering her sweet opening as our lips pressed eagerly together.

27

When we were back on the road, a large contingent of Jaguar Knights marched by us. Besides obsidian swords, the front ranks carried spear-throwers made of bamboo, which enabled warriors to hurtle spears farther. Behind them came sling-users, who flung rocks at the enemy. Sitat told me the weapons permitted the knights to devastate the front ranks of an enemy before they came into hand-to-hand-combat range.

"They have ollin," Sitat told us. "Not individually, but as a unit. The warriors of other armies follow their leaders, but once the battle begins, they fight as individuals. Jaguar Knights fight as units, moving in, retreating, and regrouping. Three olli players are a team. So are a hundred Jaguar Knights."

"They have tortillas, too," I told Ista, when Sitat was out of earshot.

"Everybody has tortillas."

"True, but carrying them is the secret of their success."

I let the comment hang until he threatened to thump me.

I was immensely proud the day Vuk announced that I was ready to play. In a brief ceremony before the midday meal, Sitat presented me with an eagle headdress and mask.

"When you wear the feathers of the eagle, you draw on the power of the great predator of the sky."

The headdress and mask Sitat gave me were grand, yet I had the feeling they were well worn. "Did another player wear these?"

"Not a player."

"It seems like it's been—"

"It was worn by a great man, one that played the ball game for sport, not professionally. But he was a great player. And a great warrior."

"Who was he?"

"You have not earned the right to know his name. If you become a great champion, the name will be revealed to you. And if you fail, worms have no right to speak the name of a great man."

"Is that all there is to life—worms and champions?"

"Champions are those who have been bestowed a gift for greatness by the gods. Worms are those who fail to use the gift." As he walked away, Sitat turned back to me. "Those of us who are lucky have never received greatness from the gods. That way we never fail."

The game was to be played in another secondary town, but I was as excited as if it were a Skull Game. I was surprised when Ixchel came in to help me dress and brought me rubber pads for my waist yoke and elbow and knee pads. Only the greatest players could afford rubber padding, and it was usually awarded them by the wealthy nobles who owned the teams.

"These are part of the eagle uniform that you're wearing. My father wanted you to have the complete uniform so that the gods would recognize it and perhaps they would bestow favor on you."

Ixchel had been cool toward me since we had coupled at the pond. I knew the reasons why—not only was I younger and of a lower social order, but lying with a man could make her pregnant. If that happened, she would have to stop playing the ball game. And would kill me.

"I also have orders for you from my father. You are to permit the other team to get the ball first, take it away from them, make the first point in the game, and play no more. You will be replaced by your friend Ista."

"*What?* That's insane. Ista can't win the game."

"We know that. The game is not to be won by us, and Ista will be told to make sure he doesn't win. The game is between two cities that have a dispute. The kings have already resolved it between themselves, but want to make their people believe that it was decided by the gods in a ball game."

"We are to deliberately lose?"

"Yes. My father believes you have the makings of a great champion. He doesn't want you to suffer the loss. That's why you are to make a point and leave the game."

I spoke to Ista before the game. "From your face, I see that you have been told to lose."

He nodded. "The lead player for the town team is the king's nephew. I have to make him look good without making it obvious."

"I don't know why Sitat chose you, he should have a more experienced player—"

"He chose me because I begged him. It works for him because he thinks I will lose anyway."

"Why did you ask to play?"

"What am I doing here? You are at least being groomed to be a player, but I am nothing but a porter. Am I to spend my life carrying other people's burdens? At least in our village I knew that someday I would take my father's place as the headman."

I hugged him. "I'm sorry. It's my fault."

"No, you didn't choose to have the wrath of the Flay Lord chasing you." Ista squeezed my shoulder. "Don't worry, I can take care of myself. Like you, I would give everything for one moment of glory."

I entered the game with two other of our players and played the role Sitat had assigned to me, permitting the other side to take the ball first. The opposing player moved the ball down toward the goal we had to protect. I kicked the ball from his control, ducked under a straight-arm to my face from the player I was told was the royal nephew, and drove the ball down-court, slamming into a blocker with my shoulder, rico-cheting the ball off the sloped wall and picking it up to drive it across the goal line.

And I was out of the game, that quickly, breathless, accelerated, excited, ready to make goal after goal . . . but instead I was on the sideline, watching Ista and the two other players. Only when I was on the sideline did I realize that everything had happened so quickly I had forgotten to be scared my first time out. Now, realizing what I had done, I was eager to get back in and play.

Ista did well, better than I thought he would. The royal nephew slammed him with his shoulder, knock-ing him away from the ball. Ista came back and got the ball again from another player. The nephew came up from the rear and kicked him behind the knee, send-ing Ista down.

The opposing team made the goal that it was ar-ranged to make. Sitat called for Ista to come out of the court because he got uneasily to his feet, but my friend shook off the order and immediately rejoined the play.

As the royal nephew drove down the court with our other two players making deliberately feeble attempts to stop him, Ista suddenly came up from behind the man.

"No!" The exclamation escaped from me when I saw Ista's angry features.

He drove in to get the ball, slamming the nephew with his shoulder. As the man staggered, Ista came in under his chin and brought up the full force of his shoulder with its wood guard under the chin of the player's helmet.

The man's neck snapped backward with the sound of bone cracking.

Iyo! I knew instantly what Ista's actions meant. I leaped forward, shouting, "Run!"

Out of the corner of my eye I saw Sitat's club coming a split second before my head exploded.

The next day all of us, the entire team, porters and cooks, were brought into the square before the city's temple. Ista was already there. Tied up. The royal nephew he had injured was dead. Because his son was unable to move his arms or legs, the nephew's father had plunged a dagger into his son's heart to put him out of his misery.

Sitat wore his obsidian dagger. "If you make a move, say a word, I will cut your throat."

My head still ached and I had an egg-size bump on it. I knew I could not express my anguish for my friend. Ixchel had put it bluntly: Ista was to be sacrificed. Nothing could save him. If another team member annoyed the king, the entire team would share the Knife of the Gods.

I kept my face blank to protect my comrades, but my knees shook and my heart bled as they dragged Ista up the stone steps to the waiting priests. No flower weaver was present to give him dream dust. They wanted him to suffer.

I tried to keep my face averted and the tears from falling, but when I heard the dagger hit his chest and his cry, I looked and saw my friend's heart being ripped out.

The priest held the heart in the air above Ista's chest. Ista's arms and legs convulsed and he stared in horror at his own heart.

Rather than honoring my friend by eating him as would be done to a courageous warrior who had fallen in battle, the father of the dead player ordered the body to be chopped up, the pieces thrown to two dogs.

So ended my first time on the playing field.

I swore on the memory of my friend that I would join him on the sacrifice block before I would play for a team that deliberately lost a game.

"That is insane!" Sitat yelled.

"That is the only way I will play. I will bring you the championship that you have always lusted for. But I will only play to win."

28

So it came to pass that I became one with the great predator of the sky, and in my eagle guise I drove the team to victories.

Sitat said, "You must wear your eagle mask before entering any town and must keep it on until we leave. Let no one see your face."

I knew why I should wear the mask. At least, I knew that the great god of Teotihuacán lusted for my blood. What the sin of my father was, I didn't know. If Sitat knew, he never revealed it. The team manager never spoke of my troubles.

Wearing the eagle mask in public would not raise the suspicions of anyone. Many great champions became the alter ego of the creature they assumed and wore masks in public, but we both knew that was not the only reason that Sitat told me to wear the mask. He knew what would happen if the Teotihuacán lords seeking me found me playing with the team. Not only would I be sacrificed, but so would all the other team members.

What game was Sitat playing that made him willing to risk his life and the lives of his daughter and others?

Was it just that he saw me as a potential champion for his losing team? Perhaps . . . but I sensed that there was more to Sitat's willingness to risk all than just the ball game. He was playing his own game, and had a secret that was in some way linked to the eagle uniform he gave me to wear.

I played hard and mean, giving no quarter. I entered the court to win. At any cost. No blow was too low, too vicious. The crowds loved the violence I brought to the court, the blood that flowed, the bodies carried off.

When I stepped onto the court, I carried two things with me. The eagle whose persona I had assumed . . . and the scream of Ista when they ripped out his heart.

What Sitat didn't realize was that I wasn't playing to be a champion. The rage that arose in me was not the lust for honors, but something infinitely more violent: revenge.

Ome, my aunt—no, not just an aunt, she was the only mother I remembered—was murdered while trying to protect me from an unnamed vendetta from the past. If we had not had to flee and been hunted like animals, Ista would still be alive.

The mighty of Teotihuacán had bloodied those I

loved. When the time was right, I would draw my own blood.

My affair with Ixchel was also over. We made love, and alas, I carried my hardened violence to our bed.

"You frighten me," she said. "I no longer know you. You are not the boy who carried my gear."

"I am not a boy anymore. I'm a man."

"No, you're not just a man. Not even just a ball-player. I am a ballplayer, too, and I have known many. I sense something different in you, something that frightens me. You've become a beast. I have never seen anyone enter the court so willing to kill. The other players sense it and so do the ones you play against— you frighten everyone."

"Good. The more they fear me, the easier my victories will be."

The only regret was that my teacher, Vuk, was not present the day we won at the Cantona games and I was chosen to play the Skull Game in Teotihuacán.

Vuk fell ill before we reached the finals at Cantona. His spirit escaped with his last breath, to descend to the nine hells of Mictlan and the challenges that lie there.

A great champion lay within the twisted body of the old ballplayer. The challenges of the underworld were many, but with his spirit freed of its crippled body, I was confident that he would surmount the hells and find the Peace of Nothingness.

My teacher was gone, but I had to keep learning on my own because before it became my turn to descend to hell and meet the challenges there, a challenge in the One-World awaited me: the Jaguar champion.

Iyo! No one had ever defeated the Flay Lord's champion at the Skull Games. His player's uniform is that of a jaguar. No one has seen his face. Some say that the "uniform" is actually his own body. That he is a Nawal. He had no name, none that I ever heard, at least. He was simply always called the Jaguar champion.

My vendetta against the Flay Lord and his dark servant Zolin could be settled by ripping out their hearts. But the Feathered Serpent was a god, and no earthly act of man could destroy him. My one chance for revenge against the god was to defeat his champion in the ball game. Such a defeat would resound throughout the One-World and grow with the retelling.

To accomplish my goal, I had to go to the city of the Feathered Serpent. But I wasn't going to Teotihuacán until I had answers to the dark mystery that had left a trail of murder in my past.

Because I had my own demons to face, I didn't go with the team when they were permitted to take a two-week rest before setting out for the great city. Instead, I left without telling anyone, sneaking away in the night.

My destination was the village in the land of the Rubber People where I was raised and spent many happy years. There I hoped to find some answers before I faced my powerful enemies. My uncle Tagat would have answers to my past. I had to find him, and the village was the place to start.

As I neared the village, I stayed back, not daring to enter. Not out of fear for myself, but worry that if my visit was reported, the entire village would be sacrificed. I also knew my welcome from the villagers would not be warm. Besides bringing danger to their homes, Ista had died because of me. For certain, Ista's father and mother did not know their son was dead. I would earn no honor in their eyes with the news.

I stayed outside and hid where I could watch the road to the village. Each morning Ista's mother walked to the next village to report to the headman there the amount of rubber processed the day before. That headman passed on the information to another village, and down the line until it reached the town of the nobleman who owned the land of the Rubber People.

When I saw her coming down the road, I stepped out from the bushes.

She slowed her pace, but kept coming, staring at me. I read sorrow in her features. Ista was not with me—and she guessed the reason.

"My son is dead," she said.

"Yes. He died with great honor as a warrior." I pointed up at the sun. "He is up there now, racing across the sky with the honor guard for the Sun God."

Tension flowed from her. She smiled and nodded. "I thought for sure that he would end up dishonored and defeated in the terrible hell of Mictlan. How did he die?"

"Fighting for a great lord. He slew three warriors before he fell. He was honored in death by having his heart eaten by a great warrior king."

"That is good, that is good, he was strong and brave. And you? Why are you not dead?"

"My feet take me on a different path than Ista. They have carried me here—"

"You're not welcome."

"I know that. What do you know about my true parents?"

She shrugged. "Nothing. We always believed you were Ome's child and she hid the fact because she had no husband."

"Nothing else? Ome never said anything about who my parents might be?"

"No. Before she returned to the village with you in her arms, your uncle Tagat told us she had become a nursemaid to the wife of a great lord in the Feathered Serpent's city. But when she came back, she said she had worked making clay dishes and that she found you after sickness killed your family." Ista's mother walked by me. "I must go."

"One more question. Is there any news of my uncle?"

She shook her head. "He has never returned to the village. One of the carriers claimed he saw him in the city of the Feathered Serpent, but when he greeted him, your uncle ran away."

"Did he say where in the city?"

She kept walking and didn't answer.

I walked fast in the opposite direction, not certain that the woman wouldn't report my presence. Was it possible that my uncle had gone to the Feathered Serpent's city? The more I thought about it, the more sense it made. Tagat was at home in only two places: among the Rubber People and in the great city of Teotihuacán. Back and forth between the two regions, carrying rubber products to the large city and trade items back to the villages, was how he had spent almost his entire life. Talk that he had a family in the far city was also tossed about by the villagers.

Teotihuacán was not only the largest city in the One-World, a thousand times larger than our village, but Tagat described it to me as a city of strangers because so many carriers and merchants flowed in and out. That made it a better place to hide than a small community where he would immediately be recognized as a stranger.

I pointed my feet in the direction of the city of the Feathered Serpent.

29

Teotihuacán

Iyo! The Feathered Serpent's abode was not a city, but the beating heart of the One-World.

On the main road to the city, I was part of a steady flow of people with their merchandise—merchants carrying loads on their backs and others with a hundred slaves or hired carriers—along with warriors, government officials, and messengers.

I had long ago learned that people in cities do not grow their own food, so it was not surprising that so many carriers heading into the city had packs loaded with maize for tortillas and mush, beans, squash, chili peppers, and many kinds of meat—rabbit, turkeys and turkey eggs, duck, deer, and dog, along with fish that had been dried.

Many items that only rich merchants and nobles could afford—cacao, quetzal and other bright feathers, and stones of green and turquoise—were being brought.

Going out was merchandise produced in the city—vessels for food and water, masks, incense and incense burners for religious observances, jewelry to be worn on the neck, hand, or ankle and made of bone, teeth, shell, silver, and gold. The two metals were highly prized because silver was the excrement of the Moon God and gold that of the Sun God.

Clothing and blankets were also produced in the city, mostly from animal skin, cotton, reeds, and maguey.

The most important merchandise was the substance that made the Feathered Serpent's city the most powerful empire in the One-World: obsidian. The material was a gift of the fire mountains that spewed flaming rock from their entrails.

Besides weapons, jewelry, mirrors, and other decorative items were also manufactured from obsidian. A merchant I traveled with for a day told me that the city had over four hundred shops just for the manufacture of obsidian items.

To blend in with the hundreds of carriers on the road, I purchased a pack filled with dried fish and mounted it on my back.

As I approached the city, the great fire mountain to the north shot smoke into the sky. The One-World was ringed by these mountains that were the homes of the fire gods who shook the earth and sent smoke and fire into the sky. An ominous sign for my arrival.

South of the Pyramid of the Sun God, a river flowed through the city. By the time the grand boulevard reached the heart of the city, it was wide enough for thirty men to walk shoulder to shoulder. Most buildings were a combination of living quarters and workshops. The buildings were one story high, but the taller of the two pyramids, with the temple to the Sun God atop it, was higher than a stack of twenty buildings, the pyramid to the Moon God only slightly smaller.

As I came down the wide boulevard that pointed directly at the Pyramid of the Moon and the Fire Mountain behind it, I walked alongside the tall wall that hid the Forbidden Compound. On the other side of the wall were the Temple of the Feathered Serpent and the domain of the Flay Lord and his servants.

From the Forbidden Compound came the laws that the citizens had to abide by and the orders for legions of Jaguar Knights to march when a rebellious ruler refused to send tribute.

With only one well-guarded stairway for access, the tall wall was obviously not only for privacy but to make the compound easy to defend.

On the other side of the boulevard was an enormous marketplace. I had passed many small marketplaces on my way in, but this open-air center was big enough to fit in it most of the towns I'd ever seen. Iyo! It looked as if every merchant in the One-World had gathered here to sell, buy, trade, and even craft—most merchandise was made in the stall that sold it.

The most amazing thing was the sheer number of

people. Vast hordes of people. Their noise and smells were everywhere. As if the Feathered Serpent had indeed opened the gates of Mictlan and breathed life into the dead to populate its city.

Near the great marketplace I passed the ball court. The playing field and the spectator area were much larger than any I'd seen before. On a stone wall next to the skull rack was an image of the Flay Lord's champion. The picture showed a man who was at least a head taller than me, and I was considered tall for most men.

The image was of a fierce creature. I say creature because his human qualities were completely covered by the mask and other jaguar gear, even to a greater extent than a Jaguar Knight, whose hands, arms, and legs were at least exposed.

I couldn't help but wonder how I would fare in a game against this much bigger player on a much larger field.

When I'd decided to find my uncle in the city, I had no conception of its size. Now I had no idea where to start looking. Streets were endless, people were a mass. I couldn't stand on a street corner and shout his name; not that it would do any good—my shouts would be lost in the clamor.

My feet inevitably took me to the most revered and feared place in the One-World: the Pyramid of the Sun God, with its magnificent temple.

Home of the Feathered Serpent's main minion, the Flay Lord, it was where thousands of people were sacrificed each year.

At the foot of the pyramid, Jaguar Knights were lined up every ten feet. They stood stiff as stone figures. Tagat had told me that knights chosen for guard duty at the pyramid were all battle-tested warriors.

Gawking at the magnificent edifice, I was suddenly knocked aside from behind. My instant reaction was to recoil and strike back, but I froze when I saw Jaguar Knights and warriors that were infinitely more terrifying: Nawals.

A litter carried by slaves and covered with brilliant quetzal feathers came down the roadway. Several dozen Jaguar Knights, including the one who'd knocked me aside, cleared the road for the procession. But it wasn't the knights that attracted my attention. The litter itself and the Lords of the Night flanking it were the stuff of my nightmares.

Though I heard many tales about them, never before had I actually seen a Nawal. Unlike the Jaguar Knights, who were simply warriors in uniforms with a jungle-cat motif, the Nawals wore masks that reflected neither man nor beast but man-beasts. Grotesque, malevolent, evil, but most of all frighteningly dangerous.

As the litter came by, the only glimpse I had of the occupant was of a pale hand with long, sharp, green fingernails that dangled from the bottom of the feathered curtain. For reasons I could never explain, that pallid hand the color of death was more frightening than the creatures flanking the litter.

"Fool," a hoarse voice whispered in my ear. "Why don't you jump in front of the litter and tell them who you are?"

The voice froze me in place. I resisted swinging around and shouting, "Uncle!"

Tagat briskly moved through the crowd that had gathered to watch the Flay Lord's procession. I pushed my way behind him. When we broke out of the crowd, he slowed his pace until I caught up with him.

"What luck!" I said. "I thought it would be impossible to find you."

Tagat huffed. "The only luck is that you weren't dragged off to the compound where those to be sacrificed are held before their day comes to meet the Knife of the Gods. Why did you block the way of the Flay Lord?"

"I didn't realize it was him until I saw the Nawals."

"Weren't you taught to play the ball game? To surprise the other player? To kill before you are killed? Remember those skills. It's a reflection of how life must be lived here in the Feathered Serpent's city."

I didn't reply because my mind was spinning. How did Tagat know I played the game? How did he find me so quickly?

"He was coming back from the mountain," my uncle said. "Visiting his master."

"Who?"

"The Flay Lord."

"What are you talking about?"

"You'll find out."

"I don't understand."

"You will soon."

We walked without words passing between us for a long way through the city. When we reached a building, he paused before we entered and faced me. His face twisted. "Tah-Heen . . . Ome would have been proud of you. I am proud of you. Word of the prowess of the eagle player is well-known even here. You're the greatest ballplayer in the One-World."

My pride surged and my eyes filled with tears. I wished Ome was here to have heard the praise.

I followed Tagat through the main door and an inside door. From campfire talk during my journey to the city, I learned something of these buildings where people lived and worked. Each building occupied a square block. No windows faced the street, but the interior was built around a central courtyard.

The courtyards for palaces of the rich had fountains and green, cool gardens. For commoners, the courtyards were places of manufacture.

It came as no surprise to me that rubber-soled sandals were made in the courtyard of the building where Tagat took me.

Someone else from the past was waiting for me inside.

"Sitat!" I yelled with surprise and joy.

* * *

I sat in the courtyard of the sandal makers and listened as my uncle and my friend unraveled some of the twisted mysteries of my life. I felt immense pride to learn that my father was a great lord and my mother the daughter of a king of the Rubber People, which explained why Ome had been my mother's nursemaid.

Sitat told me Lord Light had not only been a great lord, but "no other lord in all Teotihuacán was his match on the battlefield or the ball court."

"The eagle uniform you gave me . . . it was my father's?"

"Yes. The legion he commanded was called the Eagle Knights. I was one of his captains."

"The Eagle Knights were even more victorious on the battlefield than the Flay Lord's Jaguar Knights. His success and acclaim made the Flay Lord jealous," Tagat said.

"Worse than that. Your father questioned the ever-growing need for human sacrifice to appease the Feathered Serpent at a time when Teotihuacán was powerful and prosperous. The Flay Lord had your father murdered because he believed your father was building a coalition of other lords to depose him and stop the sacrifices."

"Was my father conspiring?"

"Yes," Sitat said, "I was his emissary to other lords. When he was assured of support from the other lords, he would have attacked and put an end to the Flay Lord and his bloodlust."

As I listened, I couldn't help but wonder what my

life would have been like had my father succeeded and I was raised as the son of a great lord rather than a rubber-village laborer.

Tagat connected the massacre of my family with the death of Ome.

"She realized Zolin, your father's steward and betrayer, had recognized your father's features in you."

"She gave her life to protect me."

"Yes."

We were silent for a moment. I had a feeling that the tale was not finished. "Is the fact that I am Lord Light's son the only reason the Flay Lord still seeks my blood?"

They exchanged looks, and Sitat pursed his lips before answering. "That is enough reason, but they have a greater worry. The memory of your father's greatness still lives on, as does the terror of the Flay Lord and the questioning of the need for thousands of sacrifices each year. The Flay Lord fears Lord Light's son would become a rallying point against him."

"What would the Feathered Serpent do to us if we didn't feed him blood?" I asked.

Sitat said, "Your father didn't believe the Feathered Serpent was as bloodthirsty as the Flay Lord claimed. He believed that once the Flay Lord was out of the way, he could approach the god and find out its true needs."

I sighed. All so complicated. "Are there more of you? To fight the Flay Lord's Jaguar Knights and those Nawal creatures?"

Sitat shook his head. "Only the two of us. But we believe that once word spreads that Lord Light's son has returned, many more will join us."

I shook my head. "I know rubber and the ball game. I am not my father. I could fight the best in the land man-to-man. I don't know how to command an army or run an empire."

Both men bowed their heads and stared at the ground. After a moment I asked, "Who exactly is the Flay Lord? I know he is the Feathered Serpent's High Priest. Is he a god or human?"

Sitat answered, "Lord Light said that the Flay Lord was a creature of the dark side of the Book of Fate. But he is neither mortal nor a god. Nine Lords of the Night fell from grace with the Sun God. The Flay Lord is one of them. His knowledge of the Book of Fate gives him the magic to command the Nawals, the man-beasts."

"You said my father thought he could reason with the Feathered Serpent if the Flay Lord was out of the way. If one got into the Forbidden Compound without being spotted, would it be possible to approach the god?"

"The compound is guarded by Jaguar Knights and Nawals," Tagat said. "You cannot simply enter and walk up to the Feathered Serpent's temple and speak to it. Your father would have marched in with an army."

"Lord Light never intended on attacking the Forbidden Compound except to kill the Flay Lord. He never believed the Feathered Serpent was there."

"What do you mean?" I asked. "That's where the god's temple is."

"True, but as a great lord, your father had access to the compound. And he believed that the temple was there to worship the god, but that the Flay Lord spoke to the Feathered Serpent at another place."

"What place?"

Sitat nodded in the direction of the Fire Mountain. "In the mountain. It has always been believed that tunnels and caverns start at the temple in the compound and lead all the way to the mountain." Staring at the mountain spewing clouds of smoke, Sitat said, "Its belly is full of fire. Soon the gods will vomit some of it."

"The Sacred Cave is in the mountain," Tagat said. "The cave is where the Feathered Serpent gave life to the dead to populate the world again after it was broken on the wheel of time."

"Your father believed that underground passages led to the mountain," Sitat said, "and that the god's lair was not in the temple in the compound, but inside the mountain itself."

That made sense, but a series of underground caverns and caves would be even more difficult to navigate by an intruder than entering the temple by going over the compound wall. I pointed that out.

"Your father believed there was another path to the Feathered Serpent," Sitat said. "There is a very small temple high on the mountain. It is the private worshipping place of the Flay Lord."

"An entrance into the god's own quarters?" I asked.

"That's what your father believed. No one but your father has ever spoken about attempting it."

No one but a madman would dare such a thing, I thought.

"As a great lord, your father would have special knowledge on how to talk to a god," Sitat said.

"True."

"And as his son, the god may listen to you."

30

The plan was simple. At least to Sitat and my uncle. To me it was more frightening than a journey through all the hells of Mictlan.

"The temple on the mountain is not heavily guarded," Sitat said. "Just a few Nawals."

I shrugged. "Of course, just a few man-beasts that are the most terrifying creatures in the One-World. That's why there are only a few needed. People would not dare go near the temple if Nawals are there. But that won't be a problem for me. I will probably just drop dead when one growls at me."

I held up my hand to stop their apologies and pleas that I didn't have to go. "I am going up the mountain. I came to Teotihuacán to find out about my family. Now that I know my family was murdered, it's my duty to avenge their murders along with the deaths of Ome and my friend Ista. So, Uncle and good friend, prepare me to meet a god and his man-beasts."

"Tonight will be a good night to go." Sitat said. "The Flay Lord is having a youth sacrificed at each corner of the Sun God's pyramid. For certain he will be there to personally conduct the ceremony. His guards will not be at the mountain, but with him. Only four Nawals stand guard at the mountain temple. Two at night, two in the daytime."

Tagat said, "They say these creatures can see in the dark like a jaguar and can smell the blood of men and animals. You must approach the temple from down-wind if it's possible."

"Most of all, you must be quick." Sitat said. "Nawals are known to be savage, but I have seen them move. They are not as fast as a champion ballplayer. Speed will be your most important weapon. You must wear dark clothing, but nothing that will slow down your movements. When I was a soldier, we put obsidian blades in the tips of our sandals. We will do that to your sandals. You can break a man's leg with a kick. You would be able to chop a leg off if you had daggers on your feet."

"I need a leather collar around my neck."

"A leather collar?" my uncle asked.

"They say these creatures first rip out the throat."

Above the obsidian fields on the Fire Mountain, I rested and looked back down at the city. The great pyramid was ablaze with hundreds of torches as the Flay Lord conducted sacrifices of two boys and two girls to appease the Rain God.

I veered off the trail before reaching the temple area, and fifty paces above the trail I studied the area before I ventured in.

I had so far established that my advisers were correct about the number of Nawals—I saw only two moving about. A hut was off to the side, and I assumed that two slept there while two kept guard.

The temple was not a great edifice. I found it surprising that this, so small and insignificant, was the Flay Lord's personal temple with which to worship the great god. It was little more than an entryway with the snarling stone image of the Feathered Serpent on its roof.

Sitat believed that the Flay Lord deliberately made the temple small to discourage speculation about it.

From my vantage point, I could see the front. After studying it, I concluded that there was in fact an opening into the mountain. The opening was square-shaped but did not have a door covering it. All I could see was the black opening.

The two Nawals on duty did not stay by the entryway, but wandered about, not alert as if they were expecting intruders, but slow and lazy, as if this had been their lot for endless nights spread over endless years. They certainly did not move with the grace of the jungle beast they were believed to be.

What does one say to a god? I wondered. One known to be bloodthirsty.

After watching for two hours, marking the time by the movement of the moon, I slowly crept down the side of the mountain, keeping downwind from the two guards. Sitat and Tagat had dressed me not only in a leather collar and sandals with obsidian toes, but in black clothing with charcoal on all exposed parts of my body.

When I was close enough to make a quick move the rest of the way, I lay down where I was hidden by an outcrop and waited for the surprise that my friends were to execute: a barking dog.

They were to bring a dog up near the clearing and get it to run into the clearing by tossing a piece of food for it to chase.

A dog's presence at the sacred site would certainly attract the attention of the Nawals. Dogs were raised for food in the One-World, a delicacy for the wealthy, and as a companion to be buried with the dead so it would help lead the dead person through the challenges of Mictlan. Again, a luxury for the rich.

When the dog barked, both Nawals on duty moved away from the temple and disappeared out of my sight into the darkness. I left my position and scurried across to the temple where a single torch was lit. I stepped inside and stood in front of the black doorway to the mountain.

Refusing to think about what I was doing out of fear that I would turn and run, I rushed into the abyss.

The air was thick and denser inside than fog. Light

was not cast by torches. A source I couldn't see cast a much brighter glow than what torches could.

The smells were strange. An earthy scent was present, and a second one, alien to my senses, was a stench, much like the sweat of a jungle beast.

My mind immediately felt queasy, almost the feeling I had when I awoke after Sitat knocked me unconscious.

I saw something moving in the fog, coming toward me. My mouth opened to ask for forgiveness of the great Feathered Serpent, but no words came out.

What I saw in the dimness coming toward me was the champion of the Skull Game, a living version of the tall ballplayer etched in stone at the ball court. The etching had the champion wearing gloves. The creature in front of me had no gloves. Rather than having normal fingers, his hands were clawed.

Iyo! It had not occurred to us that the god would have guards *inside* the mountain. I fled back through the doorway, weak and faint, gasping for air.

A great explosion erupted and the ground shook under my feet as I came out of the cave. The night lit up as fire erupted from the smothering hole where the fire gods lived.

A figure appeared before me—a Nawal. My body reacted instinctively and I kicked out with my obsidian-toed sandal.

The thing screamed as my blow caught it in the bone of its lower leg. Before it could recover, I kicked it again, this time with the bottom of my foot, hearing the bone of his leg snap.

I was already moving at high speed as the other guard came around a corner and into the clearing carrying the body of a dog whose throat was ripped out. I had elevation on him, my footing was a couple feet higher, and I leaped up, throwing myself at him to catch him in the face. Instead I flew by him and hit the ground. He dropped the dog and came at me. I rolled and got to my feet and kicked, but he knocked my foot aside and stepped in to rip out my throat with his claws. The claws hit the leather guard at my throat and slid off. I kicked him in the shin and ducked under another blow. He grabbed my arm and I cried out in pain. His head suddenly exploded with blood and the creature dropped at my feet.

Sitat saluted me with his bloody sword. "Run! They're coming!"

We ran as the two Nawals came out of the hut in pursuit. More explosions erupted and the earth shook. Sitat stumbled and I jerked him onto his feet.

I could have outrun the two creatures, but I knew Sitat could not. I let him get ahead of me and turned and slowed down to let them get closer. I went down an embankment and lost my footing and tumbled, rolling over and over. When I got back to my feet, the two creatures were rushing down at me, but they weren't any better with their footing than I had been.

I got atop a rock half my own height to get leverage

to kick at their heads. In the corner of my eye I saw a strange creature, a round, black object about the size of a giant sea turtle but with its head sticking straight up from the shell. The odd-looking head swiveled to look at me. The small face appeared to be a shiny black obsidian mirror.

The first of the beasts was upon me and I kicked it in the face, catching it under the chin, breaking its neck as it snapped back. I jumped up to avoid an attempt by the other creature to grab my leg and I fell off the rock, falling toward the strange black object.

My world suddenly exploded and I was swept into a maelstrom of black wind, a terrible black fire that stripped the flesh from my bones and threw my soul into the mouth of a fire mountain . . .

"My God! We hooked something!"

31

Los Alamos, New Mexico

Allen Holt stood at a large window and stared into the other room at the young man in the "bubble." The clear plastic isolation tent kept the patient from spreading germs or becoming infected by contact with others.

"Is this one-way glass?" Holt asked the scientist standing beside him. The woman was an infectious-disease medical expert from the National Institute of Health.

"No, but he can't see us anyway. He's strapped down and can't turn his head enough to see us. He does see people who are close to him."

The young man in the bubble was short by modern standards, but powerfully built. An artillery shell, Holt thought, that's what the young man from ancient Mexico reminded him of. Shot forward two thousand years.

The medical staff had his head, chest, arms, and legs strapped down.

"We'll slowly be giving him inoculations and introducing him to modern medical perils," the scientist said.

He's going to get a firsthand introduction to the greatest modern peril of all, Holt thought. A creature from the young man's own time, an ancient evil that dwarfed the killing power of the most resolute terrorists: Quetzalcoatl, the Feathered Serpent.

The Feathered Serpent had been worshipped as a god in Mesoamerica two thousand years ago, around the same time Christ was performing miracles in Galilee. The bane of the 2012 prophecies, the god of violent storms and a destroyer of worlds, it had been sealed in an underground mountain chamber by an earthquake that erupted at the same time the man who was now in the bubble had been brought forward in time. The action of the time device had kept the young man from being killed by the volcanic eruption that caused the earthquake.

Released from its twenty centuries of hibernation, the Feathered Serpent began its attack on the most powerful nation in the world, starting an ecological disaster in the Gulf of Mexico that quickly spread north, devastating the South and Southwestern states.

The contagion made the region almost uninhabitable. Millions had died, tens of millions had fled to northern states. When the impact on the migrating population became too much for the northern states to absorb, the affected region was sealed off. Anyone who attempted to escape the area, "the Zone," was shot. But many took the risk—staying in the Zone was a slow death sentence.

The man in the bubble had been brought forward two thousand years by the Time Explorer. The device was not a contraption racing through different time periods as H. G. Wells conceived, but a mechanism created accidentally when a megamonster cyclotron had knocked a hole in time itself.

Used only once before in a clandestine mission, the mechanism capable of time travel had been "destroyed" on paper to satisfy the rest of the world that the USA would not use the mechanism to its sole advantage. But the device was too valuable to destroy—so the destruction had been faked.

The deception had paid off because it was now being used to fight a preternatural evil from the past.

Holt had had the Explorer's tech staff send a probe back to the time when the god-king Quetzalcoatl ruled the ancient Teotihuacán empire. The young man in the bubble had been brought forward in time when the probe returned.

Holt had a feeling about the man from the past—a hunch that he would prove an invaluable asset to the mission. Holt was not a believer in signs or Lady Luck. His conclusion was based upon the video of the man's activities on the mountain just prior to his being zapped forward in time. The man had been hiding and observing. Spying, a field that Holt had more than a passing acquaintance with. Since the man didn't wear the uniform of Quetzalcoatl's minions, he might well be an enemy of the god-king. And give vital information about Quetzalcoatl's strengths and weaknesses. Right now Holt knew nothing about the enemy except legends that the god-king was a bloodthirsty bastard.

"Think our bubble boy will be of any help to you?" the scientist asked.

"Help?" Holt lit a cigarette, ignoring the No Smoking/No Fumar sign. He was wasted from too much caffeine and nicotine, too little sleep, and the burden of carrying the world on his shoulders. He told the woman, "Doc, you're looking at the man who will save the world. Suit me up in one of those sterile doctor outfits you're wearing. I want to take a closer look."

32

Iyo! I have died, my soul flung into Mictlan, the dark underworld with nine hells. Had I died in honorable combat, I would have ascended to the heavens and flown across the sky each day with the Sun God. But I suffered a straw death, an accidental death, not a glorious demise in battle.

A man and a woman dressed in white with cloth masks across their noses and mouths stood by my bed and stared down at me through the transparent tent. Was it Mictlantecuhtli, Lord of Hell, and Mictecacihuatl, his wife, the Lady of the Place of the Dead? Or their torturers?

I know I must endure eight physical tests if I am to make it all the way to the ninth hell and beg Mictlantecuhtli to turn my tormented soul into dust and scatter it in the parched lands of the north.

I had not feared the inevitable journey to Mictlan I

would have to take because it was a test of physical
prowess. But in this hazy world of people in white, I
am not allowed to fight back. They have me tied down
as they take sacrificial blood by sticking reeds in my
arms to draw blood.

Will they rip out my heart next? I will have to survive this first hell in which they have me strapped
down. Iyo! What will the rest of the hells of this
strange world be like?

BOOK VIII

I HAVE BEEN A STRANGER IN A STRANGE LAND

—Exodus 2:22

DAILY WEB NEWS

Government Barricades Devastated Region

The ecological disaster that has turned the Gulf of Mexico into a poisonous swamp has spread inland along the coast to the point the affected region had to be sealed off, the president announced today.

So many millions of people in the Gulf states have fled north to escape the contagion, governmental control and order have deteriorated to the point that drastic measures had to be taken. Farther south, the entire east coast of Mexico is a no-man's-land. Millions of Mexicans have fled north, aggravating the problem of chaotic overcrowding.

"We have barricaded off the affected region to save the rest of the country," the president said.

A new cabinet-level agency with military and police powers, the Zone Security Agency (ZSA), has been created to manage the crisis. "Martial law is in effect and anyone crossing the demarcation line will be summarily shot," the director of the new agency said.

Several million people still in the affected area will slowly die from the contagion that has reduced the supply of drinkable water, critics of the decision say. The cause of the disaster is a seafloor microbe that produces methane, the chief ingredient in the natural gas used for cooking and heating. The microbe has spread into rivers and lakes by rain and hurricanes coming off the Gulf.

The government claims that the disaster was caused naturally when the population of methane-producing microbes in natural gas vents on the seafloor increased to the point that the Gulf, which is twice the size of the state of Texas, became an enormous swamp. Methane is also called swamp gas. Conspiracy theories abound as to the possible cause, ranging from a bio-disaster created by terrorists to the work of aliens as part of a plan to kill life on Earth so they can colonize it.

MIT biologist Nelson Harriman states that during the Permian period 250 million years ago, a methane imbalance killed 90 percent of the life on Earth. "Methane's common in the atmosphere of other planets, but for us oxygen breathers, when it goes beyond one part per million in our atmosphere, it becomes poisonous," Dr. Harriman said.

Worldwide Water Crisis Grows
Thousands Die in Los Angeles Water Riots

The ecological calamity that began in the Gulf of Mexico claimed more lives today as over seven thousand people were killed in water riots yesterday. The incidents began when a water truck failed to show up at a distribution point in North Hollywood. Soon the violence spread throughout the southern end of the San Fernando Valley, leaving over four thousand dead.

Three thousand more people died at the Silver Lake reservoir when ZSA troops opened fire on people trying to storm the water storage facility.

The Zone Security Agency says that besides the death toll from the water riots that occur throughout the nation daily, thousands of people are killed each day trying to break out of the Zone, the barricaded area that keeps people in the South and Southwest from escaping north and aggravating already critical water shortages.

While there are no accurate statistics of the mortality rate in the Zone itself because the ZSA does not release them in the interests of national security, it is estimated that more thousands die there each day from dehydration and the contagion known popularly as the red death. Scientists have traced the cause of the contagion to a mutation of the methane-producing microbe that poisoned the Gulf of Mexico.

Reports from Mexico indicate that government authority there has suffered a complete breakdown. Mexico's provisional capital, the densely populated Tijuana–Los Angeles corridor, is now considered the largest city in the world.

A spokesperson for the ZSA states that stories of bizarre ritualistic murders by beasts created by biological mutation as a result of drinking contaminated water are urban legends.

NOTICE: This news report has been approved by the Zone Security Agency.

33

Waterhole #9, West Texas

They came at night, surrounding the waterhole. Briggs didn't know anything about them, except that they weren't human.

"Are you sure they're out there?" John Milner asked. He didn't know what "they" were, either.

Briggs shook his head. "I'm not sure of anything. Keep walking the perimeter, make sure everyone's alert. Tell our people to keep their hands on their guns and their eyes on the bikers."

Milner moved off and Briggs kept staring at the darkness. He couldn't describe what he'd seen in the darkness that frightened him, couldn't honestly say he'd actually seen anything. But he knew they were out there. Last night they had killed Bear, his ninety-plus-pound rottweiler/pit bull mix. Bear had seen something in the dark and gone after it. The dog went silently, like a wolf, never making a sound until it was growling viciously when its teeth were into something.

"Would've been easier to shake off a steel-jawed bear trap than that dog," Briggs told Milner after they found Bear. When the dog bit down with its powerful jaws, the teeth went through flesh and snapped bones.

This time they hadn't heard a triumphant growl, but a sharp cry of the dog's agonizing pain. And terror.

Briggs had sensed fear in the dog's cry. And it made his flesh creep.

Bear had never been afraid of anything.

They'd found Bear the next morning a hundred feet from the barbed-wire outer perimeter of the waterhole. A hole in its chest, its blood drained, heart gone . . . as if someone had shoved a fist in and ripped the still beating heart out. The dog's neck hadn't looked right when Briggs knelt beside the dead animal to examine it. The powerful neck had been crushed by someone— *something*—with a powerful grip that went beyond human strength.

He figured Bear had been held up in the air with one hand while its assailant used the other hand to plunge into the dog's chest and pull out its heart.

Briggs's knees quivered and the hair on the back of his neck rose just thinking about it. He sure as hell didn't want to meet up with anyone—or anything— that could tear out the heart of nearly a hundred pounds of badass dog. And drink its blood.

The waterhole was the lifeblood of Briggs and the nineteen people he shared it with. Water, drinkable water, stuff that didn't rot your innards, had become scarce after something got loose in the Gulf of Mexico. There was no scientific name for it yet, not even after two years, because scientists were still trying to figure out what it was. The contagion gave a faint reddish tint to water, inspiring the street names for it: *red death* from the Edgar Allan Poe tale of biological horror, and *the glow* from a rapper song about the contagion.

Scientists knew the underlying cause was an imbalance in poisonous methane gas produced by a microbe in prehistoric vents at the bottom of the Gulf of Mexico. But when it was carried by wind and rain onto land and freshwater, it mutated into something else. Everyone had an opinion as to why the imbalance occurred, from conspiracies to aliens, but Briggs knew exactly what caused it: damnation from God.

After the contagion poisoned the waters of the Gulf of Mexico, the ecological plague moved north, carried by the oceanic evaporation-rainfall weather system, infecting the nearby states—Florida, Georgia, Alabama, Mississippi, Louisiana, and Texas—killing millions, while millions more fled north as it spread.

To stop the massive migration that was overwhelming the unaffected states, the government established a military zone in the affected states, administered by the ZSA, and policed by the agency's military troops.

Anyone who crossed the line was killed on sight.

That left the Zone with a few derelict metro areas that functioned from water and food brought in by pipelines and trucks convoying from the north. The government abandoned all but designated metro areas in the Zone, along with the crumbling bridges and freeways that led to them. Outside of those areas, the region was a no-man's-land in which the scattered sweet-water wells still unpolluted by the contagion were fought over. Roving motorcycle gangs, old-fashioned outlaws, crazies, and just plain greedy, mean bastards fought the water ranchers for control of the liquid gold.

But everything in the Zone was a losing battle. Pure water only delayed the death penalty everyone was under. The ranks of the water ranchers and gang-bangers grew smaller every day.

"See anything?"

Briggs spun around, shotgun in hand, to face the leader of the biker gang he had let into the compound. "How do you see something no one has seen?"

The man facing him wore a black military uniform so dirty and dusty that it was hard to determine the original color. The uniform was an imitation of the Nazis' elite SS Totenkopf, the death's-head units that murdered millions in World War II concentration camps. He called himself Heinrich, after the fair-haired storm-trooper murderer who was assassinated in Czechoslovakia during the war. Heinrich had black eyes, dark, almost olive skin, and rotted teeth. His upper lip had failed to form completely, leaving a harelip vertical cleft above his mouth.

Heinrich's motorcycle gang called themselves the

Werewolves, the name of the German guerrilla fighters who were supposed to rise up and drive out the Allies after der Fuhrer finished biting the bullet in a Berlin bunker. The units turned out to be nothing more than the imagination of Goebbels, the clubfooted propaganda minister of the late "superrace."

Roaming gangs such as the Werewolves, bizarre, violent outlaws, had risen in the wake of the contagion. People said the gangs were mostly criminals who'd walked out of the open gates when prisons in the Zone were abandoned. Whoever they were, the one consistency was that they were trouble, especially to isolated water ranches. Water from a clean well could provide the good life for a biker gang until the well went dry or a rival gang killed them off.

Briggs considered Heinrich and his gang dangerous freaks and weirdos. In ordinary times, they would never have got past the first defensive perimeter unless they could catch bullets in their teeth. But when they showed up that morning after Briggs found Bear, he changed his mind and made them a deal to stay overnight and help defend the waterhole for a hundred gallons of water.

He regretted it almost immediately.

On the good side of his decision, he was certain that whatever was out there wasn't human, and his people would need all the help they could get to survive. Besides, there were only seven Werewolves. The waterhole had nine men, six women, and five kids, most of whom could fire a gun.

"Heard about a waterhole outside Tucson," Heinrich said, "attacked by the Rippers. Killed thirty people. Six others were never found. People say the dead got off best."

"Those stories are all bullshit," Briggs said, but he looked back out at the night, trembling inside. Until Bear got its heart torn out, he considered Rippers one of the urban legends that arose in the wake of the contagion, a bogeyman for people to talk about and scare kids with.

He'd heard other stories like the Tucson one—a waterhole or other isolated settlement attacked, people murdered, hearts ripped out, blood drained. But all the stories were just rumors spread by word of mouth. The government controlled all news, and if the stories were true, they weren't admitting it.

No one with any sense asked too many questions of government officials, anyway. Or talked indiscriminately to strangers. You never knew who was listening or if the Zone police would show up at your door in the middle of the night.

The only source of real news was a guerrilla-radio talk-show host who hacked into a broadcast satellite. He called himself Wolfman, like the fifties talk jock. People believed he had been an aliens-and-paranormal radio talk-show host reportedly killed by government cops, Zone Security agents, after he began broadcasting a claim that the Gulf contagion was the work of aliens who had taken control of the government. *Bastards.* ZSA cops ran the Zone as their private fiefs.

The official cause of Wolfman's death was the firestorm that destroyed Dallas after water had been cut off to the city. But a couple months after the city went up in smoke, someone claiming to be Wolfman—and sounding damn like him—began a guerrilla broadcast from somewhere in the Southwest.

That outlawed, underground radio broadcast from a roving RV, which moved almost every night to avoid satellite-controlled missiles, was about the only news Briggs, and most other people trapped in the Zone, believed.

Wolfman's theory was that Rippers were mutants who survived the red death but ended up like vampires, with a thirst for blood.

How do you kill something like that? Briggs wondered. Vampires? Mutants? What the hell kind of world had it become?

"It's midnight," Briggs told Heinrich. "We have less than six hours before full light. We'll have two guard shifts, three hours each. Three of your men, four of mine."

"Look!"

Briggs swung around, staring at the night. "What? Where?"

"It was out there," Heinrich said. "I saw it."

"What'd you see?"

"I don't know. Something moved. Like a shadow."

"It's nighttime, there's no goddamn shadows." Briggs couldn't keep the fright out of his voice.

"I swear on my eyes and my balls that I could see through it. It was like some kind of wraith."

"What the fuck is a wraith?"

"Kind of like a ghost. They say you see one before you die, a premonition."

Briggs gripped the shotgun tighter. "You saw it, not me. Keep watch. Anything moves, call me."

Briggs walked away, spooked. He knew there shouldn't be anything out there moving. No animals were left in the Zone except for a few guard dogs. People couldn't afford to give water to a pet—and many pets went into the pot for stew when food got scarce.

Briggs walked the perimeter, checking on his people. The two outermost perimeters were four-foot-high strings of barbed wire. One inner ring was a three-foot wall of sandbags. Behind the sandbags, next to the water well, was a concrete blockhouse built from blocks taken from an abandoned construction site.

The night was hot and dry, still over a hundred degrees long past sundown, the kind of night when it felt as if the earth were shriveling up from thirst. Maybe it was. People weren't the only victims of the contagion. Little plant and animal life were left in the Zone. First there had been the deluge, extraordinary rainfall that carried the contagion inland. After a season of record rainfall and flooding came two dry years. When farming and ranch irrigation throughout the affected region stopped because plants died from tainted water and forests dried up, great fires followed. With nothing to hold the dirt down, winds turned the entire southern and southwest region into an enormous dust bowl.

Briggs used to be able to see his cattle from the steps of his ranch house, chickens in the yard, birds chattering overhead. Now the ranch house was gone, blown away in one of the terrible dust storms that put a hazy filter on the sun. Gone, too, were flies to shoo, mosquitoes to swat—not even an anthill popped out of the ground. But to Briggs, the lack of birds really drove home how lifeless the Zone had become.

Milner was making coffee on a Thermos burner near the blockhouse when Briggs came into the inner perimeter. They had no wood to burn—there were no forests. Not even the scorched skeleton of a tree— what nature hadn't completely burned, people had.

Wolfman's midnight broadcast was coming out of the hand-cranked radio near the gas burner. Wolfman—or whoever was using his name—was interviewing a Mexican from Veracruz. The man had fled the contagion when it struck the east coast of Mexico.

Briggs paused when he realized Wolfman was interviewing the man about Rippers. From the man's voice, Briggs took him to be elderly.

"They're Nawals," the old man said, his English heavily accented.

"What is a na-wall?" Wolfman asked.

"Werejaguars, señor. Just as you have werewolves in el norte, *these fiendish creatures of the night are half-man, half-beast."*

"Werejaguars, what a bunch of horseshit," Briggs said.

"Shhhh," Milner said. "This guy was a historian in Mexico, he's an expert on the subject."

"Expert my ass."

"What support do you have for the existence of werejaguars?" Wolfman asked.

"The Olmec civilization of Mexico was called People of the Jaguar because they worshipped the great jungle cat and believed that their bite could turn a person into a half-man, half-beast. The other civilizations of Mexico, the Mayans, Toltecs, Aztecs, all copied the Olmec culture. In fact, following the conquest of Mexico by Cortés, there rose the Cult of the Jaguar that nearly drove the Spanish conquistadors from the land."

"The Cult of the Jaguar, that was some sort of murder cult, wasn't it? Like the Thugee of India and the Tigermen of Africa?"

"The difference between werejaguars and those other cults is that there is no evidence the others were supernatural. The jaguar cult is well documented by the amazing stone edifices left behind for a couple thousand years. That history chiseled in stone shows beasts with the bodies of men and the heads of jaguars."

"Tell me about—"

Whatever Wolfman wanted to know was lost in a burst of static that became a steady hum.

"They've jammed it again," Milner said, turning

off the radio. "They're getting quicker at jamming him. Wolfman says the government has missiles airborne every night at the time he comes on, hoping to track him down and hit him before he goes off the air."

"Then why do they jam him off the air? Wouldn't it be better to let him talk until they have him in their sights?"

"Because it's the government, that's why. They don't know their ass from a hole in the ground."

"Keep moving around. I don't trust these Nazi bastards any more than what's out there."

Milner's voice followed him. "Do you think that Mexican is right? That there are werejaguars out there?"

"Yeah, along with Bigfoot and Dracula. Get your ass moving."

Turning to look back at Milner as he spoke, Briggs almost bumped into one of Heinrich's biker pals. The man was as filthy as Heinrich and had the same foul smell.

Just about everything changed after the contagion. No one smelled pretty anymore because you couldn't waste water washing with it—and when everyone stank, even piss and sweat were not impolite odors. But Heinrich and his gang had a different smell to them from other people, a stench that reeked from them. Briggs found something familiar in the odor, something that struck a cord in the back of his brain, but he couldn't put a name to it.

Briggs went to each of the four men on the guard shift, quietly instructing them to keep their eyes open—with one eye on the bikers.

After he talked to the last man, he went out into the area between the two barbed-wire fences. He walked around, flashing a light into the darkness, wondering what the hell Heinrich had seen. Crazy bastard like that might have seen anything, even something that wasn't there.

Luck of the draw, Briggs always said, when the state of the crazy world came up in conversation.

The contagion wasn't the first great plague or disaster to hit the world. As many as one out of three people in Europe and the Near East were killed by the Black Death in the Middle Ages. In each century a couple of influenza pandemics killed millions around the world. The great indigenous civilizations of North and South America were wiped out by invisible conquistadores—smallpox and syphilis bacteria that followed the European conquerors and killed tens of millions. But not even the atomic age had threatened the *whole* world.

The contagion was slowly spreading, both on land and at sea. Once the contagion fouled the water everywhere, planet Earth would no longer be a green place and would instead become a desert planet with dead oceans.

The luck of the draw, he thought again. *If I'd picked better cards, I would've been born in a better time.* Maybe a time when his grandfather came West and got into cattle ranching, a simpler time when talk about the end of the world was just *talk*.

Heinrich was beside him almost before he realized it. He heard the man's quiet step and swung around, leveling his gun at him.

"Why are you sneaking up on me?"

Heinrich grinned, his harelip giving him a sinister edge. "Your mind was somewhere else. You just didn't hear me."

"My mind's on the trigger of this gun. Come up on me again like that and I'll ventilate your guts with this ten gauge."

"Everyone is on edge. They all feel it."

"Feel what? I don't feel nothing," Briggs lied. But he did feel it. A sense of impending doom. He couldn't shake it off, not since he'd seen Bear on the ground, a fist-size hole in his chest, and hardly a drop of blood on the ground—or left in the dog's body. It spooked him that there had been no footprints, either. Just that ninety-pound shark-with-four-legs lying there, easy pickings for something infinitely more dangerous and ferocious.

"Did you ever think about where they came from?" Heinrich asked.

"Who?"

"*Them*. The Rippers. Whoever they are, whatever their name is."

"Yeah, I think about it, I know where they come from. People like you make stories up about them so that people like me will abandon their waterholes."

"I don't want your water," Heinrich whispered.

Briggs got another whiff of that foul smell that oozed from the bikers, and again it stirred a memory in him.

"There!" Heinrich pointed.

Briggs swung around, crouching, leveling the shotgun at the darkness. "Where? What'd you see?"

He kept the gun pointed at the darkness. He sensed Heinrich had moved in closer to him because he got a stronger whiff of that foul smell the bikers carried.

It suddenly struck him where he'd experienced the smell before—in his own barn, when he was butchering a cow or pig for the freezer.

The smell of blood.

As he turned, he saw the fist of claws coming at him. The claws struck his chest. He didn't fly backward because in a blur Heinrich's other hand grabbed him by the neck and held him from falling.

He gawked in horror as the hand came out of his chest clutching his beating heart.

34

Twelve Thousand Feet over the Gulf Coast

Allen Holt stared out the window of the Douglas DC-3 airliner as it came over the Mississippi River delta and wetlands. Jazz-and-booze New Orleans, the city's wicked, self-indulgent French Quarter, and its impossibly absurd Mardi Gras, swamp-boat rides on the bayous, and casinos lining the beaches at Biloxi—all of it was gone. The green wetlands were a watery desert, a vast putrid, green-black swamp without living vegetation. Or people. This close to the Gulf, a breeze blowing off the water had a high content of methane.

Holt lit a cigarette and wondered what would happen if he did it at sea level. As a kid in South Carolina, he'd seen that mysterious phenomenon called foolish fire. In those days people said the sudden flash of fire over swamp water was an omen of misfortune. Now he knew it was the spontaneous ignition of marsh gas, which was produced by decomposition of dead plant matter.

Nothing mysterious about it. The decomposed plants created swamp gas—methane.

He knew the methane couldn't be that thick or lightning would ignite it, but the thought stayed with him: could he ignite the entire world with a single flick of his cigarette lighter?

He shook off thoughts of burning the world and stared out the plane window.

What hurricanes such as Katrina could not do, microbes invisible to the naked eye had accomplished: The coastal cities famous for their wet-hot green environments were either ghost towns or, like New Orleans, had disappeared, becoming just part of a vast dead sea as the levees crumbled in the wake of nature turned homicidal.

God had spit on the slate and wiped the decadent Gulf Coast off the map.

Holt couldn't resist the thought that there was something biblical about all the hell inflicted on New Orleans. If there was a Sodom and Gomorrah in America, it had been the French Quarter. But maybe it was the whole world God wanted to wash clean and start over again with.

Last night he had watched a popular hour-long TV show. Loud music, crashing cars, big-breasted women, kick-ass men . . . that was what the world had become.

He asked himself again if the world was worth saving, then turned back to the task at hand.

Other than the crew, Holt was the only person on board who was not a scientist. He had gathered a team of experts for an assault on the contagion. Thousands of scientists around the world were already working on the problem, looking for answers in a test tube.

Holt had a different game plan.

He feigned attention as a scientist with a keen interest in planes discoursed on the history of the aged DC-3 prop plane that was carrying them two miles above the dead sea. Holt's real attention was a covert study of another scientist.

"I'm surprised," the plane enthusiast said, "that a former director of the CIA, and now deputy director of the Zone Security Agency, would have a DC-3 instead of a sleek modern jet like other high officials use. Did you know that the DC-3 was the first successful airliner? A World War Two warhorse still used around the world at the advent of the twenty-first century over sixty years later? Not to mention that its most notorious claim to fame is that it had been the plane of choice for South American drug smugglers during the early boom in the cocaine trade."

Holt knew the plane was an aeronautical antique, but he had deliberately chosen it as his government-requisitioned private plane. Those sleek modern jets with high-tech engines have a habit of breaking down . . . often while in flight. As parts and complex fuels for higher-tech airplanes get more scarce, the government has been reaching back to mothball fleets and private collections for planes that were simpler to fly, land, and maintain.

Programming out more talk about the plane, Holt stared back out the window. His thoughts were on the assignment the president had given him: Give new life to the most secret piece of high-tech equipment on the planet. And use it for nothing less than saving the world.

After being hauled out of a retirement where his only goal was drinking himself to death, Holt felt as if he had once again been handed Atlas' task of supporting the world on his back.

Sighing deeply, he turned away from the depressing sight he saw below and gave his attention back to the other people in the passenger area of the plane: seven scientists—four men and three women. A *Mission: Impossible* team to achieve the goal of saving life on the planet. They had all been given the same cover story: "Think of yourselves as part of a think tank," Holt told them during their first meeting three days ago in Seattle-Tacoma, the current capital of the nation. A think tank to analyze how to reverse the contagion.

Not a very original idea to any of them, since all of them had been drawn from other think tanks with exactly the same goal. But Allen Holt had a secret weapon to deploy in the crisis. What he needed from them was a plan on how to use it . . . without revealing to the scientists the exact nature of his weapons.

The purpose of the flight over the Gulf was to bring

home to these men and women who spent their lives with their heads buried in the sands of academia the terrible wasteland that had to be reversed. All of them had experienced the consequences of the contagion—massive upheaval and chaos, water and food rationing, the services of government and utilities completely broken down or greatly restricted. He wanted to shove their noses in the crisis, making them see the no-man's-land called the Zone and the dark waters of the dead sea. But more than anything, he wanted to watch the people for hours in a confined space.

A possible deviation in his game plan had been formulating in his head for months, and it had ignited into a nuclear mushroom when he read the backgrounds of the team candidates assembled by his aides. He had almost passed over her as he skimmed through the pile and had stopped when he saw her picture.

Caden Montez. Archaeologist and astrobiologist. Expert on ancient Mexico. *Speaks Nahuatl.* That she was also a water expert meant nothing to him—he had his choice of the best water experts in the world. Hell, half the scientists in the world were studying water. He had never before planned a mission or even thought in sexist terms, but this was the time to do it: He needed her for an assignment because she was a good-looking woman who spoke an ancient language of Mexico. Those two qualities were more important than her intelligence and accomplishments.

He couldn't have designed her better if she had been molded with God's hands from clay.

What a mess, he thought, staring down at the vast, murky waters. A swamp the size of Alaska. Created by a gas that had been a boon to mankind—natural gas for kitchen stoves and factories was mostly composed of methane.

For millions of years methane got out of balance only in limited areas: exploding in coal mines, festering in swamps and sewers. Incredibly, a significant source of methane in the atmosphere was bovine flatulence—cow farts. But methane production was no longer in balance.

That the world was under siege and losing a battle for survival against a form of life that had been underfoot for eons and was too small to be seen with the naked eye was truly bizarre. Even more incredible was that about one-third of the life on the earth was not part of the oxygen cycle utilized by plants, animals, and fish, but a microbe that hated oxygen. Microscopic archaea are a life-form existing beneath the ground and the seafloor. Mistaken for bacteria until they were designated a separate life-form in the 1970s, they easily turned lakes into swamps and garbage dumps putrid. Unlike most of the earth's life-forms, archaea do not require sunlight or oxygen.

Rather than existing on the oxygen cycle used by other life-forms, archaea were either methane *producers* or methane *eaters.* The process was analogous to the symbiotic relationship between plant and animal— man and beast breathe in oxygen and breathe out carbon dioxide, which is regenerated back as oxygen by plants. If that photosynthesis process were ever to get out of balance, oxygen-breathing life would soon die.

Holt knew from scientific studies that something had happened to the methane eaters while the methane producers keep on producing. As the methane killed the oxygen at the bottom of the seafloor, and the sea life that depended on it, the process sped up until the Gulf became an enormous swamp and then a dead sea. When the Gulf current carried the contagion into the Atlantic, what began as a threat to life in the southern United States and Mexico became a hazard to the whole world.

A limitation on the spread of the contagion on land was that the oxygen in the air was deadly to the archaea. But as winds and storms carried the microbe onto land, a mutation occurred, and the archaea developed a hard shell that protected it, keeping the microbe dormant but ready to become active again if it found a suitable oxygen-deprived environment. It found that environment in the digestive system of humans and animals, eventually killing its hosts.

Holt knew how the imbalance had happened.

Now he had to find out a way to reverse it.

35

Caden struggled to keep a calm countenance and not let her fears show. Yet she sensed that Allen Holt saw through her charade. Not that she wasn't really whom she claimed to be. None of her qualifications had been doctored, though the past two years of her life had to be fictionalized to get her on the mission. It came as a surprise that Holt had chosen her when there were more qualified scientists available.

While the contagion spread in the Gulf and came ashore to make a third of the nation a no-man's-land and give the other two-thirds a crowded, water-starved third-world lifestyle, she had worked with Koji Oda and the Frogs. The belief that layers of deceit lay beneath government explanations of the contagion grew as the president retracted contentions that the disaster was set off by an earthquake or oil drilling. The current explanation—an imbalance between methane-producing and methane-consuming microbes on the bottom of the sea—was undoubtedly true. But beneath that fact were more layers of deceit.

She looked over at Holt and caught him staring at her. She smiled to cover her concern and looked back out the window.

Holt had a stocky build, a barrel chest that made him look overweight and a tendency toward a heavy belly. Her own father had that same sort of large, round barrel-chested build, and she suspected that like her father, Holt was more iron than fat. His hair was thick and dark. She figured him to be over fifty even though no salt was visible in the tousled hair.

Caden knew he had been CIA director. Koji told her that at the end of Holt's CIA career Holt had handled a scientific project so secret that not even a long-time scientist friend of Koji's who worked on it would hint at its nature.

Holt also had a reputation as a tough guy. "My friend said he's a pit bull with a brain. Cross him and he'll sink his teeth into your throat."

After Koji learned from a Frog high in the government that the president had handed Holt a top-secret project concerning the contagion, Caden and Koji had devised a plan to get her on the mission. The Frogs had a contact at NASA that could give her a work history from the time she had escaped from a Mexican hospital to the present. A completely new identity couldn't be used because she might be recognized by other scientists who knew her. And reconstructing her identity, after her life had electronically been erased, came with a risk that the people who wanted her dead would find her and finish the job.

Koji had calculated that risk as extremely small—the entire nation had been convulsing in chaos since the contagion erupted. Mexico had been hit harder and sooner than the Gulf states. The people who'd held her prisoner at the Mexican hospital were all most likely dead.

The Frogs chose Holt's mission for her to infiltrate because of his prestige. He was an intelligence favorite of the president's and a man who had led the country's spy agency. If anyone knew the truth about the contagion, it would be Holt.

So far she had learned nothing except that Holt had an unusual approach to tackling the problem. An approach that would whet the appetite of conspiracy theorists: He told the group that rather than analyze and debate ways to stop the spread of the contagion, they were to focus on ways to *start* the methane imbalance.

"Every scientific mind in the country is focusing on how to kill the methane producers or restore the methane balance by reintroducing methane eaters," he had told them. "We're not going to determine how to get rid of it, but how it was created. An accident of nature created it, but for our purposes, it'll be easier to assume that someone wanted to deliberately create the imbalance. How would it be done?"

Holt said to think of it as a form of reverse engineering.

It struck her that reverse engineering is what detectives do. They start with the crime and work their way backward to the culprit.

Caden felt that his explanation wasn't satisfying to any of the team members, but no one dared express his or her thoughts. The entire nation was under a permanent state of emergency, a shoot-on-sight mentality for any disturbance that could set off riots and insurrections in the overcrowded, food- and water-starved cities of the North. Conspiracy theories that the contagion was man-made were rampant . . . and illegal to express.

If the government hadn't lied and been so secretive about the cause of the contagion, she could readily have accepted Mother Nature as the culprit. Methane was just one of an infinite number of things that had to be kept in perfect balance for life to survive on the planet.

Besides Caden, an astrobiologist, the other members of the team included an oceanographer, biochemist, microbiologist, bacteriologist, virologist, and hematologist.

She understood the reason for each of the fields of expertise to study a waterborne microbe except for two fields: Why did they need a blood expert—a hematologist? The microbe had no blood, nor was the contagion a blood disease. Unlike an aerobic bacteria such as anthrax, archaea was not a blood invader because the oxygen in blood would be poisonous to it.

Closer to home, why an astrobiologist? The need

for that discipline tantalized both her and Koji. All Earth life fell into the purview of a scientist studying life in the universe . . . but this strange earthly microbe could be studied much better by hands-on experts such as microbiologists and bacteriologists.

Unlike biology, oceanography, and most other scientific disciplines, astrobiology was not confined to a precise field of study. Even the name was somewhat misleading. The discipline, also called exobiology, was not a field restricted to "biologists" who studied extraterrestrial life. Not only was the existence of ET theoretical, but it involved obtaining and analyzing astronomical data received by optical and radio telescopes and cutting-edge deep-space probes. The objective was to obtain data about planetary atmospheres and determine whether those atmospheres could support a form of life. The field used the knowledge of astronomers, pathologists, biologists, chemists, geologists, oceanographers, and almost every other scientific discipline.

Astrobiology, once a high priority on NASA's plate, was no longer a viable profession because the national space agency itself was on hold as the nation struggled to survive.

Ironic, she thought. She had been selected as a team member of a prestigious scientific investigation headed by one of the most powerful men in the country. But there were so many complications she felt as if her head were on backward.

She stared back out the window. Two miles above

the murky waters, there was no clue that she could not have breathed the air at the surface.

"Ever been along the Gulf coast before it bellied up?" Holt asked.

He startled her. He sat down across from her and lit a cigarette despite the profusion of No Smoking/No Fumar signs in the plane.

Rank has its privileges, she thought.

"Not a whole lot. The usual things. The Mardi Gras, a swamp-boat ride on the bayou, playing the slots at Biloxi, once down to Padre Island for spring break, that sort of thing."

"I understand that before the methane imbalance became apparent, you wrote a science article on some of the ways life could be wiped out on earth."

"Yes, but it was purely coincidental, not at all prophetic. I barely mentioned the fact that a couple hundred million years ago too much methane in the atmosphere had once wiped out most of life on Earth. It was called the Great Dying."

He nodded. "The Permian period, a mass extinction. Severe global warming, probably caused by methane-producing archaea. You hit it right on the head."

"Actually, it was more of a footnote than a prediction. It just happened to be one of the global disasters the Earth has faced over a couple billion years. There've been many catastrophic situations and many more lying in wait. In fact, methane imbalance has been a two-edged sword for the planet. Too much of it caused disastrous global warming and may have set the whole planet afire, killing most life a couple hundred million years ago, but a slight imbalance fifty million years ago may have brought the planet out of an ice age with a burst of global warming."

As a scientist who studied life-forms, Caden knew that an infinite number of contingencies could threaten life on Earth, some man-made, others the damnation of God or nature. Her favorite theory about the delicate balance of nature was that life depended upon ice floating. If ice sank in water, the oceans would freeze over and the world would be in a permanent ice age.

Another was how bacteria were kept in balance by limiting their food source. Many bacteria, such as anthrax, duplicated themselves so fast that when they had a nutrition source, if the source was unlimited, the bacteria would be a mass the size of planet Earth in a short time.

Holt said, "About every six months scientists come up with a new theory as to how the dinosaurs became extinct. If this contagion isn't conquered, a million years from now some species of intelligent life on Earth may ponder how *Homo sapiens* became extinct. They'll probably wonder how a species that sent men to the moon couldn't win a war against soldiers who can't be seen without a microscope."

"I hope I wasn't chosen for this program because of that article. It wasn't a paper with research results. I was illustrating some ways life on other planets could have become extinct."

"You wrote another paper, right before the conta-

gion broke. A theory about ancient astronauts, the
Feathered Serpent, Cult of the Jaguar. I understand
your theory caused a stir among the more . . . orthodox
in your field."

Caden cringed, but kept a straight face. *How did he
know?* That paper had been deleted when her history
had been reconstructed by the Frogs because of its
reference to Teo. The last thing she wanted was to
make a connection to her and the ancient city where
she had been held captive and under a death sentence.

"I know," he said, "the paper wasn't in your NASA
or university file. It came to light when I had a more
extensive search done about your background."

What had that "more extensive" search revealed?
she wondered.

"I, uh, don't remind people I wrote it. It was ridiculed by the scientific establishment at the time."

Holt met her eyes and didn't let them go. He was a
compelling life force. She felt as if he were peering
into her soul.

He said, "You're defensive. And you're not mingling with the others."

The job was important to her—vital. The Frogs had
worked hard and risked exposure of a White House
staffer to get her on Holt's team. Common sense told
her that she should BS the man, tell him that she just
had a little headache, and force herself to mingle with
the others, but she decided he knew the answer already.

"I'm a good astrobiologist," she said. "Unfortunately,

the world decided to come to an end before I was able to establish myself at the top of the profession. But that doesn't make me any less qualified than anyone else."

"You heard one of the old farts refer to you as *that Mexican girl*."

"Yes! I'm a woman, not a girl, and I was born and raised in this country."

Three days ago, she had walked into a conference room at ZSA headquarters in Seattle when it was announced to the other team members that Caden had been added to the group.

The question "Why that Tex-Mex girl instead of Stepenack?" had been asked by the oceanographer, who hadn't seen her enter the room.

Caden had been struck speechless. Not from a lack of words, but because she would have expressed herself to the scientist in language she hadn't used since she was in high school and a girl had called her a *taquita*.

"Stepenack is twice my age and has twice my experience, but I have two things he doesn't have."

"Which are?"

"I'm angry and ambitious. Angry because the world has gone to hell, and eager to practice my profession as it should be." Caden paused and locked eyes with Holt. "Now let me ask you a question. Why did you pick me? What interested you enough to add me to the team over people more qualified on paper?"

The oceanographer interrupted their conversation.

"Sorry, Mr. Holt, but you mentioned you wanted me to explain the nation's freshwater flow when we reached the end of the Mississippi."

"Go right ahead," Holt said.

The oceanographer began his remarks by quoting a bit of the *Rime of the Ancient Mariner*:

> *Water, water, everywhere,*
> *Nor any drop to drink.*
> *The very deep did rot: O Christ!*
> *That ever this should be!*
> *Yea, slimy things did crawl with legs*
> *Upon the slimy sea.*

"Take a look outside and you'll see the slimy sea that Coleridge's sailor moaned about. Despite the fact that nearly three-quarters of the earth's surface is covered by water, little of it is drinkable. Less than three percent is freshwater. About two-thirds of that freshwater is found in ice and permanent snow cover. Most of the rest is stored underground as groundwater. Less than one percent is in freshwater lakes and rivers. Bottom line, only a tiny portion of the water on earth is freshwater. That supply is constantly replenished by the evaporation process, with moisture rising, mostly over the oceans, and falling as rain and snow. Ultimately, the moisture flows back to the sea via a drainage system.

"In terms of our own country, the largest freshwater drainage system is the Mississippi-Missouri river system. It begins near the Canadian border and drains the entire middle third of the nation as it flows to the Gulf of Mexico, distributing water for drinking, agriculture, and industry along the way.

"As we know from the days of acid rain before the contagion struck, moisture in the air can carry pollution and spread it across land. Which is what is happening now—the poisonous microbe is being picked up in evaporation and carried inland . . ."

Caden tuned out the spiel and caught Holt's eye. The question she'd asked was still hanging in the air. She suspected that something about her was important to the mission—other than her expertise as a scientist. Knowing it would give her insight into the deceit that the government was committing.

She raised her eyebrows to remind him that she had asked, *Why me?*

Holt leaned down to answer. "You speak Nahuatl."

That left her speechless.

"From now on, I want you to concentrate on learning everything you can about ancient Mesoamerica. Concentrate on the period about the time of Christ."

"On what aspect?"

"Everything."

36

Santa Fe, New Mexico

Holt exited the DC-3 at Santa Fe and sent the team members on to Sea-Tac, where his staff would give them more indoctrination. He was no longer enthused about the think-tank concept. It would still go on, but his chief deputy could supervise it. He had changed tack after meeting Caden Montez. He got off the plane because he wanted to get things ready in Santa Fe before he called her back.

Two months had passed since a young man from the ancient world had been brought forward in time. The political game in Sea-Tac was unlike anything else in American history. Martial law was in effect everywhere. The police power of the president was absolute, and it was exercised in the Zone through the ZSA director, who had his own army and was almost autonomous from Sea-Tac.

Not a political system that Holt was comfortable

with. A student of history, he knew that the traditional way of a dictatorship's rise to power was by instituting martial law during times of crisis. He also knew that putting all the reins of power in the president's hands was born out of necessity. But he wasn't comfortable with all the talk he had heard since coming back to the government—expressions by people in power that the new political reality was going to be permanent.

President Barbara Berg didn't adhere to the notion that martial law was going to be permanent. But many in her administration, including the powerful ZSA director, did.

Regardless of Holt's personal feelings about restoring democracy, the contagion had to be controlled first or there wouldn't be a nation or a world to be concerned about.

He had left the plane to implement his plan for control.

Busy settling into his new position and learning the political ropes in the new administration, he had got briefings and videos showing the progress of the young man from ancient Mexico, but had not returned to physically see him.

"Acclimatizing" him to the strange, new world was how Holt thought of what a team of psychologists and psychiatrists were doing to the ancient-young man.

Dr. Samuel Frankel, the psychiatrist Holt had appointed to head the team acclimatizing the man from the past, was waiting as Holt came down the boarding ladder of the DC-3.

"How's our guest?" Holt asked as they drove toward the science facility.

"He's progressing." Frankel beamed. "We learned his name just this morning. Tah-Heen. A breakthrough, for sure, but just the beginning. We've had two big breaks so far with him. You already know one—he speaks an early form of Nahuatl, a language still used in some rural regions of Mexico and by a few scholars. Sort of Mesoamerica's equivalent of ancient Greek or Latin to European tongues. The second advantage is that the operation to install a memory chip in his brain went well."

"It increased his language skills?"

"Indirectly. The chip wasn't originally designed to enhance learning a foreign language, but to reduce the memory loss of Alzheimer's sufferers. Our adaptation is a chip containing a dictionary of common terms used in more modern Nahuatl and English. It's much easier to learn a language if you already have the words and just need to put them into the proper order. So far he's already able to put together a few basic expressions. Our learning-behavior specialist believes he's at about age three or four in terms of English usage." Frankel gave Holt a look. "Some of the staff have questioned whether he should be burdened with having to learn English when we can get by with pidgin Nahuatl."

"Sam, in a crisis, there might not be Nahuatl speakers around to interpret. Even if there were interpreters, we probably wouldn't have the luxury of taking the time to have his statements translated. Not to mention that Nahuatl is much too limited. It's an ancient language in a modern world, and too much of it doesn't compute."

Frankel said, "One of the most important things we've been trying to get across to him is the fact that there is a past, present, and future. It's harder for him to conceive than one might imagine. He came from a society in which little had changed in their recorded history. In fact, after his birth, nothing much would change for the next fifteen hundred years, until the Spanish conquistadores arrived and conquered the Aztecs. Getting him to comprehend that we are the future and that he has been brought forward in time is a real challenge."

"Does he seem to have any interests? Sex, food, TV—"

"An intense interest in games."

"What kind of games?"

"Ball games, anything to do with a ball: baseball, football, soccer, even tennis. By showing two different games at one time, we were able to determine that his favorite sport is soccer, with basketball a close second. We discovered almost by accident that he also enjoys watching an amateur game called kickball. Bottom line, he has an exceptional interest in ball games."

"And he has an athletic build. An exceptional one," Holt said. "Interesting. Perhaps he was a professional athlete in his own society."

Frankel cleared his throat. "Some of us are curious

as to exactly what type of mission the young man is slated for."

The doctor was not on a need-to-know basis. Besides, the mission was still taking form in Holt's head. "We're not ready to announce it yet. What else is going on with him?"

"The most difficult hurdle is trust. Although our bodies are the same, everything else about us is completely alien to him. Some of the staff believe we've built a degree of trust."

"What do you believe?"

Frankel chewed on the question for a moment. "Personally I think we have a stalemate. He's our prisoner, he's locked up, he can't go anywhere, he's dependent on us for food and water. We keep him in a room that has two-way mirrors. We permit him to see some of the staff through thick Plexiglas at the door. Food is pushed through the door.

"His only experience with the rest of the world is that one wall has changing scenes, some pastoral, others slowly introducing him to the modern world of cities and cars. When he first saw the outside world portrayed on the TV monitor that serves as the wall, he threw himself at it—"

"In an attempt to escape?"

"At least to escape the room. Per your instructions, he's had no personal contact with anyone when he wasn't restrained and hasn't been let out of the room he occupies. You told us to think of him as all the gold in Fort Knox." Frankel gave Holt a sideways glance.

Holt knew Frankel and the rest of the staff were anxious to learn his plans for the young man. But he had told no one, not even the ZSA director. The director was theoretically his direct boss, but the director was in a power struggle with the president, and Holt's loyalty ran with Barbara Berg even though he was operating in ZSA territory and was forced to accept an appointment as a deputy ZSA director.

The only purpose the added title served was to bring him under ZSA authority. That was the idea, at least. A reality Holt managed to keep sidestepping.

Frankel hesitated. "Some of the staff don't believe that we should always keep him in full restraints when we're in the room to draw blood or otherwise examine him. And we must put him to sleep with a drug in his water before coming into physical contact with him because he's no longer restrained. They believe he'd progress much faster if he didn't have to relate to us as prisoner and jailer."

"Anyone on the staff ever trained wild animals?"

"You think we're dealing with a wild animal?"

"What do you think the culture was like that we jerked him out of?"

"Certainly not a society of wild animals. They had cities, trade, art, picture writing, even a form of books."

"Might is right, survival of the fittest, that's what it and every other ancient culture was premised on. Our Tah-Heen was raised in a society in which human life lacked the great significance it has today. People were killed for looking cross-eyed at kings, sacrificed for religious purposes, invading armies were turned loose on conquered cities for days of murder, rape, and looting. Sometimes entire populations were wiped out. On an individual level, there were no guns that you could stand back and shoot. Killing was a personal thing, inevitably involving personal contact with hands or blade. One-on-one. You don't erase the mentality to react with violence to a possible threat by being chummy with him. And that's what we are to him. A threat. For all he knows, we're fattening him up to eat him."

"That's—uh—"

"Ridiculous. Is that the word you're looking for? If I recall my recently acquired history of the ancient Mesoamerica culture correctly, it was customary for the victor in a fight to eat the defeated warrior. He ate the heart himself and shared other juicy parts with his close friends." Holt leaned forward and blew nicotine breath in Frankel's face. "What would you think if you were in his shoes?"

Frankel didn't have an answer.

Book learning, Holt thought, that was what these head doctors knew. They had sent him professionals who excelled in the academic world of classrooms and lofty scientific journals when he needed people with experience in the psych ward.

Frankel cleared his throat. "You're aware that Dr. Zimmerman, a psychologist who's worked with the ZSA, has been sent to evaluate the young man?"

"Yes."

Zimmerman not only had the academic credentials Holt thought were useless in the situation, but was the worst of all worlds—he was politically connected.

Holt hadn't been consulted about Zimmerman coming aboard and knew why. The director wanted his own man to evaluate the captive because Holt did not have the director's full confidence for good reason: Holt had been the president's choice for the mission, and the ZSA director resented it. The director's reaction was to load Holt up with aides that were loyal to the director. Holt had already been told another one was on his way: Carl Stryker, a federal agent with an expertise in assassinations.

"Zimmerman disagrees with the, uh, hands-off, keep-our-distance method you've instructed us to use with the young man. He, uh—"

"What's Zimmerman up to?"

"He's been dealing with the boy on a one-on-one basis, unrestrained. With a stun gun."

"What? Why the hell is he doing that?"

"His theory is that because Tah's primitive background—"

"Primitive, hell—ancient Americans were more advanced than most of the world of their time."

"He's only done it once. And he only used light shocks as Tah advanced toward him. He's going back in today. As soon as you arrive."

Clever bastard, Holt thought. If it went well, Zimmerman could take all the credit because he went in the first time when Holt wasn't there. And if it went wrong, Zimmerman could claim Holt interfered.

Iyo! I am a prisoner in hell. I am no longer tied down, but I'm imprisoned in a small room. One wall opens to the strange scenes, demons, and monsters in cities that are more violent and dangerous than anything I was ever told about the nine hells of Mictlan. Demons in white clothing push food through an opening in the door, but never enter the room. I know what they are up to—they will wait for my guard to be down to attack me.

I have also learned that sometimes what I eat or drink puts me to sleep so they can steal my mind for a while. When I awake, I realize things have been done to me. Once they had stabbed my head, perhaps to open it and put one of their creatures inside. I know there is a demon in my head because thoughts and words that are strange to me come to my own tongue when the demonic language these creatures use is spoken to me.

They pay tribute to their gods with my blood. When I was awake and tied down, they stuck a sharp silver thorn into my arm to draw my blood into a small, clear tube. I know they still take my blood after they put me to sleep because of the wounds on my arms.

I hope their gods will favor me for making these small sacrifices—and that it will not be necessary to have my heart ripped out and blood drained to please them.

The underworld is not as I expected it to be. All in the One-World know that monsters and severe challenges are to be found in the domain of the death master, but such monsters as I have seen here were not told of in any tale I heard as man or boy.

An opening in the wall permits me to see outside this room and into their strange world. I don't know why, but for this opening on the wall the word *television* intrudes into my mind. It must be the demon they put in my head telling me the word.

I have learned from the visions created by the thing called television that the underworld I have fallen into is a place of continual violence—people attack each other with their hands and feet, with strange weapons, even crashing strange metal weapons called cars against each other. In my world, violence had two main reasons—necessity and greed. In this hell, violence is committed even for thrills.

Through that opening I have seen many wonders, the strangest of which are giant metal animals called cars, with their round rubber disks that spin instead of feet and run along black roads. People open doors and enter these animals to be carried place to place. Iyo! And the birds, giant flying silver creatures a thousand times larger than the biggest eagle, race down black roads and soar into the sky carrying people.

Fighting the best warriors the Lords of Hell can send against me holds less fear for me than battling a metal monster that rolls at high speed on a road or soars into the sky. If these are the foes that Mictlantecuhtli, King of the Underworld, pits against me, I shall at the least go down fighting. But even these metal monsters are a small part of the strange creatures I have seen in hell.

Up to now I have survived this first Hell, and I know the challenges will get more dangerous. To be free of this hell and continue to the next, I must fight and defeat these creatures of the underworld. But they give me no opportunity to kill them! I have already learned that the gods have made invisible walls of a substance called glass that I cannot pass through. People stand on the other side of the walls and stare at me.

I don't know how much time I have already spent in this first level of hell or how much longer Mictlantecuhtli will keep me imprisoned. The trickster gods deliberately made a fool out of me by making me think I could leap through the window called television that showed the outside. I slammed into the invisible wall when I tried to escape and got cut as materials as sharp as obsidian shattered.

I tire of lying back and watching the magic and terrors of hell on the television. I want to get up and do something, not watch others do it.

As I lie on the strange bed that the gods have provided and ponder what surprises will be in store for me from these tricksters, I am reminded of the story of how the two greatest ballplayers of the One-World also had to battle tricksters in hell. No tale of the ball game is better known than this one in all the One-World. Thinking about it and the game of olli, I tossed back and forth a ball I had made. I'd taken springs from my bed and intertwined and bent them into a ball shape and wrapped it in strips of bed cloth.

The tale is of the Hero Twins. It begins when two brothers, Hunhun and Vukub, are playing a ball game. They are interrupted by an owl with a message from the Lords of Hell in the underworld. The underworld gods have heard of their skills, the owl tells them, and challenges them to come to the underworld and play against them.

The two brothers enter the underworld, traveling down a narrow cavern that snakes deep into the earth. When they cross a river, to their horror they discover it is a river of blood. Once across, they fall to their knees before a figure they believe is Mictlantecuhtli.

Iyo! The image was a trick, nothing more than a stick figure put there so the lords could laugh at the brothers kneeling before cloth and wood.

Back on their feet, the brothers are chased by a vicious wild animal. Exhausted after avoiding the jaws of the beast, they sit on what they believe are stools. They jump up immediately, howling with pain. The stools are actually hot stones put there by the lords, who once again laugh at their pains and at the tricks they fell for.

When they are no longer amused by humiliating the brothers, the gods imprison the two in the House of Gloom, where they are tortured, sacrificed, and decapitated.

The head of Hunhun is taken to the upper world and suspended from a tree. So that no one will notice it, the lords have gourds the size of human heads also on the tree. But the gods failed to take feminine curiosity and weakness for forbidden fruit into consideration.

After some years pass, a princess pauses under the tree. When she reaches up to grab a gourd, the head of Hunhun spits into her hand. The head tells her that she will now become pregnant and bear sons that will become great ballplayers.

When the Lords of Hell discover she is pregnant, they send an assassin in the form of an owl to kill her. To prove that she is dead, the owl is to bring back her heart. When the princess is confronted by the owl, she talks it out of killing her. Instead, she has the owl take back the coagulated heart of the bloodwort plant.

The princess gave birth to twin sons, Hun-Apu and Xbalan, who grew up to be great ballplayers. Hearing of their feats on the ball court, the Lords of Hell invited them to the underworld for a match.

The twins know the story of how their father, Hunhun, and uncle, Vukub, were lured to the underworld to be humiliated. As the Lords of Hell throw tricks at them, they are prepared to avoid humiliation and defeat. They cross the river of blood on the back of a giant turtle, bat down the wood figure rather than worship it, and lure the wild beast sent to chase them into itself sitting on the hot stones.

Unable to trick the twins into submission, the lords

are forced to play the twins in a ball game with the celestial heavens itself as the playing field and Xolotl himself overseeing the game.

The twins win the match. As a reward, after their deaths, their souls become the sun and the moon.

The House of Gloom . . . Truly that is where I am being imprisoned and tortured. I was contemplating how I must avoid their cruel tricks when the door to my room opened and a man stepped in. I tensed—he had come yesterday, bringing with him a short stick that gave me pain when he touched me with it. He was a minion of the Lords of Hell back to torture me.

He took two steps into the room and stopped and smiled. "Hello, Tah-Heen, remember me? I am Dr. Zimmerman."

I got off my bed slowly. I recognized his words— a greeting, my name, and his name—but I was not fooled by his smile. He was dressed in white like the other creatures who smiled as they held me prisoner, stole my blood, made a hole in my head, and forced me to watch the demon called TV.

He left the door open behind him. Iyo! The only thing that stopped me from getting out the room and out of this House of Gloom was this creature, who now came toward me and held out his hand as if he intended to grab me, keeping the pain stick in his other hand. I threw the ball, hitting him in the nose. I kicked him in the knee with my foot. As he yelled and bent over, I brought my own knee up as if I were hitting a skull ball, catching him in the face. His head snapped back and his body went backward. Before he hit the floor, I was through the doorway.

More of the creatures in white were in the hallway. I ran down the hallway with the demons scattering and shouting. Two of the creatures, bigger and not dressed in white, but in blue uniforms, stood their ground, yelling at me to stop. I recognized them as warriors of the Lords of Hell. I threw myself at them, using my feet, knees, elbows, and fists as weapons. When they were both down, stunned and bleeding, I ran again to make good my escape.

A man holding a metal tube in his hand stepped out of a doorway. By the way he stood and pointed it at me, I knew it must have been a weapon, perhaps a club, but it was unlike any weapon I'd seen. It was black metal and had a barrel and a handle. In a flash I recognized the man as a leader I'd seen watching me through the glass wall. From the body language of others who stood beside him when he watched me, I knew him to be one of the Lords of Hell.

I charged him, and the thing in his hand made a loud noise. Something hit me in the chest and I felt excruciating pain. My mind and body exploded. I lost control of my arms and legs and went down, my skin burning, the pain unbearable. I felt as if my body had been stung by a thousand bees. My limbs convulsed, jerking, kicking.

My attempt to escape was over. I was bound again, hands and legs, and carried back to my prison.

The demon I had assaulted earlier was carried out

as I was brought in. Watching him being taken out on a small cot with wheels, I wondered if they were going to remove his heart for me as the victor to eat.

One of the creatures in white stabbed me with the pointed objects they use to take blood or put liquids into my body. My eyes closed and I passed into a dark place.

Allen Holt stood in the hallway as they carried Dr. Zimmerman out on a stretcher.

"He's dead," Frankel said. The psychiatrist was hysterical. "He was only trying to shake hands, and that wild man killed him. His neck is broken."

Holt nodded and tried to look sympathetic as he reloaded a dart into his stun gun. "A tragic misfortune."

"My God, it's a good thing you had that gun. The two guards who tried to stop him were severely injured."

Holt wasn't unsympathetic to Zimmerman's death, but wouldn't mourn the loss, either. The psychiatrist was part of the ZSA director's plan to take control of the project—and the country.

Holt was also pragmatic when it came to politics and national-security missions: If Zimmerman had made successful physical contact with Tah-Heen, Holt would have gone into the room, too. But unlike Zimmerman, the most important things he learned about people were not in a psychobabble session or university lectures, but on the back streets of such places as

Beirut and Baghdad. The stun gun was his backup in case the prisoner tried to attack.

Frankel wrung his hands. "What are we to do? Zimmerman was one of the great minds in the field. Now he's dead. Murdered."

"It was an accident. He's replaceable, Tah-Heen isn't. Get another project psychiatrist before the ZSA director appoints his own. This time I want a prison psychiatrist with experience in a supermax cellblock." As Holt started to walk away, he paused and turned back to Frankel. "See if you can find a wild-animal trainer, too."

"You're joking."

Holt raised his eyebrows. "Ask Zimmerman if he thinks it's a joke." He waved at the doorway to Tah's room. "Get him balls."

"Balls?"

"Soccer, basketball, baseball, football, every kind you can get."

37

Caden stared out the window of the project's DC-3 as it came in for a landing. Albuquerque's International Sunport had the war-zone atmosphere of all airports in the Zone—bristling with tanks and armored personnel carriers rather than airplanes, soldiers in battle dress rather than ground crews in coveralls. Only one runway was used, and it was lined with sandbagged machine-gun positions. The flight had been scheduled to land in a strip created in Santa Fe, but had been diverted when a gang of people attempted to hijack a plane. The plane was still there, in charred pieces. So were the people.

The airport was a derelict—beer cans, shattered wine bottles, Styrofoam cups, broken windows, peeling paint, planes and ground vehicles abandoned where they'd broken down.

No commercial flights went in and out of the Zone.

Each large metro area had an airport used exclusively by the ZSA to move troops, supplies, and civilian contractors doing business for the government in the Zone. Airports had been on high military alert since a mob attacked the Atlanta airport and hijacked planes within days after the Zone was barricaded. The three large commercial jets they managed to get off the ground were shot out of the sky before they reached airports beyond the Zone.

The taxi was an "aged" VW Bug—still functioning because it had a manual transmission, an air-cooled engine easy to keep running, and was easy on gas. As they drove away from the airport, a motorcycle gang roared by on their way into town, their choppers rasping.

"Zone Zombies," her driver said. "Fuckin' skinhead, neo-Nazi biker freaks. They have tapes of World War Two stuff off the old History Channel, and they sit around and drink Sterno beer and watch those dumbass Nazi bastards goose-stepping. They're too fuckin' stupid to realize Adolf and his boys got their asses kicked."

Her driver told her he had retired before the contagion to Santa Fe from a job with an accounting firm in Chicago. He couldn't leave the Zone when the contagion first broke out because his wife got sick. After she passed away, it was too late for him to get out—the barricade had gone up and anyone trying to cross was shot.

Like the airport, the freeway leading to Santa Fe

was a derelict. Cars and trucks and burned hunks of cars and trunks stayed where they stopped, along with whatever else the wind blew down the roadway. Some abandoned vehicles were used as metal caves for people to live in. But like everything else in the Zone, no water meant no life, and the freeway squatters ultimately died or moved on to await death somewhere else.

Albuquerque was around eight hundred miles or so from the Gulf but had been affected even more than some closer areas because most of the region was arid or semiarid, making it easy to tip the ecological scale. Unusual weather from the Gulf brought the region red rain in torrential quantities that killed forests, leaving dry trees, bushes, and grasslands that ignited into violent firestorms that left a dead world in their wake.

When strong winds blew, New Mexico's dirt became part of the nearly million-square-mile dust bowl that blotted out the sun. A place where people were always dirty and thirsty.

"The Underground says the Canadians kicked our butts in a battle outside Toronto. Those Canucks are badasses," the driver said.

"The Underground" usually meant anything that was antigovernment, though most people claimed that 90 percent of what was antigovernment was really federal agents pretending to be antigovernment.

The president had announced "mission accomplished" over a year ago in the war between the United States and Canada, but everyone knew the war was still going on. Millions of Americans had crossed the Canadian border in the desperate attempt to put miles between them and the Gulf, overpowering the limited resources of the Canadians.

To relieve even more of the population stress, the United States had invaded the much smaller country. The Canadian army was not prepared for an invasion across what had long been flaunted as the longest un-protected border on the planet . . . but the civilian population was.

Instead of the U.S. fighting an army, the war went underground as Canadian civilians took up arms against the invaders. Farmers and clerks during the daytime, guerrilla freedom fighters at night played hell on the U.S. forces, who soon discovered that the only land they controlled was the dirt under their feet—and even that dirt might become their grave.

Despite the U.S. government's frequent announce-ment of victory, everyone knew the damn war would go on forever.

The world is truly a mess, Caden thought.

Maybe another Dark Age was being ushered in, as when the lights of culture went out after the fall of the Roman empire to the barbaric hordes. Or, more likely, the end of the world. It would have been nice to be on the dark side of ninety years old when the end came.

When they were on the outskirts of Santa Fe, a small whirlwind called a dust devil swirled across the roadway, throwing sand against Caden's passenger-side window. Few people were on the streets.

"Lawrence of Arabia would have felt comfortable around here," she told the driver as they passed a man wearing a southwestern version of bedouin clothes— long, loose clothing and a corded headpiece that came down to his shoulders. His desert outfit, topped by a faded baseball cap, was not unusual dress in the Zone.

The driver nodded. "People say the clothes camel jockeys wear in Arabia are better than those BDUs, battle dress uniforms, the army developed for the Middle East wars and the ZSA troops now wear."

Caden agreed. Anyone who had researched water usage knew that bedouins had a head start of thousands of years when it came to desert survival tactics.

She knew that people who dressed as bedouins were called *a-rabs* and no one capitalized the *A*.

A woman on a camel came down the street.

"From the zoo," the driver said about the camel. "When the water went bad, the zoo turned loose everything that didn't bite. Only the camels survived."

Caden didn't think camels were immune from the contagion. That meant the woman had a source of drinking water. She might have been one of the "water ranchers" that controlled a well . . . with firepower. With gas more scarce than drinking water, a camel would be a great asset to a water rancher.

Billy the Kid and Kit Carson, both Santa Fe characters, would also have been at home in this Santa Fe. Scattered among the a-rabs were men and women wearing western-style clothes and openly packing guns.

"Long-barreled six-shooters are favored," the driver told her, "because automatic pistols are prone to misfire in the dusty atmosphere."

Dry rot, she thought, as she stared at people. The inhabitants of the Zone struck her as brittle and ready to crumble into dry powder, like abandoned buildings in an Old West ghost town.

Everyone she saw, except for members of the ZSA forces, was thin and weathered, with parchment skin and not an ounce of excess fat. They were beyond the stage of what hot and thirsty Texas cowboys used to call "spittin' cotton." There wasn't enough excess moisture in them to hock a good one.

"Crazy-crazy-crazy," the driver said, repeating lyrics to a popular song. And so it was—crazy. In fact, being crazy was considered a benefit—people who tried to be too rational and face the inevitable had shorter, meaner life spans than the crazies, who had lost touch with reality.

Caden liked Santa Fe—at least the town she knew from the old days. And the "old days" was a visit just a few years ago. At an elevation of nearly seven thousand feet, the city was at the foot of the Sangre de Cristo, Blood of Christ, mountains, which had peaks that rose above twelve thousand feet. It had a dry, pleasant atmosphere, a little high desert, a little chaparral. She thought of Taos, a touristy art colony about an hour north with a great ski area in the mountains above it, as an extension of what she liked about Santa Fe.

Founded nearly four hundred years ago as Villa

Real de la Santa Fé de San Francisco de Asís—Royal City of the Holy Faith of St. Francis of Assisi—the city was built on a prehistoric Tiwa Indian pueblo.

Besides the ghosts of Stone Age Native Americans, Santa Fe, like Sedona, attracted artists and writers, gurus and New Age energy seekers, rich people who'd fled the violence of the Middle East and wanted to live in the Sun Belt, and retirees who fled the violence of metro America and wanted to bask in the Sun Belt before they died.

The city had been fought over by Indians, Spanish, the United States, the Confederate States, and most recently a plague of real estate developers.

"Downtown Santa Fe" was about all that was left habitable of the former sprawling state capital. Squatters who held as much space as they could defend lived in buildings that had once housed the town's ubiquitous jewelry stores and art galleries. Much of the broken glass and debris from the riots and looting in the early days of the contagion still lay scattered on the sidewalks and streets.

Like everywhere else in the Zone, the city's fragile lifelines were the heavily guarded caravans of trucks carrying food and water from the northern states. When the trucks stopped, there would be no more Santa Fe. And no more people.

"Main Street" was a one-block area with most of the commerce done in Middle Eastern bazaar fashion, with a touch of *Blade Runner* bizarre thrown in—you could buy everything from Nazi daggers in an army-surplus store to salted seal jerky and black-market pint cans of water stolen from an ambushed caravan. A popular stand sold ice cones from an old-fashioned ice-cream pushcart.

"Glow cones," Caden said, when she saw the ice cones.

A handwritten sign on the side of the cart said the water came from a private well.

"But who the hell knows where the water really comes from," her driver said. "They don't call them glow cones for nothing."

But people on the street did buy them. It was part of the fatalism of the Zone. People under a death sentence weren't particular. Getting "the glow" was seen as inevitable. Thus the ice cones were a moment's relief from the feeling of having a mouthful of dirty cotton.

Everyone knew that the only way to avoid the contagion was to stay strictly away from liquids and foods that didn't come out of a sealed package from the north. But they did it anyway.

She estimated that one out of every three or four people on the streets were showing symptoms of the affliction. In the early stages the victim had increased thirst and a bright pink flush, causing the skin to glow. In a few months the color got a deeper red . . . and the thirst became unbearable. The affliction spread to the nervous system, affecting motor control.

When she was a kid and the world was less politically correct, people who had a disease with coordination difficulties such as cerebral palsy were called spastics. That word was reborn in the Zone.

The spastic phase lasted a few months before the person fell into what Raymond Chandler called "the big sleep."

But for the grace of God go any of us, thought Caden, as she watched an "old" woman who might have been chronologically younger than herself holding on to a rusted shopping cart for support as she came down the street with wobbly limbs.

She remembered the word *spastic* from childhood, something her mother would say when she saw someone who was physically or mentally disabled.

What strange paths our destinies lead us upon, she thought. So far she had been lucky enough to have been spared the glow. That Koji Oda was "one" with water had kept her and the Frog group safe.

The taxi driver took her within four blocks of her destination, the Palace of the Governors. ZSA troops had barricades blocking vehicle access from that point.

"Only authorized people are allowed in," the driver said. "The scuttlebutt is that they're conducting weird medical experiments in there, crossing humans with animals or something like that."

"Like *The Island of Dr. Moreau.*"

"What's that?"

"The H. G. Wells story where they crossed humans with animals."

Caden showed her ID to a guard at the barricade. She was permitted to enter after he found her name on a list. "Do you know how to get to the Palace of the Governors?" he asked.

"No."

"They call this Old Santa Fe Trail. Stay on it until Palace Avenue. The palace is right there. It's a five-minute walk."

"Is it near the Plaza?"

"Yeah, but the Plaza is closed off completely. No one can enter."

She left the guard station, wondering what was so secretive about Holt's project that it would create rumors of horrors. Not that there weren't already plenty of horrors in the Zone.

Plaza Santa Fe was definitely off-limits, and sealed off, with guard posts all around it. Something very secret was going on inside. Which was apt for the region—the development of the atomic bomb took place at Los Alamos not far down the road.

She'd been sent to Seattle with the rest of the project members after the trip. An order sending her to Austin, Texas, soon followed. The university at Austin had an outstanding collection of information about ancient Mesoamerica, much of it transferred from Mexico City after the contagion turned the Valley of Mexico into a ghost region.

Why Holt wanted her to increase her knowledge about ancient Mesoamerica, the region that extended from what is now modern Mexico through Central America, was a mystery to her. He even had her studying the greatest city of ancient Mexico, Teotihuacán.

Though she was familiar with the ruins, he ordered her to memorize key points of the ancient city, reconstructed by computer analysis.

All of her instructions came through Holt's aides. She had not seen him since the Gulf flyover.

The one-story Palace of the Governors was an unimposing building that ran the entire length of a block. She knew from Internet searches that it had originally been built in Spanish colonial style and that about a hundred years ago the city fathers refurbished its exterior to give it a "pueblo adobe" look. Bare timbers held up the long portico that fronted the building and poked out every few feet along the top.

Old and revered in New Mexico, it was neither a large nor an imposing building, hardly what one would expect housed a critical project run by one of the most important government officials in the land. A fact that added to the mystery.

After waiting an hour and a half in an outer office, she was ushered in to see Allen Holt. No apology was offered for the time she'd spent cooling her heels. He was the boss.

When Holt came out of his office, he was not in a good mood. "The worst contagion on Earth is the virus called bureaucracy. I spend more time pushing paperwork than creating results."

She followed him as he stalked down hallways, groups parting in his path like the Red Sea for Moses. They came out of the rear of the building to a basketball court. The court looked newly built.

Holt stopped and turned to Caden. He gestured at the players. "What do you see?"

"Uh . . . I see six players . . . a mixture of races, black, brown, white . . . all young men, different sizes . . ."

Loud rap music was broadcast from speakers on a wall.

"How many teams?"

"Hmmm . . . uh . . . looks like it's five against one."

The "one" was the shortest player, a well-built young man with brown skin. He was obviously the best player, running circles around the other players, doing fakes, bouncing the ball between their feet and moving so fast he'd get it back again.

She heard his name yelled by another player: Da Eagle.

He bounced the ball off the head of another player, retrieved the ball, ducked under a taller player trying to block him. "In your face," he yelled as he sent another player sprawling onto the concrete with a shoulder blow. "Foul," the downed player shouted.

"I'm the rainmaker!" Da Eagle yelled as he shot a basket from long range.

"What I see is an exceptional basketball player playing some kind of roughhouse basketball. Some of the moves remind me of break dancing."

"It's called Streetball," Holt said. "That's trash talk you hear them shouting at each other. And you're right, it has elements of rap, break dancing, basketball . . ." He grinned. "With a little last-man-standing thrown in. And it's easy to see who the last man standing would be."

"He's not just good," she said. "He's incredible. None of the others can keep up with him. He moves around them with the ball as if the ball were an extension of him."

Holt nodded. "Good observations."

"He's barefooted. I guess that gives him better footing, but it has to be hell on the bottom of his feet. He's the only one not wearing padding. The other players are all heavily padded."

"For protection."

"But not him?"

"He's what they need protection from. What else do you see?"

"He's the only one wearing a thick black belt. Is it an electronic device? Something that increases his ability as a player?"

"It's a stun belt. If he tries to escape, the guards press a remote that triggers a high-voltage charge that knocks him down. After he got a dose of it, he hasn't tried to run again."

"Why's he a prisoner?"

"He's wearing the stun belt because he's already killed a man in an escape attempt."

She caught her breath.

"In his mind, he killed another warrior during battle," Holt said.

"Where's he from?"

"A very complicated question. Why he's our prisoner is an infinitely more complicated question."

She locked eyes with him. "I realize I'm just a peon, a small-time scientist, and you are an important person. But it would be nice if I knew what my job entailed. So far I have been studying Mesoamerican and now the prison-basketball culture. Mr. Holt, the world is coming to an end. What can be done to save it? How can I help?"

"Good question. There's your answer." He pointed out at the court.

"A basketball game?"

He shook his head. "The ballplayer. He's Da Eagle in trash talk, but off the court his name is Tah-Heen. He's going to save the world. You're going to help him."

38

I saw the woman for the first time when I was playing the game in hell they call basketball. She stood by the man whom I have been told to call Holt. From the way others obey—and fear—him, I believe he is Mictlantecuhtli, King of the Underworld, in disguise. If he is not the mighty King of the Dead himself, he is an underling god—one that strikes with lightning. He brought me down once with his rod.

From the way he spoke to her and pointed to me, I knew that she would play a role in whatever tests he and the other gods had designed for me. I had bested the demons in their ball game and wondered what challenge they had next for me. I found it strange that a ball game would be a challenge in hell. Now they brought a more difficult challenge than wrestling a jaguar—a woman.

Iyo! I have seen other women in the underworld,

but none that pleased my eyes as this one did. What also caught my eye was her surprise at whatever Holt told her. Rather than being among those who have been keeping me captive, she obviously knew nothing of me before I was pointed out to her while I was playing. Perhaps like me, she knows nothing of what the gods have in store for her.

When the play was over, I was escorted to Holt and the woman, with two of the demons called guards hovering nearby. Anytime I was allowed out of my room, two demons always stayed close to me. Each had a small black object the size of a deck of cards in their hand. I am told that if I try to run, they will point the object at me. That will awaken the demons in a black belt around my waist to bite me with unbearable pain.

Holt was still talking about me as I came closer to them. Twice she had stared in my direction as if something he said startled her.

When I came up to them, Holt said, "Tah, this is Caden. She is a scientist on the project."

I had learned enough of the language of the underworld to understand what he said. But I was surprised that she was a scientist. I had already learned that scientists were superior demons, some were even inferior gods to Holt. All the men and women I had met were the god's minions. Something about this woman gave me the impression that she was different.

She greeted me. "Your ollin was amazing, Tah."

She spoke my language, not exactly as I spoke it,

but enough for me to understand what she was saying and to reply in the same tongue.

"I understand, Tah, that you are from a time in the past," she said. "That a mechanism brought you to our own time."

She spoke this time in English, the new language I have had to learn. I had already discovered that many things in the underworld could not be described by the language of my people.

I recognized wonder in her voice, as if she really believed I was from this place called the past and now in a place called the future. I wanted to tell her that we were both in hell and they had tricked her, too.

"That is what I am told." I do not disagree when the demons tell me that I am now in what they call the future rather than hell. I fool them by seeming to agree with whatever they want.

"I was just told about the mechanism, what we call a Time Explorer. I had no idea it existed. It's . . . it's incredible."

I nodded and smiled. I again had the urge to tell her that I was not a fool, that I knew I was in the underworld, but I merely smiled. I wondered what death she had suffered to have descended to face the challenges of hell.

"We will be working together," she said.

Working with a woman? Was she a ballplayer like Ixchel? I asked, "What work will we be doing . . . together?"

"I have not been told everything yet. Mr. Holt, our

boss, will explain what we will be doing." She looked to Holt, the question on her face.

Holt said, "All right, let's take a look at the next step."

We followed the god across the street to the place called Santa Fe Plaza. Nothing could be seen of the inside of the plaza because tall barricades surrounded it. Guards opened a door and we entered.

I heard a gasp—it was my own.

I was back in the One-World.

39

"What is this place?" Caden asked Holt.

I kept walking, listening to conversations, watching people. I nodded at a well-dressed man, obviously a nobleman, after he gave me a greeting in Nahuatl as he went by. Like the many tricks played on the Hero Twins, I knew that this, too, was a trick of the gods of the underworld.

"You're smiling, Tah, what is it?" Holt asked.

I shook my head. "Nothing, I am just happy to be back in the One-World."

"You're lying. Tell me the truth."

Iyo! You do not lie to a god. At least, you should not lie poorly enough to get caught.

"This is a trick, it's not the One-World."

He nodded. "You're right, it's not your world. But it's not meant to fool you. We have shown you TV and movies where other times and even other worlds have been re-created."

"Acting, you called it."

"Yes, acting. And that's what these people are doing. In a sense, what you see around you is a movie set and the people are actors following a script."

"Why?" Caden asked.

"The contagion is not an act of nature. It was deliberately created."

It struck me and I almost shouted it. "Quetzalcoatl!"

"Yes, Quetzalcoatl, the Feathered Serpent."

I knew that bloodthirsty god had not forgotten about me.

"We'll go over it at length later," Holt said, "but at this moment you need simply to understand that the thing called the Feathered Serpent ruled ancient Mesoamerica. A massive earthquake buried it, sealing it in a mountain. Two thousand years later it was released by another earthquake. And it set out to dominate the modern world by introducing something akin to a virus that killed off the methane-eating archaea."

"How does Tah fit in?"

Both looked at me. I, too, wondered what the answer would be—and if it would be honest. Holt's sincerity was obvious—but a god can fool you into believing it is earnest. Caden was so honestly surprised, I wondered if there was some truth to what Holt said—or if she was just falling for another trick. It occurred to me that there could be a war in the underworld between the gods, and the woman and I were being used.

"In the ancient world, the One-World, Tah challenged Quetzalcoatl. He managed to find the Feathered Serpent's nest and was battling its guards when he was accidentally zapped to the present by a probe we had sent to the past." Holt directed a question at me. "Tah, you instantly realized that this was not the One-World. Why? How is it different?"

I looked around. "The language is not correct, not so much the actual words, but the sound of it spoken. But that is not important, there are many different tongues in the One-World. To speak differently from another would not be that noticeable. But what you call body language is wrong. A moment ago a nobleman greeted me. What he said was correct, but"—I pointed down at my bare feet—"he would know from my lack of sandals that I am not of his class. Had I spoken to a nobleman before he spoke to me, I would have been beaten. Also, the smells are not—"

Holt raised his hand. "Enough. You understand, Caden? Tah is the real thing. We can't fool him with a movie-set city, but he would be right at home in the real thing."

"This thing, Quetzalcoatl, what is it?" she asked.

"We don't know. A primeval beast that existed in some epoch before mankind? An ancient astronaut? Something that grew out of a puddle of slime and developed superintelligence? A nightmare left behind by the Mayans to make sure the world ends on time? No one knows exactly what it is."

"It's at Teotihuacán," she said. "That's why you chose me. I tangled with it, too."

"We don't know exactly where it is at this moment, but we need to start someplace, and Teo is the number one choice. That's where it was trapped in the mountain. The problem is we can't guess where it's at now, we have to be one hundred percent sure. We're going to send a mission to destroy the beast. We'll only have one chance. If we fail, all will be lost."

"What do you mean?" she asked.

"It wants to dominate the world. Or destroy human life if it can't dominate us. The governments of the world have been negotiating with its representative. In essence, we're stalling in the hopes we can come up with a way to reverse or control the contagion. The second option is to kill the beast. If we knew for an absolute certainty it was at Teo and exactly where it was, we could nuke it. But if it's not there and we fail, we're certain it will unleash more hell on us. We believe it would be most vulnerable in the ancient world."

"So you've built a model of Teotihuacán so you can train people for a mission to go the city and see if they can locate Quetzalcoatl. Using the device you told me about, the one that brought Tah here. A mission back in time to the ancient world."

"Exactly."

"And that's why Tah is important and why you've

had me educating myself about ancient Mesoamerica. You want us to train the people who are going back in time."

Holt was shaking his head before she finished speaking. "Good guess, but not quite right. We don't want you to train other people. We want you to become time walkers."

"Time walkers?" Caden asked.

"People we send back to other time periods." Holt paused and gave both of us a hard stare. "We're sending you two back in time."

Back to the One-World. To face a monster and its horde of Nawals and Jaguar Knights. With this beautiful but helpless woman as my companion.

Iyo! Was this just another trick of the gods to frighten me?

40

After Holt was finished talking to us, he told the guards who watched over me with their magic devices that put lightning into my body to take us to the Greenhouse. And instructed us to speak English only, to improve my skill.

"They call it the Greenhouse," Caden told me as we walked toward a tall structure that appeared to me to be a dome of glass. "A greenhouse is a place where plants are grown in a protected shelter. But I call it a rain forest."

The building that the forest grew in was a giant transparent dome. It reminded me of the plastic bubble that had been over my bed when I first arrived in the underworld.

The guards waited outside when Caden and I entered. Immediately I felt the cool mist and smelled the sweet scent of trees and plants that have not been deprived of water.

"I've been told you watch sports," she said. "This place is about the size of a football field you've seen on television."

As we walked along a dirt path lit by ground-level lights, Caden said, "It's built for the use of high-ranking ZSA personnel and their families. There's one in every major area where ZSA people are stationed in the Zone. I've never been in one before."

I understood. It was a temple only for the gods and their high priests.

"We no longer go outside when it rains, not even in the northern areas where the contagion hasn't hit yet. Even in the north it's not healthy because no one pays attention to environmental laws anymore, so we get acid rain. You understand acid rain?"

I shook my head.

"Our factories and vehicles put unhealthy chemicals into the air. Rain picks up the pollution and brings it back down on our heads and plants." She giggled like a child. "Ohhh, Tah, I can't tell you how good this feels. I wish I could take off my clothes and run naked, letting the moisture soak into me."

"Then let's run naked." I started to take off my shirt and she stopped me, laughing.

"No, that wouldn't be permitted. We would be arrested."

I was already a prisoner anyway, but I did not want to displease her. Or have her made a prisoner.

We walked by a fountain where stone fish spit water high in the air. Such magic no longer impressed or puzzled me. The gods of this world could create anything they imagined.

She knelt by the fountain and scooped up a handful of water. She smelled it and tasted it. "It's not living water."

"What is living water?"

She stood up and we walked as she spoke. "Water in a natural state that hasn't been polluted or processed. I suppose it's like our blood. It's healthiest when it's in a natural state. There's a belief among many people that the earth operates much like an organism."

"Organism?"

"Like living creatures, animals and humans. They believe the world is an immense, vast mass of functioning flesh and tissue. If it's an organism, then the rivers and seas would be its blood, its circulatory system. And like blood, living water has oxygen and minerals that allow it to enrich the plants and animals that use it. Dead water lacks oxygen. Even when it's safe to drink, it tastes flat and empty."

I listened to what she said, enthralled by her every word. And I believed what she said. She was the first person in the underworld that I didn't immediately distrust.

"What about your people, Tah, what do they think of this place they call the One-World?"

I thought for a moment before answering. "My people believe that the world is unpredictable and unstable, that its destruction is threatened by the whim of the gods. To appease the gods and preserve the world from their anger, we make sacrifices to them."

"The blood covenant."

"Yes, blood for sunshine and rain. The One-World has been broken four times on the wheel of time. If Quetzalcoatl and the other gods are not appeased with blood sacrifices, they will once again destroy it."

"Is there a legend about how the destruction will occur?"

"Nawals will kill everyone."

"I've heard of Nawals. Shape-changers who can look human or like animals. Beasts. What we call werejaguars."

"You understand," I said, "we are helpless to keep the gods from destroying the world?"

"Tah . . . I don't believe the world is meant to end. I know we humans have done some terrible things to the world we live in, but people are capable of change. There is an incredible amount of good in people. And great talent to mend the damage we've done."

We stopped and she studied my face with her eyes. "This may be a surprise to you, but my own family has roots in what you call the One-World, especially the Teotihuacán area."

That did surprise me.

"Of course, the area looks nothing like when you were there," she said.

"I know, they showed me pictures of what they

called the ruins of Teotihuacán. The two great pyramids still stand, along with the remains of the Temple of Quetzalcoatl and some other places."

"My parents were from Mexico. It's from my mother's mother that I learned Nahuatl."

Her connection to the One-World, even to the city of the Feathered Serpent, sealed my opinion of her. The god Holt might be using her for his own purposes, but she was without guile herself.

"Was Teotihuacán your home?" she asked.

I told her the truth, about Lord Light, the Eagle Knights, and Ome, the nanny who escaped with me. Caden listened attentively, sometimes with concern and wide eyes. The truth had been stored inside me, and now it flowed out in a big gust. I had always pretended not to understand when others questioned me, but I wanted to share it with her.

"You were a professional ballplayer," she said. "Amazing. I never really thought about sport professionals in the ancient world, but I guess that's what gladiators and Olympians were." She surveyed me again with her probing eyes. "How about family? Are you married? Children?"

I shook my head.

She suddenly smiled and gave me a quizzical stare. "I keep asking you about your world. Tell me . . . what do you think of *our* world?"

No deep thought was needed. "It stinks. The air stinks, the water stinks, the ground is dry and hard and smelly. People stink. There is a body odor that does not all come naturally from a person's body, a chemical odor—"

"Yes, we don't bathe like we used to. We take what they call navy showers—turn the water on to get wet, stop it, put on soap, then rinse it off. All very quickly. We use dead water reconstituted from toilets and sinks. We wear a rubber band around our mouths so we don't drink it. We don't get completely clean, so we douse ourselves with perfumes." She avoided my eye, embarrassed.

"You smell like a rose."

She laughed. "You're right, it's the scent I use to hide the soap smell."

"Another difference is the lack of color. Your cities are that gray stone you call concrete, your roads are black. The cities of my world are colorful, reds and greens and yellows. And your artwork. None of it is made by the hands of people. Machines you call computers make pictures of people and things on TV and billboards. They look perfect, but they lack interest because they are perfect. And that monster you call television . . . why would anyone want to sit on a couch and watch *other* people do things?"

"Holt told me you watched a lot of television."

"Television is interesting, it taught me about this place you call Earth. Now all the shows are beginning to look the same."

She listened quietly as I scolded her world. When I ran out of complaints, I said, "They keep telling me that I am now in the future, that I have come forward in this thing called time. They believe I was privileged to have been kidnapped from my own world and imprisoned in yours. Let's say that I believe them, that I accept the fact that I am in the future. I have to wonder why, if you have two thousand of your years to improve upon the One-World, couldn't your people have done a better job of it?"

"Apparently we failed."

After I finished, we walked in silence, she, deep in thought. I worried that I had offended her. Finally she said, "Tah, this . . . thing, Quetzalcoatl, the Feathered Serpent. It created something, probably a virus, to kill the methane-eating microbes. Why?"

I shrugged. "It wants to dominate your world as it does the One-World."

"But why this way?"

I thought the answer was obvious. "Obsidian weapons are not powerful enough to dominate your world."

"So it's using a high-tech bioweapon that no one else has? It sounds right. That's the history of warfare, a new technology overpowering the old. Bronze weapons overwhelmed sticks and stone, iron came along that sliced bronze, now nuclear weapons are the deadliest." She shook her head. "But I still find methane an odd choice."

"A good soldier, like a ballplayer, would adjust his weapons until he found the right one. Your world is superior when it comes to atomic weapons. If it chose a weapon like that, it wouldn't have the edge."

I realized even if she was being tricked, she truly cared for this miserable world. I felt sad for her as I spoke what I knew to be its destiny. "There is one more legend from the One-World you should know. It is written that the Feathered Serpent will destroy the world again, for a final time. It will drink up all the water and people will die of thirst."

"Interesting," Holt said. He watched Tah and Caden on a video screen while they walked and talked in the rain-forest dome.

A newcomer watched with him: Carl Stryker, the director's assassin.

"Your Neanderthal has a warm spot for the woman," Stryker said. "You can see it in his face."

Holt lit a cigarette. "Thinking of him as a caveman is counterproductive. He comes from a civilized society. And he's very intelligent. His comments about the Feathered Serpent show that."

Stryker smiled and shrugged. Holt kept the reprimand low-key. Stryker was one of the director's men. It wouldn't be easy to get rid of him. Holt not only disliked the man, he wasn't pleased that he'd been chosen to lead Tah and Caden in the mission back in time. The man had the arrogance of raw muscle— muscle backed up, of course, by a gun under his coat and one strapped around his ankle. Given the option, Holt would have preferred that Tah had killed Stryker rather than the psychobabble expert.

Holt continued, "Tah's crucial for the mission. He's the only one who can actually pass for an ancient Mesoamerican because he is one."

"My orders are to observe the prisoner and gauge whether he will be useful to us. If he becomes a liability, my orders are to retire him."

Holt was both practical and expedient. He didn't have a problem with murder if it was in the interests of the nation he served. But he ordered assassinations only as a last resort. He had never met Stryker, but had checked him out with the DEA director whom Stryker had once worked for. Stryker had been a sharpshooter assigned to take out designated targets when he had been a navy SEAL. The navy found him too eager to pull the trigger even for military purposes, and he had flowed out of the SEALs and into the DEA. At the Drug Enforcement Administration, he tracked down and killed a Mexican drug lord who had killed a DEA agent.

The DEA director told Holt that Stryker took perverse enjoyment in the assignment because it required he torture and kill a series of the drug lord's underlings to get to the target.

Holt blew smoke in Stryker's direction. "As long as you're working under my supervision, you're not to take any action without informing me first."

Stryker smiled and nodded. "Of course. But you have to understand, I may get orders directly from the director."

"Of course. After they come through me, they will go directly to you. If that's a problem, you can take the next plane back to Sea-Tac."

Stryker only smiled at the challenge.

Holt knew he hadn't won a victory—the man was just not ready for a confrontation.

Stryker said, "I have to tell you that people at Sea-Tac are puzzled by the strategy of sending me back with an untrained woman and a big question mark like your prisoner. If you let me have a dozen commandos and a nuke, we'd—"

"Introduce modern weapons into the ancient world and you could very well alter world history. You'd kill off an enormous number of ancient people, which would cause a tidal wave in time. Even if your mission was a success, you'd come back to a radically changed world. You wouldn't recognize it as the world you left. At least that's what our best scientists believe."

Holt jabbed his cigarette at Stryker. "If the Aztecs had had modern weapons, Montezuma would have conquered Europe instead of the other way around. If Julius Caesar had had a BB gun, barbarians would've been pounding at the gates of Rome with atomic weapons a few centuries later. From the time of Christ, it took nearly a couple thousand years to get the hand-driven Gatling gun, the first efficient machine gun. And it took less than a century to go from the Gatling gun during the Civil War to the atomic bomb in the Second

World War. Under no circumstances can any modern technology be introduced into the ancient world."

Stryker nodded and kept a smile on his face. Dead eyes. False smile.

Holt felt a chill in his old bones.

41

The next morning I was taken to a second-story room that had windows overlooking the village built to look like a street scene at Teotihuacán. Caden was there, as was Holt and several people I am told were experts on the One-World. Being an "expert" on a place that they had never even visited seemed strange to me, but it was just another weird phenomenon of the underworld.

A new member of the team was introduced to me, a man named Stryker. He had been a soldier in a military unit called the navy SEALs, who swim like a fish, only with metal lungs. I had seen people on television swimming underwater with equipment. I understood that he was a superior warrior, like an Eagle or Jaguar Knight.

My impression was that he would be fast on his feet and uncompromising. He would have made a good olli player—but violent and unpredictable. If he were my opponent in a ball game, I would strike first, crippling him because he would give no quarter on the playing field.

I was glad he was on my side, but the lack of warmth in his eyes told me that he was not someone I should trust.

"You have maize porridge and dog meat in front of you. This will be a working lunch," Holt said. "I'll start at the beginning. You'll all have had a chance to walk through the village below. From now on it will be your home so you can get used to the lifestyle of the One-World. You'll only hear me in English, but other than when it's absolutely necessary, no one will speak to you except in Nahuatl." Holt gestured at Stryker. "We're making an exception for our newest member. He's getting a late start on the language, but like Tah, he's had a language chip installed that will speed up the process."

"Don't make any exceptions for me," Stryker said. "I can carry my load."

"Good. You'll need to do exactly that." Holt pointed to a pile of papers in the center of the conference-room table we sat around. "Consider that pile of papers on the table a campfire. Starting with your next meal, you'll squat down before a fire. That's how food was usually served in ancient Mexico, cowboy fashion, unless you were in a nobleman's house.

"From now on, you'll be eating, drinking, dressing, thinking, and shitting as if you were in ancient

Mexico. Native speakers of Nahuatl will be with you every moment. The most important one is sitting at this table."

He meant me.

Holt paused to cough, rub out a cigarette, and light another. "There's an old theater technique called Method acting. Some Russian guy invented it. It means the actor strives for close personal identification with the role. That's how I want each of you to approach the training you're going to get. Hands-on, personal.

"To convince others, *you'll have to think like an ancient Mexican*. Which means that you'll have to stop thinking about who you are and what you're doing. Like playing a sport, your mind and muscles must react without thinking. If a king is carried in your presence on a sedan chair and you must fall to the ground like a dog, you must do it instinctively, not think about it. The last thing you want is to be caught *acting*.

"Time walkers don't act. They become the person at the time and place they are flowing in."

Holt held up a ten-page schedule. "You'll see that over the next several weeks you'll get a full course in the roles you're to assume. Language, customs, sleeping, eating, dressing. You'll even learn the no-no's. The two of you will get practice in hand-to-hand combat with obsidian blades. Tah will do the teaching."

Holt tapped his temple. "You'll be expected to use your brain to get out of jams, not a gun. We can't expose the ancient world to modern technology—any of it. I understand that these ancient Mexicans didn't even invent the wheel, much less more—"

"That's not true," Caden said. "They didn't *use* the wheel because they had no need for it, but they understood the concept because wheeled toys have been found."

"Why didn't they have a use for it?" Stryker asked. "Weren't the Romans, Egyptians, Chinese, all those dudes, running around with chariots during the same time period?"

"They had animals to pull chariots and carts, horses, donkeys, mules, oxen, even elephants. The pre-Columbian Americas lacked those animals, not to mention that much of the terrain is jungle and mountains unfriendly to wheels."

Holt nodded, pleased. "Caden's knowledge of the history and customs is probably as good or better than that of the professors we've brought in from Mexico. And I'm sure Tah will end up teaching our set designers a few things. So don't be afraid to point out mistakes in what we've done. We put up this ancient Teotihuacán mock-up by having Hollywood set designers working with scholars. We want to refine it so you are absolutely comfortable walking down a street in the ancient world."

42

Holt introduced Caroline Wong, a woman in her forties. She was the head of Creative History, a Hollywood company that specialized in re-creating scenes from the past for Hollywood. She stood beside a large computer screen as she spoke.

"This computer is where the ancient city was born—or *revived*, I guess is a better word. Actually, two cities were created, both replicas. This is the first one." With a dramatic wave of her hand, Wong stepped aside as the screen behind her came alive. "What you are seeing is a computerized representation of Teotihuacán, filled with color and people, a city with perhaps a quarter million people, bustling with activity."

The film first showed Teotihuacán as it is presently, an ancient ruin, well preserved in the sense that its colossal pyramids still stand. Slowly, colors, buildings, and people filled the screen. The Pyramid of the Sun evolved from dull, brownish rock into a red-and-green monument. The scene expanded up and down the Avenue of the Dead. Dull, grayish brown monuments slowly rose from the earth in brilliant colors. The Temple of Quetzalcoatl took on vibrant shades of red, green, and yellow.

Incredibly real, I thought, but that was to be expected. From watching movies and TV, I had learned that these demons were capable of creating a bloodthirsty audience of thousands cheering in a Roman arena as gladiators fought, great armies clashing on darkling plains in ancient times, or a battle of spaceships a thousand years in the future. They created people, monsters, and cities that looked real. The marvels of the underworld were endless.

"The objective is to re-create history accurately," Wong said. "We don't let our imaginations run wild. The creation team included not only set designers and artists, but archaeologists, historians, and linguists. We have a good record of what Mesoamerica was like when the Spanish arrived. And we know that people lived pretty much the same at that time as they did for a couple thousand years before.

"Of course, Teotihuacán was even more advanced than the later Aztec and Mayan cultures. That's evident because the later cultures, especially the Aztec, who were in the same region as Teotihuacán, made little progress in architecture, language, weaponry, and agriculture over the inheritance from past cultures, most of which was passed down from Teotihuacán."

As Wong talked, a Nahuatl speaker, a Mexican university professor, repeated the words in the aged language as best she could, falling back to English frequently because many words were not translatable.

The scene expanded and Teotihuacán evolved into a city with thousands of structures. Homes, palaces, marketplaces, streets. And as I well know, the only beasts of burden were people with packs on their backs.

Scenes with "real" people unfolded. Conversations occurred between neighbors. Their language was not perfect, but I could understand that they talked about what people everywhere talked about—the price of corn and beans, rumors of war, the birth of a child, women preparing the cornmeal "pancakes" called tortillas, men working deerskin into a pair of sandals, a teacher with a pictograph book teaching boys.

"You approve?" Caroline asked me.

"It's close."

"Close enough to fool Jaguar Knights?" Holt asked.

I shrugged. "Close enough in a city like Teotihuacán. In a smaller community, some things would stand out."

"Like what?"

"The hands and feet of the men and women in your pictures are soft, like the ones of the people you have in the village outside. People in the One-World spend a lifetime being barefoot most of the time and using their hands constantly."

I held up my own hands.

"You have calluses and muscle development we

don't have today," Holt said. "There's nothing we can do about that. Hopefully the Feathered Serpent's minions won't think of checking hands and feet." He nodded at Wong. "Go on."

"Notice that in the marketplace there is poultry, turkeys and ducks, and vegetables—corn, beans, squash, peppers—but you won't find beef or pork, milk or cheese. The cow, pig, sheep, and goat are all Old World commodities. Potatoes were grown in South America, but made their way to Mexico circuitously after the Spanish brought them to Europe and then across to Mexico. There was no wheat, barley, rye, or other grains that are common today. The flour of the day would be cornmeal from maize.

"Mesoamerica may be the only place in the ancient world that achieved a high culture with an agriculture based on a single grain: maize. Most major cultures had a multigrain, multimeat diet. Because the people who lived away from the ocean didn't get sufficient salt from their diet, the control and sale of salt was important. Is it true that food was always eaten raw, baked, or boiled rather than fried?"

"Yes," I said.

"That was because it's difficult to fry foods which had little fat content."

Holt interrupted, "Each of you will be given a copy of this film to watch when you have free time. Even you, Tah. You check it again for errors. The copy will contain new scenes and different conversations. It's important to listen to the conversations over and over, especially the mumble of a marketplace. Hearing a foreign language in a classroom is always different than hearing it spoken naturally, especially in an old-fashioned marketplace where people get excited or agitated while negotiating. Language is where we would be most easily exposed. From what you've heard so far, what do you think, Tah? Can Caden pass muster?"

I shrugged. "There are many different tongues spoken in the One-World. She would be recognized as a foreigner in Teotihuacán, as I would be. But the city gets many thousands of visitors from distant lands, so being a foreigner will not draw attention—"

"Unless they're looking for foreigners," Stryker said.

"Hopefully they won't be looking for anyone. This mission is so secret, only a few people in the Seattle White House even know about it."

"What we must not do," I said, "is make a mistake that will bring attention to us. Anything suspicious or out of the ordinary can be taken as an offense to the gods. And an excuse to have you taken to the sacrifice line."

Caroline Wong said, "Just one more comment about language. While English is the common language of business and travel today, French used to be the lingua franca, and Latin before that. The expression *lingua franca* was originally applied to a hybrid language of Italian, Spanish, French, Greek, Arabic, and Turkish. In other words, scraps and pieces of the major tongues spoken by seafarers in the Mediterranean. I imagine that the lingua franca of ancient Mesoamerica would be a form of Nahuatl along with a little this and that."

Caroline looked to me for confirmation, and I nodded. The One-World had many languages, but Nahuatl was understood by traders everywhere.

Holt said, "The Situation Computer came up with a plan for the three of you to travel in the guise of jade merchants. Jade was chosen because it's easy to carry, yet costly. That way you'll have money to live on and to bribe your way out of trouble if you need to. Much of the jade came from Central America, the lower end of Mesoamerica, so that will give you an excuse to be foreigners on your way to Teotihuacán. What do you think, Tah? Sound like a plan?"

I thought for a moment and shook my head. "A bad plan. Jade merchants travel with large groups. Even at that, they carry jade secretly disguised as something much less valuable and have many guards. Jade would attract the attention not only of robbers, but of greedy kings and noblemen, all of whom desire it."

"Jesus," Stryker said, "so much for the computer."

"Should we use obsidian?" Caden asked.

"No, it's highly desirable. And the Feathered Serpent controls the sale of it. Besides, the city has its own supply not far away."

"What's your call, Tah? What should we use? Rubber balls?" Holt asked.

I shook my head. "I am from the People of the Rubber."

"So that would attract attention because they will still be looking for you."

I pursed my lips. "A god."

"A what?" Stryker asked.

"You mean a statue?" Caden asked.

"Yes, a small statue of a god, of wood or clay, taken to Teotihuacán to be sold in the marketplace or as a donation to the temple. No one would steal or harm such a traveler for fear of offending the god. And it has little value in terms of money."

"That's brilliant!" Caden exclaimed.

I glowed with pride.

"I have a question of you," I said to Holt. "You say you are sending us back to the One-World to kill the Feathered Serpent. How are we to kill the beast?"

"Good question. I'll let you know as soon as I know myself. I'm leaving for the capital today. I'll be getting your marching orders there."

43

Sea-Tac

Holt stared out the window of the DC-3 as it entered the greater Seattle-Tacoma airspace. Puget Sound was now surrounded by one huge metro area from Olympia to Port Townsend, all of it slums, much of it tent cities with dirt streets, cesspools, breadlines, and neighborhood water supplies that served up typhoid and cholera. It hadn't taken long to turn America from the land of the yuppie, preppie, and old-age-battling baby boomer to a third-world country. The only difference between it and the rest of the third world was that it had enough thermonuclear warheads and ICBMs to nuke the whole planet in its dying breath.

Hurricanes from the Caribbean generated winds that were capable of sending moisture almost anywhere in North America, but the farther north the moisture was carried, the less contagion traveled with it. Washington, D.C., on the Caribbean hurricane corridor that ran all the way up the East Coast, had been contaminated early on. The Sea-Tac area was a natural as the nation's emergency capital. It was the farthest point from the Gulf of Mexico in the continental United States with a major airport, nearly twenty-five hundred miles from the Gulf, and was further buffered from Gulf weather by the Rocky Mountains. The Rockies, extending for two thousand miles from British Columbia to part of New Mexico, formed the major bulwark of the Continental Divide, which separates rivers draining into the Gulf and Atlantic from those flowing toward the Pacific Ocean.

As Sea-Tac became overwhelmed by the mass exodus from the south, making it almost impossible to govern and subject to explosive, spontaneous riots, plans were first instituted to move the capital farther north to the newly conquered British Columbian city of Vancouver. When the war with Canada went guerrilla and sour, Canadian territory became too dangerous to house the capital. That left Honolulu and Anchorage as potential capitals. The Alaskan city was being readied to become the provisional capital for two reasons—Honolulu was surrounded by ocean, which would eventually be subject to the contagion as it spread, while the Arctic ice pack would be the last source of water available to the northern hemisphere.

Holt hadn't slept well—he'd drunk himself into a deep sleep with red wine and woke up after four hours, his mind on fire with an endless stream of problems and memories. He truly believed in the power of sleep learning because it was in these moments in the middle of the night he realized solutions to problems and remembered things that he needed to fill in the blanks on work done the previous day. And at these moments, he inevitably thought about his family.

Looking down at hell on earth, he once again wasn't sure the world was worth saving. As with the Flood, he wondered if it wasn't time for God to spit on the planet and wipe it clean.

He sighed and leaned back in his seat. He wasn't anxious to visit the capital. He lacked rapport with his ZSA boss, Director Carvis Muller. Holt was not Muller's choice to be brought back into government to run the Time Explorer program. Barbara Berg, the nation's president, had insisted on Holt's appointment. The reins of government had two pairs of hands on them—the president's and the ZSA director's. But the ZSA directorship was no ordinary cabinet-level position. The director had a better-equipped and better-trained military force than the regular armed forces.

With the regular military tied down fighting in Canada and with police duties in the northern sector, the ZSA's units were the nation's dominant internal military force. While the director technically only had absolute power over the Zone itself, a territory comprising about a third of the continental United States, because the Zone had a liquid border with millions of Americans illegally escaping into the northern states, his power of martial law extended everywhere in the nation. Emergency powers of the president and the ZSA director included the suspension of the court system, along with the power to arrest and imprison without recourse.

During his years in government in the past administration, in which Barbara Berg had been vice president, Holt would have been counted upon as a strong advocate of civil rights, considering the Patriot Act, passed in reaction to the threat of terrorism, as dangerous overkill, a prelude to the "national emergency powers" that had been the harbinger of tyranny throughout recorded history. But he didn't disagree with the current suspension of civil rights. The entire nation was under attack and reeling from a catastrophic invasion. Basic survival had become the categorical imperative.

Holt had worked with President Berg back in the days when he had been CIA director and she was chairperson of the Senate Select Committee on Intelligence. He knew her to be a reasonable, strong-willed woman who was not disposed to tyranny. As long as she was alive and in power.

ZSA Director Muller was a different story. Before the contagion struck, Muller had been given the job of FEMA director as a political payoff. His "experience" in government had been restricted to raising money for politicians. As the chief fund-raiser for the prior president, Muller's FEMA job, with its ability to parcel out government contracts—and get political donations to the ruling party in return from the recipients—was a plum pork-barrel assignment.

When the contagion struck, Muller's emergency powers rapidly increased until in one fell swoop the Zone Security Agency was created with the Federal Emergency Management Agency as its nucleus. All the political, judicial, and legislative authority for the contaminated region came into his hands.

Holt knew the president and her ZSA director were in a power struggle with the nation as the prize. The program Holt headed up was a critical pawn.

That the Time Explorer had opened another avenue for eliminating Quetzalcoatl made the program important. But Holt's well-honed sense of political intrigue—and political chicanery—told him that the currents of the power play over the mission back to the ancient world went beyond just another attempt at eliminating the threat.

Holt wasn't quite sure of all the nuances the Time Explorer created, but as a chess player—and political appointee—he knew that pawns could be sacrificed to gain an advantage.

A command car met his plane to taxi him to a nearby heliport. Gunships, run by the government, were the only practical way to get to the government center in Seattle. The armed chopper fleet was reserved for government officials and business executives who did government business. The fifteen-mile stretch from the Sea-Tac airport to the government center was more dangerous than a night swim in shark-infested waters. The freeway was gone in several places from Canadian missile attacks, forcing a route along city streets, not a pleasant task without a fleet of armored vehicles. Every neighborhood had its own gang and warlord collecting "tolls." If the bandits didn't get you, a mob of hungry, thirsty people were just as liable to ambush your vehicle for the water, food, and gas that might be aboard.

Like the airports in the Zone, the northern airports also had to be protected against the common person. Twenty million thirsty, dirty, sweaty people were in the immediate area . . . they all wanted a ride on a plane to take them to the last hurrah: Alaska.

A terminal building he drove by had recent bomb damage—it was still smoldering.

His driver told him, "Canadian guerrillas launched a Scud missile from somewhere near the border yesterday. Pretty good shot considering everyone says it was a rusty old missile."

War had been conducted over the eons for many reasons, and the buzz words for the war against Canada had been *carrying capacity.* It wasn't a new term, but was now one that everybody knew. Before the contagion, scientists used the phrase to describe the size of the population that could be supported by the resources of a given area. The number of living creatures— whether they be deer, bears, or humans—that a region could support was its carrying capacity.

The planet itself, under siege by massive populations and reduced water and food resources, had a limited carrying capacity.

When food or water in a region became insufficient

to support the indigenous population, a nation had two choices—die or conquer their neighbor. Canada had more food and water than was necessary to support its people. And its big neighbor to the south was hungry and thirsty.

A second catchword was *Darwinism*. Species that adapt the best to the environment had an advantage. A world with limited water meant a limited population and a fierce competition for the supply . . . with survival of the fittest.

"A bedouin can survive on a gallon a day," a scientist across from Holt on the chopper said to a companion. "Before the contagion, we used more than that to brush our teeth. The average American utilized a hundred gallons a day for personal use."

But no one now brushed his or her teeth using more than a mouthful of water—most people didn't brush at all. Unless you were high in government or industry, the water that was piped into your house was used only for showers and toilets, and you used bottled water exclusively for drinking and cooking.

What Holt found fascinating about the water crisis was that it was not really a crisis over drinking water. Only a small percentage of water was actually drunk by humans. Farms and factories went through 99 percent of the freshwater available—and people had to go thirsty so enough food could be grown and processed.

Water conservation was life conservation—consumption was much more heavily regulated and policed than illegal drugs ever were. And every effort was made to find alternative sources of water. Besides piping water down from the north and towing icebergs, a massive project was under way to build "pumping" stations that would crush arctic ice and push it down a pipeline where friction would melt it along the way.

Holt shook his head as Seattle Center—d/b/a U.S. Government Center—came into view, dominated by the Space Needle. The seventy-four-acre center of buildings and parks had entirely been taken over by the feds with the green areas turned into a tent city. A great deal of truth was in the urban legend that the site was chosen because the six-hundred-odd-feet-high Space Needle made a great lookout tower from which to watch the restless natives.

Strange new world, Holt thought. The traumatized world around him seemed almost as alien to him as Tah's encounter with the twenty-first century.

Of course, he was a first-world person in what was now a third-world country. People in Africa and most of Asia would not find a world of thirst and hunger as alien.

44

Protocol demanded that his first visit be to the ZSA director. As Holt sat on a chair in front of Muller's desk with the glare of hazy sunlight coming through a dirty window to annoy him, Holt knew it was an attempt to intimidate him because he was the president's man and not the ZSA director's. But seating a visitor to be distracted by glare through the window was a power play by the director that he used on everyone—he was notorious for ruthlessly dominating his subordinates. The chair technique was mild compared to more brutal techniques Holt had heard about. But the chair was effective to put people in their place—it kept the director in cool shadows while the visitor on the other side of the desk squirmed like a suspect being questioned under a hot, naked lightbulb by police.

So far the director had not tried heavy-handed supervision of Holt. Holt would have been more comfortable if he had. Instead the director had subtly spied on and undermined him by placing his minions such as Stryker in places of power and directing them from afar.

Holt was too old, too tough, and too mean himself to put up with silly bullshit.

He stood up. "Excuse me." He moved the chair so the sun would not be in his eyes. Muller's aide started to object, and the director gestured him to be quiet.

"Bring me up-to-date about your ancient Mexican and the preparation for the mission," Muller said.

The director was tall and padded, what doctors used to describe as "well-fed" in medical reports. Had Holt been forced to guess an occupation for the director based on his looks, he would have called him an insurance salesman or accountant, occupations that at least in Holt's mind drew people who were reasonably mild-mannered. But Muller's countenance was a deceptive veneer that concealed aggression, ambition, and cruelty. He had a quick mind, an ability to carry on a conversation in person, take a phone call, and crack orders to people around him without missing a beat.

Upon meeting him the first time, Holt decided that some of the man's abrupt body language was deliberate and tactical. By not listening to others, it made it easier for him to make up his mind early in regard to an issue and then shove his conclusion down everyone's throat.

Holt brought him up-to-date, knowing full well that Stryker and whoever else Muller had looking over

Holt's shoulder were keeping the director well apprised about the project. Holt was surprised when the director waved away aides and a phone call to listen to him.

"I understand your Neanderthal is quite a physical specimen," the director said.

It was the same characterization of Tah-Heen that Stryker had made. If Holt had any lingering doubts that Stryker was reporting to Muller, they were resolved.

"He has the speed, agility, and muscles of a world-class professional athlete without having resorted to steroids. Added to that, he's instinctively aggressive. His natural instinct in any situation where there's a possibility of being attacked is to strike first. He comes from a society in which people fight to the death hand to hand. That means the people guarding him have to be carefully trained to stay back. Security people are trained to kill with guns and protect themselves with their hands and feet. Tah's instinct is to kill with his hands and feet, as one of the therapists found out when he got too close."

Holt paused to leave an opening for Muller to insert a sympathetic remark for poor dead Dr. Zimmerman and grinned to himself when the director left the space empty.

"Tah's also smart and streetwise in his own way. Our university types are no match for him when it comes to analyzing real-life situations."

"I was surprised when you brought in a prison psychologist."

"It's a situation in which practical experience works better than book knowledge. Prisons are places where killing is done by hand or crude, makeshift weapons."

"Can he be trusted?"

It was a loaded question and the director knew it. If Holt said no, the whole mission would be in jeopardy . . . and a simple yes would raise questions about his own ability to judge the situation.

"Yes and no," he said, smothering another grin. "He's brutally honest, there's no duplicity in him, what you see is what you get. But he's also a prisoner who has been physically restrained, sometimes by inflicting pain on him. And the mental stress created by an abrupt confrontation with the modern world has to be mind-boggling. The key for him to be a good time walker is for us to trust him and him trust us. We're getting to the point where he needs to be tested to see if he will work for us—or run away."

"Good, there's an opportunity for a test. We had an informant who was persuaded to give information that the Beast was up to something, probably in New York City."

Quetzalcoatl was the Beast.

"Why New York?"

"An attempt to aggravate the effects of the contagion, perhaps get it to move faster into the northern Atlantic. Maybe because it's just a huge population center. We're not sure. The informant died under questioning before he gave us everything he might have had. All we really got from him was the word *Broad-*

way, and just before he croaked he said, 'Times Square.'"

"Obviously New York City," Holt said.

"True, but to cover our asses, while we concentrate on Manhattan, we're sending a unit to every major seaside city with a street named Broadway."

"San Francisco's risqué nightlife district is called Broadway."

"Right. We're sending a unit to San Francisco, one that we think won't find anything. But if you want to see if you can trust your Neanderthal and if he can work as part of the team, take him to San Francisco. It's a peninsula with water on three sides. He can't run far without being caught. You can use the excuse he might be needed to identify the Beast or his cohorts."

Muller got on the phone and waved Holt away, his signal to leave. Before Holt reached the door, a question from the director stopped him.

"What did you think of the colony report?"

"Colony report?"

"Maybe you weren't on the list. It's another think tank we have running, based on the assumption that we could not reverse the contagion even if we eliminated the Beast and would have to colonize."

"Colonize what?"

"The past, the ancient world, that era your Time Explorer is set to, the ancient empires in Mesoamerica, the Roman empire in Europe, the Persians, Chinese." The director waved his hands. "The whole nine yards."

"You can't colonize the past with the Time Explorer. It takes tremendous power just to send back a few people into the past—and power isn't something we have much of."

"How many?"

"How many could we send back? Hell, I don't know, at most, eight or ten at once, maybe in a month another eight or ten, maybe a total of fifty or so in a six-month period. That's assuming the device lasted."

Muller turned away without another comment, answering a call. It was another sign of dismissal.

Holt kept a blank face on his way out, certain that he would be filmed and analysts would give Muller a report on his reaction.

Holt knew that the "colony report" question had not just popped out of the director's mouth. It was dropped on him to get his reaction. He might have been testing to see if Holt had heard of the secret study . . . or to see what his opinion would be once he heard.

He kept his features passive in the elevator, but his mind was swirling with thoughts. *Colonize the past.* It wasn't the first time the idea had come up. Ever since the time-travel phenomenon had been stumbled upon, people had bandied about and theorized situations in which people from the present were sent back to the past. Holt believed Muller, Stryker, and the like suffered from *The Man Who Would Be King* syndrome. The Rudyard Kipling tale, and John Huston movie, portrayed a couple of ne'er-do-well British soldiers in

India who take over a small, remote mountain area as potentates. With disastrous consequences.

Thinking about what it would be like to go back in time armed with modern knowledge—and modern weapons—was fascinating even to Holt. But as the gatekeeper for the Time Explorer, he kept a restraint on his ambitions. And those of others.

Muller and Stryker would be prime candidates for the syndrome. They would have calculated exactly what type of modern weapons would be needed to defeat ancient armies. It wouldn't take much more than handguns and machine guns. The possession of the weapons alone would make men gods in the ancient world, where superstition was more powerful than knowledge.

Holt was sure Muller knew the answer to questions about how many people could be sent back. Knew exactly how many people and what they could take back with them. The world had changed so much, the basic technology they would need to build anything from a simple bullet to a spaceship could be taken back on an instrument the size of a pack of cigarettes.

Holt had to admit going back to a time when the basic knowledge of the average person today could make the person ruler of the world was an intriguing thought . . . he, too, could be a king. What was that other book and movie—*A Connecticut Yankee in King Arthur's Court*? A Mark Twain story, he recalled, a Bing Crosby movie. A Victorian-era blacksmith gets hit on the head and wakes up a thousand years earlier in Arthurian England. With knowledge of how to make a gun.

With a simple handgun, you could be a god in the ancient world.

"Take me to the White House," he told his golf-cart driver.

Chauffeur-driven golf carts is what the high and mighty had come down to in the small government complex.

The White House, known as the Opera House, was a hundred yards away.

45

President Barbara Berg saw him an hour later. She was thin, harried, and operating on nervous energy. She sent everyone out of the room but her two closest aides—her chief of staff, Lewis Yanusevich, and her national security adviser, John Bevard.

The moment Holt sat down, she said, "We're at war with Canada, not doing well, and it may soon develop into a world war."

"British helping the Canadians?" he asked.

"Britain, Australia, New Zealand, and France are all providing military aid. But the most serious problem is Russia. It's sending troops who are supposed to be hired mercenaries, but they're government-issued. The whole world is lining up against us. They believe we will try to dominate the world's water supply and are ganging up on us in the hopes we collapse before we can do it."

Holt had seen intelligence briefings about the war. Supported by clandestine arms shipments from nations paranoid about the intentions of the United States, the Canadians were making the invaders pay for every foot of Canadian space they occupied—and the only territory the invaders controlled was what they occupied.

"But that's not the only serious threat," Berg said. "An even more immediate threat is that we may soon be at war with Alaska."

"Christ—don't we still own Alaska?"

"That depends on who you talk to: people in Sea-Tac or in Anchorage. The truth is that the people of Alaska have more in common with the Canadians than the rest of the U.S., including the fact that both have arctic water supplies that could easily keep their societies alive a lot longer—as long as the U.S. doesn't keep grabbing the water. Alaskan paramilitary units have arisen to support the Canadian guerrillas, and there are rumors that the whole state is going to join the fight on the Canadian side."

"There can't be a hell of a lot of people up there."

"There's a hell of a lot of territory, over twice the land area of Texas, most of it wilderness. Before the contagion, the population density was one person per square mile, about six hundred thousand people for six hundred thousand square miles, while the rest of the country had about a hundred people per square mile. We don't know how many people are up there now, but there's still a lot of open territory because it's not a friendly environment for squatters, too cold, not to mention the Canadians opened fire on people pouring over the border.

"But Alaska's still the least affected region compared to the Lower Forty-eight. And they want to keep it that way, just as the Canadians do. Our whole damn army could get lost up there and die from frostbite. I'm constantly reminded that Napoléon and Hitler lost their armies to similar terrain."

Berg paused to take a drink of water. Her hand shook. Yanusevich and Bevard said nothing. Holt knew she had gone into the tirade about the northern wars for some reason.

"So what do you think?" she asked.

"I think that if we lose Alaska and Canada, at least the water we can get from them, we lose everything. Arctic water is not just liquid gold, it's lifeblood."

"And?"

"A ripple-down effect of having to expand the war in the north to include Alaska will be to increase the power of the ZSA. As you send troops to Alaska to protect the water supply, the ZSA will fill the void with its troops, just as it's doing now with so many troops occupied fighting the Canadians."

"You don't trust Carvis Muller?" President Berg asked.

Holt chortled, "Of course not, that's why you had me put in charge of the project for a mission back in time. You wanted to keep him out of the cookie jar. How long have you known about the Colony Plan?"

The president exchanged looks with her advisers and asked, "How long have *you* known?"

Holt checked his watch. "About an—"

"So he told you. You understand that crazy bastard wants to send a few dozen people back in time to take over the ancient world. He's offered me a seat on the trip."

"That's generous of him."

"Before you assume I immediately quashed the idea, you need to realize that there is a certain perverse logic to it. If the Beast makes the planet uninhabitable during our own time, we'd have a duty to go back in time and arrange things so that he doesn't succeed.

"That's what your mission is all about. But if your efforts fail and we have a chance for another mission, taking over the ancient world may be the only backup plan. It's not a trip that I would go on. Nor would I permit a bastard like Muller on it. NASA has spent decades studying what cross-section of talents would be best for a colony on Mars or one of the moons of Saturn. We'd fall back on that."

Berg paused at the look on Holt's face. "What don't you like about what I said?"

"I was just wondering about the morality of going back in time to take over the ancient world. The acceleration in technology would be phenomenal."

"The think tank I have working on it is very positive about the idea. With our knowledge about pollution and global warming that made our planet sick even before the methane crisis, we could direct technology to keep the planet green while we explore the stars."

Holt shook his head. "Those eggheads are real smart people . . . as long as they're thinking with a computer keyboard. The problem with their theory is that it doesn't take into consideration the propensity of so many humans to be warlike, greedy, self-gratifying sons of bitches. We'd end up just polluting the ancient world with political hacks who will immediately want to grab as much as they can."

"When you bring back the Beast's head on a platter, the colony idea will be shelved."

Holt shook his head. "No. You'd have to kill Muller to shelve it. He wants to play king. Maybe even more than his other plan: taking over the government."

The president smiled and left the remark hanging for a moment before she said, "Watch your back. Muller is angry that I put you in charge of the mission. He'll do whatever he can to sabotage it. And one more thing, something for you to keep in mind, drill into your head."

He raised his eyebrows. "What?"

"You're on your own. I can't help you, because if it came to a showdown with Muller, I don't have the resources to fight him. Not even he knows how stretched we are. If the Alaskan situation degrades into open civil war, I'll have to strip our defenses here to try to keep the water moving. When that happens, Muller could make his move. My only alternative is to try and keep a lid on the war with Canada, the crisis in Alaska, and him. That means I can't offer you any help, period. You have to keep the mission going. As far as I'm concerned, keeping a lid on the Zone and fighting the Beast is your responsibility. Don't fail me."

When Holt got up to leave, Bevard said to the president, "You were going to advise him about the rumors in the Zone."

"Yes, that's right. Allen, we don't know what's going on, but the horror stories about blood-drinking mutant creatures in the Zone are growing. We have information that's disturbing, reliable sources that confirm something strange is happening. And we can't get Muller to confirm or deny them. Either he's lying about it to us, for reasons we can't decipher, or his own street intelligence is bad and he doesn't want to admit it."

"We'd like you to keep your eyes open," Yanusevich said. He grinned. "While you're in Frisco, if you see any bloodsucking monsters, grab one for us."

Holt left the meeting with a phrase singing in his head that had become a mantra with him.

Strange, strange world.

BOOK IX

HELLCATRAZ

46

San Francisco

We flew on a giant flying animal to another level of hell, a place called San Francisco. My people would have called an airplane a great silver eagle, but I realized it was simply another strange servant of the underworld gods.

Caden told me the city had a famous old prison. "Inmates called Alcatraz prison Hell-ca-traz back when it was the toughest federal prison in the country. It means they thought it was real misery to be imprisoned there."

Worse than this netherworld of the restless dead that I have been imprisoned in? Iyo! This prison must be a hell of Mictlan that I have not experienced yet or even heard about, one that will test me beyond what I have already endured. And one that I must get Caden through. Her mind is strong, but unlike Ixchel, who was a ballplayer, she is not physically able to battle the demons that await us in this underworld region.

After we landed, we boarded another flying monster, this time one that looked like a dragonfly. Caden called it a helicopter, and I pretended that I knew nothing about it, but I had learned from watching TV that the dragonflies transported crews that filmed news and carried people wounded and killed in war.

I know from what I have seen on demon television that people like me are called "primitive" because we lack killing machines. They would have more respect for those of my kind if we also had great metal machines that could kill many people at the same time. The most advanced instrument of war we savages have is the atlatl, a piece of bamboo that warriors use to hurtle their spears farther. Iyo! The masters of hell have bombs that can kill millions at a time.

"We have to use the helicopter to get to our destination, Fisherman's Wharf," Caden said. "It would be pretty chaotic and dangerous to try and drive there."

We flew over a city pressed with people and buildings. The crowds below remind me of swarms of ants, but ants are cleaner and more industrious. I saw endless ransacked buildings and ragged tents, vehicles stalled on the streets, broken-down or without fuel, many of them burned, most of them occupied by squatters who crawled into anything that could be used as shelter.

I didn't need to be on the ground to know that the people would be dirty, smelly, loud, angry, and mean. Most were adults. Few appeared to be very young or very old. I had seen it all on the demon called cable news.

Below on the streets was what appeared constantly on television: violence. We flew over carnage—police shooting into rioters at a water truck. I saw men and women shooting at each other, too, while they ran and dodged in and around buildings and cars.

Caden followed my eye down to the action on the ground. "They're playing a game called Winner Take All. People get together and pile their possessions and food and water-ration cards on the ground. Then they start trying to kill each other with guns, knives, clubs, whatever they have. The last person standing wins the pile."

It didn't surprise me that they had Skull Games in hell.

"There's actually a method to the madness. There isn't enough food and water to go around, but enough for one person to survive."

"Was there ever a time when"—I almost said "hell" but caught myself—"when your world was more . . . peaceful?"

"You can't judge us by what you see today. It was different just a few years ago. We had problems, the food and peace and the good life weren't distributed evenly around the world, but despite wars, terrorism, and ignorance, progress was being made. But we will survive and rebuild."

"Were there always so few children and older people?"

"So few—no." She turned her head away, painful grief obvious in her voice.

Iyo! What had I said that caused her to become sad?

When she turned back to face me, her expression was neutral, but I could see that her eyes were anguished.

"Survival of the fittest. Children are the smallest and weakest, the least likely to get water, food, and shelter. They die first. Along with the old and sick."

As we came over the north end of the peninsula, bridges came into view that had once spanned across the bay to the city but now had gaping holes.

"The Golden Gate, Bay, and other bridges were deliberately destroyed by the ZSA to help control migration north," Holt explained. "Once we set down in San Francisco, unless you are a fish, the only way out is south, down the peninsula through fifty miles of that." He nodded down at the chaos on the streets below.

He gave me a look that I understood: *Don't run, prisoner, there is no place for you to hide!*

They had taken the shock belt off me before we boarded the plane that morning. Holt had said, "This is a test to see if you will try to escape. There are only two possible results—either you cooperate and assist us, or you run and are shot dead."

I understood perfectly. I had already been tested at the first hell and passed. Now I was to be challenged again. What the demons did not know was that this time I would not run, even if I was not to be killed, because that would mean abandoning Caden, and I was not going to let her down.

The helicopter hovered over a boulevard Holt called Broadway, going back and forth above the street as Holt and his demons looked down at it. A tall, round building called Coit Tower also drew their attention.

"I loved San Francisco in the old days," Caden said.

She talked about Chinatown, cable cars, North Beach Italian restaurants, and the flesh market called Broadway, where merchants called barkers stood on the sidewalk and shouted to lure customers in to view their stock of naked dancers.

I could have told her that I knew about the other Broadway, the one famous for theaters in the city on the Eastern Sea called New York. That city was the Teotihuacán of this world, and I had great curiosity about it.

"This mission is a waste of time," Stryker said. "The people we're looking for have to be in New York. There's a Broadway in more than one big city, but there's no Times Square anywhere else in the world."

I understood that demon master Holt was using the mission as a test for me. I found it curious that Stryker wasn't interested in seeing how I played the game in this level of hell. Wasn't he concerned about how I would play when we were teammates?

Holt directed his explanation to me and Caden. "ZSA is headquartered at the old Ghirardelli Chocolate building near where the cable cars used to turn around. The ZSA occupies the Cannery and everything else in the area. The occupation corridor extends around the whole Fisherman's Wharf area and the piers up to the point where Broadway comes into the Embarcadero. Anyone who tries to get over the barricades is shot on sight."

As we approached the area called Fisherman's Wharf, I saw islands in the bay blurred by fog.

"That's the one I told you about," Caden said, pointing to the closest island to the wharf, a ghostly hulk shadowed by the fog. A large complex of buildings sat upon it. "The old prison. Cold and damp with the reputation of a medieval dungeon."

"It's occupied by squatters," Holt said. "The Indians took it back in the sixties, after that it was turned into the biggest national-park attraction in the country. Now it's occupied by a group of religious nuts who are waiting to be beamed up on a comet."

"I wish they would take me with them," Caden said.

"Why would you want to ride a dirty snowball through space?" I asked. "You would not be able to breathe."

Caden and Holt stared at me.

I shrugged. "*Cosmos*. PBS."

47

We landed on a grassy field and were taken to rooms in a round building that Caden said used to be a place where people rented a room by the night.

"All the hotels and motels in the area are now used as barracks for ZSA troops and visitors like us."

After we ate lunch in a room called a mess hall, Caden asked me to take a walk with her.

I asked, "If it's not a mess and not a hall, why do they call it a mess hall?"

"I don't know. I guess they could also call it a commissary or dining room."

"Why don't they call it whatever it is?"

She laughed. "Tah, if you try to figure out our language, it will just get more confusing. We just accept words as we are taught, regardless of whether they make sense."

Caden had been tutoring me in English, helping me

understand words that even the magic seed they planted in my head to teach me their strange tongue didn't help with.

As we strolled along the waterfront, she said, "I loved Fisherman's Wharf in the old days. I came here when I was ten and then again on my honeymoon."

Honeymoon. I recognized the word. "You're married?"

She shook her head. "Was married. Big mistake for both of us. Careers sent him to one state and me to another, with neither of us willing to give up our career and stay home and play homemaker. I don't even know where he's at now. I don't know where most of my friends are or even if they're alive. I don't have any close family, and for the first time I think that's for the best, too."

I was relieved that she was no longer married. That saved me from having to kill her husband. Iyo! I was already thinking of how to get into her room tonight to bed her. Even hell must have some pleasures.

"Most of the places that are not physically occupied by the ZSA have been destroyed by riots, fire, and earthquake." She pointed to the debris left behind by the disasters. "Along here were the older restaurants and stands where you could get a crab sandwich. There"—she pointed at the burned hulk of a more modern building—"they baked what they called San Francisco sourdough bread. Something about the air, the bay, the ocean, whatever, gave the yeast used in baking bread a unique sourdough flavor."

She grabbed my arm and groaned. "Oh, Tah, I wish you could have tasted a fresh crab sandwich made with real San Francisco sourdough bread. It was delicious."

We were being followed by two men with rifles. She saw me staring at them. "Don't worry, they're your guards. They'll make sure no one harms you."

I shook my head. "Prison guards. Doing time. Solitary confinement. The hole. Supermax. *Escape from Alcatraz*. The Rock. The slammer. The big house. Up the river."

She started laughing. "They didn't know what they were doing when they let you watch TV. You're learning much faster than they realize. Your progress reminds me of an old movie."

"I know the movie. *The Man Who Fell to Earth*, 1976. David Bowie. He watched six or seven TVs at the same time. Male and female full frontal nudity. They captured him and put him in a hell at the end. He shouldn't have trusted the demons who pretended to be his friends. I watched it three times."

"A couple years ago, I would have told you not to bother watching TV, that there were over a hundred channels and nothing to watch. People used to call TV things like the great wasteland and the boob tube. But now that the whole world's turning into a great wasteland, being a couch potato and watching reruns of old movies and TV shows is mentally healthier than stepping outside and facing a damaged world."

She unfolded papers. "A ZSA officer gave me this pamphlet about the history of Alcatraz."

I leaned close and could smell her rose scent as we walked along, and she led me through the writing on the papers. While I had learned enough of the strange tongue called English to speak to others and understand them, my ability to read and write the language was primitive. That was what they called my ability back at the science facility where I had come awake in a clear plastic bubble: primitive. And what would they have called their inability to read and write *my* language?

I followed along, more interested in the smell of her perfume than the words she wanted me to read silently as she spoke them aloud. She soon realized I wasn't reading.

"All right then, let me tell you the history. It went from being an early military fort to a federal prison and finally a tourist attraction. Many infamous people had lived on the Rock: murderers, a birdman named Robert Stroud, Al Capone—who had run something called the Chicago mob—Machine Gun Kelly, and others who liked to shoot people."

"Why are so many of your people's heroes violent?" I asked.

"What do you mean?"

"Your television and movies, they are almost always about people who do violence to other people. Violent criminals kill people, violent police kill criminals. Sometimes it's hard to figure out who is supposed to be good. Like this paper with words on it. It boasts of all the terrible people who lived on an island

which was a fortress for war and a prison to hold killers. That's mostly what your television is about . . .
people hurting people."

"But they get caught."

I shrugged. "Not all the time. And the people who
catch them are often almost as bad. Even if they get
caught, it's only after they are permitted to hurt people. In the One-World, the strongest people are the
most admired, but they must also give homage to the
gods and not steal or hurt people for the sake of hurting them."

Caden shook her head. "Tah, I can't explain what we
are. You came from a culture in which the physically
strongest were the leaders. We rely on brains, but now
that everything has gone to pieces, it's too often the
physically stronger who control things, just as it is in
your time. As I told you earlier, the strongest survive."

We went a little farther to a set of buildings. Much
of it was debris and rubble, but the heart of the structure had recent repairs that made it usable again.

"This was Pier Thirty-Nine, a big tourist attraction
in the old days. It's where you bought a ticket for the
Alcatraz tour. Pier Thirty-Nine was fun, but more
modern than the rest of the wharf. It lacked the wonderful tacky old ambience."

We entered and she said, "It's looks like it's a rec
area now."

" 'Rec area'?"

"Recreation area, a place for the soldiers to come
and relax. They play these electronic games—"

"What's this?" I went to a long, narrow table that had six holes and colored balls on it.

"A pool table."

"A table with water?"

"That's a different kind of pool. I don't know why they use the word for the game."

I handled a ball. It looked like a highly polished stone. I liked the smooth, solid, round feel of it in my hand.

"That's the eight ball. I think if it goes into a pocket too soon, you lose."

I stuck the ball in my pocket and wandered around the rec area as Caden stopped to play an electronic game. The sounds of guns firing, people shouting and screaming, came from the machine, and she walked away from it. "I don't know why people would play that game; all they have to do is walk a little ways and they can see all the killing they want."

When we went back outside, the two armed guards following us were smoking cigarettes nearby.

She went over to look at a boat docked nearby as I wandered around. I stopped and attempted to read a set of fire-scorched wood signs that Caden had earlier said advertised the tour of Alcatraz that was once offered. I slowly sounded out the words in an attempt to comprehend what they said. From our discussion about the pamphlet, I recognized that WELCOME TO THE ROCK in faded red letters was a greeting.

Drawings of the buildings and prisoner caves called cellblocks filled one side of the sign. I studied that, interested mostly so I could discuss the geography with Caden, who had enjoyed her visit to the place before she died and descended into hell.

She returned as I was studying the sign and said, "Com'on, I'll show you a big old fishing boat that sank and is still visible underwater."

"Is Alcatraz part of Manhattan?" I knew about Manhattan. Good cops, bad cops, crazy murderers, and boasting billionaires from the heavily populated, tiny river island were popular on television.

"Manhattan? No, Manhattan's another island, three thousand miles from here. Why?"

"When Holt and Stryker were talking, they said there was a Broadway but no Times Square here."

"That's right, Broadway is a street that crosses Times Square in Manhattan. There's a Broadway in San Francisco, but no Times Square."

"Alcatraz has both."

"There are no streets on Alcatraz."

I pointed to the words *Times Square* and *Broadway* on the map of Alcatraz.

"Oh my God."

48

"The long hallway at Alcatraz prison between B and C cellblocks was called Broadway by the prisoners," Holt announced to his underling demons in a conference room that had a large window with a view of the prison island. "Alcatraz's Broadway corridor ended up in front of the dining hall. They called that area Times Square."

I could see that the god was not happy with his lesser demons about the discovery of the location. He gestured at me and Caden.

"And this bit of absolutely critical information wasn't provided by the finest military intelligence on the planet, not by billion-dollar situation computers that can calculate the weight of a planet in less than a second, not even by the think-tank geniuses who slake their thirst with the government dole of clear, cold aqua pura." He slammed his fist on the table. "It was discovered by some guy two thousand years old and who is probably the equivalent of a high school dropout."

I had never thought about being two thousand years old. I tried to remember if I had learned from TV what a high school dropout was. I supposed the god was flattering me.

"It's a freaky coincidence," a man named Kordian said.

I knew from the way he was treated when he walked into the room that, like Holt, he was a god and not simply a demon. The two gods were obviously not on friendly terms. When I asked Caden who he was, she said Kordian was the ZSA officer in charge of the San Francisco region and that he resented Holt invading his territory.

"It's pretty obvious that the information our investigators obtained refers to the Broadway and Times Square in New York," Kordian said. "Our people are following up the leads there. There's no reason to believe that this isn't just a fluke."

"I was sent to investigate a link between the information drawn from the informant and this city. It's obvious that there's more of a link than ZSA headquarters realizes." Holt paused to let it sink into Kordian's mind that he himself was the reason for headquarters' ignorance. "My assignment came directly from Carvis Muller. I don't argue with his commands. If you want to argue with him, I'll be glad to—"

Kordian shook his head vigorously. "We don't want to bother the director." He spread his hands on the table. "But I don't have men to spare for a mission. I have a unit trapped between two warring street gangs—I'm talking about gangs with over five thousand combatants each. Besides, the island's socked in with fog, we can't get choppers in. Tomorrow—"

Holt interrupted, "You have boats here and a dock there. We're wasting time talking about it. Stryker has ten men, we can do it with that, it's a small island. You just have to stand by with a backup squad in case we need it."

Holt gestured at an elderly man who appeared worse for wear standing at the back of the room. He was thin, emaciated from too much of the underworld's alcoholic beverages and too little food. From watching television, I knew that before the contagion, cities had homeless people who dressed from trash bins and thrift stores. Now most people looked like street trash.

"This is Bob Gleason. He was with the last batch of prisoners on Alcatraz when the prison was closed in 1963. Mr. Gleason was a young man at the time, the youngest prisoner on the island, but he tells me that his memory of the island is still sharp. It must be . . . until the contagion, Mr. Gleason was a guide working on the island for the National Park Service. Mr. Gleason . . ."

The old man stepped forward. "I can tell you about the island."

"Tell us."

"It wasn't built regular, more kind of honeycombed."

He blinked at the assembly. "You know what I mean? Rooms and corridors all over, not all in a straight line. One passageway leading into two more, and two splitting into four and crisscrossing and hell . . ." He threw his hands up in the air. "Pretty soon a bloodhound would get lost. There's old cellblocks, interrogation rooms, the hole—that's solitary confinement. Just like today, you get put in the hole for being a troublemaker. Sometimes just mouthing off to the guards can do it. You know what I mean?"

Gleason looked around and got a couple nods that seemed to satisfy him that the people in the room were following his lecture.

"Cells nine to fourteen in D Block were called the hole," Gleason said. "No windows, solid doors, steel walls, real cold concrete with just one light, and when they turned it off, you got no sound, no light, no nothing. You know what I mean? When there's nothing, it's real scary. Even with prisoners on mainline, we didn't get no visitors in person. Had to talk to visitors on telephones while looking through a thick sheet of glass. No touching, and the guards could listen to the calls."

"Tell us more about the layout," Holt said.

"The cells are still there. 'Bout ten feet long, less than five feet wide, no bigger than a closet. Real cells, not the hotel suites with television and crappers with seats on them that the prisoners got today."

Mr. Gleason was experiencing what people in this hell called fifteen minutes of fame.

"After they closed the prison, I was hired on as a

maintenance man because it was hard to get workers to live out there. The place is kind of spooky. All that fog and wind and being stuck there. But I was used to being stuck, you know what I mean? The job didn't pay much and you couldn't even buy a cup of coffee out there, but I was used to being shutdown, being in prison and all most of my life. I spent—"

"Tell us about the prison," Holt snapped.

"Sure. That's what I'm doing. When the hundreds of prisoners and guards were gone, you could get lost wandering around alone. They could look for someone in the prison for a month of Sundays without finding them. That's how we got away from doing too much work.

"When they made it a tourist attraction, I became a guide 'cause I knew the prison and its history better than anyone. And many a guide reported hearing voices . . . ghost voices. They heard screams and pleas for help from prisoners."

"There were still prisoners?" Caden asked.

"No . . . they were long gone. It was the screams and pleas of prisoners that had died on the Rock."

Gleason's story failed to bring the reaction from the people in the room he expected. "I knew all about the ghosts because they started making noises after the prison was shut down. I can tell you—"

"You're going to do more than tell us, Mr. Gleason. You're going to show us."

"Show you? I'm not going out to the Rock. There's

not just ghosts out there. I hear there's squatters who are so thirsty, they drink your blood."

"Where'd you hear that?" Holt asked.

Something in his voice caused me to perk up.

"Just . . . just around, you know, just around. But I ain't going back out there."

"You're going out with us if we have to hog-tie you. If you cooperate, you'll get a ride both ways. If you don't . . . you do swim, don't you?"

Holt nodded at Caden and me. "You two are excused for the time being. If we find anyone suspicious on the island, we'll bring them back to see if they look familiar to Tah."

As we left the building, Caden took my arm. "Let's take a walk along the wharf. I'm too antsy to go back to my room."

Fog had thickened on the bay, cloaking Alcatraz Island even more. A chill was in the air. Caden pulled up the collar on her jacket and stuck her hands in her pockets as we walked along the wharf.

I sensed something different and looked behind us. The two guards who always followed us were not there.

"They're probably in the break room and don't realize we left the building," Caden said.

It felt good to know that no eyes were behind me watching my every move. And to be alone with Caden. She was the first woman I was attracted to that

I felt comfortable with. I had been infatuated with Ixchel, but she was a woman I wanted to bed, not love. With Caden I felt not only lust but a warm feeling. I wanted to hold her, protect her.

She suddenly stopped, her eyes searching my face. "We've been really unfair to you, haven't we, Tah?"

"What do you mean?"

"You were jerked out of your world. Did you have family? A wife? Children?"

I shook my head. "My uncle was my only family left. No wife."

"A girlfriend?"

I hesitated. "Someone I was fond of, but not to spend the rest of my life with."

"What are your regrets? There must be some."

"I have many regrets. To be alive again, in a place where the air and water are not dirty, where people don't stink. But my biggest regrets are two people who I should have killed."

She shook her head and stared at me quizzically. "I don't think that failing to murder others is a good reason for remorse."

"Not murder, what you would call an execution. Xipe, the Flay Lord, and Zolin, who betrayed my father, are still in the One-World. They eat and sleep and enjoy great luxuries. I will not have peace until they are both dead."

"I don't believe in revenge."

I shrugged. "I don't believe in getting away with murder."

"Okay. Let me show you that sunken fishing boat."

We were walking along the waterline when three men examining a box by a boat with its engine idling next to the wharf suddenly turned on us. One swung an object at me I recognized to be a stick they called a stun gun. I jumped back and kicked his arm, knocking the pain-giving weapon out of his hand. Crouching low, I leaped at him and struck him with my hip, sending him flying off the wharf. The other two men had grabbed Caden and pulled her into the boat.

I jumped onto the boat's deck, hitting with my feet and flying into one of the men with my shoulder, knocking him back. Another man jumped onto my back and I threw myself backward to smash him against steel trim. He yelled with pain and let go.

I spun around to battle the third man and came face-to-face with Caden holding a stun gun. She jabbed the weapon at my stomach and pulled the trigger.

I screamed in pain and blacked out.

49

When I awoke from the dark place where the touch of the stun gun had sent me, I was lying on my side against a hot wall. My head felt as if Xolotl had used it as a skull ball in a game on the celestial field. As I looked and listened and felt vibrations against my body, I realized I was not on a boat but in an airplane.

My hands and feet were tied with the strong gray material called duct tape. I could twist and even roll, but not move my limbs.

I lay still in the dark and listened to the raspy hum of propellers. I was on my to way to another level of hell, another challenge, of that I was certain.

The sound of voices from somewhere in the airplane reached me. I couldn't make out the words, but I was sure one of the voices belonged to Caden. Was she being tortured? Killed? I had to save her. She had disabled me with the stun gun, but I realized that she must have hit me by accident instead of the man I was struggling with. There was no other explanation for her striking me down.

Struggling to free myself was useless. I knew the sturdy tape was a favorite material that murderers and kidnappers used to bind the hands and feet of their victims. I thought about the ways I had seen the victims escape on TV. A sharp object to rub against was the tool they always used.

I wiggled around and stretched my neck, but I didn't make out anything in the darkness that had a sharp edge.

The floor was cold, and the heater that ran along the base of the plane wall felt good. I relaxed and leaned against the warmth, again thinking about the tape. I could tell it was a bit flexible, a little like rubber, enough to give me an idea. I strained against it with all my strength, trying to pull my hands apart, but I wasn't able to stretch the material enough to slip free.

My arms and legs cramped and began to hurt. The cold floor added to my discomfort. I had slipped away from the heater in my struggles, and now I positioned myself back against it. When we applied heat to finished rubber, the material softened and became more pliable.

Moving from side to side, I rolled until I was on my right side and wiggled back until my hands were against the heater. The metal was warm, but not hot enough to burn my skin.

Let it stretch like your rubber, I pleaded to the god of the weeping-women trees.

As I rubbed the tape that bound my hands against the heat and metal, straining to pull my hands apart, my heart began to pound and my breathing came heavy. Iyo! I was no longer the champion of the ball court, no longer the player who could challenge the gods themselves. I felt weak, like an old woman crippled from age, an old man who could no longer control his flow . . . *aaak!* I pulled and pulled and . . . failed.

My hands were still bound. The heater was not hot enough, my power not great enough. Then I lay perfectly still, trying to breathe quietly and not signal to my captors that their victim had been exerting himself.

I couldn't stretch the material. It had to be cut. The only cutting tool I had was my teeth. With my hands tied behind me, I couldn't get the tape to my teeth. Not by the power of my arms. As Vuk would say, the movement had to come quietly from within, not as an exertion of brute force. The duct tape was stronger than me, so I had to think my way to victory—I had to trick it into setting me free.

I relaxed my body, letting my muscles go limp, hoping to find the power that Vuk said would come from within me.

Training to play olli had given much flexibility to my arms and legs. Now I used that motion as I slowly slipped my bound hands down the back of my legs. Iyo! The heels of my shoes stopped me. Twisting my body more, I was able to get my fingers on one shoelace, then the other, pulling the knot loose. Scooting my heels on the floor, I kept drawing them back until I pulled off one shoe, then the other.

When my shoes were off, I strained and wiggled until I pulled my bound wrists over my rear and down behind my legs. Pulling my knees back to my chin and pointing my toes up, I slipped my wrists over my feet.

I stared in amazement: my wrists, bound with gray tape, were now in front of me.

I quickly gnawed through the sticky tape until I was able to break it.

When my hands were free, I shut my eyes for a moment to relax my mind. I felt as exhausted as if I had just played a championship ball game.

Listening to the voices, I was certain that one of them was Caden's. A surge of rage and lethal power flowed through me as I got up.

It was time to make my way through this hell to the next level . . . and to take Caden with me.

Holt stood on the deck of the *Pike*, a rust bucket that had once been a proud eighty-six-foot Coast Guard cruiser, as it plowed against the current to Alcatraz. He had Stryker and ten men with him. Kordian claimed he was sending reinforcements to back him up, but Holt distrusted everything the man said—and promised.

Holt wasn't as convinced as everyone else that Tah and Caden were on the island. The boat that took them headed in that direction, but disappeared in the fog. Why they would be kidnapped just to be taken to a nearby island where they could easily be rescued, or their bodies found and the culprits arrested, didn't make sense to him. But it had to be checked out. He commandeered the rusty tub as soon as he'd vented his anger at Kordian for the stupidity of the guards who hadn't followed their two charges. The guards claimed they had been deceived by a phony "officer" who told them they were being relieved. Holt ordered them arrested.

Dumb bastards.

The wino had slipped away, too, more scared of returning to the island than punishment for failing to cooperate.

Holt suspected that Kordian had kidnapped the two, on orders from Carvis Muller. The ZSA director wanted to see the mission fail so he could launch his colonization of the ancient world. The temptation to play king in the ancient world was too much for men like Muller, who would be ankle-biters in a free-for-all competitive environment but bloomed in the bureaucratic jungle of big government.

Night was falling, gray, damp, and chilly, as the old cruiser bumped up to the rotting dock at Alcatraz.

Creepy, Holt thought. The place looked abandoned. Where were the comet-loving squatters?

Stryker divided the squad into two units, and Holt moved along with one toward the brooding hulks of buildings. He was about to enter a building when he saw blood on the wall. And a severed hand on the ground.

The five-man squad had already moved inside and he followed. In the building the squad split into two and three-man units, each taking a different path. Holt followed behind the two-man—actually a man and a woman—unit. He understood why the old wino had described the place as a maze.

Holt never gave much thought to the supernatural. He spent too much time dealing with the bizarre daily. But as he walked down interior corridors and cellblocks, he felt a strange phenomenon come over him.

A haunting.

Thousands of prisoners—murderers, thieves, rapists, sadists, social misfits—had over the decades left something behind in the prison. Not a physical object, but a tiny bit of their unsavory character . . . as if the walls had soaked in their essence and were contaminated by their sins.

Shivering from the cold and the unknown, he walked along dark, creepy corridors. The supermax of its day.

Flashlight in one hand, gun in another, Holt made his way into the maze. When he saw the sign for Broadway, he swept his flashlight around and realized he was alone. Then he saw the people in the cells.

Perhaps *people* wasn't the right word. The dead were no longer people, just bodies. When Jane or John Does die, their spirit escapes but the body stays behind. *The body of Jane Doe* was the expression.

Holt cast his light down the cellblock.

Bodies were strapped to the bars. Dead. Mutilated. Pale as ghosts.

Motherfucker.

No blood, he thought. *They had sucked all the blood out.*

He knew who *they* were. What had Yanusevich said in the capital? Grab a bloodsucking monster if he saw one. He hadn't seen the monster, but he had seen the victims. Throats ripped. Blood drained.

That's why none of the island squatters had been out at the dock to meet the boat. And they wouldn't meet the next comet coming by, either. They were rotting corpses, destined for a mass grave, the standard burial in a society where so many people died that it was hard for the living to keep up with burials.

It occurred to him that maybe the maniacs who did the killings didn't actually drink the blood. The Feathered Serpent demanded blood for sacrifice.

He heard a murmuring . . . a low, guttural sound that grew louder and sounded gleeful. Forms appeared in the darkness. He couldn't make out details, but knew they were human. At least they had arms and legs.

Someone—something—flashed by him. A dark thing in the darkness. A creature of the night leaving behind the stench of curdled blood.

Then there were more of them. Coming at him.

He fired. His automatic pistol boomed, and the sound ricocheted off the concrete walls, floor, and ceiling, a reverberating echo.

He didn't know if he hit anything until a clawed

hand almost ripped into his arm and he shot the owner in the face.

Someone grabbed him from behind and he fired down over his shoulder, sending bullets into his attacker's chest.

The lost patrol was suddenly beside him, the two soldiers opening up their weapons and lighting up the corridor with their fire. An attacker ripped open the throat of the male soldier and had its grotesque face blown away.

The rest of the battle was a blur to Holt—more troopers came and opened fire and the creatures evaporated into the darkness. The troops went after them, and Holt did a search for his two protectors.

From a window in a guard tower, he saw another rust-bucket Coast Guard cruiser docked and a ZSA trooper standing guard on it. And soldiers disappearing into a building that he knew led to a basement tunnel and to a boat dock on the other side of the island. Kordian's help had arrived . . . but was busy with some other aspect of the mission.

Instincts honed from decades on the back streets of rogue cities told Holt that something was wrong.

He made his way to lower levels and followed a tunnel with several inches of seawater in it to the dock on the east side of the island. Facing away from San Francisco, activities on it couldn't be seen from the ZSA base at Fisherman's Wharf.

He watched as cloaked figures—he was certain they were Nawals—boarded a powerful speedboat. A leisurely escape, protected by ZSA troops. Holt recognized the officer in charge as an aide-de-camp to Kordian.

Holt was still watching as Stryker came up beside him.

"Did you see them?" Holt asked.

Stryker raised his eyebrows. "Them?"

Holt nodded. It wasn't any use to say any more. He knew exactly where Stryker stood.

"Any sign of your two protégés?" Stryker asked.

Holt shook his head. As he walked away, he realized that if he hadn't left the Broadway–Times Square area before Stryker arrived, he might have been killed . . . by friendly fire.

Kordian didn't have Tah and Caden. Holt was reasonably sure of that from Stryker's attitude.

So where were they?

He decided it was time for a call to Sea-Tac. He had a couple questions that needed answers, and the president was the only one who could provide the information.

BOOK X

THE BANANA
REPUBLIC

50

I made my way in the plane toward the sound of the voices. One thought dominated my mind: *Save Caden.*

A great rage inside me was ready to burst out. I was no longer Tah-Heen, the greatest ballplayer in the One-World, the champion of the game of life and death, a player who could challenge the gods. I was a ghost fighting my way through all the levels of hell, but not just to succeed so my soul could be extinguished. Now I had found another purpose.

The voices came from the other side of a metal door. I ran at it, crashing against it with my shoulder. The door flew open and I burst into the room. A man standing up and two men seated stared at me in surprise. Caden was in a seat on the other side of the men.

The standing man started to say something and I kicked him in the knee and smashed his face with my elbow. I grabbed another man, jerking him out of his seat, but Caden began screaming, "Stop! They're friends."

She grabbed my arm and I froze as I held the man by the throat, ready to smash his face.

"They're friends," she said again.

"How can they be friends? They kidnapped us."

"They—they—it was pretense, playacting. They were only pretending."

"Pretending?"

"Let me go, you bastard," the man I held said. "We were pretending."

I smacked him in the face. He went down, clutching his bleeding nose.

"Pretend that doesn't hurt," I said.

She started to cry and choked it back. "Please, Tah, you have to let me explain. No one means you harm. We wouldn't have hurt you. Please let me explain."

The third man was curled up against the plane wall, frozen with terror. They had water and I grabbed the bottle and sat down, taking a big drink. After I emptied the container I threw it across the plane.

"Explain," I said, my mind swirling, my heart pounding. Caden had been ready to cry. Now I felt like crying. Or killing. I wasn't sure which way my ollin would take me. Caden had conspired to have me kidnapped, tied up like an animal to be slaughtered? Was she my enemy?

I would give her a chance to explain before I killed her. Killed them all.

She sat down across from me. Her body shook. The third man was still pressed into the corner, staring at me as if he were cornered by a wild animal. The other two men were down, one stirring silently, the other whimpering.

"You should dedicate that blood to the gods," I said, "instead of whimpering."

A woman in a uniform stuck her head out of the cockpit. She gaped at me and disappeared when Caden waved her away.

Caden started to say something, then jumped up. "I have to help them."

I sat quietly and drank more of their water as Caden made the frightened man get up and help her assist the fallen men. When the three men were upright but still cowering, she sat back down and faced me. "I'm so sorry, Tah. It was necessary. You must think I am a terrible person."

I shrugged. "I am thinking many things." I nodded at the window. "A strange plane. I have seen many on television, but not this one."

"It's an old Osprey. Half-helicopter, half-airplane. The two props can swivel to provide direct lift off the ground or level thrust down a runway."

"A bird that can fly many ways." I wondered . . . if I threw them all off the Osprey, how would I fly it?

"These men," I said, "they are not ZSA."

"Yes. How do you know?"

"They smell thirsty." I also knew that they were not blood drinkers, not servants of the Flay Lord.

She glanced at the men. "Yes, their skin is dry, prematurely cracked. From not enough water. When people dehydrate over a long period of time, their skin becomes dry and wrinkled from a lack of moisture." She touched her cheek and smiled wanly. "I suppose I smell thirsty, too."

She smelled like a flower, but at the moment I didn't want to think about that.

"Tah, you look like a caged animal ready to break out and kill us all. You need to relax. We're thousands of feet in the air."

I smiled. "It will be a long way down for all of you."

"You're thinking I've betrayed you. I haven't. We're as much victims in this as you are."

"Why have you done this?"

She appeared to give my question much thought before she answered, "To help the people of America and Mexico who are dying, the ones in the rest of the world who soon will be dying. Holt has admitted that the contagion is caused by the Feathered Serpent. We believe the Beast is an alien, an extraterrestrial. Do you understand what I mean?"

"I know. Sigourney Weaver would have made a great ballplayer, like my friend Ixchel. She killed the alien. Three times. ET call—"

"Okay, you have the idea, but we think the alien we're dealing with is more like Sigourney's than the cuddly little guy who needed to call home."

"The Feathered Serpent came from the sky, like the man who fell to Earth, ET—"

"Yes, the legend is of a fiery god flying across the sky. But that's not what our government is telling the world. They're still claiming that the contagion was caused by an earthquake. Why keep secret that it's caused by a monster, alien or not? Why would they lie to the world?"

I shrugged. "Because they are the government?"

"*Because they're conspiring with it.* Something more is going on than what they're telling us, something they know we'd rebel against if we knew the truth. It has to be awfully bad, Tah, when the truth is more devastating than a disaster that threatens the survival of the whole world. That's why we're fighting them—the government, the cover-up."

"You and these men?"

"And many more like us. It's an organization of people who believe they were abducted by aliens. We call ourselves Frogs because those are the little animals that were traditionally dissected in biology classes in school."

I didn't know what she meant about Frogs, nor did I know what to think about cover-ups, but it was not the first time the people in this strange world had left me puzzled. Caden had allied herself with others to get through the nine regions of hell. But after seeing the mettle of her three companions, I would continue to go it alone . . . and it would be better for Caden to come with me. Her companions would not have survived more than seconds as ballplayers.

"You do understand, don't you, Tah?"

"Of course. It is elementary, my dear Watson."

"Las Vegas," Caden told me a few minutes later. "We're going to Las Vegas."

She had left her seat to help nurse her friends and returned after the bleeding had stopped. The whimperer still complained that his nose was busted. If I had killed him, I wouldn't have to listen to the whining. Was I slowing down?

After watching TV for months, I knew about Las Vegas, but I wasn't aware of what it was like since the contagion had erupted. "What's in Las Vegas?"

"Everything bad. It's a cesspool where all the rot in the Zone has drained into. It's a home for murderers, thieves, and thugs. They used to call the place Sin City, but now it should be Murderville. It used to have a bunch of big casinos lining the boulevard. Nearly two million people lived in the area, but when the Colorado River and Lake Mead went red, all but a few thousand people died or fled north. There's enough water in the valley to support a few thousand—"

"There's twenty thousand," interrupted the man who had earlier crouched frightened in the corner. He now had the courage to sit down near us. "That's our carrying capacity. We have zero population growth. If someone has a baby, someone else has to die . . . real quick."

"The old casino buildings were taken over by gangs of squatters—"

"Survival of the fittest," the man said, "with the cream rising to the top."

"At the top of the crud are gang leaders. They call themselves warlords and their casinos city-states. They wage wars against other casinos for fun."

"Not for fun. The wars are for zero population growth. They know exactly how many people need to die each month so the rest of them have enough water to survive. To meet their quotas, they have friendly wars."

"Ah," I said. "Flower wars is what my people call them."

"They're murderers and thugs," Caden said. "Not even the ZSA wants to deal with them, so they stay clear."

"I know about Sin City. I've seen *Casino*, *Leaving Las Vegas*, *Fear and Loathing in Las Vegas*, *Viva Las Vegas*. I like Elvis best." I started singing and rocking to the tune.

I stopped as she broke out laughing. "Tah, take my word for it, you will never make it as an Elvis impersonator."

"Why are we going to a place you say is so bad?"

"Koji Oda."

"What is that?"

"An enigma. A mystery wrapped in a puzzle."

I shook my head. "I don't understand."

"Water. That's the word that comes to mind when

scientists talk about Koji Oda. He's an astrobiologist. Like me, his specialty is water, studying it on Earth, finding it on Mars, on Enceladus, Saturn's moon, Jupiter's moon Europa."

"He's a scientist?"

"Yes, but unorthodox, somewhat New Age. Too much spirituality and metaphysics for traditional scientists. Most scientists think they know everything, that they can find all answers under microscopes and in lab tubes. Koji knows there are places that science has never gone—and never will unless scientists use more imagination."

I felt my anger rising. "Is he your husband?"

"God no! I mean . . . Tah, Koji is like a brother or a priest."

Ah . . . no doubt a high priest like the Flay Lord. "So why is he in Las Vegas?"

"Because the warlords who run the Banana Republic can protect him on a quid pro quo basis."

She saw that she had lost me. "The Banana Republic is what they call Las Vegas now. It used to be a term applied to Central American republics that changed dictators frequently. It got passed onto Las Vegas when independence from the United States, or the Zone, to be more accurate, was declared in a clothing store of that name in a casino shopping area.

"I told you that gang leaders we call warlords took over casinos and battle each other. Koji also has a casino, at least part of one. The Stratosphere, a high tower. The other warlords don't bother him because he produces food they badly need."

"How does he do that?"

"You'll see. That's where we're headed, for the Stratosphere on the old Las Vegas Strip. It's not going to be easy. There's no longer an airport, so we have to land on a piece of freeway. After that we have to make our way through the mobs to the Stratosphere."

Las Vegas. The Strip. Another level of hell.

51

Holt used his secure satellite phone to call Bevard, the president's national security adviser, in Seattle. Talking as he walked along the wharf with a hands-free attachment to his ear, a scarf covered the bottom half of his face to protect against the cold—and to avoid his being spied on by long-range sound equipment or lip readers.

Bevard listened quietly as Holt described what had occurred at Alcatraz. After Holt finished, Bevard said, "ZSA troops providing an honor guard to the Feathered Serpent's lunatic soldiers. That's what you're telling me?"

"That's what I saw."

"Perhaps an arrangement had been made to release hostages."

"The hostages had already been released . . . to hell."

"This is a very complex situation, full of political nuances that—"

"Cut to the chase, John. What's going on?"

No answer came from Bevard's end. After listening to the sounds of silence for a moment, Holt said, "I see. Muller's made himself king of the Zone."

"It's a Mexican standoff, a confrontation neither side can win. If the president does battle against the Zone forces, everyone will lose."

"There's nothing we can do?"

"We've been working frantically from day one to develop a methane-eating bacteria strain that's immune to the disease the Feathered Serpent has created. Our people have succeeded."

"We can reverse the contagion?" Holt asked.

"If we move quickly. Each day gets closer to the tipping point when it'll be too late. But we have to stop the Feathered Serpent first because it may be able to create a mutation that's immune to our cure."

"How about nuking it? We have bombs that could take out places a thousand times bigger than Teotihuacán."

"Because we can't guarantee the Beast will be there. Muller says it moves around constantly. And we only have one chance. Right now the thing is slowly killing the world. If we try to kill it and miss, our take is that it'll wipe out most of the world. It was satisfied with a small piece of our planet in the ancient world. Maybe large territorial possessions create logistical problems for it. We're afraid that no matter what deal we make, it plans to kill off most human life anyway."

"Muller has cut some sort of deal with the Feathered Serpent," Holt said. A guess on his part, but it fit the Zone director's character.

"We think there's a problem at the Time facility."

Holt felt his soul go cold. "What kind of problem?"

"We think the Explorer's been used."

"Used for what?"

"We don't know. Communications with the facility went dead. And there was a tremendous power surge. We don't know if Muller's pulling something. Or—"

"If the Feathered Serpent's at the controls. Jesus. What about Tah and Caden? Did you have any satellite images tracking them? Were they taken to Santa Fe?"

"Las Vegas was their destination. Space command tracked a plane, an old Osprey that took off from the old Oakland airport about the right time."

"Muller's—"

"Not Muller," Bevard said. "Frogs."

Frogs. Holt knew what he meant. The secret society had been around a long time. "There are Frogs in the Banana Republic?"

"A big, croaking one. The biggest. Koji Oda, the water guru. You know who he is?"

"I've heard the name, yeah. Reminds me of the little guy from *Star Wars*."

"Japanese scientist. Once was a NASA astrobiologist. Thinks water is living stuff, that Earth's a big bug flying through space, carrying us with it like a bunch of fleas. He's the leader of that bunch of crazies. You probably dealt with them when you were CIA director."

"It's a matter of statistics," Holt said. "There's always two or three percent on the lunatic fringe. Back in the better-dead-than-Red days, they were the people preparing to defend Denver from parachuting commies. They eventually evolved into survivalists who armed themselves to the teeth as they waited for the world to come to the end and blew up abortion clinics when the world didn't end soon enough." Holt grunted. "It's probably going to be *sooner* than later, now."

"Anyway, the Frogs are a spin-off from the Roswell phenomenon," Bevard said. "It started back in '47 with the Roswell cover-up stories and hasn't ever left us. The Frogs are the cutting edge of the alien-conspiracy syndrome. The inner control group is made up of people who believe they've been abducted. The abduction incidents often involve physical examinations, mental testing, sometimes even surgery that leaves no evidence of cutting, planting of electronic monitors in the subject's body, and even incidents of sexual abuse—alien rape, if you will."

Holt opened the scarf around his face enough to light a cigarette. He blew smoke out his nose. "Why do the Frogs want Tah and Caden?"

"We think she's a plant."

"A Frog." It fell into place for Holt. He started laughing. "Those crazy bastards have been running around for years claiming the government's conspiring with aliens. They've kidnapped Tah to prove that the Feathered Serpent is an alien. And they're right, they're finally right!" Holt howled. "Don't you get it? There's a real conspiracy for these people to get their teeth into here!"

The line was dead. He had either lost Bevard—or been disconnected.

Saving the world has gotten a lot harder, he thought.

52

The plane bounced as the wheels touched down on a roadway built for vehicles. Iyo! I would rather face the Feathered Serpent's champion in a Skull Game than fly on these metal birds.

People rushed the plane, rabble who were dirty, hungry, thirsty.

"It's okay," Caden said. "We have protection."

The protection looked worse than the mob, thugs with clubs who shoved and beat their way through the crowd. A man I took to be their headman sat on a two-wheeled chariot pulled by two men.

"The Great Khan," Caden said, "Emperor of the Imperial Palace Casino city-state. He used to be a car salesman. Koji is paying him to escort us down the Strip. He brought rickshaws for us."

I refused to get on a cart. Sitting down would make it harder to defend myself. I trotted alongside Caden's rickshaw as the warriors of the Great Khan cleared the way.

She waved at the rows of tall buildings that lined the two sides of the boulevard. "As you can see, Las Vegas has lost its shine."

It needed to lose a lot more. Starting with the dirty, ragged, stinking, violent, mindless rabble who were kept back by the clubs of the Great Khan's men.

"Always thirsty," Caden said. "They're lucky, though. They're spitting cotton but the water they drink is clean. People in the Gulf states had plenty of water . . . all poisonous."

The giant, dazzling gambling empires that lined the Strip in the movies I'd seen were now ghostly hulks. Burn damage and broken windows scarred the derelict buildings. Many windows were covered with boards. Caden told me missing windows were boarded up because it gets cold and can even snow in Las Vegas.

"There's no electricity. They're cannibalizing the wood from houses and buildings for fuel and cooking. Sometimes they throw weenie roasts where they burn a whole house. There's a hundred times more living space than needed because the town has a fraction of its old population."

The region had looked arid from the plane. I asked, "How do they get water?"

"The area has artesian springs, places where water seeps up from underground. Fossil water probably, left over from lakes that receded millions of years ago. Water's the reason the region was originally settled. It was a stage coach stop in the very arid areas along the old Spanish trail that ran from Santa Fe to Los Angeles. The name Las Vegas means 'the meadows.'

"The water supply is rationed to warlords according to how many soldiers they control. As our friend on the plane said, there is exactly enough water for food and drinking for the population. If anything goes wrong, people have to die to bring the carrying capacity in alignment. The arrangement for control of the springs is called the Nuclear Club because if the supply goes south, it will have a scorched-earth effect for everyone."

People not on foot used bikes, roller skates, and skateboards. Nobles were carried on rickshaws or on litters by slaves.

"Every warlord has an exotic car from the old Imperial Palace for prestige purposes, but gas is more sacred than water. They have races with the cars pulled by slaves. Besides the planned battles you called flower wars, we even have medieval jousts. Excalibur has knights on foot; there's no water for horses, and the horses and mules were all eaten long ago, anyway. Caesars puts its warriors on chariots, Treasure Island calls its rabble pirates, the Frontier has gunfighters. It's all pretty stupid . . . but like wild animals eating people in the Colosseum to the amusement of Romans, it entertains people who have nothing left but the specter of slow death."

The structure Caden called the Stratosphere stood higher than anything else in sight.

"It's over a thousand feet high," Caden said, "the tallest building west of the Mississippi. The elevators don't work and the stairways are easy to defend. That's the reason Koji chose it. Las Vegas is a perfect place for us. The ZSA stays away because there's nothing here they want."

53

Koji Oda stood at a window of the old Stratosphere casino tower overlooking the Strip. Shaped similarly to Seattle's Space Needle, the tower stood over one hundred stories with a saucer shape perched atop a narrow shaft.

The tower was once the home of three thrill rides: Insanity spun passengers on an arm that extended sixty-four feet off the tower. Riders ended up facing down at the city below. X Scream sent riders headfirst off the edge and let them dangle above the Strip before pulling them in . . . and sending them off again. The Big Shot ride sent passengers up the tower's mast at 45 mph before sending them back down again. Young kids loved the rides.

Before electricity became nonexistent and the Frogs took over the tower, a warlord had once used the thrill rides for punishment—putting people who annoyed him into the rides without strapping them in.

Koji watched the progress of the team he had sent to bring back the mystery man he had ordered stolen away from the ZSA in San Francisco. The team slowly made its way up Las Vegas Boulevard South.

Every building on the Strip was battered and abused. Vegas had once been the brightest city on the planet, a neon colossus where anything went—*what happens here, stays here*. But now no windows on the first three levels of the hotel-casinos were intact anywhere on the boulevard.

Koji didn't think that casino warlords running Las Vegas were any more bizarre than the castled warlords that ran Europe and much of Asia for a couple millennia. In a real sense, civilization had never moved far from the paganism of ancient civilizations such as Rome.

Before the contagion, violence from individuals and gangs, from television, movies, and electronic games, had entertained people, just like the live violence in ancient Rome. People had paid large amounts of money even to watch wrestling and tough-guy contests in which combatants pretended to hurt each other. And sometimes really did.

Koji understood the thirst for blood by modern people. Violence was not new to man—it had been there from the first ancient civilizations, up through the Middle Ages, the Renaissance, the great wars of the twentieth century . . . but how does one explain the excitement—cheering, yelling, goading—of people watching other people *pretend* to injure each other?

Koji's ability to produce water to grow food in a hothouse environment high above the Strip was his ante into the high-stakes survival game played by the warlords. The Frogs produced more food than they consumed, and the extra food bought protection from the warlords . . . who used it to increase their carry-.ing capacity for soldiers.

Koji had turned the Stratosphere into a rain forest, hauling up dirt and using sunshine from the big plate-glass walls and water-making techniques to produce high-protein, high-yield crops.

Every Banana Republic dictator would've liked to capture the sky-high gardens . . . but the tower was easy to defend, and the warlords knew they lacked the technical know-how to run the system. Koji also had a reputation as a magician—a Merlin—and the mystery surrounding him commanded fear and respect.

In a sense, he was more an inventor than theoretical scientist, more Wizard of Menlo Park Edison than Einstein. He'd studied and mastered biochemistry, biology, botany, and hydrology and was an acclaimed expert on the biosphere . . . but he took degrees in none of the disciplines. Bored with details and theory, he threw himself into living science in which the things he imagined became workable.

Fifty-three years old, he was born in the Naniwa district of Osaka, Japan. The most significant thing about his birth was that he was born with the stigma of being *burakumin*. As with the untouchables of India, Japan had a caste system that stigmatized people in certain professions. Rather than focusing on race, the discrimination arose out of occupations of people, even looking back to the occupations of their ancestors. Professions in which dead people or dead animals were touched—morticians, butchers, leather workers, and gravediggers—were low in caste. His father, an engineer for the sanitation department, was an expert in water purification, but had been kept at the lowest level of pay and authority as a *burakumin*, ritually unclean, because his own father and ancestors had been butchers.

Koji's father made *taiko* drums as a hobby, but never played them. Koji grew to understand that his father's refusal to play the drums that so symbolized Japanese culture had been his father's way of dealing with stigma. At the age of ten, Koji's father had been told by a teacher that a *burakumin* was worth only one-seventh of a person.

Koji was an eclectic genius, a child prodigy, and he knew that part of the reason he had never focused on a single discipline was because he encountered roadblocks and dead ends whenever he mastered a subject. The caste system was illegal in Japan, but legislation didn't erase the prejudices of people. Insulting words, Japanese forms of the N-word—*eta*, meaning "polluted," and *hinin*, "nonhuman"—were shouted at Koji when he left the *buraku* ghetto and went to a prestigious school in a "clean" area.

In college he fell in love with a non-*burakumin* girl. Falling in love had been naïve on their part in a society in which families hired detectives to research the ancestry of their children's marriage partners. When her parents refused to permit their marriage, she was so ashamed for him that she killed herself.

He used Shinto and Buddhism to understand his place in the universe, and he understood that the prejudice against *burakumin* was unreasonable. He had gone beyond the stigma, but had never loved anyone else again.

Watching the group as they approached below, Koji used his binoculars to examine Tah. *Tah-Heen, the ballplayer.* A man from the past who, in some ways, was better adapted to the violent, chaotic present than people today.

As Koji studied the man from the ancient world, his thoughts went back to the day he had been gripped by a maelstrom off the Space Center.

He wondered who—or what—had engineered the phenomenon that left him lying on the beach with a gold plaque that should have been millions of miles away. And wondered if it had anything to do with the man from the ancient world he was about to meet.

54

I drank cold watermelon juice as I stared at the white-haired god called Koji in charge of the Frogs. He was different from Holt and the ZSA commander in San Francisco. Those two were gods of war—predators who were quick to anger and to attack. This God of Frogs was a puzzle to me. On the surface, he appeared calm and gentle, even fatherly, treating Caden and his other disciples almost as his children. But when I met his eyes and looked deep into them, I recognized strength and power. Like the other gods, he was determined to succeed. He simply showed it differently.

As I studied him, it struck me that his movements were more liquid than those of most people I had observed. He had arms and legs like me, but moved with more ease and elegance than the others. He reminded me of movies I'd seen on TV in which martial-arts fighters flew into battle rather than just walked.

Before we sat down, Caden showed me how they had turned the round, disk-shaped structure near the top of the tower into a lush garden. "All the food in the area is grown in greenhouses, places made mostly of glass. That keeps out red rain, and there's plenty of spare glass in Vegas. What we've done is make the biggest greenhouse I know of, a sky garden. Any moisture that doesn't end up actually as part of the plants is recycled and even increased in volume with Koji's techniques."

I nodded and pretended I cared about what she told me, but mostly I looked around and thought of how I would escape if it became necessary. Escape would not be easy. The single stairway we came up from the ground was the only way down. The Frogs had blocked everything else, and even that stairway was easily barricaded by them. I would need the wings of an eagle to get back to the ground. There was also the problem of Caden. I still didn't know if the Frogs were really her friends or if they were using her. For sure, I would not abandon her.

"It is natural for you to wonder about us," Koji said.

I nodded. "It is natural for you to wonder about me." For a certainty, if he was a priest, he did not appear frightening like the Flay Lord, but I was still on guard.

"Caden has explained to you that we are not your enemy, but I sense that at any moment you are going to leap at me."

Iyo! My body language betrays me. The god sees through my pretense at cooperation. I asked, "Why should I trust you? You didn't come to me as a friend and invite me to your temple. You attacked me with a stun gun and kidnapped me."

"That was unfortunate . . . but necessary. We live in a world in which violence has become not just epidemic, but part of the culture. If we had tried to bring you here openly, ZSA soldiers would have killed our emissaries."

"Our intentions are good," Caden said. "And we're running out of time. Unless the contagion is stopped, we will all die. All except the few the Feathered Serpent keeps for his slaves."

It sounded as if the entire underworld was at jeopardy. Iyo! Where would the souls of the dead go to have their souls exterminated if there was no longer a hell to traverse?

The god Koji said, "We've brought you here because you know more about Quetzalcoatl than anyone."

"Holt and the others have asked me many questions. I told them everything I know."

"Holt's a smart man and an honest one, at least he used to be when he was CIA director. Now he works for a bureaucracy and decisions are made that he may not agree with but has no power to stop. We have learned that people in high government are planning to go back in time, using the machine that brought you here. They plan to abandon us here at the mercy of the creature as it destroys the world."

I shrugged. "Worlds exist at the whim of the gods."

"We can save this world," Caden said. "The truth about the Mayan 2012 prophecy is that civilizations do grow stale and fall, but that doesn't mean we have to. We have the power to save the world and change it for the better. But we can only do that if we defeat this demon trying to destroy us."

Koji studied me with half-closed eyes. "You and Caden are the only ones who have actually been inside the Feathered Serpent's lair. I wanted the two of you here together to talk about what you saw and felt. Caden has told us surprisingly little that's tangible. We know it was a nightmare for her, but from almost the moment she stepped into the cavern, she began to get dizzy."

"The breath of the dead," I said.

"What do you mean?" Caden asked.

"In some places the breath of the dead in the underworld seeps up and is poisonous. People have died in caves because they breathed it."

Caden shook her head. "Are you talking about natural gas? Methane deposits?"

I shrugged. These people in hell knew so little about the underworld. "The gods don't want anyone to know where the sour breath is coming from. They destroy people who take torches into caves where the breath is."

Koji nodded. "Sounds like natural gas, methane, maybe some ethane, but you can't smell natural gas, that's why gas companies put an odor in it."

"*We* can't smell natural gas," Caden said, "but Tah has a heightened sense of smell. He may even be identifying it by its effect rather than odor."

"For the Feathered Serpent to put its lair in a cave with natural gas implies something very important about the creature."

Caden said, "It's a methane breather."

"Exactly."

"I don't understand," I said.

Koji smiled. "I don't blame you. We don't either, but this is what we've deduced. This colorless, odorless stuff that we breathe is called oxygen. We suspect that the Feathered Serpent breathes a different colorless, odorless gas, one we call methane. Methane is the deadly breath of the underworld."

"Why would it breathe something different than us?" I asked.

"Because *it is* different. It's a form of life, but not human life, any more than snakes and flowers and fish are human. Not all life breathes oxygen. Plants take in carbon dioxide, some life-forms thrive on methane. Titan, the largest moon of Saturn, is a prime candidate for a life-form because it has a great deal of methane in the atmosphere that may have been produced by organic matter."

Caden said, "The Teo area, in fact the whole central plateau down there, has a long history of earthquakes and volcanic activity. There might be natural caves and caverns deep in the earth that go all the way to the sea."

"Or a cleft under the area that permits the sea to reach to the mountains," Koji said. "That's a highly likely scenario. Perhaps the Feathered Serpent is even aquatic. I wish I knew what it looks like."

"Bigger than me," I said, "but no bigger than the large men who play your professional sports like basketball or football."

"You've seen it?" Koji asked.

"When I was in the cavern. I thought it was its champion ballplayer because I'd seen his image at the ball court."

"What ball court?" Koji asked.

"In the One-World"—I almost said the "world above us" and had to remind myself that these people didn't know they were in hell—"there's a match called a Skull Game. The core of the rubber ball is the head of the last loser of the game. Each year the best player of olli is sent to Teotihuacán to play the city's champion. They always lose because the champion is bigger and faster than any player."

"And they lose their heads?" Koji asked.

"Skulls games started in Teo but were played over the centuries many places in Mesoamerica," Caden said.

I tapped my heart. "First the loser is sacrificed and his heart is eaten by the winner of the match. The head comes off later after the other parts are given to Nawals to eat. But it is a great honor to lose and be sacrificed. Rather than dying a straw death and descending to the nine hells, like a warrior, you become part of the honor guard that escorts the Sun God across the sky."

"The creature you saw in the cave matches the drawing you saw at the ball court?" Koji asked.

I nodded.

He asked Caden, "Have you seen the pictograph he's talking about?"

She shook her head. "The ball court's not there. Only parts of Teo's religious center, the pyramids and the ruins of the Feathered Serpent's temple, are left."

"Have you told this story to Holt or his people?" Koji asked.

"No. They never asked me about the Skull Game."

"So what do we have here?" Koji asked Caden.

"A methane-breathing creature. But that raises another question. How does it breathe when it's out of its lair? Tah, when you saw the creature in the cavern . . . did it look any different than the drawing of it at the ball court?"

I thought for a moment. "It had on a player's uniform in the drawing."

"Was the equipment any different than what ball-players usually wear?"

"Yes. We wear gear to protect our heads and places like elbows and hips and to hit the ball better. But otherwise, we play with few clothes on, at least less clothes than we normally wear. It's too hot to play in clothes."

"How did the creature's uniform differ?"

"Most of its body was covered with rubber protection. Everywhere that we would be naked, he had rubber cloth on. Places where he would hit the ball—hips, elbows, knees—he had thicker pads."

"How could you tell it was rubber from the wall painting?" Caden asked.

"By its color. Rubber is black in drawings."

"What about his helmet?" Koji asked.

I closed my eyes and thought about the picture. "Rubber. Thick."

Caden gave my arm a reassuring squeeze. "I want you to think about something. Imagine that you put on the creature's uniform. It would be too big for you, for sure, but other than that . . . is there anything about the uniform that would be strange on your body?"

I had already thought of it. "The back. It was well padded, more than any other place on the body. A ballplayer doesn't have his back padded. The champion's uniform was very thick." I showed them a width of a couple inches with my fingers.

"Did it appear to be one large piece?" Caden asked.

"No. There were ridges, as if three separate pieces were sewed together, side by side."

"Air tanks," she said, grinning at Koji. "Actually methane tanks. That's why he can leave the caverns. He carries his supply with him. But it doesn't sound like those tubes could hold much, not as much as we'd need in terms of oxygen."

"He might not need much," Koji said. "We need a constant fresh supply of air since we breathe in oxygen and exhale carbon dioxide. He might have a closed system that reuses methane over and over."

"Does knowing these things help?" I asked.

"Know your enemy is the most important rule of engagement," Koji said. "We know the creature's very much like us in terms of its shape, but unlike us in terms of what it breathes. That's an important distinction. Methane isn't just different than oxygen, it's highly explosive in its natural state."

"We also know that it's a fish out of water once it leaves its abode," Caden said.

"It's a fish in water in the lair?"

"Sorry—that's an expression. It means it can't breathe except where there's methane, so it has to carry a supply if it leaves."

"The bladders are on its back," I said.

I heard a familiar buzzing sound.

"Punch a hole in them," Koji said, "and the creature would suffocate on the air we breathe. That's why the supply is divided into three—two are spares. If one breaks, it still has a supply."

The buzzing sound was getting louder. They would be able to hear it soon. A plan of attack had formed in my mind.

"We need to—"

I stopped as a buzzing sound suddenly became loud enough for them to hear. They ran to a window and I followed.

Black gunships flew around the Stratosphere like giant killer bees.

55

The god Holt was not pleased with Caden, Koji, or me. Holt puffed on a cigarette and stared at us as if he was thinking about sending us to the sacrifice line.

We were still in the Stratosphere, only now Holt and his lesser demons were enjoying the watermelon juice. Koji permitted the entry after Holt threatened to blow the tower down. Not even the Banana Republic rabble tried to harass the armored gunships.

"I should have the two of you summarily shot for treason," he told Caden and Koji. He pointed his cigarette at me. "The three of you, because it's pretty clear that you went along with them."

"Tah was kidnapped," Caden said, "against his will."

"I was not kidnapped, I came because I wanted to," I said.

"And who the hell said you had a right to do what *you* wanted to do? You're my prisoner—"

"Your prisoner? You said I was your guest."

"That was before you plotted with the enemy."

"We have not plotted. While you were busy fighting Nawals at Broadway and Times Square, we were devising a plan to kill the Feathered Serpent."

"Thank you, Lord!" Holt shouted to the ceiling. "Did you hear that, men? These civilians have come up with a plan to save the world." He pointed his cigarette at me again. "Listen to me, Tah. You are going to be sent back in time to guide me and one of my men to the creature. We're going to carry a small A-bomb with us. And we're going to ignite it when we get to Teo and bury that bastard like he's supposed to be."

"That won't work," Koji said. "You'd have to knock down the whole mountain to guarantee you killed the creature. You can't carry a bomb that size. And your worst enemy will be time. You'll have to walk from your entry point to the city. How long will that take? A day? A month? Three months? The world may not have that much time."

"Yes, you don't have that much time," I repeated. I wasn't sure what Koji was talking about, but I had already made up my mind as to how to fight the Feathered Serpent. "That is why I have come up with a plan."

Holt took a long draw off his cigarette and inhaled deeply, closing his eyes. I could tell that the patience of the god toward me was becoming strained.

He slowly opened his eyes and stared at me. "All right, Tah-Heen. Tell me your plan to save the world."

I puffed up my chest. Caden would be proud of me. "I will go to Teotihuacán and cut a hole in the Feathered Serpent's back."

Complete silence. The cheers I heard in ball courts when I scored points did not come from the people around me.

Caden cleared her throat. "Perhaps you should explain a little more, Tah."

"What he breathes is on his back."

"Methane," she said. "He breathes methane, not air."

"Do you want to explain it to me?" Holt asked Caden.

"He—it—whatever, is a methane breather. That's why it chose methane as its weapon. It only permits oxygen breathers to exist because it needs people to rule and apparently hasn't figured out a way to reproduce itself or other methane breathers. I suspect the werejaguars are an experiment on its part to ultimately breed methane breathers. Then he can turn the whole atmosphere into methane gas."

Holt asked more questions. After Caden and Koji fielded them, I said, "It carries the gas on its back when it plays."

"When . . . it . . . plays . . . what?"

The god was getting impatient with me again.

"It only comes out once a year in the One-World and never ventures from Teotihuacán. It comes out of its lair where it can freely breathe and carries its air with it. It comes out for only one reason: to play. And when it plays, I will cut holes in its rubber air bladders."

Holt stared at me as if I had just been beamed up from the ancient world. "What makes you think this thing that has the whole world at bay, that the greatest minds of military and science are battling, would let you walk up to it and cut off its air or whatever the hell it breathes?"

I sighed and smiled at Caden as I answered him. Iyo! What fools these gods Holt and Koji were.

"For the love of the game," I said.

Didn't they realize that the ball game was more important than even saving the world?

56

We landed at the Mexico City airport and joined a convoy of armored vehicles that escorted us to the barricade surrounding Teotihuacán. Behind us as we left, combat helicopters called gunships were being unloaded from transport planes. The abandoned airport and the ancient city were both northeast of the center of what was once the capital of Mexico.

We did not have to travel through the capital to get to the ancient city, and Holt was relieved. He said few people in the capital managed to endure the contagion—and we would not want to meet the survivors. "Like the few who are still alive in the hardest-hit areas along the Gulf states, survival of the fittest doesn't mean the prettiest. There are reports of mutants that would scare the crap out of werejaguars."

Teo had a water source beneath it that was untainted, but Holt told us that even if the city needed water, the government would have trucked it in from the Arctic if necessary.

"We pacify the Feathered Serpent, give it whatever it wants in rebuilding its city, in the hope it will keep it busy enough not to speed up the methane crisis. The creature's populated the city cleverly, drawing people from the jungle areas of Mexico and Central America who have had the least contact with the modern world."

"They don't know about your world?" I asked. I wondered if the people were also already in hell or like me had been brought from the One-World.

"They're aware of the modern world," Caden said, "but there are still millions of people who live primitive lives. They know what a car is, but have never owned one. The creature would want that type because they'd be easier to quickly indoctrinate. The quickest indoctrination and control is by applying pure terror."

"It's been using a liberal dose of that, too," Holt said.

I first saw the Feathered Serpent's city when my tired feet carried me to it nearly two thousand years ago. I next saw it in images captured by satellites after the Feathered Serpent had restored the heart of the city. Iyo! The bloodthirsty god re-created the center of the city as I remember it from the time when I had walked it with my uncle and team manager . . . including the long line of sacrifice victims at the Pyramid of the Sun.

"The sacrifice line goes for hours every day," Holt said. "We don't know what the Feathered Serpent's fascination with blood is. We never see any of it hauled up the mountain to it."

"There are tunnels under the city," Caden said. "Blood could be taken to the mountain without people on the surface knowing it. Its fascination is with the blood itself, not with killing. If this thing wanted to entertain itself and the multitudes with death, it would have people killed in more interesting ways."

"Like Roman emperors did with gladiator games," Holt said. "Instead, the long sacrifice lines are a dull repeat of the same technique over and over. Not dull, of course, to the victims."

Caden nodded. "Koji and I both believe it uses some of the blood for nourishment, that's why it created the blood covenant."

Despite the soldiers and minor demons Holt had with us, we would be entering the city alone to battle the Feathered Serpent. *We* included me, Holt, and Caden.

"What if we're all wrong? What if Quetzalcoatl isn't in Teo?" Caden asked.

Holt grunted. "There's only one way to find out . . . go in. The son of a bitch has been killing us for years. It's time to kill or be killed."

Koji also wanted to come, but his white hair and handsome Japanese features would attract attention.

"I've got planes standing by with enough thermonuclear bombs to level the whole central plateau of

Mexico," Holt told Caden. "If we spot the Feathered Serpent, I give the word. That means we will be at ground zero when the place is hit."

She nodded gravely. "I understand. What if we're able to kill it?"

"If there's a chance, I'll take a shot. One chance, one time, that's all. And even if I hit it, unless I'm absolutely sure it's dead, I give the signal and we all get blown to hell."

"I am already in hell," I said.

That caused a pause in the conversation.

"You're right. But do you understand what I just said?" Holt asked.

I nodded. "Yes. We find the Feathered Serpent, we kill it. If we can't, you will use your powers to extinguish our souls." Was this then the last level of hell that I had to surmount? "But if I can get close enough—"

"The possibility of you getting close enough to it to cut the gas supply is so remote, I'm scuttling the idea. Tah, this thing you call a god has the whole world in jeopardy. The chance of you saving the day by playing it just doesn't compute. Our one chance will be for me to get a shot at it and explode its gas tanks."

Out of the god's hearing, I told Caden, "Its weakness is not in battle but in love for the game. It wants to play. It created the Skull Game so it could play the best."

"We're not even certain that it's the ballplayer."

"I'm certain."

We came to a twenty-foot, black "fence" as wide as

it was high. It was made of a material that resembled rubber or a pliable plastic.

"Think of it as a twenty-foot-high tire surrounding the city," Holt said. "It's the same type used in barricading the Zone."

The three of us left the armored vehicle and on foot followed a Mexican army officer who took us to a ladder that led down into a hole in the ground. A tunnel had been dug under the huge fence.

"People trying to escape dig under. They're shot by government forces when they pop up on this side. Shooting them is considered an act of mercy."

"That's nice of them," Caden said.

Coming out of the tunnel on the Teotihuacán side, the restored city lay before us. The gods of hell had re-created the city as a place of color and pageantry. Green, red, and yellow buildings glittered under the sun. Soaring pyramids scintillated like rainbows.

As we came into the heart of the city, people spoke Nahuatl all around me—not the ancient tongue but the version Caden knew. Surrounded by familiar buildings, hearing the language, seeing people dressed as they did in the One-World, it felt as if I had once again entered the city where I had last seen Sitat and my uncle.

The Feathered Serpent not only rebuilt the heart of the city but its army.

"Jaguar Knights," Holt said.

"Men in knight uniforms," I corrected.

"What do you mean?" Caden asked.

"In the One-World warriors earned their pride in battle. The swagger of these men comes from the uniforms they wear, not the battles they've won."

Pausing to watch a squad of Jaguar Knights march by, I detected a chilling smell, one that I had sniffed before. I slowly turned in the direction of the stench of raw meat, coming face-to-face with a Nawal. A mask covered its face, but this was no mock Lord of the Night. A squad of knights were behind it.

The creature stared at me, not saying a word. It pointed a clawed hand at me and Jaguar Knights surrounded me, their razor-sharp, obsidian-bladed swords raised.

57

Holt and Caden moved away from Tah as Jaguar Knights moved in and took him into custody.

"They must be onto us," Caden said.

"No, they were only interested in him. We were in plain sight and nobody bothered us."

"Can't you use your gun to help him?"

Holt just gave her a look. She knew the answer even as the words spilled out—Tah was expendable. They all were.

"Walk slowly," Holt said, "don't look so distressed."

Hearing two sandal-makers talking in Nahuatl about the ball game, she paused and listened to the conversation.

As they continued walking, she told Holt, "There's a game today at the ball court. The Feathered Serpent's champion will play a Skull Game."

"If Tah's right about the creature, it'll be watching—"

"Or playing," she said.

"We have to go. If it's there, I might get a shot. If it isn't, we'll have to find that tunnel you think leads to the mountain."

"Tunnels have been found under the Temple of the Feathered Serpent. Also near where we believe the ball court once was located."

"Let's take a look at the ball court. Can you find it?"

"I think so. It's in the area we call the Ciudadela, Spanish for 'the citadel.' It includes the Feathered Serpent's temple, a huge marketplace, and a lot of other temples and small pyramids."

She led the way to the Ciudadela. The ball court was there. So was the stone carving of the champion player Tah had spoken about.

Staring at a possible methane supply concealed in what appeared to be a vest worn by the player, she said, "I think Tah's right."

"What's Tah right about?"

The question came from behind them. They whipped around to face Stryker. He grinned at them as he pointed a gun.

"Welcome to the ancient world. At least a reasonable facsimile."

"You bastard." Holt didn't try for his gun.

Stryker shook his head. "Now that's a word loaded with different connotations. I'd like to think I switched to the winning side based on reasonable expediency rather than moral judgments."

Jaguar Knights immediately moved into position around Holt and Caden.

Stryker patted Holt down and removed from beneath Holt's shirt the pistol that fired an incendiary bullet. When he reached Holt's ankles, he found a backup piece, a .38 snub-nosed revolver, and took it.

"What did you plan to do with this?" Stryker asked, examining the incendiary pistol. "Did you think you could take out the Feathered Serpent with a single shot? I hope it's got a thermonuclear warhead on it. You haven't met this guy. He catches bullets in his teeth."

"Down here doing a little business for yourself?" Holt asked. "Or did the director send you?"

"What do you think? You're the old fart they brought out of retirement because you know everything."

"I think Muller's abandoning the world to the creature," Holt said. "He's grabbed the Time machine and is planning to use it to go back a couple thousand years where losers like you and him can be kings because you have a gun."

"Not bad," Stryker said. "You've got a piece of it. Muller dropped the idea on you to see your reaction. Test the waters to see if you'd like to come along. It would have been easier because you controlled the machine, but you're too much the Boy Scout to cooperate."

"Do you really think Muller's going to let an ankle-biter like you have any real power? You're expendable."

"Don't bet on it. When we go back to a time when might is right, not many people are going to have it over me." Stryker grinned. "Maybe when we get back to the ancient world, we'll play a little Texas hold'em to see who gets the Roman empire. I sure as hell don't want this stinking place, not with the guy who comes with it."

"You can't just let the world die," Caden said.

"Who says it can still be saved even if you knocked out the Feathered Serpent? The brass up in Sea-Tac were planning to ship off to Mars. We're just going in another direction. Com'on, it's time for you to meet a guy who can scare the balls off a gorilla."

"The blood covenant," Holt said as they walked. "That's the dirty secret no one knows about, isn't it? Muller didn't just leave people in the Zone because we were already overloaded up north—you left them behind for Quetzalcoatl. He needed people for sacrifices and a deal was cut with him."

Caden stared at Stryker. "You're all animals, crazy animals."

Stryker howled. "You think I'm crazy—wait till you meet the Feathered Serpent's chief assistant. As a special favor to Quetzalcoatl, we used the Time machine to bring forward a couple of his assistants and some of those guys who look like their mothers fucked a jaguar. You're going to meet one they call the Flay Lord because he likes to skin people alive." Stryker leered at Caden. "I'll have a lampshade made out of the skin from your pretty ass."

58

Iyo! Hell is a circle on the wheel of time. The Jaguar Knights did not take me to a prison but to a sacrifice line stretched out from the Pyramid of the Sun, the line I described earlier when I started my tale.

I thought I'd been seized because I'd been recognized, but in talking to others awaiting the Knife of the Gods, I discovered that Nawals roamed the city and selected people for sacrifice seemingly at random. Because I had been placed near the front of the line rather than the back, I suspect the creature sensed something about me that told it I would be trouble.

The wheel of time had carried me back to face someone that it's my duty to kill: the Flay Lord. My watching him atop the Sun God's pyramid, wielding the Knife of the Gods, feeding the rivulet of blood coming down the stairs of the pyramid, had quickened the beat of my heart. Not from fear, but anticipation.

For reasons only the gods of hell know, I have been given an opportunity to avenge the murder of my family and the theft of my birthright.

I would only have been more pleased if Zolin were also present to taste death. But it was two black-robed priests who assisted the Flay Lord.

The Nawal who brought me to the sacrifice line left and I saw no others. Only Jaguar Knights guarded the sacrifice ceremony. I asked the boy lamenting his fate if there were many Nawals in the city.

"Only two," he said. "When olli is being played, they stay at the ball court to serve the Feathered Serpent's champion."

"Will the champion play today?"

"He plays every day. And never loses."

Two Jaguar Knights grabbed my arms and led me to the steps. The Flower Weaver waited at the bottom to throw dream dust in my face so I would be docile as I was led up the steep stairway to the sacrifice mound. Caden told me that dream dust was a narcotic that robs people of their will when they inhale it.

As the Flower Weaver blew the dust at me, I shut my eyes and held my breath while pretending that my legs had become rubbery. The Sun God's temple was over two hundred feet high, so I had perhaps as many as two hundred steps to climb—steps so steep they were almost a ladder.

Keeping a grip on my arms, the two knights led me up the steps. When we were two steps from the top, I let my legs give way. Cursing me in Spanish, not

Nahuatl, they got on the step above me and pulled me by the arms to draw me up.

"Aaaakkkk!" I let out a war cry that shook the celestial abode of the gods.

As the two startled knights let go, I grabbed them by the front of their robes and jerked them forward. They screamed as they went by me, headfirst down the almost vertical stairs.

I broke over the top, letting out another shrieking war cry as I charged the two priests and the Flay Lord. The priests ran, but Xipe *charged me* holding the razor-sharp Knife of the Gods high.

Catching his knife wrist with one hand, I forced him back until the sacrifice mount was against his back. I twisted the knife out of his hand and into my own.

"This is for my family!"

Plunging the razor-sharp blade into his chest, I jerked it back and forth, ripping open his chest. Tossing the dagger aside, I reached into the opening and grabbed his heart. His eyes were shocked open, his mouth gaped. I palmed the beating heart and squeezed. His screams made me laugh as I jerked the beating heart out. Turning, I held the bloody muscle in the air. Cheers rose from the line of sacrifice victims, but my own grin quickly disappeared.

Stryker was at the bottom of the stairs.

Two Nawals stood beside him.

I had only one way down.

59

Stryker took me to the ball court.

I was relieved to find out Caden and Holt were alive, even though they, too, were prisoners.

"Why have you brought me here?" I asked Stryker. "Is the Feathered Serpent going to play?"

"Of course. That's where you come in."

"Where I come in?" I didn't understand the remark.

"The Feathered Serpent is going to play a professional." Stryker laughed. "You play the winner."

The ball court was nearly deserted. The two Nawals and perhaps a dozen Jaguar Knights were present. The Jaguar Knights all steered clear of the Nawals, whose function was to rip out the heart of the losing player—before cutting off his head.

Four knights stood guard near the dugout where my companions and I were held.

Spotting Zolin, I grinned and bowed to him, elated that the wheel of time had brought me back to another old enemy.

"Save your courtesies," Stryker said, "he's here to see you die. Watch the match—it'll give you a preview of what's going to happen to you."

Caden spotted the blood on my sleeve. "You're bleeding."

I shook my head. "Pig's blood."

The champion came onto the court. The Feathered Serpent was big . . . a huge figure, half again my size. Dressed in its uniform, the outward appearance of the creature's equipment was the same as that of an ordinary player: helmet, protection for elbows and knees, the big waist girdle called a yoke. But while the equipment was obvious on human players, on the creature it was as if the pieces were molded to blend with its form.

He had on the one piece of equipment olli players would find strange—the methane pouches on its back. Shaped as a half-vest, it extended from above the yoke on its backside to the back of its neck. The protective pieces and guards for its elbows and knees appeared to be made of rubber.

The theme of the uniform was, of course, a jaguar.

Like other ballplayers, I played naked except for padding and a loin covering. But its uniform covered almost all of its body, leaving only a crack at the neckline that exposed scaly, snakelike skin.

The Feathered Serpent's eyes found mine and I

tensed, sensing power I didn't understand but that grabbed my attention and wouldn't let go.

"More dinosaur than snake," Caden said.

"What?"

"Something about it . . . a predatory intelligence. Snakes crawl, but dinosaurs run and even fly. They ruled the world. He's more raptor than cobra."

The skull ball lay on the ground near the Feathered Serpent. Smaller than a bowling ball, I estimated the weight at several pounds. From the rough texture of the ball's skin, I was certain the rubber was not processed by modern equipment but in the way the People of the Rubber formed it.

Olli balls could hurt or break bones. Propelled by the Feathered Serpent's power, a skull ball could kill.

The other player, the one Stryker called a professional, entered the court surrounded by Jaguar Knights, obsidian-bladed swords in hand. He was obviously a reluctant participant, and the knights were not an honor guard.

"Christ—that's David Bailey," Holt said. "He led the NBA in points for seven straight years until he disappeared last year. He's not the only missing pro athlete—champions have disappeared from football, basketball, soccer, every sport. Muller's been grabbing world-class athletes for the creature to play."

A Jaguar Knight dumped equipment at my feet. The gear of an Eagle Knight.

I looked up and caught the Feathered Serpent staring at me. If I'd had any doubt that he knew that I

was the son of Lord Light, it was gone. The gear was
a taunt to remind me that his underlings had killed my
father.

You're next, I mouthed silently. I hoped it could
read lips.

I studied the Feathered Serpent's movements as the
game began. Watching the other player would have
told me little. The basketball star had no more chance
than he would have had against a five-hundred-pound
saber-toothed tiger.

Watching the movements, I realized that the creature held itself back from playing hard against the
basketball champion.

"Deliberately slowing down its speed," I said.

"Why?" Holt asked.

"So it can lengthen the play and fool the other
player into thinking it's much slower."

"And then the creature suddenly comes alive?"

"With the speed of a jaguar."

I bent down to adjust my sandals and saw a small
piece of obsidian on the ground. A couple inches
square, it probably fell off a knight's sword. I palmed
the piece and stood up, letting Holt get a glimpse of
what I'd found.

"If I cut a hole in its methane vest, is it true it won't
be able to breathe?"

Holt's features froze as he controlled his emotions.
"One cut won't work. There's three small pouches.
That way it can still have a supply if the others get
ripped. But if you created an explosion . . ."

He took a pack of cigarettes out of his pocket, shook a cigarette out, and put away the pack. From his other pocket, he brought out a cigarette lighter. I'd seen the lighter before, a square metal box about the size of a small matchbox.

In a flash motion, Holt brushed the lighter against the side of his pants, back then forward, igniting a flame he used to light his cigarette.

"Zippo lighter. You flip back the cap and spin the flint wheel with your thumb to create sparks that ignite the lighter fluid. But it works just as well if you brush the flint wheel against a pair of stiff pants. Even better if you get rid of the cap." He twisted off the cap and dropped it on the ground. "Now you only have to worry about spinning the wheel that ignites the fluid." He spun the wheel with his thumb and the lighter flamed. "You get the idea?"

I nodded. It was similar to creating a cooking fire by striking a fire rock.

"Ignite the methane," Caden whispered. "After you cut the methane tube, you blow the creature up."

I understood. All I needed was a miracle to survive in the game to get close enough . . . *twice*—once to cut the hole and another time to ignite the gas.

I looked back at the action on the court. Quetzal-coatl let the basketball player almost make a point . . . but as the player made a desperate effort to score, it suddenly moved at speeds no human could have reached, intercepted the ball, and kicked it hard enough to send it all the way to the goal.

As soon as the point was made, Bailey ran for it. The Nawals were waiting for him. He dodged one, spinning around and almost into the arms of the other. The Nawal's arm shot forward and plunged into the player's chest with preternatural force.

Caden cried out. I put my arm around her. The Nawals were stronger than anything I'd seen—other than their master.

Zolin came to the dugout and gestured at me.

My turn.

I held up my bloody sleeve to Zolin as I went by him. "Your heart will be next."

He leered. "Tonight I'll feast on your meat."

As I stepped onto the playing court, the obsidian blade and the cigarette lighter were hidden in my right hand, with the blade between clenched fingers.

A Nawal threw a skull ball onto the court. The ball bounced and rolled up to me.

Time to play.

I ignored Quetzalcoatl as he moved into position. Taking a moment out to practice, I moved the ball with my feet, getting used to it. It was much heavier than what I was used to playing with.

I knocked it up the slanted wall, leisurely moving to intercept as it came down. From the feel I knew it was an actual skull ball. We would be playing with the head of some great ballplayer, perhaps a soccer or basketball player. And if Zolin was right, someday my head would be the one kicked around the court.

In my time, I bragged that I could have defeated the

legendary Xolotl himself in a game played on the celestial field. Iyo! It was a boast that I could beat a god. Now I had to prove it.

I had only one chance to cut the creature's methane tank. If I failed, it would kill me before I had another chance.

Pretending I was still getting the feel of the ball, I suddenly kicked it at the creature's face. He leaned out of the way but the ball grazed the side of his helmet.

The Nawals looked ready to gut me, but he calmed them with a glance.

I met the creature's eye. "I am one with Xolotl, who gives me ollin."

I turned my back and walked away so play would not yet start. I needed to get my thoughts in order. Caden and Holt watched me intently and I gave them a nod, communicating more confidence than I felt, but my mind was reeling with a revelation. Kicking the ball at the Feathered Serpent's face had exposed a weakness—it had been pleased by my dirty trick. *It wanted a challenge.* Just winning wasn't enough. That was too easy for it. It didn't care if I cheated . . . as long as I gave it a challenge.

Now I had to exploit the weakness. Like the Hero Twins who confronted the Lords of Hell in the underworld, the game I played would have to be both skillful and stealthful.

A Nawal threw the ball between us again to start the play.

Rather than leaping for the ball, I hung back, letting Quetzalcoatl lunge for it, then I leaped and slammed my foot into the back of its knee.

That startled it enough for me to boot the ball toward my goal. As it shot by me to get to the ball, I hit the same knee with a cross-body block.

I would have broken the leg of an ordinary player, but the Feathered Serpent barely stumbled.

By the time I scrambled to my feet, the god was on the ball, kicking it back at the goal behind me. I tried to block the ball with my waist yoke but Quetzacoatl hit my thigh, knocking me off my feet. My leg was injured but still held my weight.

I scrambled and threw myself on top of the ball so I'd have control for the next kick. The Feathered Serpent moved between me and the goal to block my kick. Instead of hitting it downfield, I turned and kicked it up the slanted wall.

As the Feathered Serpent flew by me to kick the ball as it came off the wall, I threw myself at the god's back, the razor-sharp obsidian chip protruding through my clenched knuckles.

It spun in a blur and shook me off. As I crashed to the ground, the chip and the lighter flew out of my hand.

Iyo!

I was not going to make it through this level of hell.

60

With all eyes on the drama on the ball court, Holt stuck his hand down the front of his pants, reaching under his testicles to pull out a .25-caliber Beretta. Stryker hadn't checked the area when he searched for guns—he was a soldier, not a cop, too macho to touch a man's crotch.

Stryker caught the movement out of the corner of his eye. He whipped around and Holt shot him in the throat. Stryker staggered back and Holt leaped forward to get the incendiary pistol Stryker had tucked in his belt.

Coming up with the pistol in hand, Holt tried to take aim at the Feathered Serpent, but the two Nawals charged, blocking his aim.

With the Feathered Serpent's attention on Holt, I grabbed the blade and cigarette lighter off the ground, one in each hand. I rose to my feet and jumped at its back. It swung around to bat me off and I caught the arm, throwing my full weight on the beast, throwing it off-balance. I sliced at the back of the methane vest and struck the lighter's flint wheel at the same time. I got hit with something, my whole body took the blow, and I went flying.

Holt stood his ground, the crotch gun in one hand, the special pistol with an incendiary round in the other, as he faced the Nawals' charge. Across the court an explosion sounded and the mock Jaguar Knights ran in panic.

When the first Nawal was almost up to Holt, he shot it in the face and stepped aside to let it stagger past him and fall. Before he could get the gun aimed at the second one, the creature leaped on him. Holt went down backward with the man-beast on top of him.

Caden grabbed the Nawal by the hair with both hands and pulled. As its head was yanked back, the werejaguar swung and hit Holt across the face. The blow to Holt made the gun in his hand go off, the bullet striking the Nawal under the chin. It rose, screaming, and fell back, convulsing in spasms on the ground.

"Are you okay?" Caden asked.

Holt's head was bleeding, his eyes glazed.

She heard the pounding of feet and turned.

The Feathered Serpent was racing toward her.

* * *

My face and exposed parts of my chest and arms were burned; my chest felt crushed. I saw Quetzalcoatl going for Caden as I pulled myself to my feet. But it wasn't moving at the superhuman speed it showed earlier. The explosion had done damage—two of the gas pouches on its back were ripped open, but the third one had survived the blast.

A scream of terror by Caden got me off the ground and stumbling, trying to get my feet moving as they usually did.

The Feathered Serpent knocked her senseless and grabbed her, tucking her limp body under its arm as it continued to run.

I followed awkwardly, grabbing a sword dropped by a panicked Jaguar Knight as he fled.

A surge of strength came from somewhere deep inside me, and my legs were suddenly driven by ollin. I went after the creature as it disappeared into a small building on the other side of the ball-court wall. The structure was too small to have more than a single room. The Feathered Serpent and Caden disappeared into the building with the door slammed shut behind them.

I kicked open the door and flew into the dark room with the sword held high, stopping a few steps in to stare around.

No Caden. No Feathered Serpent.

Did the creature have the magic power to disappear?

61

A large stone statue of Mictlantecuhtli, the Lord of Hell, dominated the center of the room. Enough light from the open doorway came through to reveal that the statue had been slid, disturbing the dust on the floor beside it.

As I went around the statue staring down at the imprint left by its having been moved, a sword blade came at my face. I jerked back, avoiding the thrust, and clubbed the wrist holding the blade.

Zolin dropped the sword but jabbed a dagger at my stomach as he reared up. We both stared at the dagger—it had struck the wooden yoke that protected my midsection.

I broke his nose with a punch and was on him before he hit the ground. I pinned him with my knee and twisted the blade out of his hand.

Holding the blade high so he could see what I was going to do, I said, "For my family."

I plunged the blade into his chest and held him back as he reared up with convulsions. Jerking the blade back and forth, I opened his chest and ripped out his heart and stuffed it in the cargo pocket where I already had the Flay Lord's heart.

A tradition in the One-World was for the victor in battle to eat the heart of the defeated foe. Eating the heart gave the victor the extra strength of the dead warrior and honored the foe. But Zolin and the Flay Lord were charlatans, not warriors. I would feed their hearts to a dog.

Tossing the bloody dagger aside, I grabbed the obsidian sword and went back to the statue.

The king of Mictlan, the underworld, was a hideous creature, a squatting skeleton with a snake coming out of his mouth. He was also heavy. Bracing my back against the wall, I pushed with my feet until the statue budged. Beneath it a stone stairway descended into a dismal chamber in which whitewashed walls created a dark, shadowy world, just taking the edge off complete darkness.

Iyo! I had been destined to pursue the Feathered Serpent deeper into hell. No doubt the creature was brother to the King of the Dead.

Sword in hand, I went down the steps.

I had been in caves before and knew the smells of earth and even animals. But this stench was scorched flesh. The beast had suffered burns in the explosion.

It stood in the cavern ahead of me, Caden on the ground beside it. When she saw me, she shouted, "Tah!" and started up. The creature backhanded her. Its helmet was gone and I saw its face for the first time. I thought it would have the head of a snake, but I was wrong. It was more human-looking than I had imagined and not unlike the masks the Nawals wore, the cross between man and jungle beast. The stone statues of it on the Temple of Quetzalcoatl showed it to have sharp, jagged teeth. It exposed them to me.

Then it charged.

My obsidian sword was a stick with a sharp edge—and I was not a sword fighter.

I pulled out the hard black-and-white eight ball I'd picked up from the pool table at Fisherman's Wharf. Winding up, I threw the ball with the ollin of Xolotl himself.

The ball nailed the Feathered Serpent between the eyes, spinning it sideways in wild surprise.

Shouting another war cry, I charged with the sword. Just before we converged, I feinted left, then zagged right, swinging at his last methane tank.

Wheeling around, it blocked my swing before the sword buried itself in its back. It grabbed me and lifted me into the air, roaring like all the legions of hell.

I kicked wildly at its chest as it shook me like a small child.

A figure emerged in the shadows behind it.

Holt lifted his incendiary pistol and pointed it.

I saw fire burst from the barrel at the same moment I was blown into darkness.

62

"You can't go back to your own time."

The god Holt spoke those terrible words as he stood beside my hospital bed in my room at the Santa Fe complex. Three days after the explosion in the cavern, I had emerged from a deep sleep that Caden called a coma.

"Our world is exciting, Tah," Caden said, "and we need help rebuilding it. You'll grow to like it here."

She didn't sound convincing. Her arm was in a cast. The blast had thrown her against the stone wall, but she had not been knocked out.

Neither of them understood. Surviving the tortures of the nine hells of the terrifying underworld, I had earned the Peace of Nothingness. No more torments should be thrown at me. Instead, the Lord of the Dead was supposed to turn my soul into dust and scatter it.

Now I was being told I was stuck in hell.

"You know too much, you've learned about modern technology," Holt said. "We can't let you go back to your time and take that knowledge."

"Things will change in our world," Caden said. "I told you, that's the real meaning of what's happened. We have been given another chance to do things right, for ourselves and for the rest of life on earth." She squeezed my arm. "Wait till you see what the world's really like. When it's restored, you're going to love it here. You said you were going to give him a world tour, didn't you, Allen?"

Holt smiled. I suppose the god thought it made him look more pleasant, but it was a wolf's grin.

"I'm afraid the world tour will have to wait. There's a problem."

"A problem?"

"Muller gave himself a ride on the Time machine."

"He made it back? Back in time?" Caden asked.

"He made it back. Now we have to go after him. That's where Tah comes in. We need you to go back and find him."

I said, "I can't go back, I know too much. You just said that."

"You can't go back to *your* time. Not alone, at least. It's not where Muller ended up. We're calculating the time period he dropped into. When we pin it down, we'll need a team to find him."

"Me, too," Caden said. "You'll need me, too."

Go somewhere else where there was trouble?

Iyo! I was wrong. There were more than nine levels of hell.

The shocking conclusion to
Apocalypse 2012

GARY JENNINGS'
THE 2012
CODEX

ROBERT GLEASON AND JUNIUS PODRUG

In Mexico the race is on for the ultimate end-of-the-world codex—the thousand-year-old prophecy of the god-king. A young Aztec of five hundred years ago and two heroic female archaeologists of today face violent foes in their quest for Quetzalcoatl's 2012 codex. But can they find and decipher his prophesy in time to prevent the apocalypse?

"Jennings fans will savor the mix of ancient history and near-future apocalypse."

—*Booklist* on *Apocalypse 2012*

FORGE

Hardcover • 978-0-7653-2260-9 • www.tor-forge.com